Nothing
SPECIAL
5

A.E. Via

A.E. VIA

Acknowledgments

Thank you to all who played a major or minor part in this book. Nothing Special holds a dear place in my heart and I'm so appreciative of everyone's input to make this book one of the best in the series. Andrea Goodell, my one and only beta. I always need and appreciate your advice. Jay Aheer for a smoking hot cover. Tina Adamski, my editor, this is truly some of your best work yet. Joanna Villalongo, for an excellent job proofreading, Casey Harvell, my formatter, who didn't mind doing a rush job, but still made the final product beautiful. Thank you Sid Lowell for the graphics and promo material. They're gorgeous as always.

3

A.E. VIA

Disclaimer

This is a M/M Romance and contains graphic content. It's not intended for readers under the age of 18.

Contents

Characters

Nothing Special
Book 1 - God and Day:
Lieutenant Cashel Godfrey (God) ~
Lieutenant Leonidis Day (Day) ~
First Officer Ronowski (Ro) ~
Genesis Godfrey (Gen) ~

Embracing His Syn
Book 2 - Syn and Furi:
Sergeant Corbin Sydney (Syn) ~
Furious Styles (Furi) ~

Here Comes Trouble
Book 3 - Ruxs and Green:
Detective Mark Ruxsberg (Ruxs) ~
Detective Chris Green (Green) ~
Curtis Jackson ~

Don't Judge
Book 4 - Judge and Michaels:
Detective Austin Michaels (Michaels) ~
Judge Josephson ~

Prologue

The proposal…

They were all full on greasy triple-meat pizza and hot wings, arguing over what the sports announcers were analyzing on the post-game show.

As they all helped clean up, Day cleared his throat calling for everyone's attention. The guys started to mumble and groan, waiting on Day to say something ridiculous, as usual. His smirk was crooked, his eyes glittering with humor. God turned and threw his big arm over Day's shoulder. "What is it, Leo? Who do you want to call out and embarrass, now?"

Day had embarrassing ammo, in the form of secrets, on all the guys, to be pulled out anytime he was ready. They all waited while Day turned slowly and faced God. They watched God drop his arm and look at Day, neither of them speaking out loud and like always, the team wondered what they were saying to each other with those looks.

"Come on, Day. What's up? Is it about work?" Syn asked.

"Nope." Day shook his head slowly, eyes still on God.

God frowned, looking confused.

"You want to get together tomorrow?" Curtis asked.

"Nope." Day put one hand deep in his jacket pocket.

"It's just really nice to be around my brothers, my family," Day said seriously.

The team looked on, nodding their heads in agreement, still waiting to see where their lieutenant was going with this.

"Yeah, it is," Green agreed. "You wanted to let us know how awesome we are and give us all raises?"

The guys cheered, liking Green's idea.

But Day looked down at the hardwood floor, slowly shaking his head again. His expression was turning more and more serious, and the room was getting eerily quiet while they waited in suspense.

"Sweetheart, spit it out," God said in his rough timbre, casually caressing the back of Day's neck.

Day turned to face God, looking up into his eyes. He opened his mouth to speak and had to clear his throat before anything came out. The lieutenant was being uncharacteristically reserved. Day took God's hand that was resting heavily on his neck and held it in his own. Steeling himself, Day's voice was calm and confident, but low when he finally spoke. Pulling a black velvet box out of his pocket, he gently stroked the soft fabric, opening the box.

"Cashel... will you marry me?"

Chapter ONE

God and Day

Day

Day put the super zoom, 3-D recording binoculars to his eyes, zooming in on the American Trans warehouse about ninety yards away. He was crouched low under the grimy window, taking pictures with the high-tech device. When he was finished, he pulled the ratty, thrift store curtains that'd already been in the abandoned two-story home when they took it over to use for their stakeout.

He rubbed his throbbing temple. Once again, that bastard Artist was setting up for a huge shipment of ecstasy into Atlanta. He'd slipped through God and Day's fingers last year, but it wasn't going to happen again. Their special task force didn't like failing. The team had been handpicked from Narcotics by him and his partner, God. A unique collection of nine absolute badasses that were either too damn crazy for any other precinct to handle or too fucking talented for God and Day to let work anywhere else but for them.

"You been doing that all day. Massaging your head and blowing hard every couple hours. Is that stress from being stuck in this house for two days or from God still not committing to a date for you guys' wedding?" Syn asked, kicking his dark boots up on one of the crates strewn about the room.

Day's sergeant was a man he trusted with his life and with his confessions. The guy was like the priest of the group. Though only in a confidant kind of way because the man was X-rated as fuck when he was around his hot partner – ex-porn star, Furious. Day could rely on Syn to give him good advice like he did everyone, but he was so fed up with this topic. He'd proposed to God in front of his whole team, and he'd said yes, but anytime Day wanted to talk details God

13

would shut down. He'd be busy, or off to a meeting, or about to start on something, too tired, the list was endless. Actually, the big man had gotten quite creative with his excuses.

For a couple months, Day was pretty silent on the issue, just happy to be engaged for the first time in his life, and feeling blessed to have a partner that understood him, loved him, and fought by his side. A lot of law enforcement officers didn't have that luxury. When they were on the streets, their team got results for the chief, which earned them special accommodations from the mayor. As long as they kept the dangerous streets of Atlanta clean, thereby helping the man get reelected term after term, them being lovers wasn't an issue for the bureaucrats.

Maybe God was thinking that if they got married, that'd change the rules for the department. *That's stupid.* Day knew he was grasping at straws. If the man thought that, he wouldn't've said yes.

"Why don't you just tell him how you're feeling, Day?" Syn said, sitting up higher, his concerned eyes turning darker than midnight.

Syn didn't like discord amongst the team, especially between the bosses. God and Day's synchronicity was integral to their successes. As the sergeant, the third in command – not only was he a skilled negotiator and interrogator – it was Syn's job to ensure everyone was doing *their* jobs. He took this responsibility seriously. There was very little Syn didn't know regarding everyone's life, and Day seemed to be Syn's number one concern ninety percent of the time. It wasn't a surprise. Day had been the one to find Syn in Philadelphia and recruit him. His intelligence and compassion rivaled Day's own.

"I've asked him to talk too many times already, Syn. I tried to talk about it over dinner. Next thing I knew, God started eating faster than a soldier in boot camp. I tried to talk to him in bed. He started staying up later than me or accidentally falling asleep downstairs. I tried while on our down time and he'd fuckin' make an excuse to get busy. I can't..." Day ran his fingers through his light brown hair, not caring how much of it stood up on his head. "I'm starting to think he only said yes because he didn't want to humiliate me in front of the guys. That he doesn't want to marry anyone... marry me."

14

"That's not true. God doesn't do or say anything he doesn't mean," Ro chimed in, coming around to Day and rubbing his shoulders in one of his amazing massage techniques. Ronowski – Ro was his first officer, outranking the other detectives. Ro was God and Day's point man and strategist, he had a master's in psychology and was often sought out by other departments to help plan seizes.

The sexy man had been a major thorn in Day's side when he was in the closet, but when he came out he became the amazing man he was meant to be. He was an outstanding detective and deadly with a shotgun – his weapon of choice.

Day was sure Ro hated seeing him so defeated and frustrated, used to Day being a comedian, the life of the party. He was going to have to get out of this funk. It was affecting all of them and he didn't want the men worrying about it, causing them to lose focus in the field, which could lead to accidents. He couldn't let that happen. Perhaps he'd just have to be happy with being engaged, even if it ended up being the longest engagement in history.

"It's alright, Ro. I'll talk to him. I promise," Day tried to reassure the handsome man. Ro had a special connection with his lieutenants. Things had changed after God and Day got engaged, but he knew Ro loved them deeply and didn't want to see anything happen to his and God's relationship. Day would fix this soon enough. For now, he needed to focus on their case.

Ro patted him on the back and took the binoculars from Day's lap, going back to the window. He stood there staring for about ten minutes, all of them silent until Ro asked, "Syn, give me a twenty on the Enforcers."

"Ruxs and Green are asking some questions at that night club on Donald Lee. Might be done by now, though. God told them to stick close by in case we needed them. They're probably five minutes away... why?"

Ro turned to face them, his blue eyes wide and serious. "We finally got some activity, boys. Looks like our informant actually came through this time. We got six black Escalades circling around the property."

Day and Syn were both on their feet, inching open the curtain on the other side of the window. "That's an awful lot of vehicles. I'm sure our rat said that *a couple* of Artist's head guys were coming to meet about where the shipment would arrive."

"He did," Syn gritted out, pulling up the audio on their laptop to listen in. The bugs had been planted three weeks ago and had remained silent since then. "All this would be happening on my watch shift."

"Yeah, this never happens to Michaels and God." Day smirked. "You got the video rolling, Ro?"

"Of course," Ro whispered, holding the binoculars as steady as a doctor holds his scalpel.

Day reached in his jeans pocket and pulled out his micro-earpiece and shoved it in his ear. "Tech."

"I'm here," the calm voice answered. Detective Murphy was their technology genius. A hacker from MIT who'd been popped for infiltrating the Pentagon's security software to find his missing brother in Afghanistan. Day got time shaved off his sentence and immediately recruited him. There wasn't a thing the man couldn't do from behind his nine monitors. He was the team's communications hub. Anything they needed – whether emergency or not – went through him.

"God in the office?"

"Yes."

"Ro has the video running on the glasses. Pull it up."

"Done," he replied almost immediately. "You're on the speaker."

God could hear Day and see what they were looking at. "We got a lot of activity over there for a simple meeting. I think you should load up."

"ETA ten minutes," God answered, his strong, bass-filled voice unlike any other man in that office. "Tech, patch him through to the radio in my truck. Day, do not engage."

"Ten-Four," Day responded, still staring at the trucks, which had stopped circling. It was silent on the deserted street; nothing on NW Cairo accept six ramshackle homes sitting across from a dusty field and an undercover chop shop. Dusk was just starting to fall across the sky. It was the time in Atlanta where honest citizens went home to their families and the bad boys came out to play. Day ground his molars; he had a bad feeling about this. None of them made a move in the dank room, understanding the importance of silence in that moment.

No one had emerged from the SUVs. Day looked at his watch. Eight minutes and God would be there.

"Fuck. It's Artist," Ro whispered sternly.

Day jerked his head up. *Shit!* "This is not supposed to be happening right now."

"Easy. ETA six minutes," Tech spoke quietly in Day's ear. "Sit tight, Lieutenant. I'm dispatching all units."

"Oh no," Syn murmured.

Day watched as all of Artist's men began to exit their vehicles. One by one, Artist's fiercely loyal minions formed a shield around him. Day counted twenty-two of them. His nerves kicked into high gear because he was sure Artist's crew was heavily armed. He didn't want any cops to lose their lives out there.

Several men broke off, going towards the warehouse, spreading out in a formation that told Day this wasn't a meeting amongst colleagues. It was a double-cross. The startled sounds of the men inside confirmed it. He kept watching their every move, waiting for the sound of sirens. *Just a few more moments.*

Artist, still surrounded by six large men, made his way down the long row of vehicles. The door to the last SUV opened and Day watched as one of the burly men, wearing an all-black suit, yanked a frail, stumbling man out of the backseat. He could barely stand and he had a dark cloth draped over his head.

"What the fuck?" Ro whispered.

The minion yanked the hood off the guy's head and Day's stomach dropped. It was their informant. The same one that'd once worked for Artist, who Day had got to turn state's evidence against the ruthless drug lord. He was beaten badly, but Day could still recognize him, he could almost feel the fear racking the informant's

17

body. The man in black put a gun to the back of the snitch's head, but not before turning his evil glare up at the window where they were.

"Our cover's blown," Syn hissed. "We gotta get the fuck out of here."

Day turned, along with his men, and took off to the rear of the house. The sound of the single gunshot – executing their informant – was loud, even from that distance. The cadence of their heavy boots taking the stairs three at a time sounded like the running of the bulls. Day turned the corner and heard Ro's loud "Get down!" and threw his body to the hardwood floor as bullets riddled the upstairs and the back of the house.

Day covered his head while drywall, glass, and dust rained down on them. There was a two-second break in the gunfire and Day pulled his two 9mms out of his shoulder holster. The bullets started again, automatic pistols firing over their heads as he and his men kept their bodies as flat to the floor as they could.

"Get to that back door," Day yelled. Tech was quiet in his ear and he knew why. His men all knew what to do. He'd let Day concentrate on staying alive.

"There's four SUVs in the back," Ro yelled. He was behind one of the columns at the back of the small townhome, turning every couple seconds to check the window. He had dust caked in his blond hair, making it look a dirty gray. He had blood on his cheek and forearm – probably from the flying glass – but Day saw the fierceness in those blue eyes. Ro was far from scared; he was ready to give these bastards a gunfight.

Day belly crawled with Syn to the front window, ducking every time a few bullets tore through the home. This place wasn't sturdy enough for this. The whole damn structure was going to come down on their heads soon. The men were probably buying Artist enough time to shake down whoever he was meeting in that chop shop and get out of there.

"Start shooting," Day ordered. They had to hold them off for as long as they could. Their only advantage was the men didn't know how many cops were in this house. They had to make it seem like there were more of them. Because if Artist's lackeys knew there were only three, they would've already descended on them. It was a tiny advantage that wouldn't hold out long. Artist was smart. He'd figure it out. If he thought for a second that God or Day was actually inside, the man would stop at nothing to kill him or his men. His entire team had been one step behind the drug lord for years and taking them out would make his shady transactions so much easier.

Day and Syn began firing both of their weapons in the front – aiming in the general direction of the men, which seemed to really piss them off because they returned fire even fiercer than the first time. The tiny home groaned and shook around them. Day dove out the way when one of the walls that made up the tiny coat closet fell down in a heap of mess around him. The shots were getting louder… closer.

"I'm getting low," Syn yelled, still firing the best he could.

"TECH!" Day yelled. "UNLEASH THE ENFORCERS! GOD… WE'RE IN HELL!"

It was their distress code. He was giving Detectives Ruxs and Green permission to wreak havoc. It meant to bring the thunder. If a miracle didn't happen soon, one or all of them was going to die.

"ETA thirty seconds," Tech updated him, his voice louder now so Day could hear him over the gunfire, Ro's shotgun, and the wailing house.

"Thirty sec—"

"I'm hit!" Ro yelled, cutting off Day's update.

Day's ears were ringing from the noise, his body aching from the physicality of the fight and his nerves being strung so tight. His vision clouded by the rising grime, he saw Ro trying to get away from the back of the house, which looked ready to crumble at any second. He was using one arm to pull himself along the ground while his other lay limp against his side. It was a bicep shot. There were so many holes in the house it was a wonder only one of them had been hit. Thirty seconds in a war could feel like an hour. But the way the meager walls were rattling, he doubted they had ten seconds before the second floor fell on top of them. Day yelled at Syn to keep shooting the one weapon he had left while he slithered on his belly to

Ro, pulling him back to the front of the house. The bullet looked to have gone through and Day was glad for small miracles.

"Ahh! Fuck!" Ro yelled and cursed from where he lay between Day's legs while he shielded the injured man from the disintegrating plaster and thick chunks of flying wood. "Where are they?!"

Day craned his neck to look out the hole where the window once was. As soon as the words left Ro's mouth, the sound of a powerful engine was heard and Day's eyes widened when a huge garbage truck took the corner at a break-neck pace, barreling down the field at what looked like its maximum speed. Syn kept his head low while he watched. "Jesus... what is—?"

"Your Enforcers are on the scene, Lieutenant," Tech said in his ear.

Day heard the gunfire lessen, replaced by the sounds of hollering men as they tried to get out of the way or get run over. "You gotta see this," Day voiced sternly in Ro's ear, clutching him hard and helping him turn to look out the window. Sirens could be heard in the distance and he knew the rest of his team was coming, but Day could see Detective Green's angry face behind the wheel of that beast. They all braced for the deafening sound as the massive truck barreled into the last SUV, its momentum taking out all six. The SUVs were thrown aside like toys by the powerful truck.

As soon as it'd cleared the row of vehicles, the men started scrambling to find shelter, and that's when Day saw Ruxs sit up in the tailgate, both arms raised, firing two 19mm submachine guns into the night, hitting whomever he saw moving. Green brought the truck to a hard stop and climbed out the door, leaping up onto the roof in a single movement. He walked down the length, firing his assault rifle, aiming high while Ruxs aimed low. Brass bullet casings flew around them like fireflies – some hitting their black leather jackets. Bodies were already littering the ground, but Day knew they wouldn't stop until there wasn't a man left breathing. He'd unleashed them – the words Ruxs and Green lived for.

"Crazy motherfuckers," Syn yelled over the firing.

Day hadn't been that scared in a long time. He watched Ruxs cease-fire, jump down from the back of the truck, and quickly turn his head up to say something to his partner. Green nodded and in a few swift, expert motions, dropped his magazine and popped another in. He fit the long butt of his rifle tight in his shoulder, his sharp eyes looking down the sight, and began firing again. Ruxs took off across the short field towards them while his partner stood on top of that truck like Scarface and provided cover fire.

Blue and red lights turned the corner and Day sucked in a huge sigh of relief. He could still hear gunfire, but there were no more bullets coming at them at the moment – the Enforcers probably scaring them – but he couldn't let his guard down because they were on a dead end street and there was nowhere for Artist's men to run. He laid Ro flat on the ground while Syn kept his gun up and aimed at the back. Day tore a piece of the destroyed curtain and pressed it hard to Ro's arm. "Gotta put more pressure here."

"Hurts!" Ro hollered.

"I know. Hang in there—"

Bullets sounded again from the back and Day ducked down, draping his upper half over his first officer… over his best friend. Syn was inching towards the back but hit the deck hard when bangs as loud as grenades pierced the night. He and Ro both flinched and gripped each other firmly. Day knew who it was. His fiancé's presence was almost frightening – even to him. Knew the sound of that overwhelming, chest-rattling firepower. The sound of Desert Eagle handguns. "You hear that, Ro? Hang in there. He's here."

Day kept his head down as more bullets were fired, his team taking out all of Artist's stooges. These men were murderers, drug smugglers, and cop killers. They'd forfeited their day in court and God and his team sent their souls to the depths of hell.

Chapter TWO

God

God sat at the table with his captain, the DA, ADA, and chief of police, along with a couple dickheads from Internal Affairs. Anytime the Enforcers were let loose those guys popped up, ready to investigate them and open a case. God wasn't in the mood for this; he wanted to be wherever his partner was. He needed to see Day, know he wasn't hurt. He needed to touch him and hold him, reassure himself he was still here with him. It'd been a long time since he'd had this close a call with his team's lives. They'd had shootouts and busts go south, but they were all together and knew how to keep each other alive.

"You said you had concrete intelligence, lieutenant. You informed your captain that you intended to only do surveillance. Now we have twenty-six dead men lying on the street, destruction of a city vehicle, and an injured officer because of your negligence," one of the IA officers stated. This wasn't the first time God had seen him. He'd actually made a point to be assigned to all of God's cases like he had a hard-on for him.

God's captain frowned at the IA officer. "Nothing is ever *concrete* in the field, or have you been behind a desk too long and forgotten that. A notorious drug lord found out that God's team was on to his current deal, and not only did he kill the informant in cold blood, but he double-crossed his contact for the shipment and tried to take out part of God's team. Are you actually trying to make a case on Lieutenant Godfrey because criminals who opened fire on three decorated police officers were gunned down in self-defense?"

"Of course, he's not," the mayor said, coming through the door with two of the city's councilmen on his heels. It was two in the morning and the man still looked sharp as a tack, as if it were noon on a Wednesday. His ebony skin was smooth, not a lick of stubble anywhere on his stern jaw like he'd actually shaved in the middle of the night. The dark suit he wore was crisp, and his blue and white striped tie was pushed snug against his Adam's apple. God knew the men with him were on the council, but he hadn't had much contact with them. He hated politics, but sometimes it butted heads with his own position... like now.

Everyone stood when they came in, including God. The kind man ignored everyone else in the room and came straight up to God, holding his hand out. God extended his and gripped the older man's firmly. This was a mayor that truly loved Atlanta as much as God's team did. The mayor grew up in the inner city, in the middle of gang territory, struggling to survive every day. From the time he was in high school, he'd only wanted to get in a position to help this city. After serving six years as city manager, he ran for and was elected mayor. And he'd implemented whatever programs and task forces were needed to help keep the residents safe. That's why he sincerely appreciated God and his detectives risking their lives every day for his city. "How are you holding up, lieutenant?"

God's back was straight, showing no outward appearance of being stressed the fuck out. His partner, his fiancé, was almost killed tonight, and he'd come too damn close to being a second too late. Never again. But he couldn't let it appear that his and Day's relationship affected him doing his job and running his team. "It's been a tough night, sir. I got a man in the hospital I'd like to check on."

"My son said there's no permanent damage to Ro's arm, they're just keeping him overnight for observation, he should be released early tomorrow," the chief commented. Ro and the chief's son, Johnson, were living together now. When Ro finally came out, Johnson didn't hesitate to scoop the handsome man up for himself.

"That's real good news. Can't have my star players going down. You all were outmanned and outgunned; yet still only one officer was injured. I appreciate the job your men did today." The mayor flashed a camera-worthy smile, clamping God on the shoulder before claiming the seat next to him. Everyone sat back down as the mayor

24

continued. "The deputy mayor is getting the statement ready for a press conference first thing in the morning – well, in a few hours. This is huge, I'm sure you all realize."

The chief spoke up again. "Of course, sir. I've been informed that Artist is dead. We injured two of his top men, both are in critical condition. If they recover we may get some more names of who's doing the smuggling on the waters and some of the dockworkers."

The mayor looked sternly at the IA officers. "Death is never to be celebrated, but I'm going to contend to the press that Godfrey's task force reacted professionally and within their scope. And make no mistake – the APD is still adamant about clearing out the drugs from this city."

"Thank you, sir," God replied.

"I think your men can take a little time and regroup, God. We have the trial coming up on that huge bust six months ago, and I need you prepared to testify, lieutenant," the DA chimed in. The man was always on God and Day's side, too. He often came to their cookouts and football nights. God wasn't surprised his friend recognized he was strung tighter than a piano wire. They'd been going non-stop for months.

"Agreed, counselor," the chief added. "Godfrey, go on and check on your team. You're dismissed."

"I'm not done with my questions," the IA officer argued, flipping some pages in his thick file.

"You most certainly are, for now." The chief glared at him. "God has provided enough details in this briefing that he can go for now. Godfrey, be available tomorrow please, just in case."

"Yes, sir." God got up and left without another word. He was glad most of the officials had his back. His team did push the rules to almost the point of fracture, but they never were malicious in taking a life and they never broke the law.

God moved through the precinct quickly, getting back to his department. The bullpen was rather quiet this late at night, but the few that he passed gave him a solemn nod. He came through the glass doors that read Narcotics Special Task Force in bold lettering, looking for only one face. Green sat at his desk, still working on his own report, but he didn't see Ruxs or Day.

"Ruxs was stinking up the office from lying in that garbage truck so I sent him to the showers," Syn said, perched on the edge of Green's desk, helping him word his statement. He looked freshly showered himself but God saw the suture strips on his forehead where he'd been hit with a piece of flying drywall, which only reminded him, even more, how close he'd come to losing his men. "Day's still down in the showers, God."

Syn knew exactly what God needed to hear. He turned on his heels and moved with determination, his chest and head aching the longer it took to get his man in his arms. God burst through the locker room doors, scanning the long rows of lockers. He saw Ruxs easing on a clean pair of jeans, drops of water still clinging to the dark hairs on his chest. When he saw God, he didn't say a word, just pointed towards the showers.

The shower area was dark, except for the lights filtering in from the locker area, but God could see steam rising from the last stall. His boots were loud on the hard floor and he didn't hesitate for a second to yank the thin plastic back and step inside the hot stall. Day's back was to him, his hands braced on the tiles in front of him, his head hanging low while the hot water pelted his tense neck and shoulders. He never flinched at the intrusion, as if he'd been expecting God any second.

"I'm okay, Cashel. I'm not hurt," Day just barely whispered over the sound of the water before he turned the nozzles to off.

"Face me," God said roughly, his throat thick with emotion.

Day turned around, pushing his hair back off his face. There wasn't a cut anywhere on his body, only a slight bruise on his right shoulder and a little discoloration on his temple. Day leaned against the stall like he was exhausted and God had to touch him. His touch was firm, but his lover was used to that. He pressed in close, breathing in the smell of Day's favorite shampoo and his body wash. God ran his nose down Day's temple, gripping him around his waist and running his calloused palms up his sides, listening for any grunts of discomfort. Day didn't make a sound. No bruised ribs. God used

26

every one of his senses, including taste, to check Day over. When God got to Day's shoulders, he squeezed them and heard the hiss Day tried but failed to hold back.

God growled and slammed both his hands against the stall on either side of Day's head. "I was late. I was fuckin' late."

"I knew you'd do this. I knew you'd blame yourself. You did your job, Cash. You kept the Enforcers close. They got there in time." Day reached up and gripped God's massive biceps, easing his hands over his shoulders and up to his neck. When he leaned in, God let Day clamp down on the back of his neck – relishing the strength of his partner – and bring their mouths together in a fierce kiss. A kiss that made a hundred apologies and answered with even more forgiveness. When they finally broke apart, both of them were panting heavily, and God wrapped Day tight in his arms, letting the contact bring him back from the edge.

"Goddamnit. I was so scared, Leo," God admitted, no longer afraid to be vulnerable in front of this one man.

"Me too," Day whispered.

Day let God hold him as long as he needed to. As long as it took for him to know that he was safe. They didn't have these kinds of moments in the office. They remained professional at all times, so neither of them moved until they were sure they could hold it together in front of their team. Stay composed long enough, until they got home. That's when he'd really show Day how relieved and thankful he truly was. He'd show him all fuckin' night long.

Chapter THREE

Detective Shawn Murphy – "Tech"

Shawn hid in the secured room that housed the team's equipment, getting his nerves back under control. They'd had many close calls in the past, especially when it came to the Enforcers – Ruxs and Green – but it'd been a while since one of the lieutenants was cornered and fighting for his life. If something had happened to Day, there was no way the team would be able to go on. Everyone loved Day, adored Syn..., and Ro, well what wasn't to love about the gorgeous man. It could've been three members of their family taken at once, and the rest of them wouldn't survive it. Especially Tech, because he'd have felt partially responsible.

He was the link between all of them. He had to move fast enough, make quick decisions that could be the deciding factor of how well a bust went down. His lieutenants and sergeant weren't always able to respond and dictate instruction, often times Tech had to react on his own for the team.

Holed up in the equipment room within their department wing, he was, at that moment, thanking the good lord above that he'd unleashed the Enforcers before Day had sent the distress call. If he hadn't, if he'd waited even another five seconds... *Jesus, I can't even imagine it.* These men were all a part of him – they were his family. He still had his father back home in the Southern Rockies, but for a few of the guys, this was the *only* family they had.

Day was a very special brother to him. He'd saved him from a lengthy federal prison sentence after he got busted for hacking into the DOD mainframe. Day had convinced the federal prosecutor that Tech wasn't malicious or a danger to society, he'd only wanted some information for himself, not to commit espionage. So he'd worked his three-year sentence with God and Day's task force and had amazed them so much, Day helped him through the legal maze to become an actual police detective. There was no way he'd have survived in prison, he was too innocent looking. A computer geek through and through. At only five foot eleven, most men stood over him. Sure, he worked out and stayed in shape, but bulking up to the size of most of the detectives on his team just wasn't in his DNA.

He ran his hands across his forehead, wiping the sweat that'd accumulated there. Tech closed his eyes and did his breathing exercises to calm himself. Ro's screams for his team were still ringing in his ears. All of their voices were in his head. He could recognize each one of them without them having to identify themselves. He kept his earpiece in at all times, even when he slept or showered, never removed it. It was as much a part of him as his right arm. The men only put theirs in if needed. He was the only one that could hear them, so he was the one who had to communicate their needs. Sure, he could put the live feed on the radio in the office or their cars, but it would be absolute chaos if all of them were able to talk through their devices at once. He'd designed the system himself and so far, it'd been foolproof. His job wasn't always this stressful; it wasn't always a massive shootout with very little assistance. God was adamant about securing complete intel and a solid plan before moving in. Safety always his primary concern. But on this one, Artist really fucked them over by pulling a rope-a-dope. And Tech wasn't the least bit sorry that asshole was dead now.

"Tech, are you back there?"

He sat up higher at the sound of his sergeant's raspy voice and made himself look like he was busy tinkering with some of his gadgets instead of getting his shit together.

"Shawn?"

"Yeah, I'm back here, Syn." Tech straightened his posture, furrowing his brow like he was reading something on the monitor.

He heard the man's light footsteps getting closer. He should've known someone would come looking for him when they didn't see him at his enormous desk full of monitors and contraptions. Tech looked around at the huge room that held the team's specialty weapons, firearms, Michaels' sniper rifles, their armor, surveillance equipment, and a ton of other stuff, all managed by him. His system was flawless and the men were constantly praising him for his ingenuity.

"You alright in here, buddy?" Syn asked, his voice always a comfort.

"Yeah. I'm good," Tech replied, picking up his 15-inch tablet, the weight of it surprisingly comforting as well – like God's Desert Eagles were against his side.

"You did great tonight. You stayed cool under the pressure and you dispatched assistance quickly. You saved our lives." Syn looked him in the eyes, making Tech shy away from that penetrating glare.

"No. You guys save yourselves. I'm just behind the desk, safe in the office, like always." Tech bit his bottom lip. He knew his job was important, he truly did. But the team were the ones that did the really hard stuff. The cut above Syn's eye proving it. Tech winced at the dark red cut. "Let me see that. It might need stitches."

"Tech."

"I'll call Vasquez to come take a look," Tech kept going. Vasquez was a paramedic before he became a police officer. He worked the third shift and didn't mind offering his assistance whenever needed. Tech raised his tablet up, about to shoot Vasquez a message. His fear of almost losing Syn tonight still heavy on his heart.

A rough hand clasped over his before he could tap on the screen. Syn gently removed it from his hands and set it down on one of the wide shelves in the room. Next thing he knew, Syn pulled him into his hard chest, securing him tightly. It only took him a few seconds to raise his own arms up and clasp them around Syn's back. His body was all rippling, hard muscles that he could feel under the man's thin APD t-shirt. He smelled clean, manly, and Syn felt safe, no longer in danger. Tech buried his face in Syn's neck and sighed his relief against him. It was amazing; Syn always knew exactly what everyone needed.

"You're an integral member of this team, and you know this by now, so stop fishing." Syn smirked in that sexy way of his.

Tech pushed his black-framed glasses up a little higher, a slight smile curving his lips. The guys did always include him. He never said he felt like an outcast, just not as important. They could always find another technology specialist.

"Come on. God and Day are back in the office."

Tech finished checking in Ruxs' submachine guns and walked back out of the equipment room, closing the door – which was only accessible by a code – behind him. He walked slowly back to his work station, his eyes locked on Day and Green as they held each other in a tight embrace. Tech could only imagine what it was like to save another man's life, unfortunately, he'd never know.

"Alright everyone, listen up," God said, his voice rough and commanding. His sharp green eyes scanned the room, making sure he made contact with each and every one of them. When he finally began to speak, it was in that frightening low timbre that always made goosebumps pop up on Tech's arms. "Tonight was one of the most difficult fights we've faced in a very long time. But we persevered, like always. Because we are the goddamn best. A message went out tonight fellas, to those motherfuckers we hunt every day. We are not to be fucked with. I don't care who comes up next because to be the baddest you gotta be capable of beating the baddest. No matter who they send, no matter how many they send... they will go down, just like those bastards did tonight. I'm damn lucky to have each one of you. We were a unit, moving as one. Even apart, we are deadly, but when combined – we are fuckin' unstoppable, and that's what those thugs saw tonight. We're going to get some negative feedback in the press – but we'll ignore that shit like we always do because they know damn well they'll have peace of mind knowing that we control these motherfuckin' streets! They'll sleep better knowing that we rule the night. We rid Atlanta of a deadly poison by taking down Artist, and they know it. So ignore it all. They stick a camera in your face, shove it down their throat. It's us risking our lives out here to keep them safe." God turned and looked at Day, his voice wavering for only a second before he continued strong, "Go home, rest up this weekend. Make love to your man. I'll see you back in here on Monday to do what we fuckin' do."

Tech loved God's speeches. They always made everyone feel like they were twenty feet tall, including him. Because when he'd been speaking, those fierce emerald eyes had locked on him as well. The lieutenants stood there talking with Syn while the rest of them packed up. They probably had a shit ton of paperwork and meetings scheduled now, not to mention going to check on Ro. Tech was going to go by Ro's house on his way out of town tomorrow. He packed his laptop and tablet in his messenger bag, shut down all his systems and left with Ruxs and Green, both of them giving him dap and a shoulder bump before they turned into the parking lot, heading towards Green's new Camaro.

Chapter FOUR

Day

Although he'd taken a shower at the station to clear away all the grime and dust from the shootout, he'd come home and poured an unbelievable amount of Epsom salt into his Jacuzzi tub and climbed in to hopefully soothe the aches that were starting to make themselves known now that the adrenaline had worn off. They'd stopped by to see Ro, needing to see for themselves that he was fine. Johnson was right there at his bedside, his hand clasped in his partner's, his head resting on Ro's thigh. They only stayed a few minutes since Ro was in and out on pain medicine. After kissing his forehead, they promised to go by his place tomorrow. That's what family did.

Dawn was fast approaching and Day was almost falling asleep in the bathtub when he felt God caress his cheek. "Come on. Time to get some rest."

Day watched God walk back into the bedroom; that huge lion's head tattooed on his back ordering him to follow. Day dried off and closed the heavy drapes in their bedroom and climbed onto their king-sized bed. God was on him before Day had a chance to climb on top of him.

"You feel okay, Leo?" God said against Day's ear, already licking his way across his jaw to his neck.

Day sighed, pushing his hips higher in answer, his cock already aching with need – it obviously not too affected by his fatigue. He needed God's touch. Needed him to make him feel alive after coming so close to death. He had to let go of the current discord in their relationship, if only for one night, and let his man's touch heal him.

"Wrap your legs around me," God told him, and Day moaned just from the way God spoke to him. Sounded in his ear. Like a force to reckoned with. He had no reservations about surrendering his body to whatever God was going to do. He trusted him completely.

He started at his head, placing the softest kisses on his bruised temple before he licked his way down the length of his body, not daring to skip his feet. God massaged the arches there with strong pressure before gently kissing his heels. God cared for his body as though worshipping a king. Treasured every part him, leaving nothing untouched, ensuring every piece of him experienced exhilaration. Igniting every nerve. He jolted those dormant sensations back to life like a surgeon would a coder after yelling "clear!"

Sometimes their sex was fast, hard, God taking him forcefully up against their bedroom wall when he wanted to remind Day of his power and strength. But tonight God was doing exactly what he'd told their men to do. Go home… make love to your man. Show your partners exactly what they mean to you. It was easy to forget sometimes, to take each day for granted. Tonight was an almost catastrophic reminder of how fast something precious could be yanked away from you.

Day tangled his hands in God's dirty-blond hair. Rubbing his scalp while he feasted on him. Dragging his hands lazily through those soft waves that stopped just past his shoulders. This was the longest he'd ever worn it; because Day had asked him to let it grow. He arched his back and sighed into the dawn as God took him deep into his warm mouth, fitting all he had inside. He didn't know which of them was louder, it was combined, continuous grunts of arousal.

"I want you to come down my throat, Leo."

Day knew it wouldn't take him long to do exactly that. They'd been arguing, disagreeing, which was what made this night so monumental. Day spread his legs wide, thrashing while saliva slid down his balls and into his seam. God was fingering him, sucking him, licking him all at the same time, and Day's orgasm hit with the momentum of the Titanic. He came like it was long overdue.

God slurped obscenely until Day was dry. Until he had nothing left and God finally rose up his body, his mouth wet and shiny, his brow damp from putting in the work. Day's head swam with euphoria while God slathered his thick cock with lube. Day was still riding high when his legs were pulled up, his knees at his cheeks, his ankles on God's broad shoulders. His lover leaned down and kissed him hard, shared his essence with him, and it almost drove him insane. They kissed with a forgotten passion – and at the same time – God brought his hips down and didn't stop until their pelvises kissed and his cock was buried deep. One continuous drive, until their balls touched and Day's mouth dropped open in a silent shout.

He shivered; his eyes rolling in his head as God gave him shallow pumps first, keeping them connected in every way they knew how. "You'll never be without me, Cash." Day tightened and clenched around God, swallowing the yells that erupted from his slick mouth.

"I want you to say that the entire time I make love to you right now, Leo."

"Never, Cash."

"Say it our entire lives." God pulled out and glided back in.

"Never be without me." He grunted after God hit a spot so deep inside him Day thought he'd pass out from the feeling. God pressed all that bulk and muscle down on him, making him sink deeper into the plush mattress. Their chests were sweaty, gliding together, the friction and emotion so overwhelming Day forgot what he was ordered to do, and God had no qualms reminding him. The full length of that cock slid out and paused like God was using a remote control. One of his legs was knocked off God's shoulder and pushed out to the side. God aimed in another direction, going deeper than before, and a rumbled growl tore through him that vibrated Day's chest. "Say it, Leo."

"Ohh. Never... never... never," Day moaned with each languid drive inside of him. God took his time, took his pleasure, loving him well into the morning.

Chapter FIVE

Steele

Damn, why couldn't people just leave him the hell alone? Steele had arrived back in Atlanta only three weeks ago and his uncle had already sent for him. He wasn't the least bit concerned about making a difference anymore. All he'd done was fight for the good, the innocent, fight for his country, and look what it got him. Look at all it took from him. Half of his battalion killed behind enemy lines. Then his partner shot and killed because his backup was a goddamn homophobic sonofabitch. But Steele's last straw was when his own department covered it up. He was turning in his shield and there was nothing his uncle could do about it.

Steele took another shot of Jack, not caring that it was only one o'clock in the afternoon. He'd heard that day drinking was the new trend, anyway. *Everyone's doing it.* He grinned at himself, kind of liking his new sense of freedom. He pulled on his tan rustic leather jacket and bent over to tie his black shit-kickers but stopped when his head protested. *Shit.* He groaned and stood back up, automatically looking around for his badge before realizing he didn't need it anymore. Ever again. *Fuck Oakland.*

His phone buzzed in the pocket of his ratty jeans, but he ignored it again. He knew who it was and he knew he was late, but he was too fucked up to get on his bike. He might not care about his own miserable existence right now, but he wasn't going to kill anyone else.

Because you care. You'll always care; it's who you are, Steele.

Steele growled at the sound of his best friend's voice in his head and pulled the half-empty bottle of whiskey back out of the cabinet, this time not bothering with a shot glass. He tipped it back and gulped a couple times, wincing at the harsh burn. He'd do it until he couldn't hear that voice anymore. Until he could get some peace, maybe even some sleep.

You won't find peace unless you're fighting for what's right.

Gulp. Gulp.

He stepped outside the broken screen door of his single-wide trailer and lit the last half of his Swisher Sweet Little cigar. The air was brisk and comfortable this time of year, reminding him that he'd always liked Atlanta in the fall. It was boots and leather coats weather, perfect for riding his bike. He needed to ride, wanted to feel the vibration against his balls, feel the freedom that came with it. But he'd have to sober up enough, first.

He looked around the rundown trailer park, kicking a couple beer cans to the side as he stood on the rickety porch surveying the filth around him. He was never a man of expensive taste or much class. Give him a decent television with good reception and a roof and he was satisfied. He didn't need a walk-in closet, overpriced furniture, or a fancy kitchen with stainless steel appliances; shit, he couldn't cook anyway, hence the garbage bags full of takeout containers and pizza boxes. He worked out enough to combat the negative effects of his diet.

"What up, cop?" a man who lived a few trailers down threw at him on his way by. It wasn't a friendly greeting or one that warranted a response. He wasn't a social neighbor and most that came across his path never had the desire to see him again. Which suited him just fine.

Steele pulled a deep inhale off his cigar, blowing half of the sweet-smelling smoke out of his nose. His phone buzzed again and he let his cigar hang out the side of his mouth while he pulled his jacket open to get it. He read the short text, frowning at the audacity of his one and only relative.

A car will be there in two minutes… get in it.

Damn. He figured he might as well get this over with. His uncle would be disappointed in his decision to leave law enforcement, but if there's one thing Steele never did, it was let anyone tell him how to live his life.

He listened to the depressing sounds of the place he currently called home, the crying babies, the fighting spouses, the god-awful heavy metal music that his neighbor blasted no matter what time of day or night it was, but still he felt no desire to be anywhere else. Ackerman was gone, his best friend, the man who he'd wanted more than anything to become his lover, was gone.

He stood there with one hand braced on the rusted overhang while he watched a shiny, black Lincoln Town Car navigate around the deep potholes of the one street that curved through his neighborhood. One way in and one way out. As the car got closer, Steele heard the door across the street bang against the side of the metal trailer, and a toddler that looked too old to still be in diapers hurried out into the yard, heading toward the street.

Steele's heart lurched and without thought, his body sprang into action. He ran across the dirt that made up his yard and grabbed the little boy before he could run out in front of the Lincoln, the fender clipping the heel of his boot. He was just able to regain his footing and not drop the kid.

The boy was at least three or four. His hair was a tangled mess of sandy brown curls and he wore nothing except his Pull-Up, which was barely hanging on since it was weighed down with urine. He had bright brown eyes and he looked at Steele like he was Superman, not the slightest bit concerned that he was in the arms of a stranger. The benefits of being young and oblivious.

Steele placed the kid back inside the front door and locked it from the inside, not bothering to notify the parents. This wasn't the first time the little one had run outside; Steele would most likely see him back out again when he came home later.

Steele climbed in the front seat of the Lincoln.

"No smoking in here."

"Fine, I'll stay here." Steele went for the handle.

"No wait," the driver hurriedly said.

"Mm hmm. Drive," Steele grunted and pulled another long drag on his cigar. He didn't care when the teen in a grown-up outfit put the window all the way down, he simply reclined and enjoyed the cool breeze in his hair.

"That was awfully heroic of you with that kid. I didn't see him."

"You should pay attention where you're going. Especially in residential areas." Steele barely opened his mouth when he spoke. He wasn't in the mood for conversation. Especially with him. The guy's perfect haircut, impeccably pressed navy blue suit and red striped tie screamed do-gooder.

"I was distracted by that piece of crap tin box you live in. But you're right, I should've been looking. You move fast. One second, you were on your porch and the next second, you were across the street. That's amazing... especially being three sheets to the wind. You smell like a distillery. I'd be intrigued to see what you could do if you weren't wasted." The man turned a cocky grin at him and Steele had a mind to knock that smug look off his adolescent face.

"How old are you, kid?" Steele tossed his small cigar out the window, watching the scenery of Atlanta's busy streets fly by.

"I'm not a kid, I'm twenty-five." The guy balked, his frown almost making Steele laugh in his face. Was that his mean look?

"What exactly do you do for my dear old uncle, huh? Besides pick up his hard-headed nephew?"

The guy didn't respond, as if Steele had hit a soft spot. Instead, he turned the corner hard onto Trinity Avenue and pulled into the parking lot of the Atlanta City government building. Tall oak trees surrounded the building, the once green leaves already turning their bright reds and oranges. Steele walked through the cold, heartless lobby, ignoring the disgusted looks of the distinguished gentlemen that milled about, and went straight to the bank of elevators on the north hall. He overlooked the classic beauty of the historical building, its tall columns and grand staircases, no longer interested in the magnificence of things. He wasn't here on a field trip – he'd been summoned.

Steele paused, staring at his uncle's last name on the glass double doors. The name his father held, grandfather, great grand..., and him. Instead of using the brass handles, he placed his large palm over the word Councilman and entered the city official's office. He walked across the thick carpet, stopping in front of the only individual behind one of three desks that made up the reception area.

A petite blonde smiled brightly and gave him a courteous greeting before she asked how she could help him.

"I'm here to see Councilman Steele."

"Do you have an appointment?" she asked, flipping open a bulging black calendar book.

"Nope," he replied curtly, sticking a well-chewed toothpick that he'd pulled from his coat pocket in his mouth.

The woman gave him a look that barely masked her revulsion. "I'm sorry. The councilman's calendar is full for today, but I'd be happy to take your—"

"Not a problem, I'll come back when he's not busy." He winked and turned to leave. He was almost home free when he heard a sharp, "Stop right there. Don't even think about it."

Steele stopped midway out the door and took a couple steps back, letting the glass close in his face. No matter how much he'd like to, he couldn't ignore that voice or its tone. One that sounded exactly like his father's.

"Come on, Edwin. Inside."

When he turned around and looked his uncle in those light eyes, his chest ached with a need to see his father just one more time. It was his twin standing in front of him, but if he closed his eyes, he'd swear it was his dad. That Estonian accent lingering just barely on the tip of his tongue but overshadowed by the extensive time spent living in America.

"Please hold my calls, Renee. Thank you."

Steele walked past the wide-eyed receptionist, her face showing her confusion. Confused that the regal councilman would consort with such a vagabond. His uncle closed the door and walked up to him, pulling him into a hug. Steele didn't have the strength or willpower not to hug him back. He embraced his father's twin with the ferocity of needing him to make everything not only right in his life but right in the world. Life was screwing him too hard and he couldn't take it anymore.

"*Vennapoeg.*"

Steele knew some of his family's native language, but he didn't speak fluent Estonian, had always run when his father started up lessons, not wanting to miss a second of having fun with his *isa* instead of learning. But he knew the word nephew. It's how his uncle always greeted him. Steele held on and closed his eyes while his last remaining family member tried to comfort him.

"You're going to be okay. You will. You're strong, *vennapoeg*. You are your father's son. You will pull through this."

"I'm tired of fighting," Steele whispered painfully, clutching his uncle's expensive suit jacket in his fists.

"You've just begun." His uncle pulled back and placed his hands on his cheeks, looking him in his sad gray eyes.

"I can't fight for that city anymore. I won't. They let him die… they just ignored his call for help. I know they did." Steele felt the need for a drink. The weight of living with his battalion's death, and now his partner's death, ate at him. Even though he'd never felt comfortable in Oakland and he and his partner never got a chance to form a more definitive bond, Steele knew his partner had been a good cop.

"I've done everything I can, Edwin. I can't prove that unit could've got there in time to save him," his uncle said sadly.

Steele gritted his teeth to keep from cursing up a storm. He'd never humiliate his uncle in his place of business. "Those bigoted bastards," he hissed. Shaking his head, his voice strong again. "I'm not going back."

"I know you're not. Because god help 'em all if they hurt you too." His uncle spoke in that fear-provoking tone that all the Steele men were notorious for. "I'll be in prison for the rest of my life. Don't let the suit fool you, *vennapoeg*."

"It never has, *onu*," Steele answered. He absolutely knew of the power beneath that suit. His uncle was still a warrior – only now he had to fight from this office because of the metal plate in his hip – he'd fought right alongside Steele's father in many protests right here in the United States before joining the Marines to fight abroad. It was in their bloodline. His great, great grandfather was a general in the Estonian Defence Forces – a peacekeeper that participated in the 1921 forming of the League of Nations. A man loved and respected by his countrymen until he saved the life of an American soldier that was being tortured by Estonian commanders.

As far back as Steele could remember, the men in their family stood up for those weaker than themselves, stood for what was right, no matter the cost. It'd not only cost his great, great grandfather his position in the military but the love of his homeland. It was a blessing his grandfather wasn't too proud to leave, wasn't afraid to call America home, that's why they fought for it.

Steele himself was a third generation Marine Force Recon lieutenant. He performed sixty-two successful black ops missions before taking bullets in the ribs and the thigh, ending his military career. The Navy doctor said he'd walk with a limp the rest of his life and would never be battle ready again.

He may have lost his unit, but he'd never stopped living for them. Living for Ackerman. Until this day, he still hadn't chased a man that could out-run him. It took him three years to heal fully, but he did it.

"Why'd you call me here, *onu*? Not only to your office but to Atlanta." Steele stared out the tall window, looking down on the parking lot full of official vehicles.

"Because I believe you need new surroundings. Because I believe if you stay in Oakland, you won't stop digging into Ramos' death. They'll never admit to stalling on the call, Edwin, and neither you nor I have any way to prove it."

"I can beat them until they confess."

"Now you've answered your own question." His uncle stood next to him, his firm hand resting on his shoulder.

"Ramos had a family. A husband, children, aunts, uncles, nieces, and nephews who loved him. Now he's gone. Why? Because he chose to have a husband instead of a goddamn wife. He was a good cop. He didn't deserve it."

"That type of hate is never deserved, *vennapoeg*. But I can't have you blaming yourself for it all. He was off duty. He tried to stop a store robbery. He lost his life, but he saved two others before he did. He did his job, and it wasn't your fault, Edwin."

"I'm still done," Steele repeated. He wasn't sure if he was trying to convince his uncle or still trying to convince himself.

"Oh, you're far from done. Joseph told me what you did when he was pulling up to get you. Your instincts, your reactions, your need to do good is in here, *vennapoeg*." His uncle held his shoulder and placed his other hand over his heart. "There's no quitting in here. There's no quitting who you are. You'll fight until your last breath, and that's a long time from now. What do you think you're going to do without your shield or a platoon? Become a Walmart greeter? Or become an alcoholic?"

His uncle's gray eyes hardened and blazed with anger, his voice a menacing snarl. "Drowning yourself in the bottom of a bottle is beneath you. You will not disgrace your father... my brother. I won't allow it. You are not tired, you're not weak. It's impossible," he hissed, close to Steele's face. "Your last name is *Raud*. Iron... steel. You think your great grandfather changed the *meaning* of our family surname... he only translated it to English. You are unbreakable. And I demand you act like it."

Steele didn't speak. His uncle was right. He'd let hurt and injustice control his actions.

"Believe me. I understand loss. I've experienced my fair share. My biggest hurt was losing my brother. He was a part of me, a part I'll be without from here on. But I'll work hard every day to continue fighting for what he believed in. He believed in this country, Edwin. Keep fighting, son. You just need a team you can fight with."

Steele snorted. "Yeah, right. Who the hell can handle my shit, *onu*?"

His uncle smiled that crooked grin, the same way his father used to whenever Steele'd fall into his trap. "I think I know someone. Come over here and sit down. I want to show you something."

Steele sat on the low back suede couch in the sitting area in his uncle's large office while he turned on a flat screen television sitting atop a cherry oak TV stand. Immediately, a black and white grainy video began playing. His uncle didn't watch the screen, instead, he watched for Steele's reaction.

He saw a column of big SUVs lined up in a row and men –
firearms drawn – getting into position for something big. As he
watched the video play out, his jaw ticked and his eyes narrowed. He
didn't understand what this was. An execution first… then maybe a
hit. Twenty or so men – gangsters – were firing in one direction.
"What the hell is this, uncle?"

"Just keep watching."

Steele wanted to pull out another little cigar but he knew better.
Instead, he stroked the rough stubble on his jaw, looking like he
wanted this footage to stop until he saw a huge garbage truck roar up
the narrow street and mow down the men that were shooting. "Jesus
Christ." He watched a man appear from the back like Houdini, firing
machine guns like he was in Desert Storm. It was two of them. They
moved as a synchronistic unit like they could read each other's
thoughts. Quickly and efficiently, they took out every thug they
aimed their weapons at.

His uncle pushed a button on the remote. "This is film taken
from the back side, at another angle that was caught by a chopper. It's
pieced together, but check this out." The image flickered a few times
before another feed began. "This is the rear view. The gangsters that
we just saw were in the front; this is the back of that house."

There were at least ten to fifteen men back there firing. "All
these guys are firing at one house?" Steele said disbelievingly. "They
were probably wasting ammo at that point."

"Nope. The officers inside were still returning fire," his uncle
said with a determined expression. "Only three of them."

Steele stood up and moved closer, unable to take his eyes off the
screen. There was no audio to the video, but he could almost feel the
chaos of that battle inside him. A silver truck appeared around the
corner – taking the curve like a NASCAR driver – with undercover
police vehicles trailing it. He watched a man slide out the passenger
window and perch his ass on the door, firing an automatic rifle over
the top of the truck while the driver spun it in a perfect three-sixty,
bright flashes of explosions erupting from his own handgun. A Desert
Eagle. It was one of Steele's favorites. He could easily recognize that

flashbang in the dark night. The man firing over the hood was an expert, a marksman. Nothing could shake him.

"Goddamn. Who is that?" Steele pointed at the man looking down the scope and knocking off men as the truck spun him in a circle.

"That's Detective Austin Michaels."

Steele pointed to the driver, a behemoth of a man who was now darting across the road – he could move fast – towards the house, both arms raised, shooting anything in his path. Wielding those massive firearms like a true beast... like a soldier. "And him. Who the hell is he?"

"That's your new boss. Lieutenant Cashel Godfrey... they call him... God."

Chapter SIX

God

"I don't like this captain. I choose my team, it's always been that way. My team is built of qualified men I can trust. You're telling me I gotta take some blacklisted cop from the West Coast, who lost the respect of his entire department. His partner's killed and he flees. Fuck that. Find him another department. Homicide or robbery." God was never disrespectful to his captain, but this was going too far. A new member. He didn't put in a request to recruit. What the hell was this? Was someone trying to sabotage his department... set him up? "I don't like this... something's off."

"Well, he sure looks good as hell on paper," Syn put in, flipping pages of the thick file that had been forwarded to them. "Came into law enforcement rather late, though – but graduated top of the class after annihilating a few records there. Took the detective's exam three years later and aced it. But there's a ton of information back here that's blacked out."

"That's from his military career." The captain sighed, rolling up the sleeves to his dress shirt. He looked as tired as they were.

It was already after six, a Sunday evening. God had called his team in at the captain's order for an emergency meeting, only for the older man to tell him this bullshit. He and Day were supposed to be home watching football right now. Enjoying their last evening off.

"It'll take time for me to get him trained... time I don't have. And what about all the evaluations and psych screenings, does he really get to bypass all that?" God argued, his fist clenched tight on the armrest.

His captain chuckled. "You mean these two actually passed psych evals?" He pointed at Ruxs and Green.

"Fuck no! But at least we were prepared for them to fail," God barked.

Green tried to cover his laugh but failed at that, too.

"I'm glad y'all are finding this amusing. But I don't see the humor." God glared at them.

"Why's he coming to us, anyway?" Day finally spoke, standing behind God, massaging his shoulders to keep him from jumping up out of the chair and throwing shit around.

"This is coming from higher up, Day. Not exactly sure who, but higher than the chief. Believe me, I fought this. I've been on the phone with every connection I have, but there's no one that can override this decision. It's done." The captain sat up a little straighter and motioned for the file from Syn. "I'm kind of optimistic, Godfrey. This guy was a Marine for twenty years, Special Forces for eleven of them. He had top-level security clearance, has three Purple Hearts, a Bronze Star, and countless commendations and..." the captain scanned some more pages. "Holy shit... this can't be right. No way. God, am I reading these initials right?"

God took extra notice now, his captain rarely cursed. God looked at what his captain was pointing at. This guy *had* received a lot of awards, but his captain's finger was hovering over the initials MH, and it gave him pause.

"What is it?" Green asked. "Damn, now I'm intrigued."

"What is it, God?" Syn squinted at him.

"He received the Medal of Honor in '09 from President Clinton." God tossed the file back on the table. "Still doesn't mean *I* trust him."

"It means he's trustworthy. That's the highest military medal there is. They don't just give those to anyone, and you know it. The guy's a certified winner on paper... let's see if he fits in with you miscreants. You say you only want the best." The captain stood up and took his jacket off the back of the chair. "I think you just got him."

God watched the captain leave, his word final. He couldn't refute this. He'd have to give the guy a shot. If he was a cowboy and refused to take orders, God would go all the way to the mayor if he had to. He wouldn't put his men in harm's way.

"The Medal of Honor." Michaels raised his eyebrows and whistled. "That's heavy."

"What's it awarded for, exactly? I'm not from a military background and I don't feel like googling it," Syn asked.

"It's awarded for valor. Going above and beyond the call of duty. Only given by the President," God informed his team. "Alright, enough stroking his dick, the guy hasn't even gotten here yet. Syn, I want you to tell Tech to get in here early tomorrow and see what else he can pull up on this guy before he arrives. Also, tell him to get the simulation programs together; let's see this guy in action."

"No problem," Syn said, pulling on his thick denim jacket.

"No need to sit here and be pissed Cash. Let's go home. Got a long week ahead of us." Day stopped touching him and just that fast the pain in his neck returned.

Chapter SEVEN

Tech

It was still dark when he pulled his Tahoe into the station parking lot. The shift change didn't start for another two-and-a-half hours so he was able to get a space close to the door, which started his early morning off right. He'd had a really good session with his personal trainer on Saturday and for some reason, when his muscles ached it made him feel strong, like the men in his team.

Syn asked him to come in a little early because they were getting a new recruit. Which he thought odd because God usually gave them sufficient notice when he was even thinking of bringing on another member. It took months of going through qualifications and testing. He had to admit he was curious and more than a little excited to see who had qualified to run with these guys.

He walked through the desolate bullpen, heading to the rear of the station where their department was located. The lights were already on, which stunned him, he was typically first to arrive if no one pulled an all-nighter or made an overnight arrest. If anything, the Enforcers would be just heading home at this hour.

He opened the glass doors, surprised to find Syn at his desk, going through a stack of papers. He looked well rested and extremely handsome in his worn Levi's and black dress shirt, that bright gold badge suspended around his corded neck. His olive skin and constant five o'clock shadow were a huge turn-on for anyone, male or female, but those dark eyes and kind smile made him an unpredictable and deadly detective. "Morning, Sarge. You're here early."

"Yep. Wanted to meet you here so we could try to gather as much as we can on this guy before God and Day get in. Last I checked in on him he was still pissed. They have a meeting with IA this morning, but they should be here by ten."

"No problem. So, how's Furi?" Tech asked while he went about powering up his computers. The loud whirring of the internal fans and the awakening of his powerful CPUs was a symphony to his ears.

"He's good. Happy." Syn smiled a smile that was reserved for mentions of his partner.

Tech nodded and averted his eyes. It had to be nice to have someone to go home to each night. Someone who understood the demands of the job and didn't constantly bitch at you about it or lord it over you. The last boyfriend Tech tried to have was over three years ago and had lasted a good nine months – the longest he'd ever been with someone. He'd loved Jason and thought they were going to build a life together, but Tech was on call twenty-four hours a day and Jason couldn't handle being second string. Tech wouldn't change his job for anything in the world, so he'd regrettably let his boyfriend go.

Now all he had was his work. If anything, Tech wanted more responsibilities, but he was currently working on that. When the time was right, he'd go to his lieutenants about it. In the meantime, this was his contribution to righting some of the vast numbers of wrongs in his home city.

"How's your dad? I saw some more pictures he posted on his Facebook page, they're so beautiful. The one with the rainbow after that thunderstorm… Jesus. I can't imagine what it's like to live in those mountains and see images like that all the time."

Tech smiled. Syn knew everything about his team, and it wasn't just his job. He really was interested in how the only biological family Tech had was doing. "He's good. Yeah, I saw them too, they are amazing. He's gotten really good. I keep telling him to try to sell his photos, get a few framed, ya know. Landscapes are used in everything from screensavers to printed calendars. But he does photography for peace. He says if he makes it a job… then it'll be work."

"I told you, Mr. Murphy is one of the smartest men I ever met. When are you going back up to visit him? I'd love to go again. We had a ball. Furi still makes fun of when I got buried in that snow

54

mound. It was freakin' April and there was still like eight feet of snow on the ground."

"I guess growing up there I forget how others see those mountains. Yeah, we did have fun, though. I'll probably go back the beginning of the year, or right after the holidays if I can get the time from God. I've been dying to put my skis back on."

"No problem. Just let me know when you're ready to submit for the time, I'll make sure he approves it."

"Thanks, Syn." Tech dropped down into his chair and turned to face his boss and good friend. "So, tell me about this new guy. Have you met him yet?"

"No. None of us have. Never even heard of him, actually. He was on the West Coast. Did it big up there, I heard." Syn rubbed the crease in his forehead. "But you know God doesn't like hearsay, so get me something concrete. You're gonna have to dig deep on this one, kid."

Tech gritted his teeth, he hated being called that. Sure, he was smaller and of course, he was the youngest of the crew – all of them were over forty and he was twenty-nine – but he had the IQ and mentality of a seventy-year-old scholar. Damnit, he needed to show them what he could do physically.

Syn rolled up a chair next to him with the file in his hand. "Let's start with name and social and work our way up. He's got a confidentiality mask in the paperwork from when he was active duty, so I guess that's not all that critical. But if he's got severe PTSD issues, then we need to know... immediately. Obviously, he's still cleared for duty because he's a police officer, but those qualifiers don't catch everything, sometimes these men can mimic exactly what needs to be said to pass. Not all that concerned with ability, I mean he got some type of Medal and Honor so—"

Tech stopped typing, slinging his head around so fast he heard his neck crack. "Did you say Medal *of* Honor?"

"Yep. That's what the file says. He's a real live GI Joe, so do what you do, kid and let me know what you find. He comes in at noon. He's here on a trial run, but still get him suited up with everything. I'm kinda feeling like we won't have much of a say on whether or not he stays. Not unless he tries to kill one of us."

Tech sat with his back to the guys while he hacked through countless databases, pulling up all the private information he could on their new guy. The more he discovered, the more impressed he became. The guy was pretty amazing. He couldn't really see what his face looked like from his military photo since his cover was so low on his brow, but he had a beautiful mouth. It wasn't hard to get more information regarding his law enforcement career since it was only four years long. Most of his adult life was spent as a Marine. He was an awarded marksman, a decorated Marine from a long line of activists and career military predecessors. Tech hit a ton of blocks when he tried to dig deeper into the man's military background. He was at the DOD's mainframe again, his inquiring mind getting the better of him as his fingers started flying over the keys. His eyes darted back and forth from one screen to the next while he moved through encryptions and firewalls. He kept telling himself that he had every right to get this information, it was for his lieutenants.

No one bothered him and he was able to tune out the incessant chatter when all of his teammates were in the office while he worked. His eyes widened when he finally got to some notes that would interest all of them, and then he heard the captain's voice.

"Everyone. This is Detective Edwin Steele."

Tech quickly clicked print and turned away from his monitors to get a glimpse of the man of the decade. Tech gulped hard, hoping no one heard it over the deafening silence, and checked out their new member. *How the hell am I supposed to stare at a computer screen when he's in here?* To say he was hot was like saying Everest was a little high. Nothing could've prepared Tech for his arrival. And the way they were all staring at the guy, his team had to be feeling the same way.

The man didn't speak, seeming perfectly comfortable being stared at by eight sets of eyes. He had on jeans with permanent grime stains, which rode low on his hips, and a threadbare long john shirt

under a rustic brown leather jacket. Tech really had to get himself
under control when he looked down at the untied, dusty black combat
boots. Steele stood there with both thumbs tucked into his jeans
pockets, flicking around a toothpick nestled in the corner of his
mouth like he was bored. But it was the eyes. Those icy gray eyes
that seemed to see all and dismiss nothing.

God was the first to speak up, his voice startling Tech. "You
smell like alcohol."

"Because I been drinking," Steele quipped right back. "I can see
why you guys are detectives."

Tech's eyes widened. He hadn't heard anyone mouth off to God
in a very long time, not without seriously regretting it. But Steele's
voice made his breath catch in his throat. It was grainy and deep like
he fantasized about in a man. Tech took a silent breath. He had to
stop looking at the guy like that, he screamed straight. Which left him
thinking the man probably wouldn't be around long.

The captain turned his eyes to Steele. "We're willing to overlook
that today, and only today since you're not officially on duty. Well,
I'll leave and let you guys get acquainted."

The captain left fast like he knew of the storm that was brewing.
God still stood there with his arms crossed, shooting furious green
beams at their new member, clearly already not liking his attitude.
And boy did he have one massive fucking chip on his shoulder.

"My name is Sydney. Corbin Sydney. I'm your sergeant." Syn
moved past God and Day, who were still staring, and extended his
hand. Tech released a breath when Steele grasped Syn's hand and
shook it before tucking his thumbs back in. Syn being the diplomat of
the group, Tech expected him to take over and try to cool the fire
burning in his lieutenant's eyes and smooth things over. "We've
heard some amazing things about you. Let me introduce everyone."
Syn began pointing while Steele moved further inside the office.
"Those are your lieutenants Godfrey and Day. God is first in
command."

Syn narrowed his midnight eyes at God, and after a couple
seconds, God stuck his big hand out and shook the Marine's hand,
Day following right behind.

Syn nodded and kept moving. "Over here is Detective Austin Michaels. He's our sniper."

"You only have one?" Steele murmured, the toothpick barely moving when he spoke.

"They only need one," Austin replied, shaking Steele's hand.

Syn quickly diverted in the other direction. "These two men are Detectives Ruxsberg and Green. We call them the Enforcers. They are experts in hand-to-hand combat and do most of the shakedowns on the street, obtaining information and arrests. By whatever means necessary." Ruxs and Green stood at exactly the same time and shook Steele's hand.

"You two were the ones in the garbage truck?" Steele asked, his expression still dark and serious.

Ruxs gave a curt nod.

"Nice," Steele gritted out and turned around to look dead at him.

Tech stood up, pushing his glasses up higher on the bridge of his nose. It was like Steele wasn't paying attention to anyone else in the room, even Syn was now behind him as he made his way over to him. *Stand up tall*. The Marine stopped right in front of him and held his hand out towards him.

"And you are?"

Enraptured. Before him stood a man who possessed a goddamn Medal of Honor. This close, Tech could smell the soldier's virility, the power, mixed with a hint of whiskey and sweet tobacco. Tech felt his cock harden and he had to breathe through his nose not to crumple to a useless heap of lust at the man's boots. He blinked and tried to prepare his throat to produce sound while he fought to remember what the hell the question was. "Um...."

Syn cleared his throat and hid his grin behind his fist, and Tech wished the ground would open up right at that second and swallow him whole. They were all looking quite amused while his pale skin overheated and the tips of his ears burned with humiliation. "This is Detective Shawn Murphy, we call him Tech. He's our technology expert and comms specialist. You and he will probably be working very closely together while he runs you through all your tests and simulations."

"I don't take tests," Steele answered, his light eyes still on Tech while he stood there chewing off his bottom lip, wishing Steele'd direct those eyes anywhere else in the room.

Chapter EIGHT

Steele

The meeting had just gotten a little better. The detective they called Tech was the only highlight in the entire department. He looked so innocent standing there, waiting to be acknowledged. A sheep amongst wolves. Steele licked his lips and watched the sexy, light pink tinge work its way up the man's long throat.

Steele didn't like tests or simulations, but if this man was the administrator, he might reconsider.

"Everyone goes through the simulations, not—"

"The streets are not a simulation, lieutenant. You wanna see what I can do, put me in the field. Where the real test can begin." Steele finally turned away from those sexy brown eyes and looked at his new bosses. "There's nothing that can come from his pretty little head that will show you what I can do. No offense." He looked back at Tech, whose ears were turning back to their natural color... oops... spoke too soon.

"None taken." The young man finally spoke, his voice deeper than Steele expected, but still gentle.

He couldn't have been over thirty. Steele almost felt like a creep, staring at the guy like that, but he was too unique, stood out too hard not to stare at him. That ivory skin and those deep brown eyes encased in long, soft-looking lashes. Even behind the black-framed glasses, those eyes were mesmerizing. Instead of continuing to fluster the sexy detective, Steele walked over to the window and looked out into the parking lot.

"I think you have the details of this job confused. There're only three bosses." God scowled at the back of Steele's head. He could feel the heat of those intelligent green eyes. Yes. He already liked his new lieutenant. He looked strong and capable of leading such an imitable group of men. The way he maneuvered his truck and shot those weapons, Steele had to respect him. God was a true commander and Steele knew the strength it took to uphold that position. The responsibility, the courage needed... the honor.

"You'll be in the field. Sooner than you think. But we are a well-oiled machine here, and if you wanna work with us, we have to trust you... and I'm sure you need to trust us."

That was Syn again. Obviously, he was the level head of the group. The negotiator. He was good at it. But how was Steele supposed to fully feel comfortable risking his life with these men? What had happened to his partner had him doubting a lot. All these muscled, testosterone-filled detectives looked like they nibbled on tits when they went home each night. Steele didn't blurt out his sexuality or have a rainbow magnet on his bike's exhaust pipe, but he wasn't in the closet, either. If he met a guy... and he liked him... he wasn't hiding him.

"Why don't you tell us a little about yourself? This is an interview of sorts," Day asked.

Steele turned around and spread his arms wide, looking directly at the shorter of his bosses. "Ask away, lieutenant. I'm an open book. I'll tell you anything you wanna know."

"What'd you do in the Marines?"

"That's classified." Steele smirked. He turned back around, holding in his laughter. He and the guys in his platoon used to love to do that to officers, just to piss them off. He thought about his men and quickly tamped it back down. This was no place to drudge up those memories. It'd been seven years. Would the ache in his heart every time he thought their names ever fully go away?

"Real cute," God grumbled.

"So you think I'm going to send my men out there with you and we don't know shit about you except you have a liking for cheap whiskey and Swisher Sweet cigars?" Day retorted.

"You guys got my file, I'm sure."

"Regardless. All that file tells us is that you were better than most of the detectives in Oakland. Your partner was killed off duty and you left. Are you grieving?" Day stepped a little closer and propped his hip up on one side of his large desk.

Steele lowered his voice to a rumble. "No. I'm not. He was a good man. He didn't deserve what happened, but he died saving lives. I don't need to grieve him. It was a good death."

"Excuse me?" Ruxs balked.

"He means it was an honorable death," God answered for him. "You were a Marine twenty years. You have nothing to say about that?"

"Nothing I *can* say, lieutenant. I fought wars." Steele turned back to the window. Day's eyes were too observant, keen and knowing.

"I can tell you some things," a quiet voice said from behind him.

Steele didn't turn around; instead, he let the sound of that sweet voice caress the back of his neck. So, Tech wanted to join in on the interview, huh. No problem there. But he still wasn't going into the details of his service and he'd never again recount the details of the night the Taliban took his brothers. The thirty-two he'd killed – their lives would never be retribution enough to ease him through the hurt he'd live with forever. The hole that losing Ackerman left in his soul.

"Lieutenant Colonel Edwin Leks Steele. Comes from a long line of Marine men, including his father – Robin Steele – and grandfather. Information here dates back four generations to his family in Estonia. He has one living relative in the United States, who also served in the Corps but was injured in combat and honorably discharged in 2003... name is... one second."

Steele turned away from the window, looking at the only man who'd managed to get his hands on more than generic personal information about his life prior to joining the Oakland Police Department. The guy wasn't rattling off the obvious; he was giving his bosses what they asked for... something they didn't already know. Tech had a binder-clipped stack of about hundred pieces of paper in his hand and stood boldly in front of him reading his rap sheet. Was this the guy's way of getting back at him for embarrassing him? If so, it was rather cute and flattering that the sexy detective had done a little hacking on his behalf. Steele widened his stance and shrugged. So they'd know a tad more about him than he usually divulged but, *que sera*. They'd never get what they were actually after… what they really wanted to know.

Tech continued when he found what he was looking for. His dark pupils moving rapidly over the text he read. "Last living relative – in the States, anyway – is Rasmus Steele. Atlanta Councilman Rasmus Steele."

"Well, at least we know who pulled the strings now," God growled. "You're Councilman Steele's son?"

Steele slowly shook his head back and forth. "*Vennapoeg.* Nephew. Rasmus was my father's twin. He asked me to come here after my partner was killed."

They waited a second for him to keep going, but when they realized he wasn't offering up anything else, Tech went back to reading. Finding out his uncle was a councilman should've been a piece of cake.

"Did a ton of black ops missions. Fourteen of them he headed up, until…" Tech stopped and Steele assumed he was stopped by all the black Sharpie that had to be all over those documents, but he kept reading. "There're a lot of initials and codes I don't understand, but it was a mission to recover a General Robert Belle. Led by Col. Steele, the Fifth Marine Regiment, nicknamed the Fearless Five, was ambushed—"

"How the fuck did you get that?" Steele's smile fell like a deflated balloon. The cocky smirk long gone. No one, absolutely no one, should have that name. The general's or his battalion's. That was a black ops mission ordered directly by the Secretary of Defense. A general with top-level clearance and infinite knowledge of a new US base being built in Baghran had been captured and taken to be tortured for the information. The Fearless Five was a myth to most. His team were ghosts… *he* was the ghost. This wasn't possible. The hacker shit was no longer cute, right now he felt like Tech was a terrorist with classified information and Steele's hands began to clench at his sides as his pulse raced. *Who the fuck was this man? Who sent him?*

"Steele," he heard someone say, but he wasn't sure who.

64

Tech kept reading off the details of the worst days of his life. For thirty-six hours, they'd held those fuckers off. Took out as many as they could before... Steele's head jerked as he tried to forcefully yank his mind back from that night.

"Steele."

Tech's head was down in the document – oblivious to Steele's reaction – like he was reading the most interesting manuscript of his life. But this wasn't the next Stephen King thriller... this was war. "There's a lot of terminology I don't know, but there's mention of a suicide bomber and a regiment of sixty or more rebel insurgents."

Steele just barely held in the growl that wanted to burst from his chest. He flicked his eyes up at the detective. He needed to stop immediately. Needed to stop talking.

"Tech, that's enough."

Steele cut his eyes over to Syn, to his sergeant. *Stop him.* He tried to convey with his eyes, because if he opened his mouth at the moment he was going to roar his rage and react. This man had broken the law, didn't matter if he was a cop or not. He tried to keep a lid on his anger. Focused to remember where he was.

"Oh," the young man blurted. "Here's why he got the Medal. He killed over thirty of them and pulled the general and two of his men to safety. But... oh... but three members of his team were killed. Marks... Ramiraz...."

"Tech, no," God hissed, but it was too late.

"And Ackerm—"

A jolt hit Steele's chest at the first syllable of Ackerman's name. No one in that room could move fast enough to keep him away from Tech. Before the smaller detective could finish the last syllable of his best friend's name, Steele snapped his hand out and grabbed the documents, slinging them into the air at the same time he moved into Tech's body and wrapped both his arms up in a clutch that was not only impossible to get out of but exceptionally painful. The man yelled out, his brown eyes blown and shining with fear. Both his narrow arms were hyperextended at the elbow, with one upward thrust Steele could snap both ulna bones at the same time.

"Hey! Whoa... Steele! Let him go! Easy... easy!"

"Don't touch him!" Steele heard the strongest voice of all of them break over the yells. If God was ex-military, he knew what he was talking about. Because if any of the others got too close, or tried to touch him, he'd take care of them, too.

He could hear the yells of the men but he kept his eyes locked on Tech. "It's illegal for you to possess that information," he snarled, his anger bubbling beneath the surface. He kept the lock on Tech's arms with one hand and shot his arm around the back of the smaller man's neck, jerking him close to his mouth. "Don't you ever say that name in your life. You don't deserve to say that name."

"Okay… okay, easy Steele. He's not your enemy," Syn crooned from a distance, his raspy voice breaking through. "He was only doing what we asked. Shawn was going to shred it right after."

Steele listened to the sergeant's words, the darkness around the edges of his vision fading back to color. When he looked closer, he could see the moisture, the panic in the detective's eyes. He also saw the man's anger, the shame at being the weaker opponent. Steele abruptly released him and Tech stumbled back, landing in Day's arms. When his lieutenant tried to look him over, Tech brushed him off and shouldered past the rest of his team to storm out of the office. Syn bolted after him, his concern for his brother evident.

That's when it hit Steele like a two-by-four to his chest. The regret. He'd used his skill on a man who hadn't stood a chance. He'd attacked a man who had meant him no harm. Tech had just been doing his job. *Fuck. Goddamnit.* Steele ran his hands through his short strands of hair, trying not to beat himself up so hard for what he'd done. But how could he not? He'd just shown these men how fast he could snap at the mention of his fallen brothers. The office held that uncomfortable, dismal vibe that was the polar opposite of what it had been when he'd entered. He'd brought despair into their team… that meant he'd never be a member.

Steele bent and picked up the documents he'd knocked out of Tech's hands. He looked at the few men still there, all of their eyes averted, not even able to look at him. There was only one thing he could say as he took his walk of shame towards the door. "Interview's over. Test failed."

Chapter NINE

God

"Damnit. What was Tech thinking?" God grumbled, dropping down into his chair. He propped his arms up on his desk, wishing the meeting had gone very differently.

"What do you mean? Tech was innocent here. That guy tried to break his arms in half, and for what?" Day paced, looking like he wanted to go after the guy and teach him a lesson. God grabbed his partner's hand, stopping him midway between laps. He wished he could pull Day into him but he refrained. "It's not like that. Those names were triggers."

Day's scowl finally receded, his look turning to empathy. He knew Day would understand. God had served as well, and he definitely had a few triggers of his own. But the rest of God's team wasn't looking all that convinced, especially when Syn walked back in with Tech close behind him. Syn held his hand up, signaling them to give him some distance. It was hard not to want to comfort him. That clutch had to hurt. It was an arm bar clutch trap. God knew it well, which was why he warned his men not to advance. The move could do significant damage, and he had a feeling that Steele was punishing himself right at that moment for using it.

Tech went back to his computer and began working on whatever it was he constantly did over there when he wasn't under specific order, and God let him. Let him get himself situated.

"So, what do you want to do?" Day asked God.

He sat there a second longer just to be sure, but he believed he was doing the right thing. He looked at Ruxs and Green. "What did you guys think?"

"I think he's a loose cannon." Ruxs shrugged. "But then... so are we."

"I don't like what he did, man." Green looked hard at God. He understood. It looked bad, and Tech was a member of their family and no one hurt their family... but this was different.

God stood up to address his men. "You guys heard what I did on a bust – before we got this task force – when that kingpin, Hansen had a gun to Day's head. I wasn't concerned about what was right... what was protocol. I put the entire bravo team in jeopardy, risked the lives of a lot of officers... to save him. I'd do it again. Syn. Do you remember what happened when Furi was attacked by his ex-husband in your house? You'd be in prison for murder right now if we hadn't shown up in time. Green, you almost pulled your firearm on that woman... that housemother, when she let Curtis get bullied in that boys' home and did nothing to stop it. You remember how you reacted when you first saw those bruises on your son's face? Ruxs, when that crackhead got the drop on Green... you went fucking ballistic, man. Then he mentioned your mom... Jesus... it was a wrap. You were suspended for a week." God looked around, noting the looks of understanding. "We all have our triggers, fellas. Steele ain't no different. He came in for an interview and got ambushed with a memory he wasn't prepared to deal with... one he had an extreme reaction to. Sometimes for those men, it doesn't matter how many they saved; all they care about is how many they couldn't. We've all been there."

Green pffted. "In my defense, I was caught off guard, okay. No one got the fucking drop on me."

"Bullshit!" Day burst out laughing. "You got your fuckin' clock cleaned."

Syn was the next one to laugh. This was how they reversed tense situations. There was always a joke that'd fit in somewhere, and it was usually Day who started it. When the laughter eased, God walked over to Tech. "You couldn't have known. I could see you lost yourself in reading what he did. I have no doubt Steele's service was—"

"Heroic... amazing," Tech finished. "I blew it, though."

"Not if you can forgive him. Because he won't forgive himself, otherwise." God gripped the young detective's shoulder.

"I can. I just don't know if he'll forgive me. It *was* illegal to get that information, God. I was showing off. All of you can do so much." Tech shrugged like this was nothing, but God was wondering if he'd missed something in Tech. "All I have are my computers. I wanted to show him what I could do, too. Why I'm even here."

"We'll all get the chance and he'll get his chance." God spun Tech's chair around and bent so the man was looking directly at him. "No one on my team is dispensable. No one is weak. No one… especially you. There's no way we could do this without you and you know it. So man up. Stop looking so damn sad. You just took an arm clutch by a Force Recon Marine and didn't scream like a bitch, so hold your goddamn head up."

Tech turned his chair back around, but God saw a little pride cross his face before he did.

"So, what's the verdict?" God looked around. They knew what he was asking. Did they wanna work with Steele? After what happened, God had a little more of a say if he wanted the man on his team. He, himself, was psyched as shit to see what else Steele could do. The guy *was* a loose cannon. A hothead and terrible with authority… but wasn't that their team motto? Steele would be uncontrollable, and God knew exactly where to put him.

When they all nodded in agreement, God pointed at Ruxs and Green. "You guys got a third. Go get your new partner."

Chapter TEN

Steele

Steele leaped up on his raggedy porch and threw open his screen, only damaging it even more. He didn't care. He'd be gone from here soon, anyway. His uncle would be hurt, but he'd screwed up, there's nothing he could say or do now. Steele pulled the bottle of Jack out of the crinkled brown paper bag and dropped down in his La-Z-Boy in front of his television. He didn't want the bottle but he didn't want the memories, either. He cut his eyes to the stack of papers he'd taken from Tech, a printout of all his mistakes.

Damn... Tech. Steele had immediately liked the guy. That shy demeanor that he could sense concealed a fearless animal. The detective was more than just a man behind a computer screen. He had the trifecta. Smarts, looks, and Steele had hoped to see his fight soon. But he'd blown it. He knew the man hated him now. He was a bully. Everyone hated bullies. No doubt, Tech's team was probably hunting him down for revenge. The bad part of it all was he actually wanted to work with those guys. Taking a deep breath, he tilted his head back against the headrest. He'd disgraced himself. His father, his uncle... Ackerman. *Fuck. Chris, if you could see me now.* His gunnery would kick his ass. Steele forwent the shot glass and took a large gulp from the bottle. Grimacing as the burn slid down his throat and landed like dead weight in his gut.

Like a glutton for punishment, he reached behind his seat and pulled out the ten-year-old answering machine that he'd kept in his apartment the entire time he'd been deployed. He took another chug on the bottle and closed his eyes, pressing play. Ackerman's gruff voice filled his tiny trailer and flooded his mind with memories and pain.

"What's up grunt? If you're listening to this, then we're finally back stateside. Thank fucking God, huh. I uh... I wanted to have you come over, man. I feel like a damn coward doing this on your machine, but... I wanted to let you know that... I think I feel the same way you do. More than brothers, ya know. I mean, I wanna be more. Fuck... this sounds coy as shit. Just get over here... I'm waiting... I uh... I love you, man."

The message ended with a click of the button. Steele was supposed to go to him, but Ack never made it home. When Steele heard that message, he'd trashed his place... everything but the ancient answering machine. Even now, he wanted to take out the tape and crush it in his hands but he stopped himself by taking another long swig of the harsh whiskey. All those nights out there with Ackerman – his straight comrade – had changed their relationship. They fell in love. So many nights of sitting up, sleeping back-to-back, with their heads on each other's shoulders, sharing secrets no one else in the world knew. Endless days of hiking through the dangerous jungles of Malaysia, trusting his best friend at his six to protect him. All those nights of sleeping in subterranean temperatures, Ack's thick body wrapped around him from behind to keep each other warm, his hot breath on Steele's sensitive ear. It was thought that love and war went hand and hand. But Steele couldn't believe that shit anymore. Because too many war heroes never made it back to their loved ones.

He turned his television up louder over the heavy metal music blasting next door. After a few more gulps, he wouldn't give a damn, like most nights. Steele scowled, staring at the replay of last night's Raiders game. He was becoming a functioning drunk. Since he'd left Oakland last month, he had to have bought at least eight or nine bottles of whiskey. The sound of heavy footsteps on his porch halted his internal berating.

A fist banged hard on his door, but he didn't bother to get up. He had the start of a nice buzz going, so whoever it was could fuck off.

"Coming in. Don't shoot, Marine."

Steele's brows furrowed as he swiveled his chair in the tight space towards the front door. A hand waved around the door, then a black boot came into focus before Green's face appeared. Steele groaned. Damn, they really were coming for him. He wouldn't fight them. He deserved whatever they dished out on their friend's behalf. After Ruxs came in behind him, Steele held his breath, wondering if Tech was with them, but he wasn't.

"Nice place you got here, man." Ruxs' pale green eyes took in the meager surroundings while he ran his palm over his buzz cut.

Steele looked at the outdated furnishings that came with the place – except for his television and stereo. "Yeah well, the online pictures didn't do it justice. Came fully furnished… can't beat it. Honestly, didn't think I'd be here long."

Ruxs grinned at him and sat on the black- and red-checkered loveseat – that clashed horribly with the sage green carpeting – in front of the window. His leather coat gaped open, showing a cool Kid Rock Snake Label t-shirt. When he sat back, Steele got a view of the blade under his shoulder and the black Beretta in a holster tight to his hip. Green stood close to the door – which was still right by the loveseat – propping one big boot on the wall. Steele could see more of the tribal tats licking up his neck under the white V-neck t-shirt. They both looked like renegades.

"I take it this isn't a social visit," Steele grunted, pulling out his little cigars and lighting one. He put the bottle next to his chair and looked at the two detectives that took up more space than the furniture. "Are you here to arrest me for assaulting an officer?"

"We don't arrest our own team."

Steele watched Ruxs for the punchline, but he never cracked a smile.

Instead, Green took over. "About what happened today, Steele. We've all messed up, so don't sweat it. Even with each other. No one's holding it against you."

Steele jerked his head back, shaking it in disbelief. "Even Detective Murphy."

"Especially Detective Murphy," Green and Ruxs said in unison.

After a couple seconds, Ruxs frowned and craned his head back to look out the dirty window. "What the fuck, man? How can you sit here and listen to that racket? That's not even metal, that sounds like a man being raped in Dolby."

73

"Want me to tell him to turn that shit down?" Green smiled like he'd enjoy nothing more.

"No. I usually just turn up the television." Steele dismissed the thought of noise and instead focused on what Green said before the music distracted him. Steele looked back and forth between them. He didn't believe it. Tech had to have a hit out on him by now.

"He's sorry about what he did. He didn't know that speaking those words would do that to you. And he's real... well... he's come down on himself pretty hard. He was just trying to show you his skills. If you watched that video of the Artist bust then you've seen ours. He wanted to show you his. I'm sure all this shit can be squashed with a handshake."

Steele still wasn't sure if he was buying the "everything's all good" speech. He wouldn't become part of a team that already hated him, just because his uncle pulled some strings. It would only lead to no back up when he radioed for it. "You guys seem real tight. Any of you ever put your hands on each other the way I did him today?"

"Pfft, yeah. It's been about a year and a half since the last incident. But Michaels clocked the shit out of God." Green chuckled.

"Oh damn. I forgot about that," Ruxs added with a huge chuckle, scooting to the edge of his seat. "I thought God was gonna kill him, Syn had to hold him back. That was entertaining. No one usually hits him. It's usually Day that gets the business. Fucker plays too damn much. He broke into Syn's apartment when he first signed on and got a shotgun shoved in his face."

Steele found himself smiling along with them. This team sounded like his old squad.

"So, like we were saying. No one's holding that against you. You got a get outta jail free on that one." Green took his boot off the wall and braced his feet apart, looking down at him. "So, you in or out? It'd mean you have to keep up with us, though. We cause a shit load of property damage and destruction on the streets, but we get the job done. You'll probably piss off God on a regular basis and get your ass chewed out repeatedly. But he's a lot of puff and smoke. Syn usually smooths things over for us. So what d'ya say, Marine? You up to roll with us?"

Steele took a deep pull of his cigar, licking his lips at the sweet flavor lingering there. He nodded once. "I'm in."

"Cool." Ruxs got up to leave, stopping right before he got to Green. "Be there tomorrow by seven so Tech can get you situated."

"Hold up." Steele stood, feeling a little lightheaded from the alcohol, and the way Green squinted at him, he saw it too, but he didn't comment. "It'll take some time, but I'll show and prove out there. Show I can be trusted. But there's something you need to know." Steele rubbed his hand over his scruff, wishing this wasn't necessary, but it was probably best. "You guys should know before we get out there on the streets. That I'm gay. I'm not ashamed of it and I don't hide it. I'm single right now, but that may not always be the case. But I'll be damned if I'm gonna go out there with a team that can't deal with that. That's what happened to my last partner."

Green's eyes twinkled with what looked like amusement and Ruxs looked flat out exasperated before he spoke. "We were gonna say something real similar to you, but we figured your uncle already informed you about us. I guess not."

"Excuse me?" Steele asked, not sure what his uncle didn't tell him.

Instead of Green clarifying any further he shot out both hands, grabbed two fistfuls of Ruxs' leather jacket, and slammed him up against the wall hard enough to rattle the entire front side of the trailer. Steele winced right before he saw Green press in hard against his partner from chest to thighs, and crash his mouth over his. Ruxs didn't even appear stunned, just melted into Green's aggression like it was second nature. *Jesus.* This wasn't something you could fake, either. They were lovers. Big ass, alpha, macho motherfuckin' lovers. Ruxs' hands came up fast and got a firm grip on the back of Green's neck, not letting him go until he was finished too. They grunted and ground against each other like they forgot they weren't alone. Steele felt his cock hardening at the live porno, wondering if he was going to have to excuse himself soon. He didn't want to interrupt. He wasn't a fool. Both of them were sexy as hell – not quite what he was interested in now – but fine male specimens nonetheless. One of Green's hands slid up to Ruxs' throat, and his partner's reaction was downright lewd. Ruxs bucked his hips and reached down for a handful of Green's tight ass in those jeans like he was encouraging him to thrust with him. Steele just refrained from letting out his own growl, the front of his pants way too fucking tight now.

"Alright, alright! Goddamnit. Being gay isn't a problem. I got it." Steele dropped back in his chair feeling like he'd just been the one thoroughly kissed. He took a long pull on his cigar, letting the smoke linger in his mouth for a while before he blew it out.

"Oh, and you're not smoking those in my truck. You can forget it. They may smell good, but I don't want to smell you every time I fuck Chris in the backseat," Ruxs said, still panting, and walked out the door.

"He was joking. We don't care about smelling the cigars in the backseat," Chris added, his face flushed, his lips red and swollen.

"Thanks. I think," Steele said uncertainly.

Green cocked his head a little and walked back towards him, looking in his eyes as he did, relaying his nonverbal communication. Green bent down slowly and swiped the bottle of Jack from beside his chair. It was still over three-quarters full. Green stared at him – daring him to protest – while he dumped the remaining whiskey out in the sink and tossed the bottle in the trashcan underneath it. Green didn't have to say anything as he turned and left right behind his partner. His message was loud and clear.

Chapter

ELEVEN

Tech

Tech pulled up to the renovated warehouse dubbed a state-of-the-art training facility for military and law enforcement. It was owned by a retired MMA fighter and three of his ex-military partners. Chen – one of the owners – was one beast of a fighter. Tech met him when he came to Atlanta's law enforcement divisions to do a demonstration of his program for any officers that could afford to take his classes. They sure as hell weren't cheap. Especially on a cop's salary, but Tech helped Chen with the business' system programming, so he got a great discount.

He walked inside and waved to Chen, who was behind the registration desk talking with one of his partners. Tech saw the frown crease his forehead but he ignored his teacher for now and went straight back to the locker rooms to change his clothes. It was five in the morning, so there were only a few people upstairs – that he could see – working on the exercise equipment. This was the only time he had available to do this training, which had now increased to three days a week. He'd come to observe after Chen's demonstration at the precinct and had hit it off with him. He was honest with Chen when he told him he hoped to get in the field one day, but his bosses didn't think he could handle himself. He wanted to prove to them that he could, but more than that, to prove it to himself. What if a suspect being questioned or a detainee on their way to the holding tanks got loose and tore through the station? What was he going to do – hide behind another officer? He just wanted to be able to contribute. Now, even more, with Steele coming in.

Damn. What was Tech going to say to him? He'd worked out a few tidbits in his head last night, after not getting near enough rest, but nothing sounded right. *Sorry I brought up your deceased brothers. Sorry I made you snap. Ya know, it didn't really hurt that much, so don't worry about it.* All of it sucked, and that move had hurt like a sonofabitch. He had dark purple bruises on both arms above his elbows and one at the base of his neck where Steele had grabbed him and growled in his ear. He'd been scared shitless then, and he still was. He brought a long-sleeved shirt so Chen wouldn't see the marks and—

"What the hell happened to you?" Chen's mild Asian accent cut through the silence, startling him.

Tech hurriedly finished putting on his Under Armour shirt, but he knew it was too late. "Nothing. Had a little accident. Hit it on the desk."

"We have an understanding, don't we, detective?" Chen stated, his voice a little sharper as he came around to face Tech. "I don't have dishonest students. I can accept any truth, but I can never condone a lie. Real men don't lie. I recognize those wounds, Shawn. Who did that to you?"

Tech slammed his locker shut, wincing at the soreness in his arms. "A man that my lieutenants interviewed yesterday. He was Special Forces and I ran my mouth about something I shouldn't have."

Chen looked disgusted. If he only knew the part that he'd played in it, he might see things differently, but right now Tech was too tired to get that deep into it. "It's fine, okay. I'm ready to begin."

"We'll work again on leg training today, sweeps and knee blocks," Chen told him, checking off a few items in Tech's file. Chen had created an amazingly detailed plan especially for him. It included marksman training, martial arts, hand-to-hand, defensive and close contact maneuvers, and a core-strengthening regimen. He'd noticed results, too. He was more toned and defined. His endurance was a lot higher than when he began training, also. He couldn't wait to show his skills, but he'd have to be patient. The last thing he wanted to do was make a fool of himself. If he couldn't take the heat out there in the field and blew it, God wouldn't give him another chance.

"Alright," Tech answered. He couldn't even begin to argue. His arms were too tender for the gun range today.

He was good at the leg sweeps. Tech was fast when he dropped to the ground to sweep Chen's legs from under him. He wasn't hurting him – Chen knew how to fall the correct way when sparring. Every now and then, he'd demonstrate other techniques and Tech would mimic them perfectly. Tech was sweating profusely by the time Chen wrapped up their floor training and told him to do his leg press reps and forty-five minutes on the treadmill at a five percent incline.

Shit.

Tech sat at his desk, chewing on the end of his pen while he looked through an on line catalog for a newer model switchblade for Ruxs. He'd forgotten to yank his last one out of his perp's thigh before he was rushed to the hospital. So it was another one lost. Tech wasn't paying attention to the comings and goings in the office. God and Day were in and out constantly, then there were officers and admin staff that would often breeze in to see if they needed any assistance. So he was surprised when he heard Steele's voice.

He sat up but he didn't turn around. He didn't know why, probably because his pulse kicked up and heat slammed into him so fast he felt dizzy. He needed to get this over with. Tech swiveled his chair around and Steele's intense gray eyes were staring right at him. Tech swallowed a gulp of nothing and stood, along with the rest of the men in the room. His legs were shaky but he didn't waver, feeling a little proud about that. Two of the SWAT team leaders were sitting at the long conference table with Syn. They often used SWAT as back up when they did a big bust, so it wasn't uncommon for Hart and his lieutenant to chill in their department.

God shook Steele's hand again and proceeded to introduce him to the SWAT members. No one acted weird with Steele – well, no one but him. Tech was having a hard time keeping his eyes on Steele as he moved around the office speaking too low for him to hear – maybe apologizing. Tech was a ball of anxiousness, but the new member didn't seem to be experiencing the same trouble, because every time he finished an introduction his eyes were right back on Tech.

Tech couldn't take this, he had a job to do, and so did Steele. If he was going to be partnered with the Enforcers, then he'd hardly see the man anyway. Which might be best, because if Tech had to look at that worn gray long john stretched tight under that leather jacket all day, he'd be in a perpetual state of hardness. Steele's entire look was exactly what did it for him. Tech's team members were hot, but he'd been around them and their significant others for so long, he didn't see them as anything but brothers now... with a little envy here and there.

He saw Day clap Steele on his on his back and point towards him. *Shit, shit, shit. He's coming this way.* Tech almost rolled his eyes. This wasn't junior high, for shit's sake. Steele wasn't the wrestling captain finally approaching him for a little extra help with his Algebra.

"Tech. You got the paperwork sent over from admin, so he can get his ID?" his lieutenant asked him.

Tech was staring at Steele, mesmerized by the gray eyes that seemed even darker now that he'd gotten closer. Or maybe it was the shirt causing them to look that way. Steele hitched up the shoulder strap of his backpack, staring at him with those exotically beautiful eyes.

"Tech?" Day said a little louder.

Tech jumped. "What...? Sir...? I'm, huh, Day." *Lord just take me now.*

Day caught Tech by the elbow and the yelp of pain left his mouth too fast for him to muffle it. His reaction to Day clamping down on his fresh bruise was not only seen but heard by everyone. He looked up to see Steele's apologetic expression and wished he hadn't. Tech looked like a wimp, for sure. He knew his neck was the color of crimson if the warmth there was any indication. He might even break out in hives if all those eyes stayed on him.

Steele put his hand up to hold Day off. "If you'll excuse us, I'd like to talk to Tech alone."

"Maybe that's a good idea," Day agreed. "Tech, go ahead and get him armed and bugged. He can do admin later."

Tech nodded and took off in the direction of the equipment room, grateful to get the hell away from their concerned looks. He had to punch in the code twice before he got it right, and waited for Steele to step inside. When he walked by, Tech could smell the lingering fragrant smokiness over Steele's cologne. The smell was a woodsy-spicy combination. Cedar, amber and the crispness of pine. He knew those fragrances well; they reminded him of the Colorado Rockies... of home.

Steele looked around as he moved around the narrow space. It looked like a bunker with a top-notch organization system. Weapons hung all around them in locked cages, and Tech felt his nervousness trying to get the best of him.

"This is pretty amazing. Did you design all this?" Steele had an edge of awe to his tone as he pointed to the 22-inch monitor embedded in the steel wall. The keyboard extended when Tech tapped a couple keys.

"Yes."

"How long it take to do all this? I've never seen anything like it. You guys got more gadgets and artillery than an infantry squadron."

"You can put your bag on that table and sit right there," Tech said, keeping his eyes on the monitor while he punched in his access code. "Took a few months."

"Wow. That's alright." Steele sat in one of the high stools, still surveying everything while Tech got the system going. "So, what are you doing?"

"First, I need to get some weapons for you. Of course, everything has to be accounted for. I can't just shove a firearm in your hand and tell you to go. Ruxs and Green require a lot, so if you'll be partnered with them you need to be prepared. Green's truck has an M16 kit under his seat. There's a shotgun in the back. In the hidden compartments in the doors is everything from throwing knives to tear gas. And I think he's used everything at least once."

"Holy shit." Steele chuckled. His laugh was softer in the confined space, but masculine.

81

"Yeah, fun, huh." Tech sighed but tried to keep the longing out of his tone.

"Do you ever go out with them?"

Tech kept his back to Steele while he answered his questions. This was good, he guessed. Getting to know each other. "No. I'm behind this desk twelve to fifteen hours a day. And everyone is partnered. God and Day. Syn and Michaels are usually with Ro. And of course Ruxs and Green. So that leaves me. But since God and Day got engaged, Ro's been with them more. I was hoping—"

"Wait... wait just a minute. God and Day are lovers?" Steele said, a little louder.

"How can you not know that?" Tech looked back. "Every law enforcement agency in the state of Georgia knows that."

"Well, I'm not from here. And I wasn't told that they were gay. It's a little hard to picture."

"Is that a problem?" Tech turned fully; ready to defend any member of his team.

"Not at all," Steele answered, a look of complete openness on his face.

"Good, then. Because everyone in this damn department is. Councilman Steele probably should've disclosed that before he placed you."

"He's a man who only discloses what's absolutely relevant." Steele shrugged his strong shoulders. "Most agencies don't permit coupling in the same precinct, so it's unheard of for couples to be in the same department."

"You're right about that. But they're not your average task force. The mayor and chief approved this department, God and Day being the first ones appointed to head it up. Wherever they go, they're going together... even into retirement. If the chief had been against their pairing, any one of the other states that know about them and their records would've snatched them up."

"I see."

Tech's fingers went back to flying over the keyboard.

"So, the sergeant, too."

"Yep. Well… Syn's only gay for one man. Before him, he was straight. It's okay to tell you this because it's no secret."

Steele laughed. Damn, these guys were really a bunch of characters. "And Ro. I haven't met him. He's gay?"

"Partnered with the chief's son."

"Damn," Steele whispered. "Y'all don't do any half-stepping here. Go big or go home. A gay task force."

Tech was wondering what all the questions were leading up to. Was Steele okay with all of them being homosexual, or not? Having a straight detective would be a change for them but they could handle it. He might get his ass slapped every now and then just to piss him off, but that'd be all in good fun. No one would make him uncomfortable. The guy was really going to have to lighten up, but it wasn't Tech's job to get him to do so. He'd do what he was required and leave the deadly Marine for the lieutenants to handle. "So, what's your weapon of choice?"

"Glocks, two of them, black on black, no chrome. I'll need a suppressor, too. I'd also take that .380 Smith and Wesson for my boot." Steele pointed to the glass enclosure of firearms.

Tech punched in a numeric code on a keypad next to the case and after the glass slid open, he retrieved each weapon he'd been asked for. Steele watched him pull out three extra magazines and turn back to his monitor to input the serial numbers.

"If you have your own blades, you'll have to do the paperwork for approval, or you can choose from those," Tech said, pointing to the adjacent wall. "I can also order one of your choice."

"Nice selection. I usually like a fighting knife in the other boot. So the F-S right there will work. But I'll need the paperwork for this." Steele dipped underneath his long john and yanked out a five-inch slender blade, the handle of it fitting around four of his knuckles. He did it so fast; Tech wondered if he'd pulled it out of thin air. He stared at it like it was foreign, inching forward, wanting to stroke his fingers down the sharp edge of the blade, which was attached to a Bakelite grip that snuggly surrounded Steele's four knuckles. An extremely rare fighting knife.

Tech feared what this man could do, but he was also turned on by him. Had he used that weapon on an enemy? A terrorist? Tech could almost see him in his mind. Moving masterfully around a man, punching and stabbing at vital organs with one hand. *Jesus*. Tech blinked out of his fascinated state. His cock was rising in his slim jeans, which could go very wrong if Steele looked down. He cleared his throat, but his voice was still husky. "I'll get that put in." He watched Steele slowly lift the hem of his shirt, a sneak peak of dark brown hair leading to his navel briefly came into view while he placed that dangerous blade somewhere near his armpit.

"It's in a sheath that wraps around my bicep." Steele smirked, answering Tech's unspoken question.

"That's very unique. What's it called?" Tech coughed again and turned to get his audio kit.

"A knuckleduster dagger. Got it custom made in England. It's saved my life a few times."

Tech nodded as he came back to Steele's side and placed the medium-sized plastic container on the table beside him. "I have to get you fitted for your earpiece. You can't be in the field long without it. It'll take twenty-four hours for the shell to harden but you'll be with Ruxs and Green, so I'll be able to reach you if I have to."

"I don't need that." Steele looked quizzically at the kit that Tech was setting up. He was sure all the tools looked like he was about to perform a type of surgery on Steele's ear, the long ear forceps lying next to his thigh.

"Unfortunately, this isn't negotiable. Everyone has one and is required to keep it on them at all times. Even if you're on a date, it should be in your pocket. You don't have to put it in unless you need me... um... the team." Tech caught the slight lift of Steele's mouth but ducked his head back down, concentrating on unwrapping a piece of putty to mold to Steele's ear canal.

"I can simply call you if I need you... or the team." He grinned lazily.

Tech took a deep breath. "Cell phones have technical difficulties, interference, and dropped calls, whatever. What if there's no signal and you need back up? You're undercover, so you can't

84

carry a radio. We only use radios when we're on a big bust so you guys can communicate. God doesn't take those kinds of risks with his team. Sometimes, time is of the essence. You might not even have time to wait for a connection before you need me to get someone to you. My phones are to communicate within the precinct. Don't worry. This will be molded to your ear; you'll hardly notice it's in."

Steele blew an exasperated breath and Tech hoped earpieces weren't another trigger or something. He lifted his left arm to show the large-faced watch on his arm. "It's a smart watch. I press the icon of who I need to speak to. You'll only hear me. I *can* sync them together so everyone can hear each other, but I haven't had *that* type of emergency in a very long time. So, there won't be seven men screaming in your ear, if that's your concern. When you put it in, you only need to say my name and I'll respond. No one else. When you need to speak to me, you'll press the computer image on it and speak, press it again when you're done."

"I already have a watch," Steele grumbled.

"Well, now you have a better one," Tech quipped right back. "I can track you with that watch. Pull up a map for you to get to safety. Send you intel… almost anything."

"Your earpiece is always in?" Steele squinted and leaned to the side, looking at his ear.

"Even in the shower." Tech turned and showed the small ivory piece tucked deep in his ear.

"How do you even get that out?"

Tech pulled out a little rubber finger from his pants pocket and pushed it on his pinky. He put it in his ear and the magnetic back gripped the earpiece and slid it out like nothing. He was used to it and it was so comfortable he rarely realized it was in. "Has to be small so it's not seen when you're undercover. When I'm off, the guys will use their cells to call me. This *is* for work only. No one alerts me on the com just to ask for the Falcons' score in Sunday's game."

"Fine. But I'll do it myself," Steele said when Tech went to reach for his ear.

"No. You don't know what you're doing. This stuff is too expensive to let you try it and mess it up. It doesn't hurt at all. The whole thing takes twenty minutes, once the mold is set, the rest I can do without you." Tech waited. When Steele finally conceded, he reached for his ear.

Chapter TWELVE

Steele

Steele looked at Tech's profile while he set out all the tiny tools to make him an earpiece. His hands moved methodically over the delicate pieces, putting each item in its place. It was way outside of Steele's scope of knowledge. The young man was a genius. As he looked around at all the sophisticated technology, he couldn't help but marvel at the detective. This was something you'd see built by an engineer that worked for Bill Gates or something, making a six-figure salary, not in an Atlanta precinct, and he found himself wanting to know Tech's story.

He looked sexy today in his fitted jeans and black, slim-fitted, ribbed turtleneck. The black, plastic framed glasses set off his entire "I'm a hot nerd" look, but the body didn't quite match. He was fit and toned in a Peter Parker kind of way. Tech probably couldn't get overly muscular, but it was clear he worked out. His biceps were probably the size of small apples when he flexed, and Steele hoped he'd get an opportunity to see them.

Tech finally moved to get to work, putting a piece of the gray putty on the end of the five-inch forceps. But as Tech's hand got closer to the side of his face, Steele could see the slight tremor. *Fuck.* Steele slowly reached up and got a gentle grip of Tech's narrow wrist, bringing his hand back down. He took his other hand and pushed back the long sleeve of Tech's shirt, locating the spot on his wrist he could manipulate with a little pressure to help calm some of Tech's anxiety over having to touch him – especially when they hadn't yet approached the elephant in the room. He looked into Tech's brown eyes behind those clear lenses while he rubbed his thumb in a small circle over the smooth skin. He lost himself in the movement; Tech's skin was so pale and soft as he caressed him that he almost forgot why he was touching him in the first place. Maybe because of their first interaction, Steele felt an extremely strong pull towards Tech.

"Don't be afraid of me, detective," Steele whispered, watching closely as Tech's long lashes fluttered over his intelligent eyes. "I'm sorry I hurt you. I truly am. I promise... I swear on my fallen brothers that I'll never ever hurt you like that again. I wouldn't've come back if I didn't think I could control myself... especially around you. I'm ashamed of what I did."

Tech's breath came out in shallow gusts while he let Steele continue to touch him. "I'm sorry, too. I didn't mean to offend you, either... or hurt you."

"I know you didn't." Steele wanted to lean in closer, somehow get better acquainted in a different way, but he'd try to establish some trust between them first. He slid Tech's sleeve up until it was bunched around his tight bicep. He stopped caressing the pressure point when he saw the dark purple bruise above Tech's elbow. Oh no. He felt even shitter than last night. No words he'd thought of seemed good enough to speak, right now.

"I'm okay. Really. I'm stronger than you may think," Tech said hoarsely, his eyes darting away. He looked upset, but for a different reason.

"I know you're strong. I felt it. But I know the joint is swollen and aching in there." Steele let Tech's wrist go and reached for his backpack. "I brought something to help."

Tech inched in a little closer and Steele took that as a good sign. Ignoring the delicious coolness of Tech's cologne, he reached inside and took out the circular metal container. He didn't take much with him as he moved from place to place but he did keep his array of natural remedies he'd acquired from doctors all over the world, from hypnotherapists to Ayurvedic physicians.

The can of presoaked bandages was the best he'd ever encountered for aching muscles and joints. It was made of so many herbs and oils; he'd never be able to recite them all, but he knew of the primary ones. He took off the tin lid and Tech's neck jerked back at the potent smell that blasted their senses, even their eyes began to water. Tech put his hand up to his nose. "What the hell? Oh my god."

Steele chuckled deeply, reaching out to cup Tech's hand, pulling him back towards him until was standing between his legs. "I know. I know. It's the Capsaicin. It's an oil extracted from hot chili peppers. I think, mixed with the peppermint it's a bit overpowering, but all the properties together do wonders in reducing inflammation."

"There's no way I can walk around the office with these on. God'll kick my ass out of here so fast."

"No, he won't. Because after the bandages are on, I'm going to wrap it in plastic. It'll contain the smell. Trust me." He looked up at Tech's eyes, realizing their close proximity. He'd done it on purpose, opening his legs a little wider. He wanted to show Tech he had a measure of gentility under all his strength.

Tech was quiet while Steele carefully wrapped both elbows. "It's cold. Feels kind of good, despite the smell." Tech's smile was gorgeous and warm.

"It's the Camphor cream. A lot of physicians say to use hot temperatures for aches, some say cold. I've found cool works best, especially for acute pain." Steele began wrapping the Saran wrap. "Out in the field, we'll try just about anything to eliminate pain. Of course, we had our corpsmen; but taking narcotics was a last resort, we needed to stay sharp."

Steele pulled down one sleeve and then the other. He closed up his canister and tucked it back inside his bag. He wiped his hand on a small towel in his backpack and zipped it up. "So, what do you think?" Steele knew the medicine well. Knew it was already working its way into the layers of Tech's skin, giving him some much-needed relief. At least Steele was able to fix a little of the damage he'd done.

"Much better, actually. Wow, it's like a miracle serum," Tech said, bending his arm, testing the mobility.

"Keep them on overnight, if you can. It'll really feel a lot better by tomorrow."

"Okay," Tech agreed, almost wistfully. He stood rooted in place, just watching him for a moment and Steele saw his eyes drop to his mouth. Steele licked his lips.

Tech blinked, dropping his eyes down, moving back to the side, in front of his kit. "I better get this going. I'm sure your new partners will be ready for you soon."

Steele tilted his head to the side when Tech reached for his earlobe again. He didn't make a sound and he fought not to react, but the hot detective touching him on his spot was making it difficult. No words were spoken now, only silence and Steel's shameless thoughts. He wanted to moan so badly when those agile fingers moved across the fleshy part of his ear, manipulating the soft substance to mold to his canal. Tech's face was so close to his he could feel his exhale while he peered into the tunnel of his ear. His breath was a mix of coffee and something else sugary… like he'd had pancakes for breakfast. Steele turned inward, wanting to smell, wanting to taste.

"Hold still," Tech whispered, close to him. "Won't be long."

Oh, damn. That erotic voice. A mild tenor, lighter than bass but far from feminine. Absolutely perfect. Steele would love to hear it right here in Tech's sanctuary. Standing in the midst of all he'd engineered with his brilliant mind. In the darkness, illuminated with only the flashing red and green signal indicators on Tech's monitors, not the harsh florescent lighting over his head right now. *Ahh.* He'd hold that taut body close to him while he caressed the petite round globes of his ass. Would Tech fit to his body the same way he was curving that malleable paste to fit his ear? Steele could feel his heart beating faster the more his fantasy played out in his mind. He closed his eyes and pictured himself coming back from a dangerous bust and Tech taking him into this room, keeping the lights off and bringing his adrenaline down with his lustful voice and feather light touches.

"Doing real good," Tech breathed quietly, still so damn close. "This is going to be a little warm now, so I can fold it easier."

"'K," Steele responded throatily, without knowing what he'd just consented to. He felt the slick piece of putty slide back into his ear; it was nice and toasty like it'd been dipped in warm honey. Still, Tech blew on his ear like it was too hot for him to take. Oh, he could take the heat. "Mmm."

"You okay?" Tech paused.

Steele's eyes popped open, the bright lighting jerking him to reality. *Fuck, did I just moan?* "Oh yeah. I'm good. Fine."

"Alright. We're all done," Tech said, putting the intricately curved piece of goo in a plastic dish and closing it. "This'll harden, then I'll put the casing with the mechanism over it and you're good to go." Tech looked back and forth before his eyes landed back on him. "I'm real glad we're square. This team... we're a family ya know, a unit. Everyone is partnered up... in love. We don't take risks with anyone's lives. It'd be devastating."

Tech was preparing to walk away but Steele wasn't ready for him to. He stood and walked up behind the smaller man while he stood in front of a row of shelves and put his kit away. When Steele spoke, Tech jumped slightly but settled right back down. "And who are you in love with?"

"My job. I don't have time for all that," Tech answered. Steele had a feeling that even Tech didn't believe that answer.

Steele's chin was over Tech's shoulder. He didn't grab his narrow waist, but he wanted to. "How warm does this job keep you at night, detective?" Steele didn't wait for an answer; instead, he turned and took the weapons Tech had placed out for him and left his space. But he made a mental note to revisit that topic real soon. As he made his way back across the office, he hoped that Ack would approve. It'd been a long time since any other man made Steele's body react this way.

Chapter THIRTEEN

Steele

"You all situated, man?" Ruxs asked him when he walked over. He was tilted back in his chair with his boots propped up on his desk. Today he wore a King of Rock, Run DMC t-shirt, his leather coat hanging on the back of his chair. Classic rock t-shirts must be his thing. He'd yet to see Green in anything but a white Hanes t-shirt, jeans, and messy black hair.

"Looks like it." Steele noticed there was now another desk pushed up to Ruxs' and Green's, forming a T. It was completely bare except for a phone and a desk calendar. Beside it was a huge box and once he got closer he noticed it was a new desktop computer.

"That's you, bro." Green nodded at the desk. "Tech will hook all that up for you. Get all the programs running… ya know. All the smart shit we can't do."

Steele shot his new partners a look. "I can do some smart stuff."

"Compared to him… no, you can't." Green laughed.

Well, there were probably only ten people on the planet that could do what Tech could with a computer. Didn't mean Steele couldn't set up a standard desktop. But it wasn't enough for him to concern himself with so he tucked his backpack inside the deep drawer of his desk and sat down.

"God went down to get your badge since you were in the cave so long." Ruxs smirked. "You guys kiss and make up?"

Steele swiveled around and leveled a hard look at him and replied with a clipped, "Yep."

Before either could retort, God walked back in with Day close behind him. He saw Steele and tossed the badge all the way across the room, and Steele shot his hand up at the last minute, swiping it out the air before it sailed over his head.

"Show off," he heard Day mumble.

Steele smirked, flipping the gold badge over. He didn't think he'd ever have one again. Not after leaving Oakland the way he did. He pulled out his wallet and clipped it to the first flap.

"Pick up your ID on the way out. I told them you'd be down in a bit."

"On my way out?" Steele frowned.

God opened a file and stood just a few feet from their cluster of desks. "Need y'all to go to Peoplestown. Artist's thug is still in the hospital but the DA was able to question him last night. He gave us the name of a dockworker that's been helping with the smuggling. The addresses to his house and job are in here. The guy frequents a tavern off Pulliam in the evenings. I'll have Tech sync the addresses to your GPS, Ruxs. Come back when you got something for me."

Steele got up and pulled his jacket off the back of his chair, watching God watch him. "Just gonna toss me into the deep end, huh lieutenant."

"Right in with the goddamn sharks," Ruxs added, throwing Steele a "you're screwed" look.

"Jumping in's the best way to learn how to swim." God shrugged.

"Do you make up this ass backwards logic off the top of your head, God?" Green shook his head, walking past them.

"God is all-knowing," their lieutenant responded with pride, ignoring the combinations of "like hell," and "bullshit" from his team. Throwing on his thigh-length leather coat, God yelled over his shoulder before walking out the door, "Sink or fight, Steele. Show me what you got."

After Steele got his new Atlanta PD identification, he met his new partners at Ruxs' truck and hopped up in the backseat. Ruxs stomped on the gas and sped out of the precinct's parking lot. He looked between the seats to the front and saw that quite a bit of technology had been added that he was sure didn't come with this vehicle – even fully loaded. Green was leaning over, tapping on the

94

large display screen, pulling up a map and what he assumed was the route to where they were headed.

"That looks, pretty hi-tech, man. Who did that?" Steele asked, still looking at the screen.

"Put Tech and Furious together and there's nothing they can't put in a car." Ruxs smiled at him in the rearview mirror.

"Who's Furious?"

"That's Syn's partner," Green answered. "Probably one of the hottest guys you'll ever see."

Steele doubted that, an image of styled preppy hair and glasses popping into his head.

"He owns a garage in Midtown with his best friend, Doug. They do all of our vehicles, and even most of the officers' in the precinct. He does maintenance, custom jobs, oh, and custom bikes are his specialty."

That perked up Steele's ears. "Really." His baby could definitely use an overhaul.

"You'll meet him, eventually. He'll breeze in every now and then. Or if you see a long-haired man riding one of the baddest bikes you've ever seen… that's him."

Steele sat there, chewing on a toothpick – since he couldn't smoke – watching Atlanta go by. He wondered if Tech liked bikes. He had to pull at his pants leg for more groin room when he thought about Tech riding behind him on his Suzuki GSX. It was strictly for going fast, and boy did it ever. Sometimes Steele had to feed the energy of his need to fly. He'd have to check in with this Furious and see where he could open his bike up here. Atlanta really was a nice city – from what he'd seen – and he hoped he could call it home. The entire four years he spent in Oakland, it had never felt permanent to him.

"Tech…" Ruxs waited for a second then continued. "Give me an image of the house address in Peoplestown you just sent, and its perimeter."

Steele hadn't noticed Ruxs' earpiece but obviously, it was in. He leaned forward and watched the screen flicker as a series of pictures appeared of a modern, two-story home with a nice lawn. The neighborhood looked pretty quiet.

"Nice setup for a dockworker," Green added, his eyes going from the road to the screen.

"Got it, Tech." Ruxs tapped the watch on his arm that looked identical to the one Tech wore. Then he noticed Green's too. He found himself wanting one, wanting his own personal connection as well.

"Is there anything Tech can't do?" Steele asked casually.

Green and Ruxs laughed and exchanged looks. "Not really," Green answered first, pushing back a few strands of wild hair that had fallen forward. "He does it all. All our training and recerts. We do our own research, but he can always find way more than we do. But a lot of information he acquires can't be used in court because of *how* he attains it, but it points us in a good direction to get what we can use. It really is because of him that we have the success rate we do, which in turn, gets us special privileges. He handles all our weapons and technology, making sure we have only the best. He's the best detective in the world that never gets out from behind a desk. It's amazing he hasn't left us and the shitty pay. But he's loyal and he loves us. He likes making a difference, not building some billionaire his next greatest Pentium processor.

"So what's his story?" Steele hoped he sounded nonchalant.

Green turned around and looked at him. He stared for a few seconds before he answered. "If you wanna know, ask him yourself."

Asshole.

Chapter FOURTEEN

God

"So, how do you think Steele's going to do out there?" God asked Day as they drove to their meeting at the DA's office.

"I think he'll shock us. Putting him with them was a good idea. He's military… disciplined. Ruxs and Green could use a little of that in their crazy routine," Day responded, his eyes watching the scenery. He was always on alert, on or off duty.

"Yeah. I hope it works out. He could be a good asset. I was reading more of his file. He could be put anywhere. On the ground, up high with Michaels. Wherever we need him." God nodded, feeling better about this new addition. "It looked like him and Tech smoothed things over, too."

Day nodded again. He'd been exceptionally quiet this morning and all day today. Usually, God couldn't get him to shut up. Maybe he was still shaken about the shootout last week. "Everything all right?"

"Look, Cash. I've been thinking." Day scrubbed his hand over his stubble. "If you don't want to get married… I'll understand. I know you said yes, but… if you've changed your mind."

"Whoa. Where's this coming from? I said yes and I meant yes," God said, barreling through the yellow light right as it was turning red.

"Well, it's going on a year. I thought we would've at least come up with a date by now. I think Vikki has emailed me every month asking for a date." Day gaped at him.

"Goddamn, that woman needs to get a life. Ever since she left working for us and joined the prosecutor's office, she's done nothing but meddle. If her life is that boring over there, then she needs to get a damn hobby and stop stirring up trouble!" God barked.

"Trouble? She asked to plan it for us so we're not consumed with details, and you just called it trouble. Cashel, this is ridiculous. I'm not gonna let—" Day stopped and blew out an angry breath like he was trying to calm himself down.

Shit. "What's your hurry, Leo? I don't plan on going anywhere. It's not a bad idea to be engaged for a while." God shrugged like it was no big deal. He had meant it when he said yes, but he didn't think they had to run down the aisle as soon as he did.

"Fuck it. I'm done talking about it." Day threw his hands up and turned to look back out the window. "You let me know when you decide for both of us."

"Day, you're being a bit melodramatic, don't you think? I just haven't had time to talk about it. I've been busy, you know that."

"You watched five episodes of *Naked and Afraid* last night, for fuck's sake! That's nothing but goddamn time!" Day yelled.

God winced. This could get bad, fast. He didn't like Day upset with him. "Just let me get my shit together, okay. And we'll talk about it."

"That's elusive as hell, Cash, but what-the-fuck-ever," Day retorted, shutting down.

At the DA's office, they were as professional as they always were. Fully supportive of each other while they prepared for the trial they had to testify in. But inside, he was torn about being honest with his partner. Day had mentioned venues, caterers, and so forth while trying to get God to open up. He knew his silence was making it appear he'd not been sincere in accepting the proposal and it was hurting Day... that wasn't going to fly. He wanted to get married. There was no other person on this Earth for him, no better fit. But God wasn't a showoff, and definitely not one for appearances. He didn't want a wedding. He just wanted to get married. How the hell could he tell Day that? He didn't know, but he'd put it off long enough.

Tech

98

The Enforcers and Steele had been gone for a few hours and Tech was always extra mindful when they were in the field. While he waited to hear any calls for assistance, he ate a quick lunch at his desk then went about getting Steele's desk set up. He'd hooked up the computer, now he was uploading the programs and the APD system. He'd even gotten him office supplies. While he waited for the files to download, he added more ink pens to the desk caddy, repositioned the stapler and Post-it holder for the fourth time. He chewed on his bottom lip, seeing if he'd missed anything... ah, staple refills. He pushed the chair back to his own station and grabbed a box from his drawer. He tucked that in Steele's top drawer, looking around again.

"I don't remember you setting up anyone else's desk like that." Syn chuckled, looking over at him from his own desk. He'd almost forgotten Syn had come back in the office, he was so quiet over there by the lieutenants' desks.

"Of course, I did. I set up everyone's computer." Tech wouldn't meet Syn's eyes, instead concentrating on the progress bar on Steele's monitor.

"Yes, computer... not supplies and decorations. And is it me, or does he have a bigger monitor than everyone else?" Syn's voice still held amusement and Tech glared at him while Syn made a point of tilting his own monitor from side to side like he was checking the dimensions.

Tech hid his smile. "Whatever. It's the same size, just a newer model. Makes it look bigger, that's all. And putting a desk organizer up here is hardly decoration."

"It's mahogany!" Syn laughed harder, getting a kick out of teasing him. He reared back in his chair, clasping his hands in front of him and scrutinizing Tech's every move.

He tried not to fidget, but it was difficult. Syn was really going to roar when he pulled out the City of Atlanta laminated map he planned to seal onto the top of Steele's desk instead of that cheesy paper calendar. Tech shook his head, he was doing his job, and he had nothing to be embarrassed about. He pulled the 27x30 inch map out of the wrapper and removed the paper calendar.

"Oh, you gotta be shitting me." Syn jumped up, his long legs quickly covering the distance between them.

Tech ignored him and went about setting the map up, placing the caddy at the top of it and at the edge of the monitor base. It fit perfectly.

"How come we don't have those?" Syn gaped, bending to get a closer look. It was an extremely detailed map that also had every law enforcement agency's location identified. "Oh, come on. I want one."

"You all don't need one. Steele is new to the area; he needs to be able to study this when he has a chance. It'll help him be a better field detective if he knows where he's going," Tech answered with a smug grin of his own. "Besides, I made this and I'm not making another one."

"Mmm. You have the hots for him. Admit it right now." Syn tried to sit on the edge of Steele's desk and Tech pushed his thigh off. "It's not uncommon to fall for a guy that roughs you up a bit… in a hot way."

"Shut up, that's absurd and I don't, anyway. I'm doing my job, that's it."

"Please. I want one… make me a map, too." Syn pouted. An absolutely ridiculous look for a man who had three different weapons on him.

"You know this city like the back of your hand. But fine… fine. I'll make you one. You're such a spoiled brat. Go on, go back to work." Tech continued to push.

"Hey, that's my line."

Tech was glad when he left. He could feel his face getting warmer. Damn, he wished he could grow a full beard sometimes, to hide when he got flushed. Unfortunately, that wasn't in his makeup either. He could grow a few strands on his chin but it was so sparse, it ended up being a source of ridicule, so he kept it shaved off. He had no problem flicking off the guys when they teased him, but he wanted to keep down the talk of him having a crush.

Chapter FIFTEEN

Steele

They'd sat outside the dockworker's house for six-and-a-half hours. From the details of his file, Samuel Walker got off his shift at five. It was almost seven. Steele wasn't a stranger to surveillance or long periods of waiting, and according to Ruxs and Green's behavior, neither were they. Every now and then, they'd make a comment or ask Steele a question, but for the most part, they were silent… professional. Which he was grateful for, because if the two of them talked non-stop about date nights or their hot lovemaking the night before, Steele might've stabbed them both through the seats.

"Let's go to that bar he hangs out at. Maybe he had a hard day and needed a drink," Green suggested. "Sound good, Steele?"

"Yeah, let's do it." Steele's throat was dry as hell. Next time, he'd remember to store some water back here for himself. "I'd rather question him outside a public place, though."

"What's the fun in that?" Ruxs and Green said, in unison again.

"Wow. How many times you guys use that line?" Steele asked drily.

"Enough," Ruxs answered. He drove the few minutes up Crew Street, circling around the backside of the bar.

The area sure looked different from the neighborhood of middle-class homes they'd just left, only twenty minutes away, where the skyscrapers off in the distance made a beautiful backdrop. But around them were run down businesses, foreclosed homes, boarded up warehouses that probably held squatters. People lingered on porches, some giving them suspicious looks as they rode by.

"That license plate was XJX-5148, right?" Steele recited what he'd seen in the file a few hours ago.

After Ruxs looked at the paperwork, he answered, "Yeah, that's right."

"He's in there. There's his license plate, but that's not the car it's registered to."

"Nice catch, bro." Ruxs nodded, pulling his big Dodge into the Burger King across the street. "Let's grab something in here, I'm starved. We can see if he gets in his car to leave."

They walked into the restaurant, looking like any other rough guys in the neighborhood. The manager was behind the register taking orders, eyeing them warily while they stood there, looking up at the board. After they ordered, the three of them went to sit in the far corner, near the back exit so they could leave fast if they had to. It felt good to be out of that truck, and even though fast food wasn't his favorite, he was going to enjoy it because he hadn't eaten since yesterday afternoon.

"So, you guys got family here?" Steele asked both of them.

"No other family but my mother, and she's in rehab," Ruxs admitted freely. He actually looked rather proud. "This is the longest she's stayed in."

Steele nodded, looking to Green.

"My mom's still in the area. Also, Ruxs and I have an adopted son who goes to Georgetown."

Steele's eyes widened at that one. *A kid!* "That's amazing. What's he studying?"

"Besides Gen?" Ruxs scoffed. "His degree will be sociology with a master's in education. He's got another year left."

"Nice. Who's Gen… his girlfriend?" Steele slurped more of his huge cup of water.

"Nope. Genesis is his boyfriend. God's younger brother."

Steele watched Ruxs to see if he was joking. He wasn't. Steele wiped his mouth with his napkin, hiding his grin. "Damn. All you guys really are close."

"Gen is cool. Great guy and he really loves Curtis, treats him like he should be treated. I can't complain." Green sat back. "You like football? You may know him."

"Hell yeah, I do. Who is he? Oh shit, wait. Godfrey's brother. You don't mean the G-Man? Genesis Godfrey. I'll be damned. Small world. That guy was a beast on the field. Played four years for the Bulldogs. Heisman trophy winner, was supposed to be the number one draft pick and opted out to work for Apple. That guy was a huge conversation topic with my squadron… all of them were die-hard football fanatics. He was a player that really stood up for who he was. That's another reason I liked him."

Ruxs and Green were both laughing the more excited Steele got. He was pretty enthusiastic to hopefully meet God's brother. He was sure their paths would cross some way or another. *Damn. Ack would be so jealous. He loved the G-Man.*

"Yeah, he's an engineer now. They got a small house in DC. They visit a lot, though, so you'll see him." Green spoke with a mouth full of Whopper, balling up his wrapper at the same time.

"That'd be cool. I'd like—" Steele's phone buzzed in his pocket, stopping him mid-sentence. He took it out and saw it was his uncle. "I'll be right back."

Steele left the restaurant and walked around the back past the drive-thru so he could hear. While he walked, stretching his legs, he pulled out a Swisher and lit it up. He leaned against a brick wall on the opposite side of the dumpsters, answering all the questions thrown at him. When his uncle finished getting all the details of his first day, he immediately segued into wanting Steele to come stay with him until he found a permanent place. There was no way he was doing that. He liked his privacy. And if he ever found a guy that'd give him the time of day, he'd like to fuck him loudly, so that was another reason.

"*Onu.* I appreciate the offer, but I—" Steele's heart jumped when a beat-up late model Buick sped into the parking lot, screeching to a halt just outside the door. Three men jumped out, pulling down their masks and throwing their hoodies over their heads, guns already drawn.

Steele didn't have time to tell his uncle goodbye. He tucked his phone into his back pocket and pulled out one of his Glocks, quickly screwing on the suppressor. As he moved along the side of the

103

restaurant, he could hear yelling and commands being barked. There was no one else in the Buick, but it was still running. Steele aimed at the tires and shot out the back two… just in case. The sound of his gun a muted pop that was impossible to hear over the chaos inside.

He tucked his firearm into the small of his back and walked back into the restaurant. It only took a three-second glance around the dining room for him to assess the situation. The few patrons that were dining in were on the floor under their tables, shielding their heads. Steele cut his eyes to Ruxs and Green, who were still sitting in their chairs looking somewhere between uninterested and angry. A hooded man with an ancient handgun that looked like it was made in the 1980s was controlling the customers. He moved around the small area and when he got to Ruxs and Green's table, he pointed the gun at them, shouting at them not to move.

"Get that thing outta my face," Ruxs growled.

Steele had to suppress a laugh at Ruxs' bravado. When they said the Enforcers were fearless, it wasn't an exaggeration.

The guy looked stunned but he clutched his gun tighter and backed away. "Either of you moves and I'll cap your ass."

"Be cool, T. Just watch 'em," the one up front yelled and turned back around to face the front. Two of them stood at the counter demanding the cash from the registers. The employees were terrified. One of them looked old enough to be a grandmother, her hands shaking so hard she could barely hit the keys to open her drawer. The man raised his shotgun higher, making her yelp and cringe back from it, and Steele had to make himself known.

"Hey! Don't fucking move, man! Get over here!" one of them barked, finally noticing Steele just inside the door. The man clutched his shotgun with both hands, using it to motion towards the counter. The guy had on a stocking cap, stretched over his face, distorting his features, but Steele was able to make out he was Caucasian and in his late thirties. His voice was deep, but he caught the slight quiver – he was nervous – and he should be. If he only knew.

Steele raised his hands and moved closer to the counter. Exactly where he needed to be. He wasn't going to let these petty thugs hurt innocent civilians who were trying to earn an honest living.

"Don't you try anything, man," the hoodlum snarled, his teeth clenched tight. "Don't be a fuckin' hero." He gave his partner in crime the nod. "Go to the safe. Quick, go."

The shortest of the trio jumped the counter and pointed his AK at the manager, shoving him hard enough to knock the young man to the ground. "Get up! Get to the safe! Now. Hurry up!"

Amateurs.

"No one move and you won't die today," the guy whispered sternly. Steele didn't know if that was the guy was trying to sound menacing, but it came off as weak. When the third man was all the way in the back, it was time for Steele to make his move. He looked over at Ruxs and Green and they both gave him an imperceptible nod that only he would understand.

Steele kept his hands up in the air. "Just get what you want and go." Steele spoke up, knowing it would piss the guy off. He needed to draw him closer.

"On the floor!" the man barked, looking at Steele like he'd lost his mind, especially when he didn't move. "Don't make me kill you, motherfucker!"

The employees' sounds of fear became louder as Steele stood motionless, watching the thug's trigger finger.

"I hate thieves," Steele snarled, his lip turning up in the corner. His disdain and disgust were real.

The guy walked up on him, moving to put that barrel to his chest... wrong move. Out of the corner of his eye, he could see Ruxs' arm moving. When the leader was in his reach, Steele snapped his arm out and caught the barrel of the gun, thrusting it up in the air – exposing the man's ribs. Simultaneously, Steele swiped his knuckleduster from his sleeve and struck his fist into the bastard's side three times before he could even react, turning his body into each blow for maximum impact. The sound of ribs cracking was louder than the customers' gasps of shock. A blow from the grip of his knife was like being hit with brass knuckles. Steele cocked his fist back and caught the man's temple once – ripping the shotgun free, sending him to the floor, dazed and disoriented. The fucker's head hadn't even hit the tile when Steele spun around at the sound of the third

105

man coming out the back office. With his knuckle-blade still secured in his left hand, Steele drew his gun from behind his back with his right, making it appear like magic, and squeezed the trigger twice, the suppressor silently sending two bullets into the man's thighs.

He'll never run in and rob another store.

Steele had ignored the sounds of pain that rang out behind him while he took out the ringleader, trusting Ruxs had his back. When Steele was sure his own perps were no longer a threat, he looked behind him to see the second would-be thief on the ground with a knife embedded in his shoulder and his gun about twenty feet away from him. Ruxs stood over him, making sure he didn't move.

Green was still sitting at the table drinking his soda. The ultimate trust in his partners.

Chapter SIXTEEN

Tech

This was the hardest part of Tech's job. Listening to his team when they were in the thick of it while he sat there in the office. He'd already dispatched Syn, God, and Day the second Ruxs called out his name but didn't voice a request. Tech heard the sound of the place being robbed and got to work. Their trackers put them at the Burger King on Atlantic Ave. and Syn took off out of the office while Tech contacted the zone three precinct in Peoplestown. He knew they had the worst response times in the city, over twenty damn minutes. A good response time was ten, that's if the call was near a zone. But a robbery happened in a quarter of that time. Tech had confidence in his team; they'd handled worse than a few desperate, petty thieves that were willing to risk their freedom for a measly few hundred bucks.

Tech hadn't wanted Steele to have a problem on his very first day out, but shit happened. He could hear the commotion and knew they were safe for now, but his hands sped across his keyboard while he used his software to scan for the IP address to tap into the restaurant's security cameras. He needed eyes in there. He didn't want to distract Ruxs, only spoke once to let him know his team's ETA. When he heard the hisses and pops of a suppressor, he closed his eyes, praying it was the one he'd just given to Steele. Most robbers didn't have silencers. After four too-long minutes, Ruxs' voice was composed and clear, "Tech. 10-24 and 10-52."

"10-4," Tech responded. They were Ruxs and Green's usual codes. The situation's been contained. Ambulance needed for suspect. They used the general police codes much of the time, but their task force also had a few of their own. Tech would need to teach them to Steele soon. He waited for his software to finish moving through the many IP addresses in the area before it hit on the one he wanted. In that time frame, he let Ruxs know that first responders should be on the scene in six minutes. It took another eight minutes after that before Tech's computer beeped and his Hydra system highlighted an address for him.

Yes. Tech quickly copied the address and fired up Kali to bypass all passwords. As soon as the footage came up Tech could see the place swarming with firemen and about six uniformed officers. His eyes darted all over the lobby, looking for his teammates. One in particular. He spotted Green talking with the officers and kept searching for Ruxs and Steele. *Where is he?* Tech had his hand on his chest the entire time, looking back and forth over the people in the grainy image. When his other monitor finally picked up the outside cameras, he realized Steele and Ruxs were outside, watching the paramedics load up a man whose large body filled the stretcher. Tech blew out a breath. Jesus Christ. After a few more minutes, he recognized God's big RAM when it flew into the parking lot.

As much as he'd have liked to keep his eye on them, his lieutenants didn't need that. Tech had his own job to do and it wasn't to stare at the new recruit. Instead, he went about getting the footage downloaded and into files so it could be reviewed by God and Day when they meet with the captain and the robbery lieutenants. His department always appreciated not having to wait for a company or city office to give them the video they needed, Tech was able to provide it himself within minutes. By the time he had everything compiled, including the closest street cameras, the men from his team – accompanied by the captain and a couple other detectives, were walking back into the precinct. Tech ejected the flash drive and inserted it into a cover.

Ruxs' hands moved animatedly the whole time they were walking across the bullpen. Steele was behind God so he couldn't see him, but the lieutenants and the rest of the guys looked pretty entertained by the story. When they got through the glass double doors, Ruxs finished with a loud, "It was some real Steven Segal-type shit, God, I swear."

God's deep chuckle was contagious, all of them smiling and recounting their own version of the scene. Tech hoped one day he'd be able to add in his own after-action account. *Not likely.* Tech turned back around to his monitors until he heard....

"Who the hell's desk is this? The Secretary of Defense? Shit, Steele. Tech really hooked you up, man."

Damnit, Day. Green and Ruxs had to pass him to get to their own desks, each of them whistling when they passed Steele's. "Oh boy, he has a little place for his pens and paperclips too... how sweet." Tech could feel his skin heating as he did his best to ignore the teasing. These guys were notorious for it and Tech usually got a kick out of it... but now he was the butt of it. He could take it, though. He put his middle finger up over his shoulder, not bothering to turn and face them.

"Tech, you got the footage yet?" God asked him.

"I got it ready."

"Nice job. Boot it up. We let a couple Zone Three detectives take the tapes from the restaurant. Let's see what's so damn fascinating."

Tech put the drive back in and pulled it up on the big monitor above his head. He had it cued to start right when the robbers pulled into the parking lot. All the men were crowded around his desk watching like it was the latest blockbuster film. He stayed seated and he could feel a strong, hot presence right at his back, but he didn't turn around, keeping his eyes on the screen.

"Where the hell are you, Steele?" God asked.

"I'm out back on a phone call," Steele said, directly behind him.

"Look at Ruxs' greedy ass, still eating while the place is being robbed." Day laughed, pulling a few laughs from the room.

"Those fries are disgusting when they get cold. Everyone knows that, Day," Ruxs said wryly. All of them laughed at that, only quieting down when Steele appeared through the front door. Tech's eyes widened when Steele put himself in front of the older woman at the register, a sawed-off shotgun pointed at his head. *Outstanding valor.*

It was so silent in their department; you could've heard a pin drop. When Steele finally made his move, a round of whispered "shit, oh damn, fuck," filled the room. Tech held his breath while he watched Steele manipulate that one-of-kind knife and his firearm at the same time. His military training showing up in full force.

"Hey! Is that my suppressor?" Day asked over everyone's shocked silence.

"Shut up, Day," God grumbled. "Damn, Steele. Those were some bad moves. I'll give you that. You move faster than Day."

"That's debatable," Day scoffed. He was joking and everyone could tell, but the look he shot God was downright hilarious.

"You wanted a test and I guess you got it." Ruxs nodded, clamping Steele on his shoulder, looking proud to be partnered with him.

"Damn, the way you threw that blade, that guy didn't even know what happened," Steele countered.

Tech had to rewind that part, it'd happened so fast. They were all watching Steele, not noticing when Ruxs yanked his blade from under his arm and flung it across the dining room. It lodged so deep in the other suspect that his arm flew back, making his weapon fly from his hand.

"Well, God. Looks like you got yourself another one." The SWAT captain shook his head, walking back towards the door. "Why don't you save some for us?"

"You got enough of your own, Hart. Now get outta here, you know IA will be down any minute." God dropped down in his chair.

"You mean your best friends." The big man laughed.

God gave his friend a middle-finger salute and turned back towards Ruxs, Green, and Steele. "Well, did you guys actually do what I asked and get some information from the dockworker? Or did you just play cowboys all day?"

"Um. Well, we went to the house—," Green started.

"But the guy didn't show—," Ruxs finished.

"So we thought to check out the bar—," Green jumped back in.

"But we figured we'd eat first—," Steele concluded.

"Then that's when—"

110

God put his hand up stopping Ruxs' add-on. Syn and Tech both were having a hard time concealing their laughter. They could only imagine what God was thinking, after hearing all three of them finish each other's sentences.

"Save it. Damnit." God huffed and ran his hands through his long hair. "You guys attract trouble like balls attract sweat. Now I have to talk with this IA prick again."

"Actually, my balls rarely sweat," Day added quietly, not looking up at God while he took the drive from Tech and labeled it.

"Day." God stared, looking irritated.

"I'm just saying. It's a bad analogy." Day shrugged indifferently, tucking the drive inside the file Tech handed to him. Anytime Ruxs and Green did anything, the lieutenants had to answer a ton of questions from IA. Usually about using excessive force, but Tech didn't see that at all. Steele could've put a slug center mass and killed the perp, but he'd wounded him instead, and so had Ruxs. He didn't throw the knife in the man's eye. He could've… but didn't.

"Come on, y'all. Let's go do the nasty." Day waved the file in the air and headed out the door with Syn and God following him towards the captain's office.

"Tech. I need a new knife, please. The paramedic wouldn't let me rip my other one out of the guy's shoulder," Ruxs informed him.

"Sure. I'll get it." Tech stood, still not making eye contact with Steele. He could see him out of the corner of his eye, studying the new map on his desk. He hoped he liked it. He punched in the code to the equipment room door and went inside, walking towards the knife shelf. He'd need to put in a new order soon. While his inventory system opened up, he went to check on the mold for Steele's earpiece. He opened the case and gently prodded the small lump.

"I like the desk."

Tech gasped and jumped hard enough to drop the plastic tool he has holding. Steele's dark voice was close to his right ear, near enough to feel his breath on his neck. "Jesus Christ. I didn't even hear you come in."

"Relax. I'm used to moving silently. It's gonna be a hard habit to break." His powerful words made their way under Tech's collar and the heat of his body washed down his back like a hot caress.

"I guess it would be," Tech replied before clamping his mouth shut. "Get to know that map, I'm gonna quiz you on it. It's important to learn the city.

"Hmm. A quiz. I guess that's better than a test... I don't like tests. But you probably know that. You've had an unpleasantly close encounter with me, you've read about me... seen that video just now." Steele's whisper was rough. "I know you read what they called me. Are you still afraid of me?"

Tech closed his eyes and let the excited nervousness settle inside his stomach. Yes, he had read more. He knew exactly what Steele could do, but no one else did. That video only revealed a fraction of his skill and agility. "I do know. And, no. I'm not afraid."

Steele was so quiet it was eerie, because Tech knew he was still there. Lurking, stalking. Tech felt like he was being hunted, but not to be eaten. He tried to calm his body, but he had a feeling Steele could sense his anxiousness. God, the things this man could probably do to him. But Tech wasn't on Steele's level and he never would be. No one was. All the training in the world wouldn't make him his equal. Steele's strength came from centuries of ancestral ingrained talent and decades of elite training. Tech was just a nerd.

"What are you thinking?"

"Nothing," Tech huffed. "Was there something you needed from me?"

Steele's laugh was predatory. "Actually, yes. But for now, I'll take more bullets, and I need a better suppressor. Day can have this piece of shit back. It's too loud. An AAC would be preferable, but if they won't approve it... a GEMTECH."

"I'll get it approved," Tech responded. He'd get that damn suppressor even if he had to sell his ass for it. *Wow, where'd that come from?* He'd move a few things around in their budget this quarter.

"Good." Steele felt so close to his body, Tech couldn't turn around if he wanted to. "How're your arms feeling now?"

Tech cleared his throat while he busied his hands with the earpiece components. "They're great. I can hardly feel the soreness now. Um… thank you for the bandages. I type a lot, so sometimes my forearms can get a little sore." *Really*. Tech rolled his eyes, did he actually just admit that? Typing, seriously. If he didn't sound like a weakling before, he certainly did now. *Damnit*.

"I can believe that. It's tedious and repetitive. I'd be happy to show you some exercises for them." Steele's hands ran up the length of his triceps and around his arms. Tech tried not to shiver at the light touches. Thoughts of what Steele could do with those hands that were now on his body were causing a lot of feelings that'd been dead for a long time to spark back to life. Steele kept his fingers on his forearms and ran his thumbs down the insides until he reached his pulse. Steele pressed both thumbs there and Tech felt his knees weaken. "Your pulse is erratic."

Of course, it is.

"You may not be afraid… but are you comfortable?"

Was he comfortable? That wasn't something he could answer. Now, if Steele asked was he confused in his company… fuck yes. However, he was also pissed at himself that he'd admitted to this FORECON Marine that typing made his wrists hurt sometimes. He didn't want Steele to treat him like a baby. "I'm not scared," Tech growled.

Steele dropped his arms and caught him around his waist, spinning Tech fast enough to make him dizzy. His breath caught in his throat when he stopped only a couple inches from Steele's face, having to slightly tilt his head up to look into those penetrating gray eyes. "You keep saying that. But your body is telling me different," Steele hissed.

Tech didn't dart his eyes away. He didn't want Steele thinking he was insecure. Instead, he held those blown pupils and majestic irises with his own interested gaze. Inching in closer, Tech fought down his tension and gently placed both hands on Steele's tight stomach. Maintaining eye contact, he slowly moved them up Steele's chest, gliding over the defined pecs. Steele's nostrils flared but he didn't stop Tech when he gripped his collar and pulled him down

113

closer to his mouth. Just before their lips could touch, Tech inched over and whispered in Steele's ear. "I can't control the way my body trembles when you're near me, but trust me when I tell you… it's not fear, Ghost."

Tech used Steele's classified identity, hoping it didn't backfire like hell. But the way Steele's hands tightened on his waist, he didn't think it had. He'd taken the gamble, hoping it'd pay off. He was confessing to Steele what he'd learned from those documents, information revealing what the lieutenant colonel had to do – had to become – to keep himself and his men safe. Yet Tech was *still* standing there in the man's arms, his cock as hard as a missile, flirting with danger… hoping he'd flirt back.

Chapter SEVENTEEN

Steele

Steele was back in the back of Ruxs' truck, bumming a ride home that evening with the thoughts of Tech touching him still searing his skin. The hot young detective had boldly handled him, grabbed him and yanked him where he'd wanted him. Steele rubbed his hand over his neck, like Tech's fingers were still there, his soft voice in his ear. *So sexy.* Now he had to go home and try to sleep with a hard-on all night. As tired as he was, he didn't need to stay up all night again. Last night, he'd hardly gotten any sleep, anxious about seeing Tech after what'd happened. But now that things were good, he'd gotten to showcase a little talent, and he got along great with Ruxs and Green; he actually thought he'd be able to rest without the assistance of alcohol.

Steele looked around when Ruxs turned into his trailer park, which was already starting to come alive with shady activity as night fell. Kids were still running around in bare feet with no jackets to protect them from the chilly weather. He shook his head in frustration when he noticed his metal-head neighbor was already setting up for company. An assortment of raggedy chairs was strewn about the yard and what looked to be a makeshift fire pit was being built. That goddamn monster boom box was blaring music that could probably be heard clear across the park.

"Man. You've gotta get the fuck out of here." Green sighed when they pulled into his cracked driveway.

"I said it's temporary, and it will be. I'll find something," Steele almost snarled, looking over at his neighbor. "I'm tired, though. He'd better not be having a party."

"Yeah… umm. Good luck with that." Green chuckled when a dusty, jacked-up four-by-four that was obviously used for off-roading roared to a stop in front of his neighbor's place. Three guys jumped down from the cab carrying cases of beer, all of them more ugly and annoying than the other.

"Hey. We got a couple extra rooms, Steele. You're welcome to one if you want, until you find your own place." Ruxs turned around, looking at him. "You don't have PTSD or no shit like that, do you… not gonna come in our room and try to fuck us into submission or no shit like that, right?"

Steele punched Ruxs' headrest, a scoff bursting from him. "Shut up. No, I don't have PTSD… much. And thank you, but no thank you. I'd rather not listen to you guys fuck like gladiators all night. I'll take the metal over that suffering any day."

"Suit yourself." Ruxs shrugged. "Don't hate that I have a healthy sex life, man. Jealousy is not attractive."

Steele dropped down and slammed Ruxs' door, leaning against it while he assessed how he was going to handle the situation. He lit a sweet cigar and blew the smoke so it'd go right into Ruxs' window, his partner flashing angry green eyes at him. He pushed off the truck and walked across the dirt lawn up to his neighbor. He already had a Budweiser in his hand, while his friends stood around talking loudly and smoking cigarettes.

There was no need to act like he was there for any other reason but one. "Yo."

"What's up? You wanna brew, man?" his neighbor asked, bending down to get one from the iceless cooler.

"No. What I want is for you to keep it down tonight. Some people around here work, including myself. I don't wanna hear that all night." Steele pointed at the radio that was blaring loud enough to make him have to yell to be heard.

His neighbor glared back for a few seconds and turned his lip up at him. "It's only eight."

"It's still too damn loud. Keep it down." Steele turned, not bothering to wait for a response. Ruxs and Green kept watching until Steele went through his front door, slamming it closed behind him. He heard Ruxs' truck drive off, but what he didn't hear was the volume of the music decreasing.

116

He looked out the window and saw a few more people had shown up, including some females. Someone noticed him watching and tapped his neighbor, yelling something in his ear. The guy waved with a smug smile. Steele flicked him off, earning him an angry look from a few of his friends before he closed the blinds.

He went in the back room that was no bigger than a walk-in closet and took his shirt and holster off. His eyes burned from the lack of sleep. All was quiet in his tiny living space, and he'd probably fall into a deep sleep if it weren't for the ruckus next door. Groaning loudly, he barely resisted going back over there and flashing his badge. After he ate his Hungry Man microwave meal, he was going to try to sleep; hopefully, he wouldn't have to commit manslaughter first.

He thought about Tech the entire time he was in the shower, seven minutes to be exact because that's the maximum time allotted for hot water consumption. He had to wash his dick and balls fast to avoid the urge to tug one out. He didn't know what was going on with him; he'd never been attracted to anyone who looked like Tech before. Maybe it was from being around so many jarheads, Tech's sweater vest and khakis were a new and exciting change. That neatly styled hair that he wanted to run his fingers through and mess up just for the sake of it. Just to see the man flustered and panting with need for him.

Steele sat down in his recliner with his dinner, ready to watch some mindless television, but couldn't ignore the loud women squealing next door or the horny men's rowdiness while they drunkenly chased them around the yard. All that, along with the headache-inducing heavy metal music.

Steele picked up his phone and called the non-emergency police number to report the noise. Hopefully, it wouldn't take long for a couple officers to get out here. After he finished eating his gourmet style Salisbury and mac-n-cheese that still had a couple cold spots in the center, he decided to look on line for apartments closer to his precinct. Maybe even one with a garage so he could get his bike from his uncle's. He wouldn't dare let it sit unprotected around the trailer park. After about an hour of searching and finding a few good leads,

Steele heard the music shut off and everything went quiet. Checking his watch, he saw it was almost eleven. The roaming red and blue lights reflecting off his dingy walls confirmed his suspicions that the police had finally arrived. *Serves you fuckers right. Partying on a goddamn Tuesday night.*

Steele yawned for the millionth time and shut everything off, feeling like he'd finally get some much-needed rest. Ruxs would be there to pick him up at six. Steele was in a dead sleep, snoring and drooling when a loud crash sounded in his living room. He yanked his Glock from under his pillow and was up on his feet in seconds. He didn't open his eyes while he listened for any movement. Another crash sounded – his damn windows breaking in the living room. He could only see behind his trailer from his back window. With his peacemaker pointed downward, he slid open the pocket door that separated his bedroom from the kitchen and peeked out into the living room. Nothing. He hurried to the window over the sink and glanced outside. His neighbor and friends were all standing on the lawn, drinking like nothing had happened. Steele surveyed the damage. Four or five beer bottles littered his front room, but what really pissed him off was that one had hit his big screen television, cracking it in the top left corner.

Steele growled and slung the door open. He realized he was only in his boxer briefs so he stood in the door, his gun out of view. His neighbor looked in his direction, a grin tugging on his mouth like he was barely holding in his laughter. The rest kept their backs to him, but when the punk turned the music back up sky high, the others couldn't resist breaking into laughing fits.

Steele closed his door and leaned his forehead against it. Taking deep breaths, he talked himself out of doing anything that'd get him suspended or worse, fired. He was a police officer; he couldn't bash anyone's head in just because he was extremely pissed. He'd have to go through the proper channels and file a report. His breathing was still elevated, air hissing out his nose with each exhale, like a bull intimidating its rider.

Mindful where he stepped with his bare feet, he went into his bedroom and called one of the very few people he knew he could depend on after the short amount of time he'd been in Atlanta.

"Hello," the raspy voice answered.

"Ruxs, I'm gonna kill these motherfuckers, man."

"We're on our way."

The line went dead and Steele sighed in relief. No other explanations, no pleading or begging for help was needed. The word partners obviously meant something to Ruxs and Green that they'd stop whatever they were doing, no matter what, and come to help with only a few frustrated words spoken. He'd only hoped he'd find partners like that again so many years after losing his squad.

Steele went about packing up his clothes and toiletries. He wasn't coming back. His television was fucked, so that only left his small stereo and his answering machine. He was sitting in his recliner, smoking a cigar when he heard the roaring of Ruxs' truck skid to an angry stop. Two doors slammed and heavy boots ascended his steps. Neither of them knocked, just busted through the door with looks of anger and concern on their faces. Once they saw he was safe and intact, the two of them looked around at the broken glass, shaking their heads in annoyance. Steele pulled on the cigar again, letting it calm his nerves. But his partners looked like they had other ideas.

Both of them went for his stuff, which was stacked by the door. "Let's go," Green mumbled.

While they loaded his few belongings into the back of the truck, his neighbor watched with satisfaction, bopping his head to his music. Steele was ready to climb in the backseat when Ruxs gripped his shoulder. "Where the fuck are you going?"

"I gotta get outta here before I do something stupid," Steele snarled.

"Oh, brother." Ruxs smirked. "You have to understand who you're partnered with now. We don't let bullshit like this slide. On my grave, it'll say 'always did something stupid... and it felt damn good'."

119

Steele smiled when Green tossed Ruxs a big Louisville Slugger over the hood of the truck. "Ever heard that song 'Rage Against the Machine'? Personally, it's one of my favorites, and so fitting for this moment."

Green pulled a shotgun from underneath the seat and Ruxs spun on his heels, walking right up to his neighbor's yard with the bat cocked back like he was getting ready to knock a ball out the park, and sent the fat end of his bat into the face of the stereo. Silence followed as pieces and parts flew around him. His neighbor sprang out of the way when Ruxs raised the bat high over his head and came down on it again. The friends went to advance, but Green took a couple steps forward and cocked the shotgun, issuing a warning. There wasn't a man alive that didn't fear that sound. Green kept it aimed in the air while Ruxs went crazy on the man's stereo until there was nothing left of it then started tearing up his chairs. When all six of the guys raised their hands and backed away, Green planted his feet wide like a bodyguard and let the barrel of the gun rest on his shoulder. Steele leaned against the grille of the truck, pulling long drags off his cigar while he watched his partners' entertaining display of retribution. There'd be no useless reports filed. Eye for an eye. Destruction for destruction.

He wasn't sure if he'd actually heard the bumping or not. He was in a deep sleep in Ruxs and Green's spare bedroom. It'd been too late to consider going to his uncle's in Buford, so he'd gritted his teeth and accepted their invitation instead of finding a hotel. Actually, it was more like Green telling him to shut up and driving him to their place despite his refusal.

Yeah, there it was again. Definitely a bump. Steele looked at his watch since it was still dark outside. September was his favorite month, the fall season his favorite time of year. Daylight savings was fast approaching, and after being deployed for so long, it was still a bitch to get used to. He groaned when he saw it was five thirty. At least he'd gotten a few hours of sleep. The place was nice – well, anything was better than where he'd been – but it was clean, and looked and felt like a home. Steele hadn't expected the huge two-story loft above a distribution warehouse that took up half a block. Enough square footage to have nice man-sized recliners and a wraparound leather sectional in front of a big screen television that looked to have every game console there was wired to it. There was ample workout equipment positioned in a nook that got plenty of sun. And an area to the far right with a pool table, a couple of arcade machines, and a bar for entertaining. It was large enough to host a decent sized house party. The tall ceilings made it a little drafty but Steele preferred the cool these days, having spent years in Afghanistan, he'd grown to despise the heat.

Steele got out of bed and dropped down to the floor to do what he'd done every morning since he was eighteen unless it wasn't possible, one hundred sit-ups and one hundred pushups. Some people preferred coffee; he used exercise and core-warming to wake him. He was able to do the entire workout in twenty minutes, taking a short breather between sets. When he finished he got up and grabbed the towel and washcloth Green gave him last night and his toiletry kit.

Walking to the bathroom at the end of the hall, he heard the unmistakable sounds of moaning and desire. His steps faltered right before he got to Green and Ruxs' bedroom door, which was pushed slightly open. Did they forget they had company? Or maybe they didn't give a damn.

"Chris, yeah. Like that." Steele heard Ruxs groan loudly.

For shit's sake. He didn't need to hear any of this. It's why he hadn't wanted to come here. The last thing he needed in his head all day was sounds of their sex. But it wasn't what he thought. Steele inched past slowly, looking through the gap in the door. A soft-looking gray cover was pulled up to their waists, leaving their naked torsos visible. Both of them were on their sides facing the door but their eyes were sealed tight with ecstasy while Ruxs moved slowly behind his partner. This wasn't the sweaty, balls slapping romp he'd imagined them having. No, Ruxs and Green were making lazy, passionate love to each other.

"I love you so much," Green whispered, pulling Ruxs' palm from over his heart and kissing each knuckle while Ruxs kept moving behind him.

Fuck. Steele kept walking before he got caught. He closed himself in the bathroom and leaned against the door. He looked down at his hard dick, refusing to touch it. It was just wrong on too many levels. That was private. It was their moment, *their* love, and he was too decent a man to try to hone in and jerk one out to it. He had to admit to himself that what he'd just saw was beautiful and inspiring. Steele pushed his erection down and closed his eyes, trying to think of anything but the hope and dream of wanting that kind of love for himself. A true partner to fulfill him in every way.

He tried to think of work, but all that came to mind was a hot geek. He smiled, wondering what Tech would wear today. Slim jeans with a dress shirt and a bow tie. He hadn't seen him wear that yet, but he was actually looking forward to it.

He turned on the shower, pleased when it heated up in no time flat. He did finally moan when he stepped under the huge showerhead that pelted his neck and back. *Oh god, that feels good.* He needed this… really, really needed it. Maybe he'd pick up a pair of headphones or something today. Green had offered his spare room for as long as Steele wanted or until he found a place. With that comfortable, plush mattress and this showerhead, Steele was having a damn hard time saying no.

After dressing in a comfortable pair of jeans and his last clean long john, he slid on his steel toes and clipped his badge on his hip, concealing it like most undercovers. He was putting his wallet in his back pocket when the combined smells of seared meat and something sweet hit him. *They got breakfast delivery here?*

Steele jogged down the metal staircase and almost tripped down the last step when he saw Green in the kitchen in front of the stove, flipping what looked like French toast while Ruxs sat at the breakfast bar, shoving pieces into his mouth and reading something on his phone. It looked crazy and extremely domestic. Green didn't look like your ordinary cook with his low-riding jeans and white wife beater. He had a shiny silver link chain riding low on his throat that made the jet-black tribal art covering his neck stand out even more. His sleeve of colorful floral tattoos was on full display, his usual white t-shirt hanging out of his back pocket. Turning dark eyes in his direction, Green motioned with his head to the stool next to Ruxs. Those two were so opposite, but similar. Ruxs' fair skin, buzz cut, and pale eyes, juxtaposed with Green's tan, tatted-up skin and dark brown hair that did what it wanted to do like Steele's did.

"Just in time. You like sausage or bacon?" Green asked, flipping the thick pieces of bread in the expensive-looking frying pan.

Steele rubbed his hand over his stubble. "Um, both, actually."

"Coming right up," Green said with his back to him.

Steele watched Green pile his plate up with several pieces of bacon and about eight sausage links next to two heavenly slices of fluffy French toast. He was definitely staying. "Damn, Green. I didn't know you could cook."

"Well, you've known me less than a week." Green laughed. "But stick around, I have many talents."

"Yeah, I heard, this morning," Steele mumbled, too low for them to hear.

"What?" Green asked, placing a tall cup of milk next to Steele's plate.

"Nothing." Steele took the warm syrup and poured it over his entire plate. If the food tasted half as good as it smelled, he was in for a treat. Looking over at Ruxs' empty plate, he didn't doubt it. "How'd you know I don't drink coffee?"

Green pffted a little. "Because if you did, I would've seen it by now. Two days with you, and you've never once fixed a cup of joe."

Steele would have to remember he was around some competent detectives now. The kind that observed everything around them. "Do you cook too, Ruxsberg?"

"I can burn." Ruxs smirked, still scrolling through his phone.

"You can burn, alright," Green confirmed huskily, winking at his lover while refilling Ruxs' coffee mug without being asked. Ruxs blushed, looking bashfully at his partner.

Steele groaned, taking a large gulp of cold milk. What had he gotten himself into? It sure was entertaining, if nothing else. He'd never seen a gay couple as macho as them behave like this. Green serving his guy. But after what Steele witnessed this morning? Shit, he'd probably get up and make his guy the best damn bagel and cream cheese he could if he was woken up like that. Good sex could make you do those things.

Steele walked behind Ruxs and Green to their truck, which sat under a wide carport on the side of the building. He was so full he almost wanted to get back in that cozy bed and go right back to sleep. They'd offered up their spare room again over breakfast and Steele accepted. It made no sense to waste so much money on a hotel that wouldn't be near as nice as their place. The only thing he'd need was those headphones, and he'd have to start utilizing Green's workout equipment because he saw him take out a decent sized pack of turkey legs, saying they were for dinner tonight. Eating like this would go straight to his gut at his age.

"God gave us the go-ahead to check out the dockworker at his job instead of trying to catch him at home. Maybe he'll get nervous around his coworkers and want us away from there. Might make him talk if his job is threatened," Ruxs informed him, backing out of the carport. "But we gotta stop by the office real quick. I need my new knife and God wants you to have your earpiece."

Tech messing with his ear again. Steele hid his smile behind his fist. His morning was looking better and better.

Chapter EIGHTEEN

Day

Day was already dressed in his usual blue jeans and t-shirt. He had his badge clipped to his studded belt and covered with the hem of his shirt. He'd slept in the den and his back was killing him, so he was already in a mood when God came downstairs looking fully rested. His long hair was still damp from his shower and tucked behind his ears. Day wanted to go up to him and smell that bold aftershave fragrance that always clung to the bottom of God's jaw, but he held back. He looked so sexy in his black cargo pants and tight as sin black APD t-shirt. His gold and chrome weapons gleamed when the sunlight from the kitchen window hit 'em. Desert Eagles weren't for just any man since most men couldn't handle them, but God could. Could handle both at the same time, his forearms bulging and tensing with each fire. Day closed his eyes and blew a defeated breath. He wasn't supposed to be getting hot and worked up over his partner right now, he was mad at him. And for God to come downstairs looking like he did made Day even more upset, because he couldn't bend over the counter for him.

Day had come straight home from the DA's office to make God's favorite dinner of ribeye, asparagus, and twice-baked potato, even throwing in a few red velvet cupcakes he'd picked up from their favorite bakery. They talked about the usual: work and schedules of what was coming up. As soon as God mentioned it'd be quiet for a couple months, Day used the opportunity to segue into some extremely minor wedding details – not even a date – just the mention of tuxedos, and the man had scarfed down his dinner and left, using the excuse of having to check on his mom. Something about her toilet leaking. Mrs. Godfrey lived in a senior facility with maintenance men on site, so Day knew it was bullshit. God didn't even bother to eat dessert with him.

Now, after a terrible night of hardly any rest, his eyes were gritty and his head had the start of what was sure to be a tension headache. But what was worse was how his heart ached when he saw the slender gold band he'd slid on God's finger when he proposed, resting there, taunting him. When God said yes, Day thought he'd buy him one as well, but he'd been wrong. He didn't think it a huge deal, knowing he'd have one when they said their I dos. That day didn't appear to be in the near future, either. Day couldn't help feeling like a sucker, and to a man like him, there was no worse feeling. Why was God even wearing it? He didn't want to get married. If God finally manned up and told him the truth, Day wondered if he'd be able to handle it. Would he be able to still work beside the man, feeling he was only good enough to shack up with? If he was being completely true to himself, he didn't think he could. Day felt his stomach drop, and an overwhelming feeling of grief hit him hard enough make him choke.

God watched him curiously while he poured himself a cup of coffee and took the sections of the morning paper Day always set aside for him. "You good?" he asked. But Day didn't bother to answer. "Did you eat already?"

Day usually fixed them something quick before they had to go in, but his kitchen was as spotlessly clean as he'd left it last night. He wasn't in the mood to eat and could care less if God was hungry or not.

"I'll pick up something on the way," Day mumbled, tossing the Life section of the paper to the side and yanking his heavy jacket off the back of his chair.

"Sounds good, let's go."

"I'm gonna take my car. You can go ahead and go. I got some stuff to handle after work."

"What stuff? Are you taking it by Furious' shop?"

Day didn't answer

"Leo." God frowned, looking like he had no clue what the hell was going on.

126

Day grabbed his duffle bag and walked out the side door that led to the garage. It'd been a few weeks since he'd even cranked up his classic Mustang – he and God always choosing to ride together – he'd feel like an ass if it didn't turn over. He climbed in and his beauty purred to life at the first turn. *Of course, you won't let me down.* Day used the remote to open the garage and made quick work of backing out the driveway and coasting through the neighborhood. He had so much to think about, but the knots in his stomach and throbbing in his head wouldn't let him.

God

God remained at the breakfast bar for another hour, trying to come up with a way to say what was way overdue. Maybe Day wouldn't care about not walking down an aisle. Even though he was far more sentimental than him, he still might be okay with using a justice of the peace like God wanted. God had never even worn a tux and had absolutely no aspiration to. They'd go down to city hall and do it one morning and spend the entire day in bed, or even have an exchange of vows right here at the house. Then a couple weeks later, he and Day could go somewhere and be alone. He'd make it up to him for not being honest from the beginning. He'd tried to work it out in his head, figure out how to just do whatever Day wanted. Until he saw the pricing. He had no desire to empty his meager savings for a wedding that'd last for a few hours. He'd looked at some prices for venues, caterers, open bar, DJs, and all that shit. The least he could see it coming to was about ten grand, and that was on the cheaper side. That figure alone scared the shit out of him. They were detectives, not surgeons. With the economy how it was, he was always leery of his department having to do mandatory cutbacks like so many others had already done. What if he took a huge loan for a wedding, which he couldn't repay?

He'd sit Day down and tell him his concerns real soon. If Day loved him half as much as he loved Day, then his partner would marry him in the middle of the Chattahoochee River on a pontoon boat. God grabbed his keys, locked up and headed to work.

Chapter

NINETEEN

Tech

Tech rolled on his back and fired two shots, hitting the hologram image of a bank robber in the center of the chest. He jumped to his feet and leaped over the concrete barrier set in the middle of the obstacle course and fired three times at the target moving on rails, hitting the image once in the thigh and twice in the stomach.

"Dive! Dive!" his instructor shouted at him from behind the bulletproof viewing window.

Tech dove behind a concrete pillar when the sound of shots being fired at him registered. When they ceased, he sprang up and fired, hitting the last image in the center of the forehead before ducking back down. He breathed in through his nose and out through his mouth while he loaded another clip into the 9mm handgun. The sound of the buzzer alerted him that his ten-minute simulation was over. Tech gasped and shook out his arms, shaking off the nerves. He loved this part of his training, mainly because it looked so realistic and the state of the art program – that he'd help design – was unlike any he'd ever seen. Although he fired real bullets that went through the holograms and hit beanbags surrounding the room, there were never real bullets fired at him. But the sounds were loud enough to portray a real gunfight and if he was hit... he'd definitely know it, and so would the computer.

"Great job, Shawn. I liked that last shot. Dead center. I think your score is even higher than last time." Chen nodded approvingly. "I can tell you've been putting in extra time at the shooting range, too."

"Yeah, I have," Tech answered. He took off the hi-tech helmet and set it down by the others on the shelf, along with the electronic vest that would vibrate if he got shot.

"When you go in the field, you'll be ready. I promise you."
Chen looked like he truly believed what he was saying. "Everything
you do now is just keeping you sharp, Tech. You've got this."

"I've been working on some new simulations, too. The
algorithms are almost done and I can send them over by the end of
the week so you can see what you think." Tech had designed most of
the real-life law enforcement simulations for Chen's training program
so that the user didn't have to enact the same scenario repeatedly. It
would defeat the purpose if the programs could be memorized. The
unexpected was exactly why his heart always tried to beat out of his
chest when he did the simulations.

"Sounds great. You're making my business skyrocket. I've
never imagined the program would end up like this." Chen laughed,
looking around the massive structure.

"I'm just glad I get the discount, otherwise I'd never be able to
afford to train like this."

"Well, I feel guilty for even charging you one hundred a month,
but you won't let me go any lower."

"Nope. That's already a crazy discount. I at least want to pay for
the personal instruction you give me. I get all the program benefits
for free. So this works for me. I spend more than a hundred dollars a
month on Starbucks." Tech laughed.

"Alright, then. We'll call it even. I'll walk you to the lockers; I
wanted to ask you about that Marine at your job. Is he giving you any
more problems?" Chen asked, looking serious. Tech appreciated his
concern, but he really felt he had it under control… especially after
yesterday.

"Oh, he apologized. Even patched me up, I guess you can say. I
really believed his apology was sincere and that it won't happen
again." Tech pushed open the heavy door to the locker room.

"Okay, if you're sure. Because I'll be happy to come down there
and do a little friendly sparring with the guy," Chen offered.

Tech didn't want anyone fighting for him. He knew his teacher
meant well, but this was exactly why he was getting up so darn early
and driving the hour and a half to Gainesville three times a week. He
could take care of himself.

"I appreciate it, Chen. But I'd rather spar with him myself."
Tech winked.

"Oh god. Okay fine, too much information, Shawn." Chen
waved dismissively at him. "I'll see you on Friday."

Tech made his way to the sauna to relax before he had to head
back to Atlanta. He tilted his head back against the warm bamboo
walls, sighing and letting the heat encase him. Tech's mind
immediately wandered to Steele when all was calm and quiet. He
wondered if the man would be surprised by Tech's skill if he'd seen
his shooting. Maybe he could invite him to see it one day. No, that
was dumb. They weren't partners at work or privately. He was
probably far from Steele's type, although Steele seemed to love
flirting with him. That was kind of trending right now if he recalled
correctly. Dating nerds. Tech shook his head at his silliness. A man
like Steele probably wouldn't mind bedding him a couple times
before he moved on. And not just to the next buff lover, but to the
next city. The guy just didn't strike him as the settling down kind.
Steele had lived in six cities in the four years since he'd been
discharged.

Tech had tried a relationship and gotten burned hotter than the
coals of hell. He wouldn't put himself through that again. Maybe just
tapping that fine Marine a few times wouldn't be a terrible idea –
he'd just leave his heart out of it.

Chapter TWENTY

Tech

He no longer needed the bandages Steele wrapped around his elbows yesterday. The bruises were gone and both arms felt wonderful, maybe that's why he'd done so well in target simulation this morning. But now he was hiding in the equipment room, pretending he was checking inventory. God and Day came in separately this morning and it was clear they weren't in good moods. Tech liked the funny, teasing Day. Seeing him hurting and depressed was not only affecting Tech but their entire team. He shook his head and tried to think of a way he could help, but nothing came to mind. He'd just do his job as efficiently as he could, in hopes of making things flow easier for his lieutenants. Besides, he was confident Syn would take care of everything.

Tech sat on the stool, making a few adjustments to Steele's earpiece when he felt a warm presence close to him. He didn't flinch this time. He smiled and kept his back to him when he spoke. "You must like doing that. I prefer a person to announce themselves when they enter a room. It's rude to stalk."

"If you say so. I don't mind a little surprise." Steele's dark voice was full of amusement.

He was closer than Tech had thought. He pivoted on his stool and looked up at him, immediately getting lost in those deep eyes. "Good morning, detective."

"Good morning," Steele answered, the corner of his mouth lifting slightly. "You look good this morning."

Tech looked down at his tan Polo vest over his pink- and white-striped dress shirt. The beige Levi's were nothing to write home about but they were one of his favorite pairs. Was Steele making fun of him or was he really pleased with his look? Did Steele look forward to seeing him like he did Steele? Tech wouldn't, but after his thoughts this morning, he wondered – if he asked Steele to his place – would he refuse him? He didn't want to know if he was the big Marine's type, just if he was interested in a little fun while Steele cooled his heels here in Atlanta for the time being.

Not ready to go there just yet, he chose to stay on small talk. "How was your night? Do anything fun?" Tech cinched his lips together. That question sounded probing. Like he wanted to know if Steele had company or something. He didn't wanna know that.

"My plan was to get some much-needed sleep." Steele seemed to move in even closer, his thighs brushing against Tech's knees. He never took his eyes off Tech when he spoke. "That day I hurt you, I didn't sleep at all. The next day was kind of the same. I was looking forward to resting, but my neighbor had other ideas. I had to go stay with Ruxs and Green when my neighbor threw beer bottles through my windows in the middle of the night."

Tech sucked in a sharp breath and began looking Steele over. It sounded horrible to him. Waking up to some crap like that. "I'm sure Ruxs took care of your neighbor."

Steele's smile told him he was right. "You sure know your teammates. How'd you know it was Ruxs and not Green?"

"Because Ruxs is the one that likes to have fun. Green likes to watch Ruxs have fun." Tech shrugged. "But don't tell me what he did. I don't wanna be an accomplice."

"Nothing too bad, but I don't think the guy will report anything." Steele stood there staring at him and Tech fought not to squirm.

"I have your earpiece ready and your watch is programmed. God said you guys would be out all day, so I'll be monitoring you today." Tech turned and busied himself pulling the device out of the protective case.

"You can see us?" Steele asked, sitting in the same place he had before.

"Ruxs has a dashboard cam that points outside, but I'm able to tap into video feeds or street cameras when they're on a chase so I can get a bird to your location." Tech stood next to Steele, focusing on keeping his hands steady. Being so close to him was intoxicating. He still couldn't believe he'd confessed that to the man yesterday but was glad Steele hadn't brought it up again.

"You can run the world from behind those monitors, can't you?" Steele's voice held a smidge of amazement, like *he* was impressed with what Tech could do when it was so much the other way around.

"There's a lot I can do with them." Tech sighed. "But it's not all—" Tech stopped himself. Cut off before disclosing his far-fetched dreams. Steele didn't need to know this. Didn't need to know how he longed for the same opportunities God gave his other guys. How he wanted at least the chance to prove his brain could be useful out there as well as in here. His lieutenants looked at his body and wrote him off as a man that belonged behind a desk. Instead of confessing this to a practical stranger, Tech picked up the small cream-colored earpiece and placed it inside Steele's ear canal. There, done. He turned to walk away when Steele's hand shot up and caught his wrist.

"Finish," Steele whispered gravely. "What's not all?"

"It's not important." Both their voices were low, as if there were someone else around to hear.

"I didn't ask if it was important."

"This is my job and I do what I'm required."

"But...."

"There's no but. It's nothing. I'm happy where I am." Tech looked down at his wrist, which was still in Steele's grasp, but instead of just holding it, Steele was rubbing his thumb across his pulse, carefully watching him. Tech exhaled slowly. He could feel himself vibrating with hunger for this man. He wished he could stop it. All he could do was pretend he wasn't fazed by it all. By Steele's magnificence. Yes, he was just a man. An amazing man who wasn't afraid to risk his life for a stranger. Who fought for something bigger than himself. That meant something to Tech... it meant a lot. Steele was the exact type of man, soldier, like the ones that'd tried to save his brother in a war he should've never been in. Even though that black ops team wasn't able to save his brother's whole squadron, they'd saved a lot of them. Steele was that type of man, and it made

Tech feel empowered just being near him. Not wanting Steele to see his infatuation, he tried to appear casual.

"You are lying to me." Steele stood up and crowded into Tech's smaller frame, moving him back against the cool brick wall. Trapping him there, Steele's chest persistent against his own. So close together, Tech could feel the solid planes there. Could smell the scent of the masculine soap Steele washed with this morning. He held the back of Tech's neck in one hand and pressed the back of his other hand up under his chin, just to the left of his Adam's apple. Two fingers pushed against the pulse now throbbing just beneath the tender skin. Steele's touch burned in a delicious way. His head was lowered, that raspy stubble scraping against Tech's smooth temple, his intense eyes closed in deep concentration while Steele broke apart the lie Tech was trying so desperately to construct.

"What's not all, Tech?" Steele spoke. His mouth moving against his temple, his voice coarse and smooth at the same time.

"I told you. Nothing. I misspoke." Tech shook against Steele's proximity, begging his lower body not to react. He felt the back of the two fingers push in deeper, forcing him to lift his head.

"You're lying," Steele hissed. He flipped his hand over and spread it out over Tech's throat, those two fingers still pressed over his pulse while the others rested over his Adam's apple. "The way I'm touching you right now. Is it turning you on?"

"What? No." Tech laughed nervously, his hands lying limp by his side, unsure what to do with them.

He felt Steele's lips curve up. Did he know Tech lied about that too?

"Do you like your job, Tech?"

"Yes."

Steele's fingers twitched against him before releasing a little of the pressure. Tech wanted it back. Steele's next question gave him what he wanted. "Are you happy sitting at that desk every day?" Steele ducked his head lower, his mouth right by Tech's ear. "Every day?"

Tech didn't answer. He wasn't sure if he should tell the truth. He didn't want to come off as a whiny brat wanting more than he was capable of doing.

"Answer me." Steele pressed his forehead against the side of Tech's head.

"No. I'm not. But I do what I was hired to do."

"You were hired to be a detective," Steele whispered. Then his voice dropped to a deep octave. "If you were put in the field... and you had to fight... would you be afraid... could you fight to the death, Detective Murphy?"

Oh gosh. He wasn't expecting that kind of question. Tech thought of all the simulations he'd done where gunfire erupted at the drop of a dime and Tech had to dive for cover. Steele's fingers dug in deep and even Tech could feel his pulse beating so hard it was practically audible in the silent room. It may very well be frightening, but he'd never stop fighting by his team. If they needed him, he'd be there. Steele waited for Tech's answer, the grip at the base of his neck and throat just shy of incredible. Tech was practically panting when his answer rose from deep inside him and left his mouth on a firing gust of breath. "Yes."

"Yes, what?"

It felt like a ghost of a kiss on his cheek and Tech sank into Steele's brawn and power like he was drawing off it. "Yes, I'd be afraid... but... yes. Absolutely, yes. I'd fight until the end." He didn't know why but it felt so good to say that.

"I know you would." Steele's grip moved from Tech's throat to his chin, jerking his head up so their lips were only a hair's width apart. "Life's too short to live with regret. The only guaranteed way to get what you want... is to take it."

Steele's mouth was on his before Tech could let those words sink in. He instinctually clutched hold of Steele's waist, moaning into the man's mouth like the slut he wanted to be, just for him. Steele licked the roof of his mouth and sucked hard on his tongue, tasting him in a way no other man had. With his chin still under Steele's control, he moved Tech's head in the direction he wanted and deepened the kiss even further. It was like he was only along for the ride, but damn if he wasn't enjoying the hell out of it. But way too soon it was over and Steele released him, stepping back and taking all that passion right along with him.

"Have a good day, detective," Steele told him and turned to leave his room.

Tech stood breathless and confused as to how Steele was able to get him to say and do the things he did. He couldn't figure it out. But he was sure about one thing. He wanted that man.

Steele

Steele put on his new watch while Ruxs and Green stood by the door waiting for him. He walked by them, ready to start his day.

"You finished?" Green leered with a knowing grin.

"For now," Steele told him with a serious expression and led them through the bullpen and out to the parking lot.

Parked a couple hundred yards away from the small commercial dock on the Savannah River, Ruxs watched the activity through video recording binoculars. They were quiet while keeping up surveillance until Green looked at him in the review mirror.

"So you got a thing for our little Tech, huh?"

"There's nothing little about him," Steele quipped right back.

Ruxs chuckled but kept his eyes on the dock. "Well, well, well."

"I didn't mean it like that…jackass. I just think y'all see him as this fragile, *little* thing… and I don't think he appreciates it. He doesn't have a weapon on his side and a badge clipped to his hip for nothing."

Green turned around. "You think Tech belongs in the field?"

Steele shrugged. "I don't know. Like you said earlier, I've only been here a few days. But I do know when I was a lieutenant I gave every man an opportunity."

Steele was happy to see his partners' surprised looks instead of disbelief and doubt.

"Wow, Tech in the field. Out here with all this crazy shit going on. Who would do all the stuff he does, though?" Ruxs looked at Green.

"It'd be nice to know if he's satisfied, man. You remember Vikki left because the desk got too redundant for her. She needed the excitement of the field. Although she still works behind a desk, she does get to go out to crime scenes, gather statements, prep witnesses... whatever. Besides, Tech could easily train another officer to do what he does. He could still do the hacking, though. I think we should talk to Syn about it," Green contemplated.

"Hey, don't overstep," Steele addressed both of them. "He's a man. Let him handle his own business."

"You sound a little protective, Steele," Green told him.

"Maybe. But I know he wouldn't appreciate us sticking our noses where they don't belong. If he wants it, he'll go for it."

"I guess you got a point, Steele," Ruxs conceded and started the truck. "Let's go question this guy. Everything looks standard from what I'm seeing."

"Cool. But let's not destroy the place. Simple questioning, only... Ruxs," Green barked his partner's name, making Steele laugh in the backseat.

"What? Why you singling me out?" Ruxs feigned surprise.

They parked at the end of the structure, ignoring the no parking signs, and bypassed the security office, Green flashing his badge as they did. They had a picture of their worker and since there were only a few men milling around, they didn't think it'd be too difficult to spot him.

When they were halfway through the loading area, Steele pointed to a man in a green, collared work shirt and a bright orange utility vest. "There he is." As if the man could sense he was being watched, he glanced up at them, a look of fear quickly registering across his face.

"He's about to run," Green murmured.

"Twenty says he doesn't," Ruxs answered.

"Thirty says he does," Steele countered.

They'd only taken a few more steps when the man dropped his clipboard and bolted in the other direction, towards the back door.

"You owe me thirty." Steele laughed and turned to run back towards the front while Ruxs and Green chased the man towards the back, ignoring the confused stares of the other workers.

Steele ran back out of the warehouse and was about to turn the corner when he heard heavy footsteps approaching. As soon as he got to the edge of the building, Steele lowered his body, pushed off hard with his back leg, slamming his shoulder into the runner's sternum like a linebacker hitting a quarterback. The hit was hard enough to lift the man off his feet and send him crashing down to the pavement. A hit that prevented him from getting back up and running again. The man rolled on the concrete, clutching his left side and coughing, trying to get the air that was knocked out of him circulating again.

"Nice job, Ray Lewis." Ruxs came to a stop, showing no signs of being out of breath, while Green grabbed the man by his collar and dragged him back towards the building.

"It wasn't me. It wasn't me!" the man yelled, while he was half dragged. "I did what he said. I cleared the log, man. I don't know how Artist got popped. The boat is still clear to arrive."

"That's good to know." Green smiled, pulling his shirt up so the rambling man could see his badge.

The guy groaned like the pain wasn't only in his ribs anymore. "Fuck me. I thought you were his guys… shit."

"What's coming in and when?" Green got right to the point.

"I don't know." The guy coughed and spat out the words at the same time.

Green yanked the man to his feet as if he weighed nothing and slammed him against the side of the building, another grunt of pain and a curse exploding from him. "Don't fuck with me. I have zero tolerance for bullshit today. Start talking."

"Hey! Let him go or I'm calling the cops," a man yelled. Two of the guy's coworkers came from around the back of the building. One of them was carrying a large metal pipe.

"Shut up! The cops are already here, idiot," Ruxs yelled, pulling his out badge, hanging from the chain around his neck. The guys didn't utter another word and quickly backed off like they wanted no dealings with the law.

140

Steele leaned against the wall, watching their surroundings and listening intently to the crooked dock manager.

"I didn't mean to run. I thought you were with those gangsters that showed up at my house a couple days ago." The guy sounded like he was on the verge of crying. But Steele had no sympathy for criminals. Don't do the crime. It was that simple. The payoff was never worth it. He'd never met an honest criminal. No matter how much he did for Artist, the man would've never honored their arrangement. The dockworker was lucky he wasn't dead already. Now that Artist was dead, it'd only be a matter of time before the next guy moved up to take his place.

"We're not gangsters. We're the good guys." Green smiled charmingly. The next second his smile fell and, gripping the worker by his collar, he jacked him up higher on the wall and growled, just inches from his face. "Now start talking. What's coming in and when? Say it fast because I plan to be home in time for Judge Judy."

"It's guns! Guns, okay! Um, assault rifles and Uzis. Just help me and I'll tell you everything. I have names, even bank accounts. But I need protection." The man looked as pitiful as he sounded.

Green jerked his hands back, letting the man crumple into a heap of blubbering weakness at his feet. Steele wanted to have a go at him. This piece of crap was helping put illegal weapons into the hands of felons and gangbangers so they could keep killing innocents and terrorizing neighborhoods, all for a lousy buck.

"Seal him up." Green nodded his head at Ruxs. Ruxs pulled out a zip tie from his inside coat pocket and bent over to pull the man's hands behind his back.

"Hey, what are you doing? You said you'd help me. I can't go to jail." The man struggled uselessly, Ruxs got his arms secured and pushed him back against the wall.

"How many people do you think lost their lives on the wrong end of the weapons you've helped smuggle in here? Women, children, cops. I hope you get sentenced *under* the jail, asshole." Ruxs turned around, shaking his head in disgust.

Ruxs tapped on his smartwatch. "Tech... need a unit for transport... notify ATF to send over a few guys."

"ATF? We don't interrogate him?" Steele asked, feeling like there was way more this guy could tell them.

"Yeah, we will. But we go after the drugs, Steele. ATF will have to be brought in for the weapons." Ruxs lowered his voice so only Steele could hear him. "We'll shake him down for everything we can. Probably try to cut him a deal, if he has something good enough. God will take the lead if he can tell us of any drug shipments he knows about."

Steele nodded. It was ATF's jurisdiction and they'd be able to set up a sting to intercept the shipment of assault weapons. The collar was a good break for all departments and Steele was glad about that. Lives would be saved because of it. After the cruiser showed up to take their perp downtown, they left to head back to the precinct. Steele felt good. In only a few days, he'd seen more action and made more of a difference than he had the entire time he was in Oakland. He'd have to thank his uncle soon. God's team was the absolute truth… and now he was a part of it.

Chapter TWENTY-ONE

Tech

Tech sat at his desk most of the afternoon because he fluctuated between half hard and a raging erection since Steele had taken the kiss he wanted from him earlier that morning. He was glad God was out of the office most of the day and Day was consumed with his own thoughts, so he wasn't required to move too much. Steele's lips had branded him, but his words had penetrated his mind, as well. He wasn't going to get the chance he wanted without going for it. If his bosses didn't know, then it was no one's fault but his own for not telling them. Chen said he was ready. Tech had been taking the classes and training for more than two years. Longer than any other enrollee. He felt ready to defend himself, his team if need be, and handle himself if shit got real. With his mind made up, he was going to talk to Syn.

The day was winding to a close, although none of them had checkout times. Tech definitely wanted to see if Steele was willing to come by soon and finally scratch the itch he'd been suffering from for months. Toys were such a poor substitute for the real thing. He needed the warmth, the hardness of a man's body pressing down on him. A lot of guys were turned off by his look and even more by his profession. When he first made detective he thought he'd have to beat guys off with a stick – damn, he'd been so young and naive – but he realized his job was demanding and it took a very strong man to handle it. He hadn't met that man yet and feared he wouldn't. He'd still have to keep things casual with Steele. There's just no way he could do heartbreak again. Hell, look at Day, for heaven's sake. The man was a mess right now. Everyone knew why, too.

Tech didn't bother Steele when he came back in from their briefing with the captain and two of the ATF sergeants who the Feds sent over. The Enforcers had interviewed their suspect then they had tons of paperwork and statements to complete, so he stayed quiet and worked on his algorithm for Chen. He was watching the code run through again when he felt the back of a chair bump into his. He turned around, a broad smile spreading across his face when he saw Steele leaning as far back as his chair allowed, peeking around Tech's shoulder to see what he was doing.

"What is all that?" He looked at Tech's laptop. "You hacking into the Matrix?"

Tech's laugh burst from him, causing Syn and Day to look over at them from their desks. Day just dropped his head back down to his work, but Syn threw Tech a quick wink. He tried to hide his blush, turning his attention back to Steele, who was still crowding his space.

"Real cute. Don't you have work to do, detective?"

"I'm finished. You said you were gonna quiz me on the map. I'm ready." Steele didn't care who was around or who was watching him. He was brave and upfront with his flirting. Tech guessed after seeing God and Day and Ruxs and Green paired up, that he'd probably not be frowned upon for making his interest known, but Tech still preferred privacy. He wanted to ask Steele to go to the breakroom with him but the tightness in the front of his pants prevented that, he couldn't let Steele ask him to step out of the office right now, either. The way the sexy Marine was staring at him, his chair arm to arm with Tech's, he felt like Steele would lean over and take exactly what he wanted again.

Tech quickly hit a few keys on his keyboard and turned back to look at Steele. The expression of shock and humor on his face made Tech chuckle and shrug his shoulders. With only a couple clicks, he'd sent a voice message to Steele's earpiece asking him what Tech couldn't voice in the open:

Will you meet me in the breakroom downstairs in 20 minutes?

Steele's grin was doing nothing to help Tech's little problem. As if he got the hint that Tech didn't want to make a show of the little dance they were doing, Steele nodded and mouthed, "Twenty minutes," and rolled back over to his desk. He didn't know why, but Tech released air that'd been trapped in his chest. Steele made him

144

feel overwhelmed with feelings he hadn't had to deal with since his last relationship. The excitement of something new, the anticipation of a kiss, a touch, was all there again, but he didn't want it to be.

Steele left immediately, but Tech sat there thinking about women giving birth, letting his erection recede so he could get up. It only took a few minutes, but he waited a full fifteen before he got up, taking his YETI cup with him. When he got downstairs, there was no one in the breakroom. He didn't expect to see any other officers because this was the one that never had fresh coffee. The television was broken and so was the refrigerator. Most of the officers used the breakroom on the first floor. He *did* expect to see Steele. He opened his cup and dumped the water off the ice, grabbed one of the warm Pepsis out the cabinet and poured it in. When he turned around, Steele was standing there leaning against the doorjamb.

"Are you out?" Steele led off, his face impassive and difficult to read.

Tech frowned. Where did that come from? "Of course. What am I, sixteen?"

"Why the secrecy, then? I don't think your boss cares if I see you personally." Steele walked inside and pushed the doorstopper aside, letting the heavy door slam shut behind him.

Tech ran his hand along the side of his hair. He kept it parted on one side and combed back with a little mousse to help it stay put. He refused to use gel and have his hair as hard as a helmet, but he didn't want to cut it or let it hang in his face. "Some things are private to me. And God is against displays of affection in the office. If he'd seen what you did today, you would've been reprimanded."

"Reprimanded," Steele snorted.

"Yes. He has no problems with couples. But he doesn't want us to get into shit; you know – hate from other officers about seeing us all over each other. He's professional, that's all. Nothing more."

"I can respect that." Steele nodded. "So have dinner with me Friday night. Privately."

Tech chewed on his bottom lip. A date sounded good and he had no doubt he'd have a great time, but Tech needed to set the ground rules early. "I think… how about you come over to my place Friday night?"

Steele squinted at Tech, inching forward as he did. Instinctively, Tech wanted to move back, but with his ass already against the counter, he had nowhere to go. "Your place?" Steele's voice had dropped even lower.

Tech tried to hold that piercing iced glare but it wasn't as easy as it sounded. "Yeah, I thought we could finish what we started in the equipment room," he said as casually as he could and shrugged for added emphasis.

"I kissed you. I've been wanting to since I first saw those pretty lips. But that's what it was. Now I want to get to know you outside the office." Steele was practically standing on top of him, and when he cupped Tech's jaw to lift his eyes to his, he tried to muster the courage he'd shown the other day.

"I really don't have time for dating, Steele," Tech said, too low for it to be believable.

Steele didn't look like he liked the sound of that whatsoever. "You don't have a hour for dinner but you have time to fuck me."

Tech flinched inside. Steele's words made him sound slutty as hell. He guessed when he thought about it, that's exactly how he was coming off. But he didn't sleep around or give himself to just anyone. He just didn't want to get invested in a relationship that would go south, leaving him still having to work with Steele or worse, Steele packing up and moving on to his next adventure. He couldn't deal with any of that, but god help him, he wanted so badly. "I didn't say that."

"I beg to differ."

"I meant let's keep it causal. A coworkers with benefits type of thing." Tech put on his best sensual smile, but the coldness in Steele's eyes told him it fell way short.

"So you're a tramp," Steele huffed at him.

"Excuse me?" Tech felt his face heat so fast, he thought it'd combust.

"Wow, I certainly wasn't expecting this bullshit. But if it walks like a duck and it talks like a duck, then what the fuck… call it a duck."

"Do you think insulting me will get you somewhere? And it's not bullshit."

"I'm already confined to nowhere. Right? Coworkers with benefits… really? Just because you took a dump in a box and wrapped it in a pretty bow, doesn't mean it's not still shit, Tech!" Steele barked.

Tech's eyes widened and before he could think better of it, he planted his back foot and shot his hands up to push Steele back, but the FORECON Marine was faster and caught both of Tech's wrists. Gritting his teeth, Tech flipped his hands and yanked them upwards, slipping out of Steele's hold. As fast as he'd practiced it, Tech looped his arms around Steele's, throwing him off, and shot his hands out again, hitting Steele in the center of his chest, pushing him back hard enough to make him stumble into the tables behind him.

Tech's heart was racing fast as the adrenaline flooded his body with the first act of aggression he'd attempted on another person. Why the hell he picked a black ops soldier to do it on was beyond him. But he straightened his back and kept his eyes locked on Steele's stunned ones.

"I'm impressed, detective. Didn't see the counter move coming." Steele's voice was dark and deadly, like that first day.

"I'm not afraid of you, and I know you won't hurt me."

Steele straightened and began to close the distance Tech had put between them. "Do you really believe that, or are you trying to convince yourself?"

"I know it." Tech met Steele half way, watching him closely.

"Where did you learn that?" Steele dragged his heavy palm down Tech's arm until he was cupping his hand.

"I have a teacher."

Steele's eyes darkened. "And what else does he *teach* you, Tech?"

147

Tech shook his head in exasperation. "It's not like that. He teaches law enforcement officers tactical and survival techniques. Look, let me explain about the—"

"You've made your decision. You don't need to explain yourself... especially to me. I asked for some of your time, you said no." Steele pressed Tech's hand to his cock, which was so hot and hard behind those worn jeans, Tech's knees almost gave out at the mere thought of that thickness penetrating him. "But you're out of your damn mind if you think I'm giving you this without it."

Steele jerked the door to the breakroom open and left Tech standing there with his cock tenting his Levi's. He guessed he'd met one of the few men in his life who actually wanted to get to know him and Tech had played the guy for an easy lay. He'd led Steele on, flirted and caressed, only to shoot him down as soon as he took a chance and asked him out. Tech was a wolf in geek's clothing. *Nice job, idiot.*

After spending ten minutes in the bathroom rinsing his face with cool water, he thought he looked a little less flushed, but it still took a few more minutes to muster up the courage to go back to the office and face Steele. Thankfully, he wasn't in there. *Did I already run him off?* Feeling like the world's biggest prick, he avoided everyone's curious eyes and went straight to the equipment room to pretend he had work to do in there.

Tech was counting the bullets and triple checking his inventory when Syn walked in, clearing his throat. *Of course.* "Didn't go like you thought it would?" Syn asked knowingly, settling himself on the stool beside Tech's computer.

"What do you mean?" Tech frowned.

"Shawn." Syn sighed, leveling his midnight eyes on him, giving him a look that said, "Seriously."

Tech plopped down on the stool next to Syn. "I said something stupid... as usual."

"Which was...?" Syn prompted.

"He asked me out." Tech paused for a moment, the words made more mortifying by confessing to his sergeant. "I basically told him... I told him... I don't have time for that."

148

"And that's so horrible." Syn rubbed Tech's forearm. "I think you're being a little—"

"But I told him we could have sex," Tech cut Syn off, the words spewing from his mouth in a hurry.

Syn didn't try to cover his wince. "Ouch. Okay. I think I get it now."

Tech squeezed his eyes shut and turned back around, dropping his head into his hands.

"Why don't you want to go out with him? He's a good-looking guy... if I'm being honest, he's hot. What's the problem?"

"I've done the relationship thing, Syn. That shit sucks when it all goes sour. A few years ago, I took two weeks off, told God and Day I had the flu but I didn't. I was so devastated Syn, after Jason left. I'm just trying to not go through that anymore. Casual hookups. That's all I can do." *Although I haven't had one in six months.* He barely had time for those.

"You really believe you'll be happy like that forever? I've seen the way you look when we're all hanging out. When God and Day are all over each other, or Ruxs and Green."

Tech chuckled humorlessly. "Actually, you and Furi are the worst."

Syn reared back and laughed loudly. "So I've heard."

Tech wished he could laugh at all this, but he failed to see a silver lining.

"That's my point. You deserve someone all over you, too. And from the looks he gives you... it's pretty safe to assume he would be."

"He's a flight risk," Tech added.

"What the hell, Tech. We all are. Nothing's guaranteed."

"I work long hours."

"Now you're just coming up with stuff. You'll both work long hours... in the SAME office." Syn yelled the last part in Tech's ear, making him shrink away.

"I don't know." Tech slumped in defeat.

"Think about it. It's your call." Syn patted him on his shoulder and left him sitting there. Alone.

Chapter TWENTY-TWO

Steele

Steele sat on top of one of the picnic tables on the side of the precinct building smoking the rest of his sweet cigar. He didn't know what had just happened in there. One minute they were kissing and feeling each other up, then the next minute he's calling Tech everything but a child of god. *Why'd I say that to him?* He was worse than those guys that asked a girl out and when she said no called her a stuck-up bitch. He understood their situation was a little different but he never thought Tech would only want his dick. This wasn't a college frat house. What was with the guy? Sure, Tech was younger, but not that damn young. Was he not capable of having a relationship? All Steele asked for was dinner, not his hand in marriage.

Christ.

"You're just screwing up every which way."

Steele turned around to watch his lieutenant approach. Day hadn't said much to him since he'd arrived. The guy always seemed to be lost in thought; either that or he was fine with letting God take the lead in everything. Maybe he was experiencing some post-traumatic stress – he was just in a deadly shootout a few weeks ago. So Steele had given the guy a wide berth. But he'd heard good things.

"Not sure what you mean," Steele said when Day stood in front of him. He watched Steele with pretty hazel eyes like he could read a person on the spot. Looking him up and down, Day reminded Steele of an underdressed Simon Baker.

Day sat on top of the table at the other end, propping one heavy Timberland boot up on the seat. "I think you do know. We're a family here, Steele. Tech is a brother to all of us."

Steele looked over and frowned, flicking his ashes in the other direction. "And I'm not?"

"No." Day balked, throwing his hands up in the air in exasperation. "You're like a third cousin, twice removed right now. You have to earn that respect, man. But you keep hurting Tech and you're gonna be downgraded to a redheaded stepchild."

Steele pulled on his cigar to hide his smile.

"None of us are stupid. We can see there's some weird power-play-tease-me-love-me-hate-me shit going on between you two, and God and I aren't exactly against you trying to develop something, but we won't have it become a disruption. We need Tech focused on his job. We need you one hundred percent out there on the streets. You feel me?"

"Yeah, lieutenant. I feel you." Steele couldn't argue.

"Alright. Go home. We're done for today."

Day walked away, having put on his boss hat and issued his warning. Steele already knew God wasn't a man to be trifled with, but behind those sharp eyes of Day's, he had a feeling he wasn't either. His lieutenant had a very valid point. Tech was family to them, and blood was thicker than water. There was no way they were gonna all sit around and let Steele call Tech names and hurt him like he'd done. He'd gotten a pass that first day, now it was as if he hadn't learned his lesson the first time.

Fuck. He had to fix this. All Tech said was he didn't have *time* for a relationship... he never said he didn't *want* one.

Steele took another amazing shower in Ruxs and Green's guest bathroom and changed into a pair of gray sweats and a short-sleeved USMC t-shirt. He sat at the breakfast bar watching Green move around in his kitchen preparing a meal that looked rather complicated. Steele took a gulp of his longneck Stella, savoring the refreshing brew after a trying day. Ruxs was in the living area with his bare feet propped up on one of the most comfortable recliners he'd ever seen, taking a nap with his mouth wide open while he waited for dinner.

"Do you cook every day?" Steele asked him when Green poured a box of crazy-shaped pasta into a pot of boiling water.

"I try to. And I know what you're thinking. But it's not like that. This is a stress reliever for me. I enjoy it a lot. When I'm cooking, I don't think about the scum I arrested that day or any bull that I had to endure. It's just me and my kitchen." Green stirred his sauce while he looked back at Steele. "What do you do to relieve stress?"

Steele took another drink and popped another olive from those that Green had set in the middle of the bar with cheese and crackers. "Nothing, really."

"Well, you need something. That's why you're sitting there driving yourself crazy over what to do about Tech and how to fix it." Green's look dared him to deny it.

"I'll handle it," Steele said drily. He was thinking about how to approach Tech again, or how to apologize yet again, but nothing was coming to mind.

"I'm sure you will." Green reached under the island and pulled out a cutting board, placing it in front of Steele. He placed three different color gutted peppers and a chef's knife in front of him.

"What the hell do you want me to do with that? Throw the knife at you and toss these peppers across the room to see if I can get them in Ruxs' mouth?"

"No, smart ass I want—" Green stopped midsentence.

Steele and Green shared a quick look of mischievousness at the exact same time their mouths curved into matching devious grins.

"Think you could get it in there?" Green struggled to whisper in between his hushed laughter.

"Hell yeah. Cut a piece." Steele turned and looked at Ruxs across the room, laughing already at the thought of him leaping up, confused, spitting out whatever was in his mouth.

"Here." Green handed him a piece a little bigger than a half-dollar coin.

They both had to work to get their laughter under control while Steele took aim. When he thought he had it good, he sent the yellow piece of bell pepper sailing into the air across the living room. It didn't land in Ruxs' mouth, but it did smack the side of his cheek, making his eyes fly open. The way he smacked his own cheek had Steele and Green almost falling over each other in hysterics.

"You fuckin' assholes," Ruxs grumbled, still half asleep, looking around for what had just slapped his face. When he gave up looking for it he flicked them both off and turned his back to them and curled up on his side.

It felt good to laugh. Once they settled down, Green set the board back in front of Steele, and after he massacred the bell peppers for Green's sauce, he was more than fine with being demoted from sous chef to taste tester.

"It makes no sense, Steele. You can slice tendons and muscles on a human at the perfect angle for maximum damage but you can't make a semi-straight cut in a bell pepper." Green shook his head, talking to himself.

They ate their dinner of baked turkey legs and red gravy pasta in front of the television. It looked like he had similar taste in movies to Ruxs and Green, all of them easily agreeing on an old sci-fi flick. Green told him there was a store-bought pie in the refrigerator but it was one of their favorites, and some butter pecan ice cream in the deep freezer. Steele didn't make him have to say it twice. He made three plates and brought them into the living room. If Green kept up this kind of hospitality, he was never leaving.

They watched the news at ten, all of them laying around like beached whales. Steele had no clue how Ruxs and Green stayed fit. Maybe they were the kind of guys that no matter how much they ate, they never gained too much weight. Shit, he definitely wasn't one of those guys. He could practically feel his muscle definition diminishing as he laid there.

After Ruxs finished helping Green clean up the kitchen, they said they were turning in.

"You mind if I work out a little, first?" Steele pointed to the equipment in the corner.

"Not at all. Be nice for someone to use it." Ruxs shrugged, holding Green's hand, leading him upstairs.

Steele cut off most of the lights downstairs and headed towards the back of the loft. Natural moonlight filtered in from the bay window, allowing him to look around the decent sized alcove. He realized there was enough equipment there for him to keep up a pretty good regimen until he got his apartment. Several sets of dumbbells, a weight bench. There were a treadmill and an elliptical machine. They even had a jump rope and exercise ball lying neatly on a yoga mat. Steele thought to do something light for now since it was so late and his belly was so full. He'd do a few reps on the bench and then a half hour on the elliptical. That should take care of a quarter of the calories he'd consumed at breakfast and dinner.

The workout was nice but way too short. It felt good to stretch his muscles and get his heart rate up, but it wasn't enough. It also wasn't long enough for him to decide what he wanted to do about Tech. This was the hardest he'd thought about any man since—

Steele finished his second shower, just to rinse off the sweat from his workout, and went back to his room. He had a television in there but he was in no mood to watch anything else. So far, it was quiet next door, but that would probably change any minute. Steele grabbed the headphones he'd made Ruxs stop by Best Buy for and plugged them into his cell phone. He reclined back on the soft covers, scanning his music selection. He tucked one earbud in his ear, frowning when he couldn't put in the other one. He'd completely forgotten about his earpiece. Damn, it really was that weightless in his ear that he never noticed it… all day. Tech said it didn't muffle sounds, so he'd forgotten all about it. He got up to get the magnet-tipped finger to get it out and paused with his discarded jeans in his hand.

Chapter TWENTY-THREE

Tech

Tech rubbed his tired eyes. He'd been playing Assassin's Creed on his PlayStation 4 all evening, trying not to keep replaying his refusal of Steele's date request over and over. He did want him, but he knew, deep down, he was doing the right thing. Sometimes the mind had to prevail over the body's wants. Tech got in the shower, hoping the hot water would heat him up enough to keep him warm in his cold bed.

He was scrubbing his bar of soap over his chest when he heard his name whispered in the roughest, sexiest voice he'd ever heard.

"Shawn."

Tech dropped the soap, almost slipping in the wide shower, just barely catching himself on the wall. He pressed his earpiece. "I'm here," he breathed nervously. He knew who it was. *Jesus Christ.*

"I guess I wanted to see if you really had that thing in at all times."

"Steele." Tech's voice revealed his flustered state. He was in the shower, wet, hot, naked, with Steele's dark voice in his ear.

"Yes."

"I… What… Is something wrong?" Tech tried to bring his breathing back to normal, he sounded like he'd just finished a race.

"No. Just wanted to test out my new device."

Tech huffed. He was still bracing himself on the shower wall like Steele's voice alone was enough to put him on his ass if he wasn't careful. "You wanted to test it now… right now… after midnight?"

"I didn't catch you at a bad time, did I"?

Tech rolled his eyes. "I'm trying to finish my sh—" Tech stopped. Did he want Steele to know that he was bathing right now?

"You're in the shower... I can hear the water."

Steele's voice had gone even lower, accompanied by a seductive huskiness that Tech knew he'd added on purpose.

"This is not what the earpieces are for." He tried to move his thoughts away from anything naughty.

"Can you still hear if there's an emergency?"

"Yes."

"Okay, then. Why don't you finish your shower...? I have something I wanna say."

"You can call my cell phone."

Steele replied slowly. *"Hmm. I think I'd like to keep testing my earpiece, wanna be sure the acoustics are just right. You go ahead and finish bathing. I'll just lie here patiently and keep you company."*

"Oh god," Tech groaned and picked up the soap off the shower floor. He needed to hurry up since his cock was already thickening.

Steele started speaking again while Tech ran the bar of soap over his thighs. *"It's been bothering me all evening how I spoke to you. How our conversation ended."*

Tech stayed quiet, lathering his body.

"I was never great at rejection. I guess I got a little cocky and thought you'd definitely say yes. Especially after that kiss we shared" He heard Steele let out a soft sigh. *"The way you clung to me. The way your body reacted to me. It felt good, ya know. It felt right."*

"Oh fuck," Tech whispered, unable to stop it.

"Yeah. It felt good. I hadn't been kissed in a while. You're good at it. The way you move your tongue." Steele sighed again, his breath stuttering a bit. *"I couldn't help but be greedy. I wanted more... I still do."*

Tech moaned before he caught himself. He ran his soapy hands over his balls in the pretense of washing them but he never lingered on them this long. After the tenth or so brush over, they surely had to be clean by now, but he didn't stop.

"But I respect your decision, Tech. I said some things I didn't mean. I just want... I want you so bad. You're a beautiful, smart, sexy man... a strong man—"

Tech whimpered, one hand stroking his shaft while the other kept up lazy circles over his balls. No one called him strong. No one called him beautiful. He was eclectic at best. Tech rested his back against the warm tiles and spread his legs. Steele couldn't see what he was doing, thank god, while he let that sinful voice penetrate his mind.

"Tell me you want me too."

"I do. I want you so much," Tech breathed out, lost in the trance Steele was luring him into.

"I'm willing to do the work, Shawn. To have you all to myself." Steele's breathing was picking up, too, his words still sensual, but distracted, pained... like he was—

"Oh. Unh." Tech could imagine Steele fisting himself just like he was. It was so crazy what they were doing, but damn if the image didn't make him pick up the pace, his back arching off the wall as his need to orgasm made itself known. The steady pressure of hot water beat on his chest, the feeling glorious on his erect nipples.

"Slow down, sweetheart. Not yet."

Without thinking, Tech did as he was told. His fist had been flying over his engorged dick, the urge to come overwhelming now. He gasped and panted while he stroked a little slower, keeping himself right on the edge; knowing Steele's words, his voice, could send him crashing over any minute. The Marine knew exactly what Tech was doing now. There was no denying it. But Tech knew Steele was doing it, too. Oh god, he'd never done anything like this. A modern type of phone sex. Steele groaned long and hushed in his ear like he was sneaking around. Tech's legs shook, his body was seizing up at the thought he was turning Steele on without even saying anything. He was letting Steele run this... whatever this was. Tech was confused how they'd gone from shoving and storming away from each today to jerking off together tonight. He was leaking like an adolescent, using most of it to make his hand glide easily along the flushed skin.

"Are you hairless, baby? I'm picturing your tight body, naked and glistening." Steele's breath gusted once, twice, followed by a sensual growl. *"I can see all that pale skin, pink from the steam...*

159

and from your arousal. You're hot for me… I like that… unnnnh… I need that." Steele moaned so deep the vibration resonated in Tech's ear and down his body. Steele sounded like he was close. Tech closed his eyes, fisting himself with quick shallow pumps, easing his other hand behind him, teasing his hole while he listened for every hitch in Steele's breath, every sharp intake of air.

"I know I need to slow down, give you some space, but… oh god… I'm so fuckin' hard for you. You have no idea how much I wanted to take you up on your offer today… and I will… but not until—"

Tech pushed the tip of his finger inside his pulsing hole. Just the thought of Steele being in there one day was enough to make him shoot hard and long. He cried out at the first jolt of his built up release, then whined Steele's name on the next.

"That's it… call out to me…" Steele's words were rushed and Tech could easily imagine Steele's strong hand fisting his hard cock. *"Yeah, yeah, yeah… oh fuuuck. You sound so sexy when you come, sweetheart. Fuck, I'm 'bout to come so hard…unnnnnh fuuuck, baby."*

Tech sagged against the wall; still squeezing and milking the head of his cock while he listened to the most amazing man he'd ever met come from just thinking about him in the shower. Tech felt dizzy and sated, having come harder than he had in years, and Steele hadn't laid one finger on him. God help him when he did.

Tech knew Steele could hear him trying to recuperate, and he could hear Steele was panting hard and murmuring little curses in what sounded like another language. *"Jesus. Shawn that was… see oli hea… go to sleep now, Shawn. I want you to dream about me. Goodnight, minu armas armuke."*

Tech knew the line was clear; Steele was gone, but it took him a few more seconds to get himself together enough to get out of the cooling shower. He leaned against the door to his bathroom with a silly expression on his face. He couldn't believe they'd done that. Was that the way the man apologized, because if so, Tech wouldn't mind Steele insulting him a little more often. He'd ended that call perfectly. What had Steele said? What language was that?

Tech hurried into his bedroom and pulled up the earpiece's software. It automatically transcribed all transmissions. After he figured out what Steele said to him, he needed to delete that particular transcript forever. This was not a conversation that would be recovered by WikiLeaks. Tech smiled foolishly while tapping a few keys, his towel cinched at his waist with his other hand. When he clicked on the link the transcript downloaded and Tech went through everything that was said, shaking his head when his cock started to jump again as he got further along. Some of the words were "inaudible" and he knew those were the sounds of their grunts and moans. When he got to the last sentence – *minu armas armuke* – Tech opened the language converter and clutched his hand over his chest when the English translation appeared.

"Goodnight, my sweet lover."

Chapter TWENTY-FOUR

Day

Day sat at Syn and Furi's small dinette table just a little after dawn, gulping down his fourth cup of coffee. His temples throbbed and his stomach ached after he'd foolishly chosen imported beer as his dinner the night before. He hadn't been able to go home last night. His brain and his heart were going head to head with each other, leaving him in a constant state of confusion and disappointment. After work, he'd gone to Furi's garage to hang out with him and watch him work. Furi's job was fascinating, regardless of him being a mechanic. The shit he could build was remarkable, and Day knew he was currently rebuilding a '73 Norton for his showroom floor.

Furi was one of Day's best friends. From the moment the man had stepped into Syn's life, Day knew he'd be a part of the family. He'd been married before to an abusive shithead that stalked him while he was dating Syn, and the entire team provided him with protection, which quickly solidified a bond between them. He was a great guy and one of the most talented mechanics in Atlanta. His business had been a success from the moment he opened his bay doors.

When Day showed up at his garage, Furi took one look at him and dropped the heavy wrench in his hand, walking straight up to Day and hugging him fiercely... just like he'd needed. They'd downed a couple six packs while Day assisted Furi with his work. Passing him the occasional tool here and there while he vented his frustration about God. It was late by the time God texted him, asking him to come home, but he ignored it. He couldn't... couldn't deal right then. He was tipsy and depressed, never a good combination for him. Furi locked up Day's Mustang in his shop and took him to his and Syn's home, listening to him blubber and curse all night about being stupid enough to propose.

"Morning, Leo. How you feeling?" Furi asked, walking into the kitchen in nothing but a pair of loose basketball shorts.

"Like a bitch that's been rode hard," Day grumbled, taking another long drink of the black liquid.

Furi almost choked on his own cup of coffee, laughter bursting out of him. He sat down in the chair next to Day's. "Okay. That doesn't sound great, but you promised you'd talk to God today. Put your foot down. All this skirting around the topic and trying to casually slip in a conversation about a wedding date here and there is bullshit, Leo. You deserve an explanation for why God is putting you off like this. Don't take it anymore. Enough is enough."

"I agree," Syn added, walking into the kitchen already fully dressed for work. He bent down, gripping a handful of Furi's long, brownish-gold mane and pulled his head back, laying a long, loud kiss on his mouth.

"Umm. Should I get up so you guys can use the table?" Day dropped his head in his hands while Syn slapped him on his back hard enough to make his head pound louder.

"Nah, go ahead. We can at least wait until you finish your coffee," Syn threw over his shoulder, filling his travel mug with orange juice. That meant Syn was ready to go.

Furi walked them to the door, his arm draped over Day's shoulder. "Leo, you know I love God and all, but you know what, if God won't get his shit together, maybe you should leave him."

Day's head snapped to the side like he'd been popped. "Leave him," Day grumbled. "I don't wanna reward him... I just want him to tell me what's up."

"Yeah. Leave him. Show him what he'll be missing. Let him know you won't be taken for granted and jerked around. There comes a time when you have to take what you deserve. Respect." Furi crossed his arms over his tattooed chest like his idea made perfect sense, but the way Syn was scowling at Furi made him bring it down a notch. "I just want you to be happy, Leo."

164

"That's enough advice from you, Tony Robbins." Syn pushed Day out the door like he didn't want him to hear any more of Furi's empowering rhetoric.

"Hey, you sure you don't wanna pick up your car now?"

"No. Furi said he'd tune it up for me later this week. It was riding a little rough. I'll ride back with God."

"So you're going home tonight?" Syn stopped at a light and turned to face him.

"Yeah, I am. This is getting crazy. If Cash won't give me an answer tonight, I'm telling him the engagement is off... done... taken back. Whatever the fuck you call it. I thought about it all last night, and if all we can be is boyfriends, not husbands... then... then, I can deal with it." Day shook his head, groaning. "I think."

"You can. We got your back, you know that," Syn said, pulling into the station's busy parking lot. The shifts were changing and cars were pulling in and out, but Day saw God's big silver truck already there. Feeling his eyes cloud with moisture and frustration, he climbed out of Syn's car and headed for the front doors without looking to see if his sergeant was with him. As soon as he walked through their department doors, God swiveled around to face him, a look of anger washing across his stern features. Tech looked back and forth between them, then got up and bolted to his equipment room, closing himself inside. If Day hadn't been so beat and worn, he would've laughed.

"You never came home last night, Leonidis."

Day dropped his bag on the floor next to his desk. "Whoever said you weren't a great detective, God, was out of their damn mind."

God rose up from his seat. "You're going to joke... NOW?"

"And you're going to come at me... NOW?" Day threw back.

"Take it down," Syn hissed, finally coming through the door.

"I'm finished," God said through clenched teeth.

"The hell you are. Both of you go home." Syn set his mug on his desk hard enough to emphasize that he wasn't playing and it wasn't a request, it was an order. "No one is dealing with this shit another day. You two go home and fix it. Immediately. You got everyone around here ducking and hiding when you're both around, either that or it's

165

as quiet as a library, everyone too afraid to tell a joke because you're acting like the world is coming to an end. Now get gone. Both of you. Come back when you've come to a solution…" Syn bored God with a hard, dark glare. "Come back after you've been completely honest with each other."

Day swallowed hard. Syn had to know why God was stalling. Syn knew everything but Day didn't pressure him for answers. Not like Syn would tell him anything anyone told him in confidence. But Day felt a small sliver of hope spring up in his chest. If Syn was sending them home, he must believe that God had something he needed to confess, and it couldn't be that disastrous because he said to come back when they were honest. Did God want him? Did he still want to marry him?

God closed up the file he'd been reading and tucked it in his desk drawer, mumbling the entire time. "Being thrown out of my own department. *I'm* the head of this task force."

"Well come back when your *head* is in the game and out of your ass." Syn didn't flinch when God slammed his drawer shut, shoved his chair back under his desk, and stood toe-to-toe with him. Syn looked almost bored when he responded. "If you've finished your tantrum… get out."

Day wanted to run up and kiss Syn, but instead he turned and left. Syn had been recruited from Philadelphia by them for a reason. He knew how to take charge if he had to, and if something happened to the amazing team that was God and Day, they could count on Syn to run the task force.

Day waited by God's truck, rehearsing in his head how he wanted this to play out. Being an asshole wasn't going to cut it. Neither was being reserved. All he wanted to know was where he stood. God unlocked the doors and both of them climbed inside, not yet ready to talk. The heat radiating off of God was enough to almost suffocate him, and that horrible feeling came back full force. That feeling that his life was about to change for the worse. A complete one-eighty from how he'd felt when he'd proposed.

God turned into their driveway, which was only ten minutes from the precinct, and killed the engine, finally looking at him, but

166

Day couldn't look back. Couldn't look into those gorgeous green eyes that held his heart. He felt God brush the top of his hand with his fingers, but Day still couldn't turn to look at him.

"Leo, let's go inside and talk."

Day got out of the truck without a word or a glance. He held in his smart comment about God finally wanting to talk and went inside. It was only eight a.m., still early, and his stomach was starting to protest from the copious amounts of liquor still sloshing in there with no solid food to soak it up. "Are you hungry?" he asked, going straight to the kitchen.

"Sure. You can cook, I'll talk. It's time I get this out before it destroys us."

God

He'd never felt more like a coward. His stomach was in his throat and his hands were sweating enough for him to have to wipe them on his jeans several times. Not much could get him upset or off his game. But Day being mad at him left him flustered, and Syn had been right to send them packing until they got their shit together. He was weak when he and his other half weren't of one accord. His strength lay within that man. It was almost biblical. Even Sampson – the strongest man in the bible – had one weakness… his woman. Day could destroy him if he left him. God needed to get the conflict out of their relationship.

Day set a bottle of water in front of him on the breakfast bar where he sat watching Day move around his gourmet-style kitchen.

"So talk," Day said softly, pulling items out of the pantry.

"Leo. I um… I should've said this before… I don't… I don't want a wedding."

Day froze, standing outside the pantry, and God could see his hand shaking on the door, his body trembling. *Oh shit.* God hurried off the stool and clasped Day around the waist, pulling his strong back to his chest.

"You don't wanna marry me?" Day asked, sounding broken.

God spun Day around, his words faltering and his heart shattering at the pain in his partner's eyes. "No! Yes! Yes, I want to marry you, more than anything. I don't want a *wedding*, Leo." God gripped Day's shoulders when his look went from painful to surprise or was it horror? "Please listen for a second. The moment you proposed I'd never felt so damn special. Never thought anyone would want a man as damaged and fucked up as I was. You knew... you knew what happened to me growing up and you still wanted me to be your partner, for life." God let Day go and turned around, heading back to his seat, running his hand through his hair while he tried desperately to say the right thing. "But then you and Vikki started meeting and talking about a wedding and a guest list of seventy to eighty people – fuck, Leo, I don't even like a third of those people she was inviting."

Day kept watching God with a confused expression, but he never interrupted him. He just sat on the stool opposite him, looking on with a completely unreadable expression. Damn, he hoped Syn hadn't set him up to fall flat on his face. Syn had been telling him for months to just spit it out, it'd be no big deal.

"Then there was an email for a deposit on the venue... that place, The Ashton. Day, they wanted five thousand just for the deposit. Then all the other stuff just kept adding up on me. I can't afford it, baby. Even going half and half on a twenty-five thousand dollar wedding – and Vikki said that was on the cheaper scale, it'd probably be more – is way over what I can do. I know you didn't know because our finances have been separate this whole time, though we share the house expenses. Maybe you forgot about my financial problems early on when I became a detective, or maybe you thought I was good now. I just got all that debt off me a couple years ago, so I haven't had time to build up my savings like I'd like. Leo, I tried to come up with some ideas, even thought of taking a loan on my pension, but I've already borrowed once to help my mother. If I borrow again, I won't be able to retire until I'm ninety. I should've been a man and told you up front, but I was... I was scared you'd take the proposal back or say we'll just wait until we *can* afford it. So I was trying to stall on the date to come up with a way I could get the money up. But, if I'm being honest, I don't ever wanna spend that much money on something that'll last for a few hours. I know... I know, I'll remember it forever." God got back up and stood between Day's legs, cupping his face, staring down at the love of his life; splaying himself wide open for him. "But being with you... all the years of partnering with you is all I'll ever reflect back on... it's all I need."

Day dropped his forehead to God's chest, shaking his head. God closed his eyes, hoping like hell that being honest was, in fact, the best policy. "Please say something."

"I wanna strangle you right now." Day's voice was muffled by God's thick pecs, but he still heard him. "I wanna just... ugh!"

Day's head shot up. "That's what all this has been about? You've been avoiding me for four whole months because... Jesus, Mary, and Joseph... I can't believe this."

"You mad?" God asked nervously.

"Yes! Not about you not being able to afford a wedding, but for you not trusting me to talk to me about this. Damnit, Cash. I'm not fuckin' Kim Kardashian, what the hell did you think I was gonna do if you told me it was too expensive?" Day frowned. "You thought I'd take the proposal back?"

"No... I don't know... I didn't wanna find out. You looked real excited about everything when you and Vikki were talking about it."

Day shook his head. "I'm not that superficial. You have to know that. I was excited about marrying *you*... that's it. I could care less where or how."

God dipped his head and captured Day's mouth in an apologetic kiss.

"You put me through hell," Day whispered against his lips, kissing him again.

"I know. If you'll just marry me in a real private, modest ceremony, I promise I'll spend the rest of our lives making it up to you."

Day leaned back, that gorgeous teasing smile back on his face. Oh, how he'd missed it so much. "Okay. Short, simple, and cheap.

With a name like Cash, you'd expect more, but hey, whatever you say."

God laughed, the wonderful feeling making the hard lines that'd been etched in his forehead ease just a little. When the humor died down, they stood there holding each other, gazing thoughtfully. "I'm so sorry. I should've known better. It was my pride, sweetheart. It's not easy to tell the person you love that you're too poor to give him what he wants."

Day looked at him the way he always did. With respect, not pity. "You're not poor, Cash. But instead of spending too much on the ceremony, why don't we spend a fraction of what the wedding would cost and go on a nice honeymoon somewhere quiet and alone."

God's eyes lit up. *Hell, yeah.* That's exactly what he was talking about. Yes, just him and his man. "I'm glad that's straightened out and you're not going to kill me. I have something for you." God raced into the den like an excited kid and came back a few seconds later, holding the black ring box that'd been hidden inside the entertainment stand for a couple weeks. "I bought this a while ago. It's not as nice as the one you gave me, but I liked it a lot. Picked it out myself."

Day took the box and opened it, his beautiful hazel eyes shining brighter than God'd ever seen before. He watched his partner pull out the simple gold and chrome band, squinting to read the inscription inside.

God's special Day, November 19, 2016

Day looked up in slight confusion before a broad, sweet smile slowly spread across his face. "Is this…?"

"Yeah. It's our wedding day." God took the band and slipped it on Day's ring finger. "That's nine weeks away… right after the trial. All we have to do is plan it, *us* plan it. Just me and you. Don't need anyone's outside influence. After the trial is wrapped up, we'll be on down time at work… shouldn't be too hard, huh? What d'ya say?" God pulled Day to his feet, wrapping him in his arms. He could see Day's emotions riding him as he swayed them back and forth. He put his mouth against Day's temple, kissing him while he whispered what he had in mind. "Maybe a ceremony here at the house, just our

170

family, your brother standing beside you, mine by me. And of course, the guys. We have a few vittles, some beer and cake, and then… I'm whisking you away, to Cancun, or Aruba – somewhere where no one can reach us by earpiece."

Day chuckled and sighed against his neck. "Sounds perfect."

They'd decided to play hooky the rest of the day instead of going back to work after breakfast. Things had been so strained between them, they needed a day to themselves. "They can function without us for one day. What do you wanna do?"

"How about a movie?" Day shrugged, climbing back into God's truck.

God smiled. "Is it too early? It's like eleven thirty."

"Shouldn't be." Day pulled out his phone and searched for show times. "Nice. There's a Western I've been wanting to check out."

God held Day close to him while they paid for their refreshments. He'd been so upset last night when Day hadn't answered his calls, hadn't come home. They'd never had this big a fight, where his lover had packed a bag. He admitted he was terrified. If Day left him, he'd be lost. Inside the dark theater, they realized there wasn't a soul in there with them and the movie had already started.

"Wow, is there really no one else? That's funny. Never been in an empty theater."

Day laughed, climbing up to the top row. "It's not even noon and it's a work day. But I'm feeling this."

God sat down beside Day and opened his bag of Twizzlers. "Yeah, me too. Let's enjoy."

"Oh, I plan to." Day gave God a look that was as clear as ever. This was about to be the best movie he'd ever been to.

About forty-five minutes into the film, feeling confident that there'd be no late arrivals, Day lifted the armrest and leaned into God's body, alternating between kissing and biting at his jaw. God let Day pop the button on his jeans, chuckling against Day's soft hair

171

while he worked his way down. "You're seriously about to do this in here?"

"Damn straight. Raise up."

God lifted his hips and pulled his jeans down enough to free his dick. He was already excited, his heart racing at the thought of two police officers getting busted for indecent exposure. That'd sit well with his captain. He could only hope that he could right himself before an employee came around with a flashlight.

"Fuck," God hissed when his length was taken to the back of Day's throat. Sucking hard and slow, Day came off with an audible pop.

"Baby, I've missed you," Day murmured, nuzzling the thick hairs around the base. Inhaling him with long deep whiffs.

"I've missed you, too."

"I was talking to your dick," Day said breathily, going down again.

God leaned back with a wide smile. His sweetheart was back.

Chapter TWENTY-FIVE

Steele

Steele tried not to hurry through their office doors, but Ruxs and Green moved slow as hell. He wanted to see Tech. Syn had radioed and told them to get in their time at the gun range since God and Day were out of the office today, and finally called them back in to interrogate a dealer that was picked up by a beat officer.

Steele sat there while the low-level dealer snitched on every contact he had, begging not to be sent to prison, that his dad was gonna kick his ass. Ruxs gritted his teeth as he took notes. The guy was nineteen, still in high school, trying to hang with the big boys. But still afraid of his father. Steele noticed that Green had a soft spot for the young ones. After they'd finished their questioning, Green stopped one of the city prosecutors in the hall to tell him how cooperative the kid had been and to go easy on him. Steele didn't think the boy a hardened criminal either, but he needed to be taught a lesson. Either way, they had some good information about a few dealers recruiting school kids. Steele definitely wasn't gonna go easy on them when they caught 'em.

Steele walked inside the bullpen, making a turn towards their department, opting out of lunch with Ruxs and Green.

"You don't want a burger, man?" Ruxs said, walking in the other direction.

"No, you guys go ahead. I'm still too traumatized from the Burger King incident." Steele winked.

"Yeah, whatever." Green waved him off. "See ya."

No one was in their office when he walked through the double doors. Looking over Tech's area, he saw his screens still on and a half-eaten container of yogurt and a few apple slices on a napkin. He turned in the direction of the equipment room, seeing the door was cracked. His balls tightened at the thought of what he and Tech had done last night. He wished Tech had made more noise, but the way he cried out his name when he orgasmed was forever branded in his mind.

When he walked inside, Tech was sitting hunched over a long spreadsheet, chewing on the end of an ink pen, his full concentration on the document. Steele didn't want to scare him again so he—

"Good afternoon, detective," Tech said in that soft bass that Steele was growing quite fond of, while still staring at his documents. He liked that Tech was picking up on his presence now.

"Hey. How's it going?" Steele stood behind him, waiting to be acknowledged.

"Fine."

Steele twisted his mouth in confusion. Was Tech still pissed at him? "About yesterday. I really am sorry. It was… that was stupid and childish. My ego took a hit, that's all, and I reacted like an ass."

"I liked your apology last night a lot better." Tech smiled, finally turning around. Steele took his time looking his desire up and down, taking in the ivory skin contrasted by those jet-black glasses. He wore all black today, making his beauty glow even brighter. Those pink lips that he knew were as soft as cotton. His pants were corduroy and slim-fitted, but not too tight. The black 9mm and gold badge on his side added an air of danger to his sexy nerd. Tech was a fantasy out of every geek's dreams. He wondered how the hell he'd get anywhere with him. Steele wasn't dumb, by any means, but he wouldn't say he was a genius. He had street smarts, survival instincts; he hoped that meant something to a man as brilliant as Detective Shawn Murphy. Because together, he thought they'd make one helluva team, especially after last night. He couldn't remember being that hard or coming so fast.

"Stop looking at me like that," Tech said, trying to cover his bashful smile.

"Like what?" Steele's voice had gone husky from his lewd thoughts.

"Like you wanna eat me." Tech laughed lightly.

"I think I do," Steele growled, making Tech laugh even louder. He kept moving until he stood in front of him; Tech put his hand up and held him back from pressing his body against him. Tech had told him he couldn't help how his body reacted to him... well, ditto. He wanted Tech in the worst way, but he knew he had to act with some tact and poise. He always hated those words.

"You're going to get us suspended. Stay back. God made it clear there's to be no inappropriate behavior in the office. Trust me, he means it. Ruxs and Green have been suspended like six times for screwing around in the parking lot, the locker room, twice in an interrogation room."

Steele could definitely believe that. Those two were crazy about each other. "I'm not trying to get us in trouble. Besides, God and Day are out for the day. I just wanted to make sure my apology was accepted." Steele ran his thumb across Tech's smooth chin.

"It's all good, alright. I understand if my rebuttal option pissed you off. I want you to know that's not the only way I see you. I guess I'm trying to be careful." Tech broke eye contact with him. "My option did sound a little slutty."

"I don't mind slutty." Steele moved in closer, taking Tech's hand and moving it around his own waist. "How about we slow things down a bit? Get to know each other. That way, we're not constantly apologizing to each other. I won't ask you out on any more dates... for now. And you don't proposition me like a harlot."

Tech scoffed and socked Steele in his stomach, a teasing glint of anger and amusement in those big brown eyes.

"Just conversations. Maybe a little light touching and flirting." Steele licked his lips, moving back into Tech's space. "Deal?"

"Yeah, deal." Tech nodded. His shy smile quickly becoming Steele's reason for wanting to be in the office.

"Okay, then. Since I think it's gonna be quiet the rest of the day, how about I order us some food because I'm starved and it looks like you ate like an anorexic. Are you hungry? Just so I'm clear, this is not a date." Steele put on his most professional corporate-like voice, making Tech rear back and laugh. "Two colleagues sharing a work related conversation over a meal. I can sit and watch you do what you do. Maybe learn something in the process, but understand. THIS. IS. NOT. A. DATE."

Tech nodded again, rolling his eyes. "Shut up. I had a sandwich earlier. But I can eat a slice of pizza or something. But you need to be working on your map. You have a quiz soon."

Tech stood up and Steele liked that the man was just an inch or two shorter than his own six feet. He wasn't as packed in the muscle department, Steele having a little more mass on him, but it didn't make Tech any less dangerous. Soon, he'd get the little fighter in the ring and spar a few rounds with him, see what that teacher was teaching him. Even show Tech a few of his own moves. Something that involved rolling on a mat.

"You're giving me that look again."

Steele's look was serious when he growled, "I wanna kiss you again."

"Do it." Tech's nostrils flared and his eyes shone with lust.

Steele gripped Tech by the collar of his polo shirt and pulled him to him, covering his mouth with his and burying his tongue inside like he'd been starving for it. He had. Steele wrapped both arms around Tech's neck, keeping him close until he was good and finished. Tech moaned and wrapped his arms around Steele's waist. Kissing him back with passion and an urgency that matched his own. Damn, he felt right pressed against him. Tech fit him perfectly. Obviously, physical attraction wasn't their problem, that's why Steele wanted to get to know Tech first. Find out if they'd be compatible any place beside a bedroom. Steele was forty-five years old. He'd served his country, fought in wars, he was too old to bed hop. He refused to be one of those creepy men in the club stalking the boys, a vulturine stench radiating from him. No, he was the type of man to go to a jazz bar with his man on his arm and treat him to a good time. He was ready to have what everyone else had and he'd like to give the man in his arms a chance. No one was the settling down type until they found a reason.

"Fuck, you taste good," Steele moaned, sucking on Tech's sweet bottom lip, a hint of peach yogurt lingering there. "I could kiss you all day."

Tech smiled up at him, his face pink from his arousal, his lips plump and wet. Shit, he had to pull back. But damn if he didn't want to reach down and grip that firm bulge that was pressing against his thigh. They had time. Steele was acting like he was shipping off again soon. He didn't have to rush this and he didn't want to make it harder for his hot geek to fight his tramp-like ways. Smiling against Tech's lips at his inner thoughts, Steele stole one last bite before pulling Tech out of the room. Steele had to be strong and wait, but he was happy to drive the man absolutely crazy while he did. He wanted to reveal the side of Tech that wanted to have something real and lasting.

Tech

He was glad that it took Syn a while to come back to the office because he didn't want anyone to see the way Steele was acting. The guy couldn't stop staring at him or wiping sauce from the corner of Tech's mouth with his thumb and licking it off. When Steele said flirting, Tech expected the occasional wink or pat on the ass. This was crazy.

After they finished half of a medium pizza, Tech sent Steele back to his own desk to work on familiarizing himself with the system instead of staring over his shoulder asking him what he was doing over and over. It was cute and annoying at the same time. A slight smile curved his mouth, which he'd had to wipe away when Syn came back in around three. "Hey, Tech. You said you wanted to talk to me today. I'm free now."

"Yeah, sure." Tech stole a glance at Steele and saw he was watching him with interest while he and Syn made their way back to the conference table.

"So, what's on your mind, Tech?" Syn sat in one of the tall black chairs and turned to give Tech his full attention.

"Well, this is a situation that will have to be discussed and ultimately decided by the lieutenants and you, but I wanted to adhere to the pecking order and voice my concerns to you." Tech's voice was strong and steady. Steele's voice lingering in the back of his mind, telling him to take what he wanted. He sat up straight and focused on keeping eye contact with his sergeant. "In addition to the responsibilities I have now, I would like an opportunity to use the skills that I've acquired over the years... in the field."

Syn's dark brown eyebrows raised almost to his hairline. He pushed his chair all the way up to the table and clasped both hands in front of him. "You're a comms and technology specialist. Let me be sure what you're asking. Are you requesting a different position, that of a field officer? Or are you proposing fieldwork in conjunction with the duties you currently perform?"

Tech wasn't used to the formal Syn, but he knew the guy had that side to him and used it when needed. Tech nodded. "I don't want to abandon my position. But honestly, I can do both, as far as the software developing and the research. I can teach someone with a low-level computer degree to do the communications aspect. We had another comms specialist for two years until he transferred. Radioing and dispatching aren't difficult to train another officer to do. There're several specialists in our precinct with engineering degrees and previous dispatch experience that have approached me about providing me with assistance, but I have someone who I think would be a much better asset. Someone who wouldn't need an ounce of training and will absolutely blow your mind with his skills."

Syn nodded like he was agreeing, but he wasn't saying the actual words. "Let's talk about the newly acquired skills you mentioned earlier... elaborate on that."

Tech told Steele about studying and learning under Chen's tutelage for the last two years, and Syn's reaction was as expected. Surprised and impressed.

"I looked into that program. It's extremely expensive. Even for my paygrade. You're not moonlighting on the side, are you?" Syn teased him.

Tech smiled at his long-time friend and brother. "Whatever. I've done some work for Chen, upgrading his systems and so forth. So he gives me a substantial discount."

"Nice. So you've been training with him for two years?"

"Yes, sir. Three days a week. It's been crazy, but nice, ya know. He feels I'm ready, but most of all, I know I'm ready," Tech said confidently.

"Alright, then. Let me talk with God and Day and see how they want to approach this. You know we believe in making sure you guys are happy here, and if you're not feeling satisfied or are even slightly under-challenged or not performing to your full potential, then we need to reevaluate."

Tech liked what Syn was saying, though he figured he would. His bosses were fair. Always had been. Michaels was the last one to come on to the team before Steele, and once he'd shown his skill and dedication to wanting to join the team, Day had done everything he could to get the beat officer moved through the ranks and promoted to his team. He was positive they'd do the same for him. But, no doubt, there'd be a test first.

"Anything else?" Syn asked him, a sly smile tugging on his lips. "Any confessions or personal matters you'd like to discuss?"

Tech fought to keep a poker face. "Hmm. Nothing comes to mind."

Syn reclined, linking his hands across his stomach. "Really? Nothing at all? Because I'm all ears."

"Don't sell yourself short, Sarge." Tech winked.

"You little shit. Spit it out. How's it going with our decorated Marine?" Syn chuckled, throwing a balled-up piece of paper at Tech's chest.

He swatted it back, no longer able to hide his smile, especially when thinking about Steele. "It's going to be slow going for a while, Syn, and I'm good with that. Like I said to you already." Tech lowered his voice, comfortable with confiding in his friend. "I don't want to start anything he can't finish."

"Do you still feel he's out of your league?"

179

Tech bit his bottom lip. "I never really thought that. We do have extremely different backgrounds, but we both can bring different things – unique things – to the table. And that's a good foundation. At this point, I just need to know he's here for a while and Atlanta isn't a pit stop on the winding highway of his well-traveled life. I have to weigh the pros and cons and deduce the potential risk."

Syn grimaced at him. "Where do you get this stuff? Life, relationships can't always be looked at so analytically, Shawn. Sometimes you have to go with your gut... with your heart." Syn narrowed his eyes. "Did you read his entire military file?"

"Most of it," Tech said, looking away.

"Okay then, holding that part of his life against him is not right. What he had to do as a soldier to defend his country, what he had to do to stay alive, or even what he had to do when he came back home to cope with society, shouldn't be weighed against him. He's entitled to find happiness. I think, more so than anyone." Syn stood up, looking down at Tech with compassion and understanding. Typical Syn. "I don't know him well enough to say give him a shot. But I do know he's not the type to tuck tail and run, or quit. And that seems to be your primary concern. So... make your own conclusions."

Tech could only nod.

Syn walked around the table and squeezed both Tech's shoulders. "I'll talk with God and Day soon... if they haven't killed each other today."

"Thanks, Sarge," Tech said softly, his mind reeling with the advice he'd just received.

Chapter TWENTY-SIX

Steele

The next four weeks flew by. He and Tech did exactly what they'd agreed to. They held back and got to know each other. It was different because Tech was the only one who knew classified information about his life, so he was able to open up to him. Tech respected that he didn't care to talk about his life overseas and instead, they focused on what the future held for both of them. They talked on the phone, texted suggestive messages, and had lunch most days at their desks. The team noticed, but no one showed any disdain for Steele's obvious intentions.

But damn if he wasn't having a hard time keeping his hands to himself. Tech was delicious. His look, his body, his style, his smell, and especially his genius. It all drove him crazy. That's why he was in the precinct's gym trying to tear a hole in the heavy bag with his fists. He'd been working out down there regularly. Eating Green's food was going to have a negative impact on his stomach if he didn't stay on top of his regimen. The station's entire bottom level was designated for working out. It was, by far, the nicest precinct gym he'd ever seen. Pretty modern cardio equipment, weights, mats, and a full-sized boxing ring.

Horny didn't begin to describe what he was feeling. Even though Tech hadn't offered him his bed again, his body language screamed at him to take him hard against the first sturdy surface they could get to. Steele grunted and threw a four-piece combination at the bag, then stepped back to regroup. He bobbed and ducked then threw another set, snapping his fists back after each connect. The fact that Ruxs and Green engaged in some type of sexual activity daily didn't help him either, and he was tired of blasting music in his ears every night. He would've come out better staying at the trailer park. *I need my own place, pronto. Maybe Tech will help me look for a place in a decent neighborhood.* Steele hissed with each punch he threw.

"The bag doesn't hit back, Marine."

Steele stopped and stood up taller, turning to give his boss a no shit look. "You're always so insightful, God."

God's hair was pulled back in a ponytail and covered in a black and white bandanna. Wearing only a pair of long nylon shorts, Steele got his first good look at the huge roaring lion tattooed across the entire right side of God's muscular back. *Jesus.* The guy was definitely in shape, and it was no surprise that men and women stared as he moved across the floor to the ring in the center of the gym. There were a couple of guys in there were unwrapping their kickboxing gloves and the gym managers were cleaning it for the next match.

"Come on, Marine," God yelled, loud enough to turn heads. "Looks like you're already warmed up, let's go a few rounds."

Steele turned and propped both hands on his hips. Honestly, he wasn't in the mood for that strenuous of a workout, he was just trying to release a little excess energy. "I'm good." Steele waved God off, who was now shadowboxing and moving around the ring gracefully. He was light on his feet and could snap his fists out faster than Steele would've thought.

"Come on, don't be nervous. I'll take it easy on you," God taunted him. Steele was never good with being baited. He walked across the floor, pulling off his drenched tank top and tossing it beside the ring.

"That's the spirit." God chuckled, still bouncing.

Steele climbed inside the ring, already noticing that a few of the other officers had paused their workouts and made their way closer. He doubted they were there to watch him. He had a sinking feeling that most people enjoyed watching God destroy whoever dared step inside the ring with him. His body was like a statue, hard and chiseled to perfection. Steele had been around men like that for over twenty years. It didn't intimidate him, and he was confident that he could give God a damn good sparring match. Steele put on his protective headgear and let one of the trainers wrap his fists up before slipping on the kickboxing gloves. He took the offered mouthpiece and met God in the center of the ring. God had at least four inches on him, and his arms were long; he'd have to adjust for that. His tactic would be to stay low and go for God's ribs and stomach. Make him swing and hope he tired quickly.

"Alright, guys. Let's keep it clean. No hits below the waist, high kicks, or wrestling," one of the gym managers said, and stepped outside the ring. There was no bell, only the shrill sound of the whistle around his neck. Steele tucked his chin a bit and took a couple steps back, wanting to get a sense of God's style. He wasn't surprised when God moved around him, doing the same. Both of them feeling each other out.

Steele watched fierce green eyes follow him. God's form was good, similar to his own. God threw out a couple test punches before striking out with a powerful combination that resulted in a hit grazing Steele's left jaw. Full-on impact would've hurt like hell. He'd have to be fast to dodge the blows. If God got more than a few good hits to his face, he'd be dazed. Steele was never one to go down easy; he ducked God's right and dipped, catching him twice in the ribs on the left. God stepped back and frowned, immediately dropping his elbows to protect them. Steele moved in the other direction in an attempt to confuse God and come in at another angle. With God's height, he'd assume Steele wouldn't go for his face, but he was going to fool him there as well.

Steele took a step in and danced back before he made his next move. Swooping in quick, he threw a right to God's side and caught him with an uppercut, but not before God clipped his chin when he tried to get back out of his reach. His lieutenant was smart, he'd give him that. He'd already figured out Steele's strategy of sneaking inside then quickly getting out. A few yells came from the sides, including a few encouraging him. Steele kept his eyes locked on his target. He was charged and ready, now. *Let's dance, God.*

Tech

Tech swiveled back and forth in his chair, waiting for his program to finish running a diagnostic check on his inventory system. For some reason, he kept getting duplicate orders. While he waited, he listened to Michaels on Ruxs' speakerphone, talking about the trout he'd caught while fishing with his partner, Judge, in Virginia. He'd had a two-month leave planned to travel with Judge, to connect with some of his deceased father's relatives. He put in the request seven months ago and left right after the shootout with Artist. He was scheduled to come back next month. But on this team, you took a vacation with the understanding that it could end any time God, Day, or Syn said. Being on call was a requirement. Even if you were out of the country, you'd better figure out a way to answer the call.

Ruxs was telling Michaels about Steele and what it was like working with him. Steele was already getting a reputation on the streets, too. But being partnered with the two crazies… how could he avoid it?

"Man, I look forward to meeting him. Alright guys, I was just checking in. Tell Ro I said stop faking like he's still hurt and get his ass back to work." Michaels laughed and hung up.

Tech smiled. He missed Michaels' rough charm. He was one helluva sniper. When he took aim – just like the rest of them – he didn't miss. He could fire from six hundred yards with absolute accuracy. Needless to say, he'd won the lieutenants over in no time, as had Steele. Steele was making friends quickly, and not only in their department. Hell, he was living with Ruxs and Green. That counted for something. They trusted him already. He hoped that meant Steele was sticking around.

Tech turned and looked at Syn, wondering when he was going to get back to him on his request to get out in the field. It'd been quiet the past couple weeks, but the Enforcers had made two arrests and had assisted SWAT with two raids. Tech was never even asked to go and observe. He wouldn't think Syn would ignore him; surely, he had to have talked to God and Day by now.

Things were back to how they'd always been in the office. Day was back to his fun self, and nobody had missed the shiny two-tone band on his finger. They'd wondered if the two had run off and

184

eloped, but Day was proud to announce the official wedding date to everyone. There was a collective sigh of relief when he'd finally put that doubt to rest. Tech wasn't the only one who'd thought Day was going to either leave or shoot God in his balls for stringing him along. His lieutenants were finally getting married. They were all invited but had been instructed not to tell anyone and not to bring anyone. The ceremony would be at Ruxs and Green's home, an intimate setting and a couple hours afterward a few invited guests would come for the reception. That way, God and Day could simply leave when they were ready and the rest of them could party and celebrate. Invitations to the reception had already gone out and a few coworkers had been by the department to either RSVP in person or rib the guys.

Tech was getting ready to go over to Syn and Day when one of the homicide detectives burst through their doors wearing a pair of sweats and an APD tank top, his face sweaty and flushed but his eyes as wide as saucers. "Your new guy, the Marine, is sparring with God downstairs!" he yelled, and took off back through the bullpen, a few of the beat officers racing along behind him.

Ruxs and Green were already in motion, taking off like two bats out of hell. Tech was right behind them and he could hear the heavy steps of Syn and Day on his heels.

"Hey, what's going on?" The captain frowned from the entrance to his office, looking confused at all his officers scattering like rats.

"The Marine's in the ring with God," someone yelled.

"Oh hell," the captain said and joined in the crowd.

Tech's heart was beating frantically, taking the stairs two at a time, all of them sounding like a cattle stampede. It was no secret around the precinct who their new addition was, a lot of them having seen the footage of him at the fast food robbery, so the thought of him going head to head with the baddest cop in Atlanta, that was something to run and see.

When Tech came through the swinging doors, the first thing he saw was the goddamn crowd. Everyone was down there, even a couple of the officers from booking. *What the hell?* Then he noticed all the cell phones that were pointed in the direction of the ring, recording. The noise was crazy like they were watching two heavyweight champions. His breath stopped when he saw God shove Steele into the ropes and hammer away at his ribs. Steele tucked his elbows in tight, a look of determination and pain etched on his sweaty face.

"Get outta there, Marine!" a deep voice shouted. "Get off the ropes."

Tech watched Steele wrap God up in a bear hug to halt his punches. God stumbled back, pushing Steele off him, but to his surprise, Steele came at God with a combination that would've made Ali proud.

"Yeah!" The crowd cheered when God stumbled back into the buckle, his big biceps flexing as he tried to defend against Steele's hits.

Tech swallowed hard. He was amazed and extremely turned on by how fast Steele moved. God swung a quick left hook, the crowd erupting again when Steele ducked and returned the same level of punishment on God's ribs. Steele jumped back, meeting God in the center of the ring. Tech didn't know what round this was, but both of them looked like they'd had the workout of their lives. He'd seen God not even break a sweat in the ring, but large droplets poured off his chest and shoulders while he brought his hands up, squaring off with Steele again.

"Come on, Cash! Show him who's boss."

Tech craned his neck and could see Day was standing beside the ring, yelling louder than anyone else. *Of course*, he thought, not sure whether knowing his fiancé was watching gave God a boost of confidence or a need to show off, but God gave Steele a come-hither sign, telling him he was ready for more.

Steele brought his arms back up and Tech's mouth watered, taking in Steele's strong upper body, his broad shoulders and ripped back. His pecs were thick and dripping sweat profusely, making the large tattoo there glisten in the dim lighting. The huge bald eagle clutching the world in his sharp talons with USMC beneath it, done masterfully. But the best part was Steele's knuckleduster piercing the image, the words Death Before Dishonor wrapped around the blade.

Tech's skin heated and he eased back into the corner to silently keep watching and also hide his reaction.

God and Steele traded punches back and forth, so evenly matched it was impossible to see who was winning. Cheers and spurring were yelled for both of them and Tech couldn't help but feel special that the man up there, showing just how dangerous he really was, only had the hots for him. For a geek. The women watching were no doubt praying that Steele might be the one and only man on God's team that wasn't bi or gay. All he could do was smirk. Tech was the only one in this state who knew what Steele tasted like, felt like, sounded like when he was turned on because he was the one to do it.

"You've got to be shittin' me," the captain hissed, coming through the doors.

Tech shrunk back further into the corner at seeing the captain's anger that all of his officers were down there acting like crazed wrestling fans instead of doing their jobs. The strong man shouldered through the crowd, pushing and barking at people to get back to work. Tech laughed when he saw the older officer jump up onto the ring and climb inside. He motioned for the manager to blow the whistle. Despite the captain standing there, everyone continued to clap and cheer, calling out to God and Steele for such an amazing display of skill.

"Get back to work!" the captain bellowed. "Where the hell do you think you are, Caesar's Palace? Move it! Now! What do you think the chief would say if he walked into the precinct right now?"

The captain didn't turn back to face God and Steele until most of the officers tucked away their phones and quickly begin to clear out at the idea of being caught by the hard-nosed chief.

Tech watched God and Steele exchange friendly pats on the back and teasing blows while they cooled down. God's smile was broad, having obviously liked the chance to really test his new team member. Other departments complained that God always got the elite officers, but the team he'd built made him proud – it was why God got up every day at o'dark thirty.

Tech needed to get back to their office, but he didn't want to. He wanted to go into that locker room and towel dry Steele's strained muscles, then meet him in the shower to show him just how much that display of power turned him on. While one of the trainers unwrapped Steele's wrists, his eyes scanned the small crowd that remained, not stopping until his gray stare met his. Tech's heart skipped a beat at the slight smirk and wink Steele threw his way. It was obvious Steele didn't give a damn who saw it because a few heads turned to see who Steele was looking at. Tech's neck heated as he turned away from the knowing looks and made his way from the gym. Hopefully, he wouldn't have too hard a time hiding his erection as he made his way back to his department.

Chapter TWENTY-SEVEN

God

After an extremely long shower, God walked through the locker room and dropped down on the bench, leaning back against the lockers. He felt like he was still trying to catch his breath. When he'd invited Steele into the ring, he hadn't expected the man to give him that much of a challenge. It only proved that bigger doesn't mean better. While God didn't feel he'd lost, he damn sure didn't win. Most were calling it a draw, but that'd never happened to him before. He smiled then grimaced when he flexed his abs to sit back up. Steele had really hammered at them good.

God hadn't realized he'd closed his eyes until he heard Day's deep chuckle in front of him. "You okay?"

God smirked, shaking his head in disbelief. "I can't believe how fast and strong that fucker is. His fists feel like goddamn bricks, babe."

"I'm sure he's saying the same thing about you." Day shrugged, standing behind God, rubbing his neck.

"I hope so." God pulled Day around to stand in front of him. He wrapped his arms around his waist and rested his forehead against the soft material of Day's sweatshirt. "I wish I could just go home and lay my head in your lap. I'm exhausted."

"Only got another couple hours. We have to go back to the DA's office. It'll be time for us to testify next week. Gonna be long days of sitting in the courtroom and waiting."

"Augh. Don't remind me," God murmured, rubbing his face into Day's warmth. He was so glad he'd confessed what'd been eating at him for months. He was finally able to really be excited about them tying the knot. There wasn't another man or woman on this Earth he'd rather spend the rest of his life with. The planning was coming along, especially with the guys chipping in. Tech made some really nice invitations for the reception and sent them by e-vite. They were keeping it to no more than thirty of their closest friends and coworkers, with only their teammates and family watching them exchange vows. God took Day's hand and linked it with his, kissing the finger he wore his engagement ring on.

"You wanna go grab a bite before we head over?" Day asked while stroking his hand over God's wet hair.

"No. I wanna go home and shove my—"

"Shh." Day cupped his hand over God's mouth. "Not here. What if someone hears you?"

God stood up, walking Day backward until he was pressed against the lockers. "Then they hear me."

"You're a hypocrite." Day smiled up at him. "You're breaking your own damn rule. No sexy stuff at work. That includes us."

"But I'm fired up," God groaned, pressing his towel-covered dick into his lover's jeans-clad one. "I need. Need you right now."

"Oh my—" Day let his head fall back when God dipped down and sucked hard on his throat. He felt Day reaching for his cock while he kissed his way back to his mouth.

"Damn," God hissed at the first heated touch of Day's palm on his shaft. "Yeah, stroke it, sweetheart. Mmm, just like—"

"You're both suspended."

God jumped backward like the guilty man he was at the dark sound of Steele's gruff voice. The stealthy man stood leaning against the lockers like he'd been there a while. How the hell had he snuck up on them? Evidently, he hadn't been known as the ghost for nothing. Day plopped down on the bench in front of the lockers and buried his embarrassed face in his hands. God turned away, feeling like the biggest jackass. Day had warned him, but the presence of his partner – always with him – made it hard to fight the urges sometimes. For the bosses to get caught by the new recruit was mortifying. God yanked his boxer briefs from his bag and pulled them up over his ass.

"Tech told me about your extremely stiff…" Steele looked down at God's straining erection, flicking his nose and sniffing before he continued. "… um, policy on getting off in the workplace."

"Shut up, Steele," God grumbled with very little authority. He was busted; he couldn't be pissed at Steele about it.

"Lieutenant. Was it the sparring with *me* that really got you going, or was it Day's—"

"Steele," Day hissed, his face still in his hands.

"I'm flattered, really." Steele coughed to cover his laughter.

God finally leveled a look on Steele that told him he wouldn't be wise to keep this up much longer.

"I was just on my way back up, so I think I'll continue that way. Wanted to make sure you were good, God. Annnnd, I see that you most definitely are." Steele smiled smugly. "See you when you get off… oops… I mean get up there."

God watched Steele saunter off. He couldn't help but curse under his breath. What did you do when one of your employees got the drop on you… just sucked it up. "No wonder he gets along so well with Ruxs and Green, the bastard."

"Let's just go get this meeting over with." Day sighed and stood up.

"I'm sorry. I know that was stupid. It won't happen again."

"Yeah, right." Day shook his head at him, but God saw the spark in those bright eyes.

Chapter TWENTY-EIGHT

Steele

Steele was glad that everyone was gone by the time he made it back upstairs. Ruxs and Green were going to visit Ruxs' mom and Syn was sitting in on an interrogation. Since Steele doubted Day and God were going to show their horny mugs again today, that left him alone with Tech. He walked through the doors and ate up the distance with hurried steps. Tech turned around just as he got to him, surprise registering on his face when Steele grabbed his hand and pulled him from the chair.

"What are you—?"

Steele dragged Tech to his equipment room and quickly punched in the numeric code. After entering, he didn't bother turning on the lights, instead, he pulled Tech inside and plastered himself to his sleek body. He sealed his mouth over those soft lips and had his way with them. Tech didn't fight him at first, instead returning the kiss with eagerness and fire. When Steele began to go for Tech's tucked in shirt, he finally met resistance.

"Jesus Christ," Tech said, tearing his mouth away and catching Steele's hands. "What is going on? We'll get caught."

Steele caught Tech's wrist and walked him deeper inside the narrow enclosure. The minimal lighting came from Tech's screensavers and the recessed lights in the weapons cabinets. "I wouldn't worry about that. I think we might get a pass if we do."

"No, we won't, trust me." Tech snickered, still fighting Steele's persistent hands.

"Go to dinner with me. I'm done waiting. It's going on a month. I've been understanding… and patient." Steele's voice dropped lower and lower as he watched Tech try to get away from him, but he was trapped and that spiked a whole new level of hunger within him. He could eat Tech right there. He didn't know what had gotten into him, maybe the adrenaline of the match still flooding his body, or seeing his hot as fuck lieutenants getting down and dirty. Whatever the cause, Steele was burning with an uncontrollable yearning.

"I... I... okay. Yeah, I'll go out with you." Tech smiled like he'd actually been waiting on Steele to ask him again. "But can I just ask one thing?"

"You can ask whatever you want to," Steele whispered, crowding into Tech's space.

"Why me? I know we've been talking for a while, and I've been immensely enjoying it. But you set your sights on me pretty early, and I never even asked you why. Of all the men around here... and in Atlanta. Why do you want me?" Tech gestured at his sweater vest, jeans, and Vans. "I'm sorry if it offends you but, please. I have to know."

Steele's fire cooled at the look of pleading and misunderstanding in Tech's eyes. He thought about how he wanted to word this so that Tech best understood. Steele wasn't the most articulate at explaining his feelings; he was an actions kind of man. But if Tech wanted an explanation, he'd do his best.

He motioned for Tech to sit on the stool while he stood between his spread legs. He made sure his focus was on him before he spoke. "Shawn, I like you for so many different reasons, I'm not sure where to start." Steele rubbed his hand over the prickly hairs on his jaw while Tech continued to stare. "It's simply because you're you. Because you are amazing and complex in your own right. You may think, because of who I am, because I'm strong, that I'd only be attracted to buff, weight-lifting maniacs, but that's wrong. I've been around men like that for a very long time. When I first saw you, standing amongst Ruxs, Green, and God... babe... I thought you looked like a glass of lemonade in the middle of the Sahara. Refreshing and completely unrealistic."

Tech frowned before his mouth quirked into a wry grin.

Steele ran his thumb down Tech's face, not able to stop himself from leaning in and kissing Tech's cheek, just so he could feel the smoothness on his own rough face. "I say unrealistic because there

194

you were, in the middle of all those roughnecks. Looking so sexy and beautiful. Don't misunderstand me. You are all man. Strong, confident, not an effeminate bone in your body." Steele pressed in closer, growling his next words. "And that fuckin' turns me on. No one can get me as hard as you do."

"Edwin," Tech whispered his name like he was in pain. "I could barely speak when I first saw you. You still take my breath away."

Steele's lips curved provocatively against Tech's cheek. "Now that you know I'm not fucking with you just for the sake of having something to do. Have dinner with me." Steele gripped Tech's chin and licked his way back inside his mouth. "Then, I'd love to see your place... particularly your bedroom."

"Yes. When?" Tech held him tighter, pulling him in until he was practically rubbing himself on him.

Steele whispered between delicious kisses. "So damn needy. I love it. I'm going to give you what you want, Shawn... don't worry. But I don't want to rush. I'm not going anywhere... especially now."

Tech

Finally. Steele finally said what Tech had been battling with for the past several weeks. If he fell for Steele, would he end up left alone again? Their jobs were unpredictable, time-consuming, and extremely demanding, but if he and Steele were together, that would solve everything. They'd see each other all the time. Sure, Steele was on the streets a lot, but Tech saw him often enough. The divorce rate for police officers was depressing, almost as bad as the military. All Tech wanted was a chance to be happy, like his team members.

"When?" Tech repeated, tightening his thighs.

"Tonight. I'm not waiting any longer," Steele murmured. "Kiss me."

Tech wasn't sure how long they were in there making out, but he was ready to move this to the next level. At first, he'd been unsure if they had more than just physical attraction, but after weeks of conversations and shared laughs, he knew they did. He could listen to Steele talk for hours, and though he could still hardly believe it,

Steele enjoyed listening to him, too. Sometimes Steele didn't want to get off the phone at night to let Tech get some rest. Smiling against Steele's lips, he asked him, "Are you picking me up?"

"My bike is still at my uncle's. I'm sure I can borrow Green's car."

"No. I'll drive."

"Okay, then. How's six?" Steele kept his arms over Tech's shoulders, their foreheads pressed together while they ironed out the details.

Tech peeked at the digital clock on the wall. "That's only an hour and a half away."

"I know. I told you. I'm done waiting."

"I have to get home and get changed."

"No, you don't."

"Yes, I do. Eight o'clock."

"I'm not waiting until eight." Steele gripped Tech's neck, closing his mouth back over his, silencing his protest.

Tech pushed Steele back after a few seconds. "Yes, you will. I'm gonna finish up here and head home. I'll pick you up at Ruxs and Green's. At. Eight."

Steele wore excited and horny so well Tech wanted to change the time back to six. He walked out the door, glad they were still alone in the office. He was playing with fire, allowing Steele to get him riled up like he had at work, but the feeling of sneaking around, the stolen touches, was exhilarating. Now he knew why Ruxs and Green couldn't help themselves.

Steele walked up behind him while he was powering down his system. "I'll see you soon. Don't be late."

Tech shook his head, not bothering to turn around. *So demanding.*

Chapter TWENTY-NINE

Steele

Green whistled at him when he came downstairs into the kitchen and pulled a bottle of beer out of the refrigerator. "Kinda snazzy for eggrolls and fried rice, Steele." Green teased him while he flipped his rice around in the wok like a professional.

"I'm not eating with you guys tonight. I've got a date." Steele couldn't stop his pleased smile. He was sure he looked like a smitten fool, but he didn't care.

"Oh yeah? Anyone we know?" Green mocked.

Steele gave him an irritated look while he hoisted himself on the stool to wait. He still had an hour until Tech was supposed to show.

"'Bout time," Ruxs barked from the couch, not taking his eyes off his video game.

"Shut up. We're taking things slow. You two wouldn't know anything about that." Steele took a gulp of his beer, glancing at his watch again. He was tempted to get his earpiece and fuss at Tech to bring his ass.

"Ruxs and I took things slow. We were partners for years before we found out that there was no one else that could stand us so we might as well fuck each other," Green said nonchalantly, standing at the island, scooping out the vegetable mixture for his eggrolls.

"Sounds like a classic love story," Steele replied mirthlessly. He looked at his watch again and almost dropped his beer when the door buzzer sounded. He jumped up and ran to the door, ignoring his partners' laughter behind him.

He swung the heavy door open, ready to pull Tech into his arms, when his smile fell and an annoyed grumble followed.

"I'm sorry, were you expecting someone else?" Syn rasped humorously, stepping inside, a long-haired Adonis behind him.

197

"Aren't you all gussied up and spit-shined? Did you shave, too? Aww. This is serious, fellas," Syn teased.

"I hate you guys," Steele grumbled.

Syn laughed loudly, his deep chuckle echoing in the huge loft. "Steele, this is my partner, Furious. Furi, this is him."

"Nice to meet you, Steele. Heard a lot about you. Cool name, by the way." Furious shook his hand and Steele returned the shake with equal strength.

"Likewise," he replied simply. Ruxs and Green were right. This guy *was* porn worthy, that's for sure. Steele knew Furi was out of the adult industry now, and he'd never disrespect his sarge's partner by asking where he could find some old footage of him. Furi was just that fine.

"I thought we'd swing by since we were in the neighborhood." Syn's midnight eyes mocked him, walking inside and placing the twelve pack he'd brought with him in the refrigerator, quickly making himself at home.

Steele knew not much got past Syn regarding the team. But how he'd found out about their date so fast was beyond him. Tech had to have squealed. Still, nothing could bring his mood down. He sat on the stool beside Syn, watching him try to hide his smug grin.

"I'm glad you guys got it worked out, for real. Tech's a good guy, man," Syn acknowledged.

Steele agreed. But he didn't need Syn to tell him that. He already knew. Oh, he couldn't wait to have the man all to himself, tonight. No one to interrupt them while they were talking, no one a few feet away, listening and teasing. He'd give him what they'd both wanted from day one.

This time when the door buzzer rang, he was a little cooler. He didn't run to the door, but he didn't make Tech have to ring it twice. He was early, which meant Tech couldn't wait any longer, either. Steele smiled, pulling open the metal door. "Oh, fuck no." Frowning angrily, he slammed it back shut.

The door reopened. "Now, that was rude." Day grinned, sauntering inside. "Is that how you're going to greet our Tech?"

"What is this? Are you guys serious?" Steele fussed, staring incredulously at his lieutenants.

"Slam the door in my face again and watch what I do to you," God said, shoving past him. "I was invited for eggrolls. If you don't mind."

"Yeah, everything ain't about you, Steele." Day pffted.

Steele leaned against the front door, looking at his co-workers. What had he gotten himself into? Was his date going to be on the local news too? The door buzzed again and Steele's heart began to hammer in his chest, but he still played it off. "Who is this, the chief of police?" He scowled at his team before opening the door.

"Were you expecting the chief?" Tech asked, standing there looking more stunning than he'd ever seen him look.

Steele's gaze raked him up and down. From his casual brown leather and suede oxfords, up his long legs encased in denim to his extremely soft-looking beige sweater. Was it cashmere? It looked cashmere. Steele loved the Burberry plaid collared shirt underneath. He wanted to rip those preppy clothes off him so he could get to that enticing smell. Tech's style was matchless. He felt underdressed now, in his best jeans, which meant no holes or tattered fringe at the bottom but still kind of faded on the knees, and a solid green, button-down shirt. At least he'd thought to steal a pair of Ruxs' leather boots out of his closet instead of wearing his combats. If Ruxs had noticed them, he didn't comment. Tech looked like Ivy League slumming it with a trade school student. Steele loved it. He wasn't insecure in the least. Tech was crazy about him… he was sure of that.

"You look great… come on, let's go." Steele yanked his leather coat off the hook, gripped Tech's shoulder, and tried to hurry and close the door behind him.

"Hey! Hey! Hold up!" He heard yelling behind him before he could fully shut the door.

Tech turned around, looking confused. "Is that Syn? Who else is in there?"

"Um, no one. That was the TV. Let's go." Steele tugged Tech around his waist, almost dragging him.

Syn opened the door with a huge smile. "Hey, why you rushing off?"

Tech maneuvered out of Steele's hold. "Syn, what are you doing here? Is Furi in there?"

"He sure is. Come on in." Syn hooked his arm around Tech's lean shoulders and pulled him away from Steele, giving him a gotcha look over his shoulder. Steele flicked Syn off while he trudged back inside.

Tech looked pleasantly surprised when he walked in and found everyone there. Not pissed like Steele. This was *their* night. He saw these meatheads every day, all day. He wanted his time alone with Tech. He watched his date walk right up to Furious and wrap him in a brotherly embrace.

"Hey, you. Wow, you look gorgeous," Furi said, giving Tech a Hollywood smile.

"Thank you. What are all of y'all doing here? I didn't know there was a get together planned." Tech turned, looking at his teammates. "How come you didn't tell me?"

Steele shook his head in disbelief. Tech could be so sweetly oblivious sometimes. He loved his team so much he couldn't even tell that the guys were fucking with Steele by trying to cock block him. They all knew how much he wanted Tech. Like hell, he was letting this happen.

Tech's eyes lit up when he peeked in the kitchen. "And Green's cooking... Steele, let's stay here," Tech yelled over to him. "Oh Day, are you cooking, too?"

"Sure. I can," Day agreed.

"What? No way." Steele took long determined steps and clasped Tech's hand before he could make his way farther into the kitchen. "Nope, not staying. We're going to Atlantic Station, they got food there. Come on."

Tech let Steele pull him back to the door. Tech waved frantically behind him, telling Furi he'd call him later with all the details. Steele could still hear them laughing and Ruxs hollering something about letting him get a picture first, but Steele slammed the door shut.

"You in a hurry?" Tech provoked him, slowing their steps to the parking lot.

Steele jerked Tech into his arms and kissed him hard, letting him know just how anxious he was to get this date started. "Unless you want to be bent over in front of our friends, I suggest you get moving," Steele urged, sucking behind Tech's ear.

Tech wrapped one arm around Steele's waist, the other cupping his jaw. "You look good, too." He held his head higher, guiding Steele's mouth to a spot next to his Adam's apple. "Mmm. More."

Steele reluctantly pulled back. "Later. Lots more, later. But we gotta go, or we'll be late for the next showing."

Tech led him to a shiny, all-black Tahoe parked next to Green's Camaro. "This is your truck?" Steele stared disbelievingly.

"What'd you think I drove? A Volkswagen Beetle?" Tech hit the key fob, unlocking the doors.

"No," Steele said, climbing inside. "This is nice. Holy shit!"

Tech laughed, closing his door and fastening his seatbelt.

"Tech, what is all this?" Steele pointed at all the equipment, including the twelve-inch display screen that lit up when Tech pressed the ignition button.

"Good evening, Shawn. What is your destination?"

Steele looked at Tech with the funniest expression he could probably make. "Your car is talking to you."

"Yeah, he does that. I'm going to navigate myself, though." Tech tapped a few keys on what looked like an iPad and waited until their current location displayed. He turned on the radio and classical music started quietly as he put the truck in drive.

"This is crazy," Steele said, still looking around. "Is this… is this a laptop in here?"

Tech looked over at the woodgrain dashboard on the passenger side, while Steele tried to figure out how to open it.

"Yeah. I guess I was kind of bored when I put that in." Tech shrugged like everyone could have one of those.

"Did you do all this?" Steele asked, finally settling back and enjoying the smooth ride.

"Well me and Furi. There's nothing that guy can't do with a vehicle. I bought this bad boy about a year ago and took it to his shop for him to look over. I started telling him what I wanted to do and he told me I was free to come there and work on it in his shop, anytime. And since I have no life outside of work, I went there often. He helped with the bodywork and his shop partner Doug helped with rearranging the interior to accommodate everything. He had to redo the dash and the entire front panel so I could insert the new system. It quickly became a hobby. I wanted to use it if I ever got in the field."

Steele noticed the change in Tech's voice, the want. He reached over the raised center console – wondering what kind of surprise was in there, probably a cappuccino maker – and rubbed his forearm. "You talked to Syn, right?"

"A while ago, but I haven't heard anything. Maybe he's still trying to convince God to give me a shot. I don't know. Let's not talk about that. So, we're going to the Station. I love it down there. The storefronts and bars. I don't go often but I always liked it." Tech headed onto the freeway.

"My uncle told me about this movie in the park that they do. There's a really nice restaurant with outside booths. I thought we could eat outside, talk, watch an old classic." Steele hoped Tech was into that. He'd mentioned liking action and old-time films.

"That sounds real nice. I've never done that." Tech's smile was beautiful, and Steele was glad he'd chanced asking his uncle for help.

"Is your uncle married?" Tech asked.

"No. No wife, no kids."

"Is he gay?"

Steele barked a laugh. "No. He's married to bettering the community. That's all he does. Oh, and working out." Steele huffed. "Maybe he is gay."

Tech's laugh was infectious and they made small talk for the duration of the drive. He liked Tech's truck; again, it was something unexpected from him. Steele looked over when he heard a loud beeping. "What's that? You out of gas?"

Tech looked at him like he was silly. "No. It means someone's riding my ass." Tech looked up in his rearview mirror.

"Okay. This car is like Kit," Steele joked.

"You mean from *Knight Rider*?" Tech grinned. "Damn, how old are you?"

Steele punched Tech in his shoulder. "Shut up. That show was great."

"Um. Sure. Thirty years ago."

Steele scoffed. "That wasn't thirty years ago."

"You're right, probably more. I bet the episodes are only available on VHS."

"Oh, fuck you. That show isn't that old."

Tech raised one brow at him. "Secret."

"Yes, Shawn."

"How old is the television show *Knight Rider*?"

The car responded immediately like it'd been expecting the question.

"Knight Rider first aired its pilot episode September 26, 1982. Thirty-four years ago."

Steele could barely control himself. That was crazy. "You show off. Damn, babe. Did you install that?"

"It's just the Google app installed in the car's computer. Same way it works on your smartphone." Tech bit his bottom lip again but little did he know, that drove Steele wild. "Annnnd, I kind of borrowed some of Tesla's 2019 software, and a smidge of Mercedes." Tech gestured with his forefinger and thumb.

"Did you steal their technology and put it in your truck?" Steele's eyes widened.

Tech looked out his window. "I didn't steal it… I borrowed it. Taking it on a test drive, if you will. Besides, there's no crime here. I'm not using it to make a profit or trying to copy it and sell it. It's for my own personal use. Like downloading music from a free site. As long as you don't make a CD and sell it, it's all good."

"Yeah, I'm pretty sure neither of those companies would think it's all good."

"Who are you, the police? I thought I was on a date," Tech taunted him.

Steele was liking Tech's playful side. The things his brain could do astonished him. He was riding in a loaded vehicle with highly expensive, stolen technology, which, from what Steele could understand, wasn't even available, yet. "Why do you call it Secret?"

"Because it's one of my best kept ones."

"Well, not anymore."

"But I trust you." Tech looked at him and Steele saw he wasn't joking anymore.

"Thank you."

"Do you know where we are?" Tech asked out of nowhere, probably to tamp down the seriousness.

Steele looked around. "No."

"You haven't been studying your map."

"I do know." Steele sat up. "Um, let's see, that's Georgia Tech, right...? So we're on, seventeenth, no, tenth street. Up there is Northside."

Tech nodded that he was right.

"See. I told you. I'm ready for my quiz, anytime."

"If you say so. It's not going to be an easy one."

Steele turned his body towards Tech, eyeing him suspiciously. "Did you give everyone else a quiz?"

"That's not important," Tech answered.

"Uh-huh. Like I thought."

Chapter

THIRTY

Tech

Steele told the hostess that Councilman Steele made a reservation for him. She nodded and hastily showed them to a secluded booth on a romantically lit patio at the back of the restaurant. It backed up to the park and the screen was plenty big enough for them to see. The movie was already playing but Tech didn't mind. He was too busy taking in the ambiance. There were a few booths outside but there was only one other couple, at the other end. He slid into the high-backed, curved booth that had a small fire pit in the middle, giving them just enough warmth against the brisk fall air. The lawn wasn't packed like it was during the summer. Most of the movie watchers were in their folding chairs closer to the screen with blankets draped over their shoulders or laps. With Steele nestled in close to him in the comfortable, leather-padded booth, he had the best seat available.

Steele made sure they were close enough that their thighs were touching and opened the menu, sharing it with him. A young waitress came over with a pleasant smile and filled their water glasses. "Can I start you gentlemen off with something to drink?"

"I'll have a Corona," Tech ordered.

"Let me get a double shot of Crown on the rocks."

"Sure. Be right back with that for you," she said, turning quickly and heading back inside.

"You hungry?" Steele asked him.

"I'm very hungry," Tech almost moaned. He didn't know why he said it like that, but he let the double meaning hang out there.

Steele gave him an inviting look before he finally responded, "Me, too."

"How about an appetizer? You said you liked shrimp."

Tech nodded. "I do."

"Wanna share a couple orders of the cocktail?"

Tech took a sip of his water, nodding. He was suddenly nervous and his mouth felt as dry as dust. It had felt like Steele was so far out of his league at first, but as Tech got to know him over the weeks, he began to realize just how amazing they could be together. It was as if the man didn't know how dangerous he was. Tech was still reeling over the sparring match he'd seen that afternoon between Steele and God. The man was incredible. Tech found himself wanting to be pinned under him, helpless and writhing.

"What are you thinking?"

Tech jumped at Steele's deep voice, feeling like he'd been caught with his hands in his pants. Though it was chilly out, he could feel the warmth of embarrassment licking up his throat. Steele's sharp gray eyes locked in on it and Tech shivered under the strong glare. *Jesus.* Before he could answer Steele's question the waitress returned with their drinks on a small tray. She set Steele's short tumbler of amber liquor in front of him and Steele passed Tech his frosted mug with his beer already poured in it.

"Are you thinking of starting with one of our delicious appetizers tonight?" The waitress looked expectantly between them.

Steele answered for them and Tech watched Steele reach in his inside coat pocket and pull out a pack of those sweet cigars and a silver Zippo lighter with the Grim Reaper on it while giving the waitress their starter order.

When she left, Steele lit the cigar and took a deep pull, narrowing his eyes when he blew the smoke out of his nose and mouth. After drinking a quarter of his drink without so much as a grimace, he turned and faced Tech again. He wanted to jump up and straddle Steele right then and there, darn whoever decided to turn and watch.

Steele's mouth curved in a knowing leer. "Never mind. I think I know what you're thinking." Steele pulled on the cigar again. A hint of the fragrant aroma making its way to him. He was never one to get into the habit of smoking, but he always thought it looked sexy. And

Steele wasn't smoking a typical Marlboro, the slender brown cigar looked hand rolled and smelled intoxicating.

Tech couldn't hold it anymore. He grabbed the back of Steele's neck and pulled him the few inches that separated their mouths and kissed him forcefully, tilting his head to get a better angle. He didn't ease up the pressure until Steele slid that whiskey-flavored tongue inside his mouth. Tech's dick hardened and filled to capacity as he swooned in the erotic aroma of sweet tobacco and top-shelf liquor. Tech moaned inside Steele's mouth and felt him react, pulling him closer with one arm and deepening the kiss. He shuddered, and it wasn't from the cold. He needed Steele to take him so badly it was killing him. Tech reached down and squeezed the rigid bulge between Steele's legs, already imagining it spreading him wide open.

"Easy, baby," Steele whispered huskily after breaking the kiss. "You don't want me coming just yet, do you?"

Steele turned to look around, maybe to see who was watching, but Tech didn't care. He hadn't had sex in… Jesus… he wasn't sure how long. Way too long. He pressed his forehead against Steel's jaw, trying to calm his raging libido. Even though Steele had shaved, his cheek was still rough with prickly salt and pepper stubble. Tech gave him a soft kiss and burrowed further into the crook of his neck, lingering close to where Steele had dabbed his spicy cologne.

"You're going to get yourself in trouble," Steele growled, reaching around and easing his fingers inside Tech's waistband. He couldn't go far, but the tips of his gun-calloused fingers grazed the top of his seam and Tech let out a combination whine and moan, while he tried to mold his body to Steele's entire right side.

The waitress came back with their appetizers and placed them on the table. "Are you ready to order your entrees?"

Steele hadn't removed his fingers, but from where she stood she couldn't see exactly where they were, and Tech felt a surge of naughty excitement flood his body when Steele reached a little farther and used his middle finger to tickle him… however, the feeling it gave Tech was far from funny. Steele didn't let on what he was doing as he asked the waitress to give them a little more time. When she walked away, Steele turned back to him, that same smoky

207

passion blazing in his eyes. "I want in here," he groaned, caressing the top of Tech's ass.

"Anything you want," Tech answered breathlessly. That sounded slutty, but oh, well. He was sitting in a public restaurant, outside, wishing his date would get his finger closer to his hole. It didn't get any sluttier than that.

"You're so bad." Steele nipped at Tech's bottom lip.

"Me? Everything about you screams bad, and it's making me come up out of myself."

"I'm not a bad boy." Steele nudged at Tech's throat with his nose before licking a hot path up to his chin. "I'm wearing a button-up shirt."

Tech laughed, while Steele continued to tease him with his fingers.

"We better stop. I can't eat shrimp cocktail with one hand down your pants, and you can't eat with one hand on my dick."

Tech didn't want to remove it either, though Steele was most likely right. "I can't stop."

"Try." Steele stole another kiss like he was having the same problem.

"I don't think there's anything that can get me to go down right now. I'm so fuckin' hard," Tech groaned.

"How's your father doing?"

"That'll do it." Tech grimaced and slid out of Steele's hold, dislodging the calloused hand from his pants in the process.

Steele picked up his glass and downed the rest of his drink, took another couple pulls before he put out his cigar on the side of the fire pit and tucked it back in his pack for later. Tech rolled his eyes. He wondered if smoking was even allowed, but technically, they were outside, so maybe so. Tech picked up the lemon wedge and squeezed some over his shrimp then dipped it in the cool cocktail sauce. When he looked up, Steele was staring at his mouth like he was envious of the shrimp. "You told me to stop, so quit looking at me like that."

"I will, for now. So, really. How's your dad?"

They'd talked about Tech's father still living in the Rockies, alone. He'd told him about his photography hobby and how Tech tried to go see him as often as he could. "He's fine. He's getting the house ready for winter. He needs to have the windows and insulation checked and the fireplaces swept. Snow doesn't come in for a while, but he's always prepared early."

"Can he handle that? You said he was sixty-seven. Can he chop wood and stuff?" Steele asked. Tech appreciated that he was genuinely concerned.

"No, he doesn't cut his own wood, but he probably could. He's still as strong as ever. He buys his firewood and the company brings it out and loads it in his woodshed for him. When I go there, I do a lot of things around the house for him."

Steele finished another shrimp and wiped his mouth before asking, "Do you think he'd approve of you dating me? A mere high-school educated cop who's sixteen years your senior. He might think I have pedophilic tendencies."

Tech pretended to ponder the thought. "Hmm. You have a point. When you were in high school, I wasn't even born yet."

Steele looked like he wanted to run and Tech quickly stopped making fun of him. "Hey, you know that line of thinking is ridiculous. I'm a grown man, Steele. I'm almost thirty, so what – you're forty-five. And you're much more than just a cop. I was more concerned with my father thinking I was too undisciplined for you. He'll love you… I mean… you know… if we get to that point. He wanted to go into the military but he got my mom pregnant and she wanted him home. There was no way she could've lived on that mountain with two boys and him gone six months out of the year. He'd like you a lot, I'm sure. I've always been more mature than my age. When other kids were going to dances and hanging out, I was building computers and earning scholarships. It won't surprise him in the least that I'm attracted to a mature man."

"Yeah, I guess it's a little early, but I'd love to meet him when the time is right."

"Seriously." Tech tried not to sound like he wanted to book the first flight out of Atlanta and show off his guy to his dad. He knew his father would be proud of him. Once he saw how enthralled and happy Tech was, coupled with Steele's accomplishments, his dad would be wanting to call Steele son in no time.

The waitress came back and took their dinner orders. She asked if they were enjoying the movie and Tech had forgotten there was one even playing. Steele's company was far more entertaining.

"Yes, we are; thank you," Steele answered, while she cleared away their finished appetizers and refilled their water glasses.

When she left, Tech asked Steele the question that'd been on his mind the entire time he was getting dressed for his date. "What was it like sparring with God?"

Steele barked a laugh. "Painful."

Tech smiled. "I'm sure. I've never seen anyone go at him like that. Most guys are intimidated before they even climb into the ring. But you... you were... great."

Steele kept his body turned into him while he stroked Tech's thigh with one hand. "Thank you. Maybe when you have some time, we could go in the mat room and you can show me some of your moves. I'd love to see what you can do. See if you can pin me down."

Tech's cock was rising again at the thought of using a few submission moves on Steele. Sure he could probably get out of most of them. "I could do that. I doubt you'll get as good a match as God gave you, though."

"I haven't had that kind of match up since Ack—" Steele paused his rubbing and looked up at the movie screen, his eyes shadowing over.

"I'm sorry," Tech whispered. "I didn't mean to stir up—"

"No, it's okay," Steele cut in, his voice rough from the reflection. "I know I didn't handle it well before, the mention of his name, but I'm good. Really."

Tech was unsure if he should ask, but his inquiring mind wanted to know. "Was he your partner?"

"Not how you're thinking. He was my comrade... my gunnery. One of the greatest men I'd ever met. We met in Bagdad when he got his orders to my platoon. We hit it off right away. Anytime you saw me, you saw him. Without him, we wouldn't've have been the

Fearless Five. It wasn't until it was too late that I realized he wanted more... more with me."

"I'm really sorry, Steele. You loved him."

"I did. But I never got the chance to show him." Steele leaned in and kissed Tech, murmuring against his parted lips, "I'm not gonna make that mistake again."

Steele didn't know how much his words eased the guilt and doubt in Tech's head. He didn't want to wonder if Steele was settling – having lost the one he truly wanted.

"He would've liked you, ya know." Steele smiled, the light in his eyes sparking again. "He loved reading and learning. Was smart as a whip. Anything he read, he retained." Steele laughed. "Had so much useless information in that big head of his, it was ridiculous. Always said he was auditioning for Jeopardy when he retired."

Tech ducked his head until he felt Steele's rough fingers grip his chin and lift it back up. "He was different from you. Big. Fuckin' huge, and blond. Different from the dark and hairy that I typically like. He was one of a kind. Like you."

Their soft, languid kissing didn't stop until the waitress cleared her throat, setting down two steaming plates of food in front of them. Both of them dug in with gusto, ready to move on to dessert. There was never a lag in the conversation as they spoke about work and ambitions.

"Are Ruxs and Green still driving you crazy?" Tech asked, taking another bite of his chicken Marsala.

"They're not so bad. The food is delicious. Going from MREs, to the microwave, now to Green's cooking. It's heaven. But my gut won't handle it if I don't work out enough. Although, I think I worked off about a million calories in that ring today. My abs are still screaming. Ruxs and Green really are great, and I'm good for now, as long as I keep my headphones in at night."

Tech could only imagine what Ruxs and Green's house sounded like in the wee hours of the night.

"I want to look for my own place and was hoping you'd help me with that," Steele asked, cutting a huge chunk of his Delmonico.

Tech's eyes widened. That was good news. Looking for a home meant he was staying. "I can. I know of few neighborhoods that would probably interest you."

"Good. Sooner rather than later, while we're on our down time."

"Okay." Tech drank some more water, feeling satisfied. He pushed his plate away.

"You finished?"

"I am. That was delicious." Honestly, Tech didn't want to get too full, he had rigorous activity planned for later.

Steele finished the last of his meat, having cleaned his plate. "You want to see the dessert menu?"

"I have brownies at home. Get the check," Tech demanded.

Steele's loud laughter made Tech's cheeks flush, but he was done pussyfooting. He wanted Steele in his bed in the next fifteen minutes, which would be a challenge since he lived twenty minutes away. They needed to move it.

Chapter THIRTY-ONE

Steele

He realized that Tech was breaking most of the traffic laws while racing his big SUV along the freeway, taking the exit ramp at an alarming speed. Steele hid his grin behind his fist as he watched the scenery speed past. He wasn't about to tell him to slow down, that's for sure. His cock had been confined painfully inside his jeans for the last two hours; he didn't think he could take much more, himself.

He hardly noticed the street signs as Tech skillfully maneuvered into the parking lot of a small condominium complex. The community was well lit and the lawns looked nicely maintained. He saw what must be a residents-only clubhouse with a gated pool on the side. "This looks nice."

"Thank you. It is. I've been here for three years." Tech waited until Steele got out, met him at the back of the truck and took his hand. "I'm right there."

"Good thing you're on the bottom floor." He flashed a starving look at Tech to make sure his meaning was clear.

Tech sped up, practically pulling him across the street. Tech hurried and got his key inside the lock and shoved the door open. When he crossed the threshold into the dark condo, he heard the door slam, then Tech's body pushed into him. Steele took control, grabbing Tech around his narrow waist and turning him so he was pressed against the front door. "You're ready right now, aren't you?" Steele asked, his voice deeper in the darkness. He reached down and grabbed Tech's ass with both hands, finally having those ripe mounds in his clutches.

"I am," Tech breathed, between frantic kisses. His long fingers pushed at Steele's coat and he let it slide down his arms and drop to

213

his feet. Next were the buttons on his shirt. Steele braced his hands on the door, trapping his catch, while Tech eagerly undressed him. Finally, his eyes adjusted to the dark and he could see the fire blazing behind the clear lenses of Tech's glasses. After he finished the last button, Tech ran his hands up Steele's chest, lingering over his nipples, biting his bottom lip while feasting his eyes on him.

"Goddamnit," Steele hissed, grabbing Tech's hands and slamming them over his head, pressing them hard against the door. He thrust into Tech's groin, rubbing their stiff erections against each other. The thick denim blocking the friction when he really wanted skin against skin. "Bedroom."

Tech nodded and waited for Steele to release his hands. As soon as he did, Tech moved through a well-furnished living room and past the dining area that'd been turned into an office. He cut down the hall that had two doors on the right and one on the left. Tech opened the last door on the right and turned on the light switch. The light wasn't too bright like Tech kept a low-watt bulb in the fixture. A ceiling fan came on overhead, blowing some much-needed cool air over their burning flesh. He looked around briefly, catching a small entertainment center that held a few plaques and awards on top, beneath it a flat screen television. He'd have to get a closer look at those commendations later.

Tech dropped down on the low bed, pulled his .22 from his waistband, and took his glasses off, placing them on the nightstand. With his shirt wide open, Steele placed his own firearm next to Tech's and walked over to him, his spread legs looking so welcoming. He stood there looking down on him in wonderment. He caressed the side of that soft face while Tech reached for his belt. It felt like he'd been fantasizing about this moment for a very long time. But he was glad they'd waited because it made this night all the more special. He cared for Tech and felt like they were smoothly transitioning into a relationship. They were both ready to take this to the next level, each getting what they'd wanted from the very beginning. Steele wanting a date and Tech wanting him buried deep inside him.

He ran his hands through Tech's hair, the strands gliding through his fingers, while his pants were unbuttoned and spread open. Tech buried his face against his stomach, rubbing his cheek along the dark brown hairs below his navel. Steele groaned, dropping his chin to his chest so he wouldn't miss a thing. Tech looked lost in himself as he rubbed his face back and forth over Steele's stomach, working his way lower and lower until hot, damp breaths ghosted over his thick pubic hair.

Tech's nimble fingers pulled at the waistband of his boxers like he wanted to slowly reveal his prize. Steele wouldn't rush him, for him this was all about Tech, showing him he could be what Tech needed. He could be a man he could trust, a man that would stand by him and a man that could give his body what it'd been craving. "Take your clothes off," Steele commanded, realizing Tech was still fully clothed. He wanted to see all that smooth, ivory skin.

Tech pulled his sweater over his head, looking up at him with desperation gleaming in his brown eyes as he next began unbuttoning his plaid shirt. He looked so gorgeous, unveiling himself just for him. Finally, he saw slim but toned shoulders and a smooth back that he couldn't resist rubbing his hands over while Tech went back to freeing his dick from inside his boxers.

A sigh of relief left his mouth when his pants were pushed down further and his cock sprang up, bumping Tech's chin. Tech's mouth watered, Steele cupped his cheek gently, urging him to do what he wanted. Tech licked a long line from the base of his dick to his weeping head, making him fight to not buck his hips. "Oh god."

Tech continued to torture him with light licks and brushes of his cheeks along his shaft before finally… finally, taking him fully into his mouth. Steele's eyes fell closed but he quickly opened them. "Yessss."

Moaning and slurping around his balls, Tech went all in, leaving Steele's groin slick with his spit. "Fuck." Steele pulled away and Tech grabbed his hips, pulling him back to his mouth like a crazed man, shoving his dick back in, groaning loudly as the head bumped the back of his throat. "Ahh. Shit, baby. Not ready to come, yet."

Steele had to push Tech back, pulling him up the bed and covering him, pressing him into his soft comforter. They stared at each other for a couple seconds, catching their breath. Steele ran his thumb over Tech's lips, smearing the slickness on his finger then pushing it inside. Tech's eyes closed while Steele pressed his thumb further into his mouth, moving it in and out, matching the thrust of his hips.

"You feel good on top of me," Tech rasped, his soft tenor turning to a deeper bass that was driving Steele insane. Tech spread his legs wider, growling when his pants restricted him. Steele rose up and began removing the rest of Tech's clothes. Sliding his underwear and jeans off at the same time and adding his own to the pile. He stared at Tech's long, practically hairless legs – such a stark contrast to the dark bushy hair on his own – and ran his hands down his thighs, gripping the backs of his knees and spreading him open. His hair was trimmed around the base of his engorged cock. Steele had never thought he cared about grooming, but he liked it, especially on Tech. He took care of himself, took pride in his appearance. Steele knelt and wrapped his mouth around the head of Tech's cock, descending until his nose was pressed firmly against the short hairs.

"Unnnh!" Tech's back bowed off the mattress and Steele pressed him back down.

Damn, he tasted delicious. Just as Steele thought he would. Masculine and sweet at the same time. Steele tucked his hands under Tech's ass and lifted, forcing him deeper inside his mouth. Tech whined like he had when he'd jerked off in the shower, but it sounded a lot sexier in person. "Where's your lube?"

Tech was flicking his own nipples when Steele looked up, and he had to squeeze his own balls to keep from coming all over the blanket. He was so lost in Tech's flavor that he hadn't looked up to see Tech's tongue peeking out between his shiny lips as he stimulated himself. Steele gritted at the sharp need in his balls. "Get it – now."

Tech moaned and reached for the nightstand, pulling out a bottle of slick and setting it beside him. Steele reversed their positions, easily settling Tech on top of him. He could see Tech was enjoying Steele taking the reins, submitting to whatever Steele wanted and right now, he wanted Tech to feed him that lengthy dick while he got his hole ready.

"Climb up here, *minu armas*. Want you to push that cock down my throat," Steele said hoarsely.

Tech crawled up Steele's body and settled his ass on his thick chest, rubbing his cock over the course hairs on Steele's chin before raising up and easing his dick inside his mouth just like he'd been told. Tech gripped the short hair on top of his head while he fucked his mouth with shallow thrusts. Steele picked up the lube and messily dumped some on his fingers. He was too overwhelmed to do anything with finesse at this point. Using both hands, Steele spread one cheek and grazed Tech's seam with his lubed fingers, slicking him up and down before nudging at his tight entrance.

He let Tech's cock slide from his mouth, then eagerly began nuzzling and lapping at the crinkled skin covering his balls. The clean smell of soap mixed with Tech's own musk had Steele ready to plunge deep inside and claim this man.

"Don't be gentle," Tech hissed, pushing his ass down harder on Steele's fingers.

Steele had traveled the world, had bedded enough men in his lifetime to know what did it for him, but he'd never lost his mind like this. He was sure with the slightest touch he could blow like a geyser. Tech was ticking off everything he wanted in a lover. Wanton, aggressive, eager, throwing in a bit of dominance. Steele's tongue was right there, pushing Tech's ass higher so he could lick that sweet hole. Tech went crazy on top of him, driving his ass down on his mouth while Steele fucked him with his fingers.

"Ohhh. Steele, you're gonna make me come like this. Don't stop, please."

Keeping Tech's legs around his neck, he flipped them again, placing him down on the mattress with his legs gaped open. His dark pink hole was wet and pulsing for him. He groaned for Tech to give him a condom. He pushed on the tight latex, careful not to stroke himself too hard. He hoped he lasted long enough for Tech to enjoy himself. He was young and virile, lying there squirming, his body begging Steele to wreck it. Tech's eyes were hooded like he was high. He gave Steele a lazy grin and tucked one hand behind his head while pinching his nipple with the other. He was teasing him, taunting Steele to show him what he had.

Dropping back down, he propped himself up on his elbows so he could see Tech's face when he penetrated him for the first time. Tech wrapped his legs around him, his heels high up on his back, placing his hole in perfect position. Steele lined up his cock but he didn't push, drawing on every ounce of self-discipline he possessed.

"Edwin," Tech crooned, wrapping his arms around his neck, his fingers caressing the short hair at the nape of his neck. "I've waited for you for a long time."

Steele didn't know how to respond. He thought he understood what Tech was saying, but he had no words to relay what *he* felt. He could show him. He leaned in and slanted his mouth over Tech's, whispering soft words in Estonian while he pushed his dick just past the first ring of resistance. Tech gripped his neck, squeezing his eyes closed at the first bite of exquisite pain.

"No. Look at me, *armastaja*." Steele inched in further, called Tech his lover, his sweet lover. It's who he was and if he had any say, it's who he would be for a long time.

Tech just barely opened his eyes and Steele pushed in an inch more. Tech was constricting the head of his dick so hard he thought he might not get any more blood flow to it. "Baby, you're tight. Tell me you're okay," Steele gritted through clenched teeth.

"Yes, yes. Keep going," Tech moaned, his mouth pressed against Steele's chin. His breath was hot and labored, his body trembling under him. It wasn't nerves because Tech used his legs to push Steele in deeper and cried out in bliss, his neck arching, the tendons straining as he took the length Steele had to give him.

If only he really knew how much else he had to give. Steele may not be the hottest man out there and damn sure wasn't the trendiest, but he knew what honor meant. He lived it, it was ingrained in him. He could be a good man to Tech if he let him. A good partner. He'd treasure the man in his arms until his last breath. Thinking those things while he was inside Tech made the sensations that much greater. He could just stare at Tech for hours and not get bored. He could talk to him for four-and-a-half hours on the phone – like they had the other night – and still not want to hang up. Tech's insight was endless and he had a quirky sense of humor, a way of making Steele feel like he was twenty-five again.

"I love it when you speak that language," Tech sighed, rolling his hips so Steele was in a better position.

Steele added his own sounds to the dim room. Sounds he hadn't made in a long time. Sounds of pleasure… and happiness. *"Ma ei ole kunagi mõelnud, mida tunneksid, nii hea."*

Tech mewled in his ear then licked his shoulder. Steele wished at that moment he'd not blown his father off when he tried to teach him Estonian, but he did know a few endearing phrases. *"Sa oled nii ilus."* Steele thrust one last time so he was fully surrounded by Tech's heat.

"Tell me. Please tell me what you said." Tech's eyes were a lighter brown without the dark-framed glasses. Steele found himself mesmerized, staring down at him.

He'd tell Tech anything, everything if he could make Steele always feel like this. Steele inched out a little and pushed back inside like he couldn't stand not being as deep as possible. He captured Tech's leg behind his knee and pulled it up to his shoulder, growling at the man's flexibility. He kept their chests pressed together, leaning his forehead against Tech's. He whispered, "I said I never thought you would feel this good." He kissed Tech deeply and increased the speed of his thrusts, but only by a fraction. He didn't want this to end, but the racing of his pulse and the pressure in his balls made him terrified to continue. Tech may have wanted Steele to devour his body, but the man was doing a number on his heart. "You are so beautiful. You feel so soft and smooth."

Tech's mouth spread into a wide, gorgeous smile, then dropped open in a silent cry when Steele ground himself against him. "Yessss," Tech hissed.

"Damn, I need to come," Steele groaned and kissed the inside of Tech's knee. "Come for me."

Tech took one hand from behind Steele's neck and eased it between their stomachs. "Do it. Make me come. Make me come for you."

Steele closed his mouth over Tech's sensual words, spread his legs wider, and pounded at the place inside of Tech that caused him to arch his neck and yell out with each contact. He screamed Steele's name as his fist moved rapidly between them. It was the hottest thing Steele had ever seen. This proper and perfect genius giving a devil dog like him the ride of his life.

Chapter THIRTY-TWO

God

"I wonder how the date's going." Day smiled while he helped Green with the last of the dishes.

God rolled his eyes. "We know how it's going. It's almost midnight and he ain't back yet." They'd eaten dinner and sat around bullshitting like they always did. They really were a degenerative band of brothers who could hardly stay away from each other, even on their nights off.

"Tech gettin' down and dirty on the first date. Who would've thought?" Ruxs added.

"He's a gorgeous man. I figured the Marine would have a hard time keeping his hands off of him tonight," Furi said from Syn's lap.

The guys stared at him for a moment, probably all of them trying to see Tech as a sexy guy and not just their little brother. God couldn't see him any other way.

"Are you good with this, God? You look perturbed." Syn grinned.

"It's fine. As long as they can hold it together. Not let shit get outta hand. Like dumbasses." God pointed at Ruxs and Green. "Can't have any more fuckin' in the parking lot. Jesus."

The guys laughed, all of them remembering Green's ass up in the air in Ruxs' truck, thinking no one would see them.

"That was over a year ago, when are you gonna let it rest, man?" Green ground out, spraying Lysol on his counter.

"Never," they all replied in unison. Another round of ribbing was thrown the Enforcer's way.

"I'm happy for them, and Steele really looks like he's taken with Tech. Did you see the way he was looking at him tonight? I thought he was gonna throw him on the floor right here." Furi's smile was contagious. Even God had a hard time not showing his amusement.

"He zeroed in on Tech his first day," Syn agreed. "Not God, not Day... nope, straight to Tech. It was a rough start but I think most of us have experienced those before."

"We said we wouldn't hold that against him, so it's not to be brought up anymore," Day told them.

God's official phone rang – not his personal one – silencing everyone. He hit speaker. If it was police business, his team needed to hear it.

"Godfrey," he answered.

"We got a problem at the safe house. Someone's trying to knock off the witnesses in the case you're testifying in," the captain told him, sounding like he was running.

God was on his feet, his men right behind him. "On our way. Get whoever you can over there!"

"Be careful," he heard Furi yell, before closing Ruxs and Green's front door.

"Get Tech and Steele moving, now," God told Syn while they closed themselves in God's RAM and sped towards the highway.

"Damn, what a way to end a first date," Syn murmured.

"Police chase and gunfire sounds like the perfect ending to a date to me. Call 'em up." Day smirked.

"That's why I'm fuckin' marrying you." God winked and floored it down interstate eighty-five.

Tech

He didn't ever remember coming so hard. Spraying his seed all over their chests and his throat. He'd known Steele would be amazing, but he had to admit he was shocked. He'd prayed Steele wouldn't get inside him, thrust too hard too fast, and be done before Tech had a chance to get off. Unfortunately, he'd had more than a few guys like that after having high hopes. But he should've known better. They'd gone about it the right way this time. Gaining a mental connection before conquering the physical. His body was still humming while he washed Steele's muscular back under the massaging showerhead.

They'd laid there for a long time after, exhausted and satisfied, looking at each other, touching and holding. Steele was amazingly gentle and attentive. He'd wrapped Tech up tightly in his arms, making him feel safe and protected. He didn't mind it. Steele knew he was strong and capable, but right there, right then, he'd needed the man's strength surrounding him. He had made their first experience all about him, and Tech made a note to make it all about Steele next time. And oh yes, there'd be a next time, very soon.

Steele turned around and took the thick rag from Tech's hands before turning him to return the gesture. Tech placed his hands on the tile, resting his forehead against the backs of his hands. Solid but gentle hands massaged his shoulders and back, caring for him like he was precious. The way Steele looked at him, those piercing eyes said so many words that his mouth hadn't spoken.

"You were amazing," Steele whispered in his ear, rubbing the rag between his ass cheeks.

Tech spread his legs, sticking his ass out, soundlessly begging for more.

"God, look at you." Steele smiled against Tech's cheek when he turned his head. "So goddamn hot. You want some more already?"

Tech keened when Steele pressed his groin against him and he felt that thick cock hardening against his slick ass. He was sore, but he might bite his lip and take the sweet pain. Steele was that sexy. "You're turning me into a slut." Tech lowered his eyelids when Steele dropped the rag and spread his ass, nestling his soapy shaft inside, nudging at his hole. "Oh fuck."

"I don't mind that at all. I like the slutty Shawn. I think he's beautiful. And no one gets to see him but me." Steele pressed harder, pushing Tech's chest against the wall.

The man was trying to lay claim so soon. Tech didn't think they were ready to speak of monogamy, but it wasn't like he had an active social life where it'd be a challenge to ignore all the many suitors knocking down his door. Steele had finally put an end to his sexual drought. If he wanted the job full time, Tech was happy to slap a no vacancy sign on his ass.

Steele reached around and took the body wash off the shelf and poured some in his fist. Tech bristled, knowing what was about to happen. Steele closed his thick palm around Tech's hard dick and began to pump him slowly like they had all the time in the world. When Tech felt like he was going to lose his mind, Steele pushed one finger inside him. Tech's body shook; he locked his legs to keep them from buckling and rocked his hips back and forth, taking his pleasure from both ends. He felt Steele bend his finger and rub over his prostate. Tech moaned loudly, pushing his ass back hard, wanting Steele to punch that spot with a little more force. As if he could read his body, Steele pumped his finger inside hard enough for his palm to make slapping sounds against his ass.

Tech leaned back against Steele's chest, dropping his head on his shoulder. "Fuck. Like that. Just like that." Tech reached up to flick and pinch at his sensitive nipples, heightening the sensation tenfold.

"I love it when you do that, *armastaja*. Looks so erotic. Pinch'em harder." Steele's voice had gone throaty and rough against the bend of Tech's neck. "Wanna see you explode for me again."

Steele pumped his ass and his dick in perfect sync. Tech pinched his hard nubs with more force, just like Steele asked while Steele ground his cock against ass, his rhythm faltering as his orgasm built. Tech felt him bite down hard on his shoulder, the feeling of Steele's hot come running down the back of his thigh catapulting his orgasm to the surface. Tech cried out and sprayed the steaming tiles in front of him, Steele trying hard to keep jerking him while he battled through remnants of his own orgasm. Goddamn, it was crazy how turned on they were for each other.

Tech could barely hold himself up, making Steele support both of them. He chuckled when Steele clumsily turned them around and let the water rinse the last of their sex off their spent bodies.

"You're going to be the death of me, *armastaja*."

When he could finally put more than one thought together, Tech reached down and turned off the taps. As he got ready to step out of the shower, he heard Syn's raspy voice in his ear.

"Tech?"

"I'm here," Tech breathed quietly, trying to keep the sound of being well-fucked out of his voice.

"Get Steele to this address fast, we got a situation. We'll meet y'all there."

Steele had a large towel wrapped around his waist, watching carefully for Tech to finish.

"Ten-four," he answered his sergeant then looked back at Steele. "We gotta go, right now."

Steele didn't grumble or bitch, just ran back to Tech's bedroom and hurried to get dressed.

Chapter THIRTY-THREE

Steele

They were dressed in five minutes and outside racing through the parking lot to Tech's SUV. "Here, drive," he tossed the keys to Steele.

He looked at Tech like he was insane. "I don't know how to drive this thing."

Tech jumped in the passenger seat while Steele stood there gawking. "To accelerate use the right pedal, the brake is the pedal in the middle, use the large circular thing to steer in the direction you wanna go."

"Funny," Steele snapped, got in the driver's side and started it up.

Tech already had the laptop open and powered up on the passenger side. He tapped on the keyboard and had an address up on the large screen in the dash. Red and blue lights flashed around them in the dark – Steele had no clue where the emergency vehicle lights were hidden on the outside of the truck – when Tech ordered him to "Go!"

Steele got a feel for the vehicle pretty quickly and it wasn't long before he was speeding down the main street towards the safe house. "What are you doing over there?" Steele asked without taking his eyes off the road. It was midnight so there wasn't a ton of traffic, but enough to remain extra vigilant.

"Have you had to stop at a red light yet?" Tech asked calmly.

"Nope. Wide open."

"That's what I'm doing."

"You're controlling the traffic signals?" Steele gasped.

"For us, and God and Ruxs, too. I told you I could do anything in this truck that I can do in the office. I can see them. We'll get there before they do, though. We're not that far away. God's about five minutes behind us."

"Okay. We need a—"

Tech put up a finger, cutting Steele off. "Yeah, Syn. How many...? How many officers are inside? I'm going to see if I can get a visual... Ten-four."

Tech turned back to Steele. "There're three officers inside, holding them off. Two down outside. God said to make some noise to scare them off." Tech reached over to the dash and pushed two levers, a loud siren began piercing the air as they sped through green lights. They could hear other sirens in the distance, probably 911 responders. "Make sure your earpiece is in."

Steele's eyes widened. "I left it home."

"Oh shit. You are going to get bitched out by God for that." Tech shook his head, his eyes still on the computer screen. "I don't have enough time to get into the surrounding buildings' surveillance cameras but I can get street cameras to see if I spot them running away." Tech's fingers kept flying over the keyboard and he yelled out, "I found them. They're on the run, God. Two of them, I lost the street cam when they turned southbound on 12th Street NE. We're coming in the north end. If you're coming in south we should be able to block them in."

Steele jerked to a stop, honking the horn like crazy. There were people all over and a traffic jam at the intersection of 12th and Piedmont. Some type of concert letting out at a bar. "Shit! Move! Move!" Steele yelled, laying on the horn. It was just too much commotion.

"They should be coming up that alley over there at any point." Tech pointed. "We can't lose them, God's two to three minutes off."

Tech spoke into the earpiece again, telling God their situation while Steele tried to get through the crowd. Next thing Steele knew, Tech jumped out of the truck and took off through the crowd, his long legs eating up the concrete. He ran like a goddamn gazelle. *Jesus.* Steele couldn't get through, but he couldn't let Tech run up on two armed suspects alone.

Steele jumped out and took off in the direction Tech had run, his heart beating a mile a minute while he pushed startled people out of his way. He remembered 12[th,] so he looked up at the next block, wondering if Tech cut through the buildings or if he went around the back. *Shit*. Now he understood why they had to keep the earpieces in. If he called Tech's cell, he certainly wouldn't answer, and there was no time to call God, he had to keep running. The sirens got louder and he knew the others were avoiding the crowd Tech had alerted them to, instead approaching from 10th Street.

Tech

God was bellowing in Tech's ear to hold off, but he ignored it and kept moving. Why, he had no clue, maybe because he was finally in the field and this was his chance. He knew where the perpetrators were, and if they waited for backup, they could lose them.

He jumped a low fence, ran through some bushes, and saw them running behind the fitness center at 11th and Piedmont. A wave of nerves hit Tech over being completely alone with two full-grown men running towards him. *Shit, shit, shit.* "Behind the fitness center," he blurted his location and kept running towards the guys. They couldn't know he was police, especially dressed as he was – in a long-sleeve gray t-shirt and a blue and black Argyle sweater vest. Lights lit up the alley as a vehicle came up behind him, giving him the light he needed and blinding the shooters. He hoped it was God or Steele and not an accomplice. Either way, he couldn't look back and couldn't second-guess. He'd been training for this, he knew what to do with any sized opponent, he needed to trust himself and his abilities.

Running at a break-neck speed, Tech locked his fist and bent his arm at the perfect angle. Using his momentum, he sidestepped at the last second and threw his arm up to catch the first guy in a devastating clothesline, knocking him to the ground. Before he could do anything else, the second guy was on him, slamming into his midsection, trying to mow him over. The man's weight was powerful and he wasn't afraid to use it. Tech dug his heels in and bowed over the man's shoulder as he was shoved back against the dumpsters, but he held tight, refusing to go down. The sirens were deafening behind him, but Tech could hear the man in his grasp growling with anger. Tech brought his knee up and crashed it into the larger man's midsection. He knew it wouldn't be enough. The guy was thick, maybe six one or six two and full of muscle. Like the kind you got from pumping iron in the prison yard. Damn, why'd he pick this big sonofabitch to showcase his skills on? His back was to the brick wall, trapped by this wild animal. Fighting not to let fear cloud his training, Tech ducked a wild punch that he knew was coming, balled his right fist and used his entire right side to put as much force into the blow as he could, striking the man in his ribs. The hit was good, but still not enough. Another right hook came at his face – a hit that would've rung his bell – but Tech shot his left forearm up and blocked it while he reached with his other, grabbing at a beer bottle in the trashcan next to him. He reared to the side and slammed the thick end of the bottle directly over the bridge of the man's nose, hitting him where he knew it'd cause the most damage. Thick shards of tinted glass shattered around them as the man clutched his nose, stumbling back in pain. His eyes shut tight, blood flooding his palms. The first guy Tech hooked was back on his feet, looking up and down the alley, trying to figure out which was the best way to run when he was tackled by a man flying through the air. Tech blinked, recognizing Steele's jacket as they rolled several feet from where he stood. Busted nose took off dazedly in the other direction but ran right into another fist to the face. Ruxs' punch had to have permanently rearranged the guy's nose. If it didn't, Green slamming him to the ground face first certainly did.

Steele already had his guy under control, but Syn and God assisted him, anyway. That's when it finally hit Tech what he'd just done. His chest was heaving hard and fast and his stomach felt like it'd been hit with a two-by-four from that huge bastard slamming his shoulder into his solar plexus. Still, Tech stood up tall. Day was in front of him, a look of concern on his lieutenant's face while he looked Tech up and down. As soon as Day realized he was alright, there was that shit eating grin of his.

"God is going to kill you, but holy shit. I don't know where that came from, Tech… but… but, holy shit. When Syn said you wanted to go in the field, God and I were hesitant. But you knocked that guy on his ass and then went right for the next one without missing a step. You looked like one of my Enforcers out there, Tech." Day smiled, clamping Tech on his shoulder and pulling him away from the trash. "I can't save you from the beating you and Steele got coming, bro. But, good job, Tech. Damn good job."

Tech didn't look directly at God as they watched the uniformed officers Mirandize their suspects and load them into squad cars. The cool night air did nothing to quench the heated glare his boss was firing at him. He knew he was going to get it when they all got back to the office, but he'd take it. The compliment Day just gave him was worth any wrath God leveled on him. Tech had waited years for a compliment like that and he didn't think anything could ruin it. What a way to end a date.

"You two must've fucked each other's brains out because I've never seen either of you act this goddamn stupid!" God fumed at them. His green eyes were bright and blazing down at them while Tech and Steele sat side-by-side at the large conference table. Their boss paced angrily in front of them, Day sitting on the edge of the table looking sad for them, but not daring to interrupt God's tirade, as Syn sat in the chair on the other side, his hands steepled in front of him.

"What the fuck were you thinking?!"

"We hit traffic. I knew you were still a mile and a half away. I didn't want to—"

"I ORDERED YOU TO STAND DOWN!" God's powerful voice boomed over top of him, causing him to flinch hard and clench his hands tightly under the table. He'd seen God angry before, but he'd always watched from a distance, never having had his fury directed at him… it sucked, to say the very least, it was a monumental embarrassment at most, as officers in the bullpen peered

231

inside to see who was catching hell this time. Tech deserved his lieutenant's rage; he'd disobeyed an order, end of point.

"Those men were armed and dangerous! I do not allow any member of my team to act recklessly, no matter the circumstance!" God looked at Steele. "Steele, I don't understand why you didn't advise him of the risk before he took off on his own. Do you fully understand the severity of this act? He was on his own! WITH NO BACKUP! The only reason those men didn't draw their weapons and open fire was because they didn't recognize him as a police officer. Which is another fuck up to add to the pile… he never once identified himself before he started kicking ass. These types of mistakes can't happen!"

Steele rubbed his hand across his forehead, he didn't look stressed, he looked disappointed in Tech, and it made him feel like an ass that he'd gotten Steele in hot water all because he wanted to prove something. If Steele had tried to advise him, it fell on deaf ears because he was out of that truck so fast, his mind could hardly keep up with his legs. Tech spoke up before Steele could. "He did try to warn me. I was out of the truck before he even—"

"I'm not talking to you anymore!" God hollered. "I said, Steele. Is that your name, huh? Do you think I want to hear anything else you have to say?!"

"No, sir," Tech mumbled.

"I should suspend you both. How can I trust you in the field, Tech, if you can't follow commands? Going off half-cocked will get you or a member of the team killed! I won't take that risk."

"He didn't go off—"

"SHUT UP, STEELE!" God exploded, his voice a deeper bass than Tech had ever heard. Dominant enough to make Steele snap his mouth closed so fast his teeth clicked. "We couldn't connect with your ass the entire time because you didn't have your earpiece. So, shut. The. Fuck. Up. Don't try to effectively communicate now, it's too late!"

"It won't happen again, sir," Steele replied, not making an excuse for his own mess up, the Marine in him shining through.

232

"You better damn well hope it doesn't! This is both of your one and final warning. Next time, you'll be suspended for two weeks without pay, *with* an official write-up for insubordination," God barked, jerking open the door so hard Tech was surprised the glass didn't shatter. God stormed through the bullpen, officers rushing to move out of his way.

Day sighed, dropping into one of the chairs. "I guess that covers the scary part of the discipline."

Tech looked over at Syn. His sergeant had been talking him up, and now he'd made him look like an ass. "Syn, I'm sorry. I don't know... I don't know what I was thinking."

Syn sat up higher. "I know you're sorry. And it's unfortunate God had to come down on you like that your first time out. But technically, *you* weren't supposed to be out, Shawn. God's specific instructions were for you to get *Steele* to the location, he didn't say for *you* to engage, Tech. You scared the shit out of him... all of us. If something had happened to you, he wouldn't recover from that. When we saw you cornered by that guy, God was out of the truck before he even brought it to a stop. He was frantic and out of control, screaming at Ruxs and Green to get to you, but Steele burst through the tree line and was demolishing the guy before God could get to him. We work as a unit. We strategize and plan before we attack, it's how we stay alive. You know this; you've worked with us long enough. Ruxs and Green do dangerous shit, but they're always together to back each other up. You took off and left Steele, knowing he didn't have a way to communicate with you or any of us."

Tech brought his shaking hands up and dropped his face in them. He knew his fair skin was beet red from shame. "I can't believe I did that. I let everyone down."

"No, you didn't. Yeah, you acted like a gung-ho cowboy, but what you did was impress the hell out of us and earn a shot out there in the field with the Enforcers. You showed you could provide technical assistance and be a physical asset on the streets. With that said, you're our new field rookie as soon as you find a replacement for yourself in the office. We'll discuss further details when God has cooled off."

233

Tech looked up with wide eyes, unsure if he'd heard Day right. "Are you serious?"

Day stood up. "Congratulations, Tech. I'm proud of you. You've been working hard and it showed."

Tech stood and let Day embrace him in a strong hug before he gathered his belongings. "I'm going to go downstairs and administer some oxygen to God while he's waiting for Ruxs and Green to finish interrogating the guy you didn't send to the hospital. See you in the morning."

Tech looked at Steele to see a look of extreme pride and relief on his face. He'd obviously been thinking, like Tech had, that'd he'd blown his one shot.

"I hope you have someone in mind to replace you in the office. You'll start shadowing the Enforcers immediately. We got to get you properly trained how to react in every situation. You got the chops, Tech, you just need to know how to reign 'em in, control them, and use them collectively with the rest of us. Promise me, no more caped crusader acts." Syn smirked.

Tech nodded, his throat tight with relief. "I promise, Sarge."

Syn put his coat on over his gun holster and walked towards the door. "I gotta say. I thought I was gonna keel over from shock when I saw you take down that first guy. Un-fucking-believable. I haven't seen a Russian Sickle since my days of watching wrestling in the eighties."

Steele laughed, clasping his hands together. "That was the move to end them all," he agreed with Syn.

"Damn straight." Syn waved a lazy salute and left them alone in the office.

Tech smiled when he felt his chair yanked closer to Steele's and maneuvered so their thighs were intertwined. "How are you? You had a big night."

"Yeah, I guess I did," Tech said softly.

Steele got up and pulled Tech with him. "Let's go. It's after three and we have to be back in the morning. Besides, Ruxs and Green will probably be in interrogation for a while if this guy is slow to sing. I need a ride."

234

Tech wanted to beg Steele to come home with him, he didn't want to be alone. He was right, it had been an extremely eventful night and his body was exhausted, his mind restless. If he could curl himself up against Steele's warmth, he might actually get a little sleep. But it was their first date and their first time being intimate; he didn't want to appear clingy.

"Stop me by Ruxs' so I can grab a change of clothes since it's on the way, and you won't have to bring me by there in the morning," Steele said matter-of-factly.

Tech hid his smile while they walked through the parking lot. He was thankful to have the decision of asking Steele to stay the night out of his hands. He wasn't ready to leave his company yet.

Chapter THIRTY-FOUR

Steele

Their hands still clasped together, Tech let them into his home, and they walked inside for the second time that night with one word that started with S on both their minds... and this time it wasn't sex. It was sleep... well, two words... shower and sleep. If they were lucky, they'd get a good three hours. Steele put his weapon under one of Tech's pillows while Tech put his in his nightstand. He followed Tech into the bathroom while he turned the nozzles on. He undressed quickly and waited for Tech to finish. When Tech reached his arms up and pulled off his shirt, he heard the sharp intake of breath and the grunt of pain.

Steele was in front of him in a heartbeat, looking for the damage. The pain coming from the action of lifting his arms, he'd say it was Tech's midsection or ribs. "Where are you hurt?"

"I'm not hurt," Tech bit back.

"Don't do that. It's not necessary. Did one of them get a hit in on you?"

"No. He charged me. It just knocked the breath out of me, that's all." Tech turned to step into the shower and Steele let him since he'd be following right behind him, anyway.

He stayed behind Tech, letting the large showerhead relieve some of the strain of the fight. A street fight was rough. Once the adrenaline wore off, your body was quick to take notice and remind you of every hit you'd received and thrown. He wrapped his arms around him from behind and it wasn't long before Tech sagged back against him. Steele kissed him gently on the back of his neck, feeling Tech's wound-up body tremor against him. He needed to breathe and calm down. "Relax. It's okay. Breathe, Shawn."

"Oh god," Tech gasped, his chest rising and falling erratically under Steele's hands. "Oh no."

"Don't fight it. Let it go."

Tech spun around, wrapped his arms around Steele's neck and pulled him into him just before the wave of tears hit him hard. Steele held him as tight as he could, knowing exactly what Tech was feeling. He'd experienced his first taste of action and his body had flooded with excessive amounts of hormones, with adrenaline and cortisol. But when the mind realizes the danger has passed and the fight or flight response dissipates, then the psychological reaction appears… tears.

"Edwin," Tech cried to him.

"It's okay, just let it happen," Steele whispered, rubbing his hands up and down Tech's back. "You'll feel better after."

"Oh my god. I'm crying like a damn pussy," Tech said between hiccups.

Steele couldn't help but chuckle. He slicked Tech's hair back and buried his lips just beneath his ear. "You know, as smart as you are, how do you not know what your body is going through right now?"

"What?" Tech asked, easing back to look in Steele's face, his body flushed from the rush of stress tears, not the steam from the hot shower.

"Come on, that's enough rinsing. Let's get in bed."

Tech tried to hide his face while he dried off. Steele took his hand and guided him back to the bedroom, the comforter still wrinkled and half hanging off the bed from earlier. Steel pulled back the heavy blanket and the sheet, helping Tech get settled underneath before he slid in behind him, pulling him into his chest.

It was dark in the room, quiet except for Tech's occasional sniffs. "I was in Nahdah, Oman, the first time I fired my rifle at an enemy. We were doing a transport with a couple commanders that had to be escorted to a base in Yemen. We'd quadruple-checked the intel and then double-checked it again. Though we were always safe, I'd been itching for a fight ever since I'd enlisted. I was trained… ready. But it's not until you're in the thick of it that you realize your

238

body is never geared for a fight. It acts on instinct. Sure, you can move fast and dodge hits, but the mind is always screaming to survive and it floods your body with what it needs to do just that.

"When we got out of there with our lives, leaving dead men scattered along the deserted road, we got the commanders into the base, and we headed to the nearest empty corner and cried like babies all over each other."

Tech turned in his arms to face him, a slight frown line between his eyes. "Why? Were you scared? Did you feel bad for killing them?"

"No. None of us felt bad. It was them or us. And the reaction is the body's way of bringing you down. Technically, they're called florid tears, infused with endorphins, charged with a kind of calm down cocktail. That's why I was telling you to let it happen, not fight it. It literally has nothing to do with being a wimp or a pussy. Your amazing brain sent those tears to help blunt the situation and bring you down. We used to call it the battle cry. Whenever it happened to any of us, I just held on to my brother or they held me until it passed. We'd rumble a gruff, 'Thanks, Jar' and move on." Steele grinned, thinking back on it.

"Wow." Tech stared at him, those beautiful eyes pulling at Steele's heart every time. "I was trying to let the water calm me, but I felt myself getting more and more wound up."

Steele kissed Tech's pouty lips. "The more you fight it, the harder you'll cry. I bet you feel better now, don't you?"

Tech waited a few seconds before looking back at him. "Yeah, I think I do."

"Good." Steele pulled Tech's long leg up on his hip and sealed their pelvises together, fitting them together like an erotic jigsaw puzzle. He kissed Tech on his forehead and closed his eyes, sleep claiming them both in a matter of minutes.

Chapter THIRTY-FIVE

Day

It'd been several weeks and he and God were pulling all-nighters trying to tamp down the shit storm that had become their – now delayed – trial after someone tried to knock off their primary witnesses in the case they'd worked on for seven months last year. They'd gotten the dickheads – well, Tech had – that were hired to take the witnesses out, but the DA had to work fast and get the case transferred to another jurisdiction, somewhere out of the powerful kingpin's reach, before he got that close again. More and more thugs were popping up, trying to find their witnesses, hitting old safe houses. They were getting too close. God and Day didn't know who was on the inside helping them, but it had to be someone with access to their databases. That was for the cyber crimes department to handle, all God was focused on was keeping his star witnesses safe. Unfortunately, this wasn't a headache they needed right now, with their wedding only a couple weeks away.

The case was a slam-dunk on the narcotics distribution, but they had two witnesses to testify to six or seven murders, as well. They wanted this guy away for life, not just fifteen to twenty. Of course, the kingpin's lawyer was fighting the motion for a change of venue.

Day walked back into the office with his seventh cup of steaming black coffee in his hand. Their team should be filing in shortly, except Ruxs and Green, they'd been interrogating all night – more like intimidating – their latest arrest, so they probably wouldn't be in until later.

He pushed through the doors and saw God leaning back in his chair, his mouth hanging open, asleep. Day was glad no one else was there to see it. He set his cup down on his desk, eyeing God's wide lap, wishing he could sit down on it and relieve some of his own stress. Instead, he walked over and cupped God's cheek, the coarse brownish-blond hairs scraping his palm. God cracked one green eye open, looking up at him. When he opened both of them, Day saw the redness from exhaustion. "You've got to get some sleep or you'll be useless. You had about three hours the night before last. You can't function like this, you know it's dangerous."

"I know. Let's wait for the DA to call with the judge's decision and see what it'll mean for our case. Then we'll break for a bit and come back." God scrubbed his eyes and sat back up just as Syn came through the door.

"We know anything yet?" Syn said as his good morning.

"No. You know judges don't rush for anyone. We should know by nine or nine thirty today, if defense counsel doesn't try to get another continuance," Day answered, checking his watch for the fifth time. At seven thirty, Tech and Steele came walking into the office, looking a lot more rested than the lieutenants. Tech in camel-colored jeans and a soft-looking sweater, like it came from one of those popular college student stores, Abercrombie or American Eagle; his black 9mm on his hip looking like an out-of-place accessory. Steele wore a black long-john that had a few tattered holes at the bottom and a pair of low-riding jeans. "You two look happy this morning."

Tech shrugged but failed to hide his bashful smile or faint blush. He was obviously enjoying his new responsibilities and being out in the field. God still didn't let him go on the rides that could potentially become dangerous – like last night's – but he'd gained a lot of knowledge in a short period of time and there'd been no more mishaps.

Tech sat at his desk and powered on his systems. Steele didn't even try to act like he wasn't dick-whipped already as he stuck close to Tech, standing over him while he got ready to start his day.

Day shook his head, looking between the two of them. The start of a new romance. He was happy for Tech, he was. Day noticed a lot, and he hadn't missed the longing in Tech over the years to have a partner, someone to take his mind off the day-to-day rigors of the job.

"Where are Ruxs and Green?" Tech asked.

"They'll be back later. As soon as we get some answers, we'll be gone too, but everyone be here at one for a meeting. It's more than likely God, Syn and I will have to leave the jurisdiction for this case, so make sure whatever you got on your calendar for today is wrapped up by then." Tech and Steele both nodded, still unable to wipe the cheesy grins from their faces.

"Good lord," God grumbled, waking up his monitor like he wanted to look at anything but them.

Steele

How was he supposed to keep his hands off of Tech for the entire day? Their morning was nice, no sex, just the domestic experience of dressing for work together, eating a light breakfast, and a slow, lingering kiss to last them through the day before commuting to the precinct together. Steele ended up staying at Tech's at least four nights a week, which still wasn't enough for him. He liked what they had, what they were building. Nights of dinner and talking, movies, video games – which he sucked at, but didn't mind losing – and long, steamy nights in bed. Steele wasn't sure if Tech was feeling the same way, but he loved the whole idea of having a life with one man, sharing everything. He'd watched Ruxs and Green doing it and had wondered in the back of his mind the entire time if that'd ever be him.

"Hey."

Steele's thoughts slammed to a halt when he heard Tech's voice beside him. "Yeah."

"Get to your desk; I'm going to load up your map quiz." Tech grinned.

Steele rubbed his hand over the short strands on his head. "Now?"

"Yes, now. What else are you doing, besides sitting there daydreaming?"

"That's what I was thinking." Day pffted from his own desk, throwing Steele an irritated look.

It was quiet in the office while they waited for answers. God wasn't going to put them on the streets to dig into any new cases until he knew what the rest of their month was looking like.

"Fine." Steele sat at his desk and turned on his computer.

"Okay, it's in your email." Tech looked over his shoulder. "And cover up the map. No cheating."

"I don't need to cheat. I got this."

"It's not easy. This isn't a ninth grade geography quiz."

"I've been staring at this map for two-and-a-half months. Bring it."

"No one says bring it anymore." Tech chuckled, shooting a hot, pointed look at him.

"I do, and you like it. You like whatever I say." Steele swiveled around, staring back.

"Okay, it's up. It's timed, too. Did I forget to mention that?" Tech smiled – that wicked one that made Steele's balls throb.

"Bring it," Steele whispered. "You wanna place a bet that I won't miss a single question?"

"Hmm," Tech all but purred. "What d'ya have in mind?"

"If I lose, I'll give you a good, hard—"

"Shut up and just take the goddamn quiz!" God yelled, cutting off their sexy banter.

"I was only going to say massage." Steele and Tech burst with laughter, having been in their own little teasing world, forgetting they weren't alone. Steele turned around, loaded up the quiz and began knocking out the questions. He wondered how long it took Tech to create; it was like something out of the SAT test. Tech had included everything from rivers and lakes to highways and major landmarks, not forgetting every government office, hospital, and emergency department. He held in his groan when he saw he was on number ten out of one hundred and two. *Damn, Atlanta ain't even that big.* He looked up briefly when Ruxs and Green came in making a shit load of noise about Tech's skills on the streets lately.

Steele kept his focus on his test clock while also keeping one ear peeled as Tech spoke on how he felt about chasing down those shooters a few weeks ago. It was still the hottest topic in the office.

Tech was proud of himself and Steele loved that. Although he'd made mistakes, he still got those guys and saved the team who knew how many man-hunting hours.

Ruxs and Green sat down, both with wet hair like they'd just finished showering together and came to work.

"Steele, you must got some creatine muscle powder in your dick, man. You guys went on one date, next thing we know, Tech comes back putting motherfuckers down!" Ruxs' strong voice was loud in the office and had all of them rolling with laughter; being the usual rowdy, crass bunch that they were.

Each of them went through their experiences of that night... again... Tech beaming while he added his rendition and how he felt being on the streets now. Syn even joked how he got his ass reamed – probably for the second time that night – by God when he got back to the office.

Steele cringed, looking up briefly, flicking Syn off for his crude comment, only to get the same gesture in return.

"Steele's new name is dynamite dick from here on." Day laughed, his feet propped up on his desk. Ruxs' and Green's deep, carrying laughter could probably be heard clear across the precinct.

Steele groaned loudly, dropping his head into his hands for a brief second before looking back to his monitor. He still had a hard time keeping in his laughter, especially when he could hear Tech behind him laughing hysterically.

"You can call him that your-fucking-self, because I'm not," God added, looking fatigued while he reclined with his hands linked behind his head.

Steele guessed his personal life would no longer be personal around these guys. Everyone was in everyone else's business. Tech never once tried to conceal the fact they'd had sex that first night, so he didn't either. Day, Ruxs, and Green were still tossing around "dick" names when a uniformed officer came through the doors. Steele eyed him for a second, figuring he was a friend of someone's in the office.

"Oh, this morning just got a lot more entertaining," God murmured, looking at Steele with mischief glittering in his tired eyes.

Steele went back to concentrating until he heard the man's smooth voice greet Tech in an entirely different way than he had the others.

"Good morning, Shawn."

"Hey, Vasquez. How's it going?" Tech's voice was normal, the tone he used when he spoke to anyone… except for Steele.

"I've told you to call me Ramon." The guy sounded like he was trying to infuse a little more bass and sensuality in his voice, making the hairs on Steele's neck rise. The stocky man pulled a chair from the conference table and pushed it right up to Tech's desk. Getting nice and comfortable. Steele kept his cool, not wanting to make any assumptions. But one thing he'd never been good with was encroaching. What was his was his.

"It's a habit. So used to last names. How you been, Ramon? Just getting off shift?" Tech asked.

"No, actually I had to switch from nights for a few weeks. So I missed all the excitement. Everyone's talking about you being out with Ruxs and Green now. That's nuts. I've never known you to be out in the field with these crazies," Vasquez said in a slight Hispanic accent, his tone still laced with sex and a now a hint of amazement. "I wanted to congratulate you and of course, check to see that you're alright."

"Of course, I am. Took a shoulder to the gut that first time, but nothing to complain about." Tech sounded a little offended by the guy's statement. Steele hadn't turned to intrude on the conversation and he wouldn't unless he had to.

"Maybe I should check you out, just to be sure. You wanna go up to the med station and I can get a closer look?" Vasquez said suggestively, and Steele had heard enough.

"Hey! I'm trying to take a goddamn quiz, here," Steele blurted out before he could think of something a little more intimidating.

Steele heard Day spray his coffee all over his desk and part of God's while he hacked and coughed through his laughter. Even God had turned away, his big shoulders shaking with his deep chuckling. Ruxs and Green didn't even try to hold theirs in.

246

"Maybe you should go finish it in study hall, Steele, where it's a little quieter." Syn made fun of him.

Steele ignored the look of shock on the officer's face and cast his annoyed glare on Tech. He didn't look amused at all; in fact, he looked a little pissed. "Sit down and finish, Steele. Time is ticking."

"Yeah, you don't want afterschool detention," Day quipped, still stirring up laughter from the team.

"I must've missed something." Vasquez's nervous laughter was met with more heat from Steele. The officer stood and held his hand out to him. "Ramon Vasquez. You're the new member, right? I saw you sparring with God a while back. Nice. I didn't hear God and Day were recruiting. Maybe I'll apply again – for the fifth time."

Steele gripped his hand and applied enough pressure to make the man wince and jerk his hand back. Tech narrowed his eyes at Steele while Vasquez shook out his hand. "That's some grip you got."

Steele didn't say a word, just sat and turned back to his monitor.

"I'll get out of you guys' way. Tech, I wanted to see if you felt like hanging out this weekend. I know you said you were busy with work before, but I'm nothing if not persistent. Trust me… I'll just keep coming back," Vasquez said, adding a slight stroke of his thumb over Tech's shoulder blades.

Steele shot up out of his seat, but somehow Syn was there, clamping a firm grip on his shoulder and pushing him back down in his chair. "Not in here," he hissed and kept walking past. Was the guy psychic? Steele wondered how often this guy come in here and poached Tech for a date. It seemed his entire team was waiting for Steele's reaction as soon as the pretty cop with perfect light brown skin and manscaped eyebrows walked through the door.

"Vasquez if you wanna flirt, do it in someone else's department." God finally said something, ten minutes too late for Steele's liking.

The officer stood and pushed the chair back to the table, his thick biceps bulging under the tight, navy blue polyester shirt. Why did all those guys have to choose their uniforms two sizes too small? So they look bigger. He watched Vasquez's tight ass make its way back to the door. He turned and looked in their direction. "There're donuts in the breakroom, Tech."

"Get out," God said drily.

After the smooth bastard had been gone for five minutes, Steele was still gritting his teeth, his jaw clenched tight with the urge to pull Tech away and drill him. Was he considering going out with that guy? They hadn't defined what was between them yet, but that was trivial to Steele. They'd been all over each other for several weeks, that had to mean they were dating but did Tech wanna still be free to see other people? The thought made Steele want to chase after that guy and offer him a sparring match. He'd talk to Tech soon about this... today, actually. Steele was the one in Tech's bed almost every night. He'd say whatever he damn well felt like saying.

About thirty minutes later the phone rang and Tech notified the bosses that they needed to get over to the DA's office.

"After we finish there we're going home for a few hours. Remember, meeting at one," God reminded them on his way out the door with Day and Syn.

Steele was glad he only had seventeen questions left. He hurried through them, the last few concentrating on the division lines of the precinct zones. When he finished he clicked submit and sent it back to Tech. He turned off his computer and got Ruxs and Green's attention. With his back to Tech, he motioned for them to leave him alone with Tech for a while.

Green nodded once and got up with Ruxs doing the same. "Hey Tech, we're gonna go up the street and grab some breakfast sandwiches, you want one?"

Tech turned, his eyes darkening when he looked at Steele. "Sure. Ham and cheese croissant."

"Steele, the usual?"

"Yeah. Plain bagel with French onion cream cheese."

"Got it. Be back in a few."

As soon as they were gone, Steele got up and stood behind Tech.

"They just got here an hour ago. Green cooks breakfast every morning. I'm pretty sure they're not hungry already. So why'd you send them away?" Tech asked, finally turning to face him.

"I need to talk to you in private." Steele tried to keep the strain out of his voice.

"We are in private."

"Not here, in there." Steele nodded his head towards the equipment room.

Tech got up and moved quickly to the room, accessing it with a few taps to the keypad. As soon as they got inside, Steele was in Tech's face before he could walk over to the light switch. "Who was he?"

"He's an officer who was once a paramedic. He's come over and checked out a couple bumps and bruises on Ruxs and Green in the past. He wants on the team, so I'm sure he was just trying to be nice," Tech said nonchalantly.

"Oh, he was being real nice," Steele uttered sternly.

Tech hopped up on the table, watching Steele with an amused expression. "You're jealous? After what we've been doing, do you think I'm going to go out with him? Is that why you're snapping and snarling like someone pissed in your cornflakes? Is that why you tried to break every metacarpal bone in his hand? You were acting like an idiot."

"I didn't hear you say no to his request."

"You didn't hear me say yes, either."

"I don't share." Steele stood between Tech's legs and yanked him to the edge of the table.

"I don't want you to, Steele. I'm just not the best with rejecting. He asks me out every blue moon and I say I'm busy. It's nicer than saying no, I'm sorry, I don't feel any chemistry between us."

"Figure out a way. The next time he wants to be *persistent*, you can simply tell him you're taken."

Tech draped his arms over Steele's shoulders, linking his fingers behind his head. "Am I?"

"Yes," Steele whispered, then closed his mouth over Tech's peach lips, sucking them gently before the kiss turned aggressive.

Steele pulled away, pulling in a sharp intake of air. "You knew what you were doing. You wanted to see me get pissed, didn't you?"

Tech smiled a cheeky grin and shrugged noncommittally. Steele pushed Tech back on the table and grabbed both wrists, pinning them above his head. He moved too fast for Tech to even realize what he was doing. Before the slender man knew it, his sweater was pushed up under his chin and Steele had latched his mouth over his left nipple and sucked it hard into his mouth. Tech yelled out in shock and pleasure.

Steele was going to show Tech what he did when he was toyed with and coaxed into a reaction. Tech's legs were around Steele's waist, he reached under Tech's back and hooked his shoulder, slamming him into his pelvis while he simulated fucking him hard, slamming his hard dick into him over and over while he sucked as hard as he could, wanting a dark red and purple mark over Tech's sensitive nipple. He knew the feeling was explosive, mixed with a bite of pain. Tech's cry was loud as he bucked and kicked under Steele's assault. He could yell as loud as he wanted, no one was there to hear him. Steele pulled and thrust aggressively between Tech's spread legs, punishing him in the perfect way. No matter how high his back bowed or how he tried to pull his hands free, Tech couldn't get away and his struggles only made Steele thrust harder.

When he was satisfied Tech's nipple couldn't take any more abuse and would be tender for hours and marked even longer, he pulled his mouth off with a loud pop. Tech moaned when Steele laved it lovingly, an apology to the sensitive flesh that was now swollen and dark purple.

"Oh god. I can't believe you did that. Motherfucker," Tech groaned, sitting up, staring at the angry mark. He glared at Steele and gingerly pulled his sweater back over his chest. "Oww."

"Now you think about that mark when he comes back later for his answer. Or next time I'll put one where he'll be able to see it." Steele grabbed the back of Tech's neck and surged forward, clamping his mouth over his, dominating him, before Tech jerked back. Steele gave him a look that said, "Don't make me have to mark you again."

Chapter THIRTY-SIX

God

"We won't start anything new right now. We'll provide assistance to other departments as needed until we finish with the case. It's in Spartanburg the beginning of next year, so the witnesses will be transported tomorrow morning and I've asked Hart and his team to assist with transport, that way I know the job will be done right. I'm not taking any more chances. These witnesses are trusting us to keep them safe and we dropped the ball."

"Do you want us to shotgun with Hart's team?" Ruxs asked.

"No. Hart's got it. So, with the trial postponed, that gives us another couple weeks of down time. And I think we all can use it. Besides, Leo and I have a few final things to organize." God couldn't hide his smile. With everything worked out for their wedding, he was thrumming with excitement. Now that they had answers about their schedule, God was booking their flight to Aruba. "We're going to do casework, reviewing—"

"Aw. Come on." Ruxs and Green were the first to complain – like always. None of them liked the mundane tedium of going through files. It was boring as hell. But God didn't have time for whining and bitching. He stood there staring at the guys, the expression of pure exasperation on his face finally making them close their traps.

"Who's that?" Steele nodded towards the glass wall, looking out of their department.

"Wow!" Tech's eye's widened, sitting up higher in his chair.

"Damn," Syn whispered.

Day's smile spread across his face and God already didn't like anything about was getting ready to happen. The entire bullpen was on their feet, staring and moving towards the trio of men walking

251

directly towards their department. God wished he'd stayed home in bed with his fiancé so they wouldn't've been here for this surprise visit.

"You don't recognize him?" Tech asked in awe, leaning into Steele's shoulder.

"No. Why? Should I?" Steele frowned, looking around at everyone, but no one could take their eyes off the ridiculously handsome men entering their office. With them came an air of confidence and extreme wealth.

"Hey. No superstars allowed." Day smiled and damn near jogged over and threw his arms around the man in the middle, holding him tight to him as the guy whispered something in Day's ear that had him throwing his head back and laughing affectionately.

His classy trench coat was matched perfectly to his two-tone shawl collar shirt. It was masculine and the logo was one God didn't recognize, probably too posh to be found where he shopped. His slacks looked custom made for him and his shoes looked Italian. The guy finally let Day go, his billion-dollar smile brighter than any light in their office. Day moved over and hugged the tallest one, looking him up and down like he liked what he saw. Who fucking wouldn't? He wore dark slacks and a cream sweater with a thick gold herringbone decorating his neck. God kept his mouth pressed tightly together, not wanting to do anything that would make Day upset. The third guy was drool worthy. He'd seen him more than once, modeling in a culinary magazine or charming the pants off the female chefs on television. A sleek body encased in anther tailor-fitted blazer and matching slacks. The man oozed style and perfection, his light hazel eyes scanning the room, charismatic personality radiating from him, causing half of God's men to melt in their fucking chairs just looking at him. The cool man held out his arms, the right side of his mouth curving up into a sexy grin while he encouraged Day to step into his embrace. Day hugged him more intimately than he hugged the others like the man was too beautiful to grab and manhandle.

"What the hell are you doing here?" Day finally asked, moving back to stand in front of the one in the middle. "Let me introduce you to everyone, first. I don't think you've met the other guys."

"No, I haven't," he said, too smoothly for God's liking and he barely stopped his eyes from rolling to the heavens.

Day began pointing out everyone. "You remember Syn, Ruxs, Green, and Tech. This is our newest member, Edwin Steele. Michaels is on leave. And, I know you remember Ro, but he was injured so he's home soaking up a lot of unnecessary pampering." Day clasped his hand on the man's broad shoulder. "Everyone, this is my best friend and frat brother, Prescott Vaughan, and beside him are his partners, that's Dr. Edward Rickson, and this stunning man beside him is Blair McKenzie."

"Being sex on a stick must be a job qualification to join your team, Leonidis. Looking around this table at all these strapping men has me considering a change in careers," Blair said in a southern drawl that had each of the guys gushing at him and sticking their chests out a little further.

God looked at his guys, giving each of them a stare of disdain, which none of them saw because they were too busy gawking.

The trio made their way around the table shaking everyone's hand, Prescott moving around until he was in front of God. He didn't dare try to hug him, there was no use pretending they liked each other. God didn't like the idea that Pres was the one that got away from Day. His fiancé had been in love with Pres the entire time they were in college. Had fooled around all four years, but Pres wasn't ready to admit he was gay back then. By the time he was, Pres came back for Day, but he was with God. Irrespective of how long ago it was, God never shook the feeling that Pres was the one Day really wanted.

The man was everything God wasn't. Cultured, educated, rich and crazy famous. And nothing short of a walking miracle in the eyes of the public. He'd won countless culinary awards in his twenties, and then lost his sight in a terrible car accident, forcing him to learn how to be a chef while blind. Somehow, with that handicap, he managed to grow a successful food critiquing business that was known around the world and sought out by every chef that wanted to make a name for themselves. Pres came out late and acquired not one, but two gorgeous men to stand by him and keep him warm at

253

night. Then, as if touched by an angel, his sight reappeared. Making him a culinary motivational superstar. He had television cooking shows, hosted reality shows, had so many cookbooks God lost count and restaurants from here to London. And even with those two runway-worthy men at his side, he still looked at Day differently than he looked at anyone, and God couldn't blame him.

"It's been a long time, God. How are you?" Pres asked, shaking his hand. God didn't sneer at the baby softness of the man's hands, like he moisturized every twenty minutes, instead he clasped his hand back.

"I'm good, and you?" God said stiffly.

"It's been going, but I wouldn't say good." Pres' mouth stretched tight like he was uncomfortable, looking anything but camera-ready, and up close, God could see the faint darkness under his sky blue eyes and the worry lines etched in his forehead. Suddenly the smiles faded from Pres' partners' faces and anxiety appeared on theirs as well.

"What's going on?" Day asked, stepping closer. "Why are you in Atlanta?"

"I drove in yesterday. I had a new restaurant to review. The one that opened a couple months ago next to the Botanical Gardens. While I was there, someone tampered with my car… cut the brake line. Then, last night, someone bypassed the alarm, came into our condo and shot at me. Ric was able to disarm him, but he got away. I've been receiving threats at my home in Virginia and at my office, but I thought it was someone who just didn't care for my lifestyle or simply envied my fame. I didn't mean to bring this to your door, Leo. I actually wanted to surprise you when I came into town, but unfortunately, this is no longer a social call. Someone's trying to kill me, Leo. I came to ask you and your team for help."

Day

Day felt his legs try to give when he heard his best friend say that someone was trying to kill him. Day's life without Pres would be dark. There'd be a hole in his heart for a very long time if something

254

happened to him. They talked at least three times a week, sometimes more than once a day. No matter how busy Pres was, he always had time for him. They had no secrets and Pres was a confidant. Day had told him all about God's stalling after his proposal and Day knew all about some vengeful nurse at Ric's hospital that claimed he sexually assaulted her. Being one of Prescott's lovers sometimes came with a negative spotlight. Still, Day knew information the media would never know about Prescott Vaughan. They were privy to every detail of each other's lives. They were brothers. They'd long gotten past the "I wanted you and you didn't want me then you wanted me and I no longer wanted you." A romantic relationship just wasn't meant to be for them, and being with their current partners, they knew why it'd worked out the way it did. Rick and Blair were the perfect balance for Pres' larger than life persona. And God was everything Day needed in a partner. His wild life in law enforcement could only be handled by one man and he was standing next to him. When Pres had come in, his fiancé looked like he'd rather get a root canal than be in Pres' company, but the look of concern God wore the moment Pres said he was in danger touched Day's heart. Even though Pres wasn't God's favorite person, his partner knew what Pres meant to him. Day didn't know why Pres had withheld critical information from him about being harassed, but he was going to get to the bottom of it.

"Pres, sit down. Blair, Ric, come on, have a seat. Tell us what's going on. You can trust these men, I promise you."

"I know, Leo. It's why we came."

Pres sat in the first chair and Ric and Blair sat in the next two, putting Blair right beside Tech. Day watched the tall man lean over and take a generous sniff close to Tech's shoulder.

"Well, hello there. You smell heavenly."

Tech blinked like an owl before he finally thanked him.

"You'll have to forgive me, handsome. I have a bit of a fragrance fetish. You smell like…" Blair inched even closer, his nose practically on Tech's ear. "Clean… the brand. Amber Saffron… no, no, that's Blonde Rose, right?"

"Right," Tech said, sounding fascinated.

"It's one of my favorites. You're a man of good taste, Mr. Tech, but the scent is mixed with something a little spicier. A natural scent, which I'm picking up a little further down." Blair finally leaned away and rubbed his hand down his jacket lapel, returning his attention to Day.

"I see you're still smelling men and making them extremely uncomfortable," God mumbled at Blair.

"Never made you uncomfortable, God," Blair said seductively, raising a brow. "It's okay to be honest."

Day remembered Blair practically crawling up God's body once to smell him at the base of his neck. Stating God's potent, dominating scent was a testament to his strength. God called Blair an out of control sex fiend, which only earned him a disgruntled look from Blair's other lover, Ric. God just couldn't understand how Pres trusted that hot minx, and Day had to agree. He didn't think he could have a lover that flirted with any and everyone he came into contact with. Maybe it was from Blair's days as an escort, where he'd learned how to pull a sensual reaction from whomever he encountered, including their team. Even Steele was awestruck by the man.

Day pulled up another chair beside God's. "Your nose is even sharper than it was a few months ago, Blair. I think that's the last time I saw you."

"Not as good as Pres' nose, but I'm working on it. Being in a room full of strong, good-smelling men is making me—"

"Blair," Ric barked, his deep voice cutting off what his sexy partner was about to say. "Let's stay focused."

Blair didn't look reprimanded; he looked excited at having pulled such a strong reaction from his bigger partner. He brought his loafer up and propped it on his right knee, and let Pres continue with the details.

"Three weeks ago, we came home from a charity benefit to find someone had shoved a threatening note under our door. I put it in a folder and gave it to my manager, just in case anything came of it. It was the first of many. I get two or three a day."

"What do they usually say?" Steele asked.

Day was happy that Steele was here now. He was experienced in personal security and isolated threats. His expertise would be critical for this.

"Just that I'm a deviant, a has-been. In a nutshell, they always go on about a rerun that recently aired or a restaurant I did a write up for. Everything from I'm illiterate to I can't cook. It was all so damn elementary. I concluded it was some deranged fan, but most likely a homophobic, backwater hillbilly who thinks it's his responsibility to harass gay people," Pres gritted out, rolling his eyes at the absurdity in this day and age.

Pres was getting angry and Ric rubbed a large palm over Pres' back, silently encouraging him to keep going.

"Then, we came home from dinner at Blair's restaurant to find that someone had jacked off on a pile of my clothes that they'd dumped out of my dresser."

"You said 'they'," Syn interjected.

"Well, I don't know how many there actually were, or if that event is even connected. But the guy poured bleach on it, so the lab wasn't able to get an identity from it." Pres wiped his hand over his mouth like recounting the act made him sick to his stomach. "We have a state of the art security system and cameras inside and out, but all of it was disabled somehow, and the security company can't figure it out."

Day saw Tech get up and retrieve his laptop and squeeze back in between Blair and Steele. "What's your address, please?"

Blair whispered it to Tech while Pres kept going.

"I have the same system in my Atlanta condo as in my Virginia home. Somehow, this man got in last night. I never even heard him inside my home, Leo. Blair and I were making love. Ric was at the gym. If he hadn't come home when he did." Pres rung his hands together, the fear of someone wanting to hurt him, or heaven forbid, one of his partners, was aging his friend right before his eyes.

"Why didn't you call me earlier?" Day bristled. "This has been going on for weeks, Pres.

"Up until last night, it's been a lot of talk, notes and one act of disgust. I called the police but they—"

"How come the shooting wasn't on the news?" Ruxs interjected.

"My publicist is keeping it quiet for now. Not wanting to flush out any copy cats."

"Smart," Ruxs added.

"I'm sorry, Leo. You have your work here, and I know your job is already so demanding, I didn't want to add to it. And then your wedding's right around the corner. I didn't want to impose." Pres shook his head, frustration all over his face. "I was hoping the special victims unit in our police department could handle the notes, but their delay is frightening. They've put several detectives on the case and I was thankful that they've considered my situation a priority, so I hate to say this, but they move too slowly. I'm sure they are doing all they can, but they've yet to give us any definitive answers."

"Do you know of anyone who'd want to kill you?" Green asked.

"I have no idea. I move around a lot but I live in Virginia. I still have my food critique headquarters here in Atlanta. As you already know, Leo, I've scaled back on doing television and have put most of my attention into the new restaurant in the Town Center in Virginia Beach. But, to answer your question, collectively, I have thousands under my employ. Maybe it's someone who was fired. But I've never fired anyone, personally. Or, like I said, some crazy bigot." Pres sighed and deflated in front of them. "Hell if I know, I've never had anything like this happen. I don't even have bodyguards. I never needed them."

"I recommended he get one, but we hadn't had a chance to interview any good companies, and the guy his manager sent over a couple weeks ago was more concerned with meeting other famous people than protecting Prescott. It was under his watch that someone broke into your office. You didn't mention that," Ric inserted.

"Oh yeah. Someone was in my office. It looked like they just sat at my desk and went through my things. Nothing was stolen and the computer was still locked. But I don't know if that's related."

"Right now, we have to treat everything like it's related," God said. "Any fingerprints from the office?"

"No. I had it cleaned. I just thought someone was wanting to mess with me since nothing was removed." Pres looked a little embarrassed at that admission but he kept going. "I'm more concerned with how someone can get into my security system at our home. Even kill the surveillance to the building."

"Tech, anything yet?" Syn looked over at him.

"Give me a minute," Tech said, his eyes darting all over the screen, his fingers moving so fast it was amazing he was touching only one key at a time.

"I should've come earlier, Leo. But that gunshot, that was… that was enough. I canceled all public appearances for the next couple weeks and came straight here."

"It won't take us two days," God said confidently. No one on his team was shocked by the deadline he threw out.

"Last name Carter. Ring a bell?" Tech asked. "That's the name the IP address is registered with."

"Carter." Pres placed his manicured hands on his forehead like he was scanning his brain for any memory of the name. "No one that works close to me. There could be an employee with that last name."

"I'm looking in your company's HR records and those of all the charities you're on the boards of, and a few Carters are coming up, but none that I think would fit the description of a criminal. Give me a couple minutes." Tech clicked away for another few seconds then said, "It looks like this person who got into your security system did it from an IP registered to a café. It's owned by a Manny Carter, only a few streets away from your condo here in Atlanta. I'm still digging. I doubt the owner is the hacker. Most of the cafés in the ritzier parts of town have the newer computers with built-in cameras. Maybe he's not as smart as he thinks and didn't disable the camera, thinking he covered the address…."

Everyone was quiet while Tech talked them through a hacker's mind. "He didn't disable the camera. Image appearing in three, two, and one. On the big screen." Tech spun around with everyone else, and a clear image of a guy in maybe his early-thirties appeared. He was Caucasian, had a plain black ball cap low on his forehead and his beady eyes constantly scanned back and forth while he worked quickly.

"He was on there for sixteen minutes, which means he's a dabbler. Running his face through the facial recognition software now." Tech tapped his pen on his chin while he waited. "It'll take a while for that, maybe ten to twelve hours. There's a ton of databases to search, not just law enforcement."

"Oh, you are good, cutie pie," Blair said, giving Tech a pleased stare.

"You have no idea," Steele added, his eyes locked on Tech's face. "Oh, you were talking about his computer skills. Sorry."

Tech choked and turned to scowl at Steele. "Be professional," he whispered sternly, then went back to his computer.

Day couldn't imagine working with a better group of guys. They were definitely some characters, but they'd get to the bottom of this bullshit amateur tormenting his best friend and have him arrested in no time.

"Sounds good. Great work, Tech." Day nodded.

"Yes, very nice work, Techy. Looks like I butted in right on time," a slightly British-accented voice added in. The sound came from their interoffice intercom and all of them, including Pres, jumped up to look around the room, expecting someone to walk in... Or appear out of thin air.

Chapter THIRTY-SEVEN

Tech

They probably thought this was the stalker they were hunting, but they couldn't have been more off. This was a friendly, albeit an annoying friendly, who loved to use shock factor. Tech smiled and put his hands up to settle down the team. He knew exactly who the fucker was that hacked into Tech's own system and was communicating with them from wherever the hell he was. He'd recognize that snooty accent anywhere.

"It's alright, guys. I know him, this is—"

Tech was cut off again. "I think you ignored something critical there, detectives. Your famous friend said he'd been receiving threats in Virginia, more personal, intimate attacks on his belongings and office, but when he came to Atlanta was the victim of a completely different form of attack. A deadly one. Who knew you were coming to Atlanta for a few days? How many people did you inform… your manager, secretary, maybe a couple others? Your entire staff wouldn't know of one critique you were coming to do. A fan wouldn't know that, either. Critiques aren't announced, usually, the chef doesn't even know when a reviewer is appearing until he or she is there. So we can ignore the employees and fans for a minute—"

"We? Tech, what the hell is going on?" God growled, cutting the speaker off.

"Hold on, God. Let him keep going," Tech shushed God, only to be given a threatening look, but they had to know the speaker was starting to make sense.

"Thank you," the speaker continued. "The nasty stuff was definitely related, but was merely a decoy, a distraction, you understand. To detour your thoughts from the real culprit… the mastermind. Make it look like this is someone who has a personal vendetta... a weird fan. But a weird fan doesn't typically escalate from petty vandalism to cold-blooded murder. Who knew you were here, Mr. Vaughan?"

Pres looked at Day and when he got the nod to answer, Pres rattled off a few names. His assistant, his driver, Ric's boss, two managers, and his business partner in the critique business. "Except for my driver and Ric's boss, the others are right here in the Atlanta offices."

"Dig deeper, Techy. This organizer isn't an idiot; he's someone with a little clout, aware of confidential comings and goings, with enough money to hire flunkies. So start from the top and work your way to the bottom," the disembodied voice suggested.

"Okay, enough. Who are you?" Syn spoke up.

"I'm your new Tech," the speaker announced.

"Excuse me?" God looked at Tech for answers.

"It wasn't the introduction I was looking for, but he does like to make an entrance. God, Day, this is Lennon Freeman. He's a technology freelancer. Free, this is the team." Tech glanced at a still-pissed-off God and hurried to explain. "You guys only work with the best, so I found him. Syn said to get a replacement, quickly. Free prefers to work behind the scenes. You won't find a better man – skill wise – for the job."

"I haven't agreed to the job, Techy. I'm simply here on a trial basis."

"You got that right. Might be the shortest trial ever," God said loudly.

"Do forgive my intrusion, lieutenant, just wanted to get a feel for you guys. I may be a bit daft but I'm not that bad... really. By the way, sounds like congratulations are in order on taking the vows. I do love weddings."

Tech walked over to his station. "Free, where the hell are you?"

"I'm at the airport. I thought I'd get myself acquainted with your system, Techy, while I waited for you to pick me up. You know you always leave footprints right to you and a gaping backdoor."

"Bullshit," Tech blurted, still scanning his system to see where Free was hacking in from. The guy always was sneaky. "What do you mean, waiting for me?"

"I could always remote-drive your truck here. While I was having a look around your system, I noticed the Tesla autonomous software—"

"Okay, okay, shut up. I'm on my way," Tech rushed to cut his friend off.

"I thought so. See you in twenty." A click resounded and Tech wasn't sure if Free was really gone or not.

Tech turned to look back at his team. They wore mixed expressions, ranging from indifferent to impressed.

"Syn said to find a replacement, and fast. Why would I bring someone in here who'd need a bunch of tutorials and training when I could bring in the man I learned from? He's amazing, as you can see, and he happens to be available. Not only can he hack anything in the *world*." Tech stressed the last word. "But he's also smart as a whip. He was only listening for a few minutes and look at the direction he took us in."

"I was also thinking of who else knew you were in Atlanta," Day said, sitting back down next to Pres.

"See. Free's mind works like that constantly. He'll fit in. He can do the technical part of this job with his eyes closed," Tech told them.

"If he's so brilliant, why isn't he employed?" Syn asked.

"He doesn't have a degree. We were at MIT together, but he left shortly after I did. There was nothing he could be taught there, anyway. He hardly went to class but still aced everything. We were both getting the degrees only to have the paperwork. But neither of us made it through to the end. You know what happened with me, and he kept having family issues."

"Anything, Tech, that would get us in shit for hiring him? He's not wanted by the FBI or some shit like that, is he?" God asked.

"No. He's not a criminal. Moral to a fault. He's brilliant enough to hack a bank and reroute millions into an offshore account, but he'd never do it. He lives in an RV and travels the country installing networks and upgrading software systems."

"I heard a slight accent, is he here legally?" God asked, again being careful.

"He was born here. Yes, he's a citizen. His father was British, his mother's African American. He spent his first ten years in Peterborough before his mother moved them back to the States."

Tech's computer pinged an announcement and some files started downloading. He read through some of them, knowing where they were coming from. He smirked and turned around to look back at Pres. "Did you know your business partner, Adam Carbone, is hundreds of thousands in debt? It looks like Free decided to start digging, too. Beginning at the top. He's still sending information. Looks like Mr. Carbone's been writing substantial checks to bookies associated with illegal gambling sites."

"He's part owner of the business if anything happens to you, it all goes to him, right?" Day looked to Pres for confirmation.

Pres nodded gloomily. "I'm seventy percent owner. I've never drawn up documents to transfer my shares to Ric or Blair. We weren't in a rush to do it, but I will now."

"Sounds like motive to me," Ruxs said. "He might be thinking along the same lines because he attacked you in your home while you were with your partners. In an attempt to take out all of you. If he'd been trying to kill only you, he would've waited until you were alone."

"This is that guy Free doing this?" Day asked.

"Yes. He's using my system, but yes," Tech answered.

"Go get him, Tech," God ordered. "Steele, Ruxs, Green. Ride with him."

Tech pulled up to the curb at Atlanta International, scanning the thin crowd. He inched forward a few more spaces when a shuttle pulled away and put his truck in park. A lot attendant waved them forward, yelling about no stopping, but Steele held his badge out the window. The attendant moved on to the next vehicle, aggressively motioning for cars to keep going.

"Where is he?"

"He knows we're here." Tech was practically bouncing in his seat. He couldn't believe Free was here. He'd missed him. He wasn't sure Free had gotten his encrypted message since he hadn't responded, but here he was. It wasn't easy to contact him; he wasn't on any social media, nor did he use any registered emails. If a company was looking for help with their servers, Free heard about it, researched them, and if they were on the up and up, he contacted them... not the other way around. He preferred to stay off the grid and unfortunately, his caution was warranted.

He knew Free felt like he owed Tech after what he'd done for him before Tech was arrested by the Feds, but he didn't want Free to feel indebted to work for God and Day if he didn't want to. This wasn't a job you could do out of obligation. But he knew Free liked to help people, enjoyed righting wrongs. He was good at it, which was why he'd found the man behind Prescott's threats faster than any of them did. Free had been righting the wrongs done to him and his mother all his life, so he knew how a vicious person thought, making him very skilled at finding them.

"There he his." Tech pointed. He watched his long-time friend emerge from the automatic doors with only a laptop bag on his shoulder, pulling a small black carry-on behind him.

"That's him?" Ruxs gawked.

"You like what you see?" Green stared, too.

"I'm just saying. I wasn't expecting, ya know."

Free didn't look like your usual tech guru; he was striking. Blair's earlier comment about having to look like sex on a stick to work for the team was proving to be an odd coincidence. Free had filled out in all the right places since Tech last saw him, two years ago. He was thick and toned. He'd always been tall, about six one, but Tech didn't remember the defined chest and nice-sized biceps. Free wasn't as big as the Enforcers, but goddamn, he did fit in with the team. His tan skin was smooth and healthy, his dark eyes and even darker lashes made his eyes look exotic and mysterious. In simple plaid trousers, a snug brown V-neck t-shirt and scarf, he looked like a sexy hipster. Free smiled, displaying pretty white teeth when he saw Tech coming around the truck. He set his laptop bag

265

down and wrapped both arms around Tech, holding him close for a long time.

"Missed you," he whispered softly in Tech's ear.

"I've missed you too, Free. I'm so glad you came."

"Did you think I wouldn't? I owe you my life, my mother's life." Free squeezed Tech even tighter.

"You don't owe me a damn thing. I was already going down, might as well have helped a friend before I did." Tech finally pulled back and looked up at that handsome face.

"I know your boss was the one who helped you. Kept you out of prison. He sounds like someone I wouldn't mind meeting… possibly working for." Free smiled, a nicely trimmed, black goatee framing thick, kissable lips. His shoulder-length, textured hair was held back from his face by a thick elastic band.

"You cut off your dreads." Tech smiled.

"Could never get them to fully lock, hair's not nappy enough. So I took 'em out." Free shrugged, running his hands through the thick, dark waves. "Now it's just a nuisance."

"Come on. Let's go. God's eager to meet you."

Ruxs' massive frame stepped out of the truck and pushed the middle row up so Free could climb into the third row. Free was hesitant to approach, but Tech put a gentle hand on his shoulder. "Free, in the front is Detective Steele, that's Detective Green inside, and this is his partner and boyfriend, Detective Ruxsberg." Tech lowered his voice behind Free so only he could hear him. "They're the greatest men I know. It's okay. I promise." After a few seconds, his friend finally moved closer to Ruxs and climbed inside.

Chapter THIRTY-EIGHT

God

"Tech is on his way back. Once they get here, we can go. We'll take you to get a couple things and bring you back to our place. You can stay in one of the guest rooms. Once we get an ID from the facial recognition software, I'll send Syn and few officers to pick him up."

"He'll probably lie through his teeth." Ric looked between God and Day like they should know that.

God tried not to take offense, this guy obviously didn't know who they were. He ignored the outburst for now. "He'll talk."

"You want Green to interrogate him?" Syn asked.

"No. I'll do it," Day said with his arms folded over his chest, looking like he couldn't wait to get his hands on anyone who'd hurt his friend.

"No. You're too close to this," God refused him.

"I want Leo to go after this guy," Ric countered.

God had heard enough. "I don't care what you want. You're not running anything in here, doc. This is my department. You came to us for help and—"

"We came to Leo for help," Ric cut God off, standing to his full height, his big body pulsing with anger.

"You think you get him without me?" God thundered over him.

"Rickson, calm down." Pres stood up too, holding onto his partner's arm. "God is right. Let him do what he needs to do to get this guy, okay. Leo trusts God with everything in him, and I trust Leo, so *we* can trust God, too."

"Ric. He'll get this guy. Let him. I won't question his judgment. It's either his way or no way," Day said. Any doubt God had about Day settling for him over Pres fled God's mind like it'd never belonged in the first place. The way Day stood beside him made him feel like the luckiest, strongest man in the world. He had a true partner in every sense of the word, end of story.

Ric finally sat his big ass down, his other partner, Blair, settling his arm around his shoulders. God could see the man was scared for his lovers, but fighting his only help wasn't the way to save them.

"What do you want to do, God?" Day asked.

"Call Ro. Tell him to get in here. He's recovered enough, now he's just milking it. I need to talk to the captain, let him know what's going on. I'll be back." God left the room, hoping this would be over fast. He didn't want anything postponing their wedding. No, he *wouldn't* have anything postponing their wedding. He'd done that enough himself.

Day

"It's going to be alright, Ric. Blair, I promise you. God's been entrusted with this department because he's the best." Day clasped his hands together on the table in front of him.

"Better than you?" Blair asked.

"Better than all of us," Day and Syn said at the same time.

"Just to prove God was right, that I am too emotional over the situation, I hadn't even thought about our first officer, Ronowski. Ro is our lead detective and interrogator. He has a master's in criminal psychology and has gotten confessions from the most closed-off suspects there are. He'll get the information we need."

"Aren't you a profiler, too?" Pres asked Day.

"Yeah, I am. But Ro can get a confession in half the time I can. He can gain a handle on the situation with one glance at the file and a brief look in a person's eyes."

"Sounds like the guy with the accent was pretty good, too," Pres said.

"No kidding. He'll still have to be able to work well with us. We all have our areas of expertise. That's why we get the results we do. We each bring what's necessary to the table. I don't know the guy Tech found, but yeah, he sounds smart. I'm just hoping his background is clean, but I don't think Tech would bring him on if he wasn't hirable," Syn commented.

"Will your captain not approve of you working this for me? Is that a possibility?" Pres was rubbing at the tension in his neck until Blair got up and took over the massage.

"No. Not likely. If we can keep it contained, he'll let us do what we need to do. With your status, we'll need to move quickly, though. Our captain won't want paparazzi on us. It's dangerous and, most of all, he won't want anyone with a camera following our Enforcers. It's really not a good idea for the media to catch *anything* they do on tape," Day said seriously.

He heard the door open and turned to look towards it, expecting to see God, but it was Hart and his lieutenant. They were in full-on SWAT gear. Either they were getting ready to go on a bust or were just coming back from one. The man knew how to fill out that uniform. His head was shaved bald, but he had a well-groomed full beard with at least five to six inches of bushy lengthy under his chin. It looked hot on him. He looked scary and dangerous, especially geared up in all black. If Day were just walking down the sidewalk, he'd move out of the guy's way. But if you knew Hart, you'd know he was all teddy bear... as long as you stayed on the right side of the law.

"You guys aren't superstars enough; you had to have Prescott Vaughan cooling his heels in here?" Hart's laugh was husky like he smoked too much, but Day knew the man didn't put anything toxic in his system.

Day stood up and introduced the huge SWAT captain properly. "Pres, this is Ivan Hart. Captain of the SWAT team in this precinct. Hart, this is my longtime friend, Prescott and his partners, Blair McKenzie and Dr. Ric Edwards."

"It's a real honor. I heard you guys were here. You know how fast news travels around this place. Got all the girls running around applying lipstick and shit." Hart laughed again, slapping Day so hard on his back he practically fell against the table.

Day looked out into the bullpen, noticing it was buzzing with way more activity than usual; every few seconds heads would turn to look his way. Day shook his head. "Didn't these girls get the memo?" Day looked at Pres.

"I didn't come for an autograph, my lieutenant did, though. And some of them out there want to know if Mr. Vaughan would come out there and take a few pictures," Hart asked.

"How'd you let them talk you into asking that?" Syn smiled up at Hart.

"You know I'll do anything if I'm asked nicely enough." Hart shrugged. "Which is another reason I'm here. I wanted to tell God I'm moving his witnesses today."

Syn frowned. "I thought it was tomorrow morning."

Hart gave Syn his patented captain's glare. "I know. I changed it. No one knows they're moving now, except my team and you. I'll notify the DA of the change when I get there, but *he* won't even know the new location."

"That's why I trust you, brother," God said gruffly, coming through the door with a slim file in his hand. God clamped his hand around Hart's huge one and pulled him in for a shoulder bump. "Thanks for the transport, Hart. I appreciate it. I wouldn't entrust this responsibility to anyone else."

"Yeah, yeah. Kiss my ass when we don't have an audience, Godfrey." Hart chuckled with a crooked smile.

Pres stood up. "I'm going to go take a couple pictures, Leo."

"That might not be a good idea. Word could get out that you have police assistance," Syn noted.

"Everyone knows I have a best friend in the Atlanta PD and so does you know who, if he's behind this. This is normal activity for me. Anytime I'm in Atlanta or close to it, I stop in and see Leo. It'll look like I'm going about my regular routine." Pres took Blair's hand and walked out of the office. Ric stood there watching them go, a look of uneasiness still masking him.

"You don't want to go with them?" Day asked.

"No." Ric grimaced and sat back down. "I don't do the pictures and fan thing. That's all Pres and Blair. They were made for the camera."

270

"What's going on? Why does he want to look like he's not doing anything differently?" Hart questioned.

God spoke first. "Someone's been issuing threats. Last night a man broke in his condo and took a shot at him. Ric tussled with him before he took off. We believe he'll keep trying until he succeeds."

"You got any leads?" Hart frowned.

"I'm pretty sure we got a good one, and a solid plan. We found the one who's been breaking in, tracked him backward from his hack into Pres' security system. We're gonna pick him up as soon as we get a ping from Tech's system."

"Alright, God. I'll be back by seven, at the latest. I'll accompany you to get him."

God opened his mouth, but Hart snapped his huge arm up, cutting him off. "Not a word. Unless we get a call for my team to go out, we're there with you."

"Thanks, Hart. I appreciate it." Day nodded.

"So do I." Ric stood and shook Hart's hand again.

"There're your guys coming back." Hart craned his thick neck to look through the glass. "Who's that with them?"

Chapter THIRTY-NINE

Tech

"Free, this is the bullpen. Other detectives and officers work in this area. It's usually not so full, but that's Prescott and his partner over there taking pictures, so I'm sure that's why. You can meet him when he comes back inside."

"He's more handsome in person," Free said.

"He's alright if you go for the Hollywood type. I'm more into the rugged look, myself." Tech grinned, noticing Steele's smile as he kept his eyes forward while they walked. "Downstairs are booking and holding cells and the basement level is the gym and locker rooms. Upstairs are other departments, homicide, robbery, cybercrimes, special victims, ya know." Tech kept pointing as they moved through the large precinct. "That's the captain's office. He has an open-door policy and is always available. And straight ahead is our department."

Free stopped so suddenly, Ruxs had to dodge him to avoid running into his back. Tech turned to look at his friend, wondering about the haunted look in his face. "Who's that in there?" he whispered harshly, his voice sounding strained as if he had to struggle to say the words.

Tech looked closer, noticing God standing there with Day and… oh… Hart. Tech told Steele, Ruxs, and Green to go ahead. They looked confused but didn't question him. When they were out of earshot, Tech stood there alone with Free since most everyone was crowding around the star in the room.

"That's SWAT Captain Hart and his lieutenant, Roberts. I know he looks intimidating from here, especially in his gear, but he's really a great guy. God and Day use his assistance when we have a big bust. There's no reason to be nervous. He's extremely sweet and surprisingly gentle. There are female officers who actually prefer to train with only him," Tech said, rubbing Free's arm.

"I'm sorry. I'm acting insane. I know we're in a room full of cops, but you understand, right?"

"I know your dad was an asshole cop who abused his authority, but you won't find that around God or Day." Tech looked into Free's eyes. "I wouldn't've called you here if I wasn't hundred percent sure you'd be safe. You've commented about my job before, how special it is. Well, here's your chance to have that. You can do my job even better than me, but we won't broadcast that." Tech gave Free another sad smile. "Don't let your dad continue to control your life. You've beaten him already, it's time you moved forward, Free."

Free closed his eyes and took a long breath and turned to head towards their department with his back straight and his eyes focused. Tech was proud of him already. He'd come a long way.

Tech moved around introducing him. The looks Free got were interesting. He was definitely a sight to see. Couple his trendy look with his fascinating mind and he was incredible. Tech moved him over to Hart. "Captain, this is a school buddy of mine from MIT. Lennox Freeman. Free, this is Hart." Tech inched back to let them shake hands. Free had his hand out for an uncomfortable while before Hart finally snapped his mouth closed and clasped his hand. Tech didn't miss his friend's slight flinch at the contact, but when he spoke, his voice was strong.

"It's nice to meet you, Mr. Hart."

"Call me Ivan," Hart said, more softly than Tech ever heard the man speak. Tech could see Hart's grip wasn't firm, either; he was just barely grasping Free's hand. "I hear the accent. Where are you from?"

"Born in Baltimore. My father is from Peterborough, it's ninety or so miles from London. I was raised there until I was eleven, then I came back to America," Free answered, his eyes only having to lift a fraction to look into Hart's ice blue ones. His body unlocked and his posture took on a relaxed stance within seconds. What was going on? The two interacted like there was no one else in the room with them.

"So, you thinking of working for God and Day, huh? You into action and adventure?" Hart smiled genuinely, staring down at Free.

"I wouldn't say I'm into that. I'm more of a background player. But Tech called... so I answered. I'm willing to give it a shot if they'll have me," Free said cautiously, and finally took his eyes off Hart, only to turn his gaze right back.

Tech felt Steele lean against his back and murmur in his ear, "Um, what's happening?"

"I'm not sure." Tech noticed everyone was standing there watching the interaction with fascination. Tech was ninety-nine percent sure that Hart was straight. He'd been divorced from his wife for three years and he'd dated a couple other women, but Tech didn't think it had amounted to much. The man was a dedicated officer, like many of them, which meant not much of a social life. All Tech ever saw was the man at work. Every blue moon, he'd accept one of their invitations to a game night, but rarely.

Prescott and Blair came back into the room, putting an end to Hart and Free's extremely long introduction.

Hart cleared his throat. "Well, I got a transport to do. I'm making sure God's witnesses stay safe. Good luck, Free. Hope to see you... umm... see you lat—... yeah, have a good day... evening." Hart shook his head like he was confused and stepped around Free, leaving the office without saying goodbye to anyone else.

Free moved over to Tech's station and sat down, awakening the computers like he already belonged there. The facial recognition software was still running, the progress bar only a quarter of the way through. God and Day moved a little closer but stayed quiet. All of them did. Free was looking around for his laptop bag when Green hurried and set it down by his feet. Free reached inside and pulled out a small electronic device that looked like an eight-by-five external hard drive. But Tech knew it wasn't, it was something spectacular created by Free's brilliant mind. He inserted the USB into Tech's main system and watched the screens flicker a second before the progress bar on the facial recognition sped up times one hundred. Codes were running through so fast Tech had to squint to try to follow them. Seven seconds later a face appeared on the big screen.

All of them stared at the face of the man who'd been hacking Pres' system.

"Do you recognize him?" Day asked Pres.

"No, I don't. Not at all," Pres answered.

Still working in silence, Free pulled his own laptop from his bag – it was about three inches thick and looked like it was old and outdated, but Tech knew it was specially made. Not available in any store, anywhere – and plugged it into Tech's. The screens synched and Tech's pulse raced as he watched Free do what he did. It'd been a long time, but he always got a rush anytime he saw the man work. Like watching a brain surgeon operate. Magnificent.

The systems whirred loudly in the room while Free's powerful computer pushed Tech's system to capacity. His hands danced across the keyboard, manipulating the screens and codes to show what he wanted to see and go where he needed to go. Another couple seconds passed and a red signal appeared on the screen to the far right, flashing on a map of the entire world. Free was showing them he could find damn near anyone. Tech's printer spit out a couple pieces of paper. Free grabbed them and turned around, handing them to the closest man beside him... Day. "That's your man. Robert James Mercer." Free turned back to the computer. More screens were appearing and reappearing, Mr. Mercer's life and personal information being hacked and reviewed while he was none the wiser. "He got a wire transfer of ten thousand dollars nine days ago. Unless he got one helluva bonus at his Cannon Systems technical assistance operator job, he was just paid off for doing something quite naughty."

"That's a helluva way to apply for a job," Pres said, sounding shocked, still watching Free. Holding his chest, the star looked relieved, probably to be a few steps closer to figuring out all this mess. "I'd say you're hired, but it's not my decision. If God won't hire you, I can use a man of your talents."

"Too late. He already has a job... if he wants it," Day spoke up before God could. "That was amazing. I see why Tech is so good. We'll need to iron out some details, but the job is yours if you want it."

"I don't carry a gun and I won't." Free pointed at Tech's hip.

"We need a technology specialist. You don't have to be an officer of the law for that position. Tech *chose* to become a detective. You'd just have to be okay with the pay grade," Day told him.

"To what? Pay for my summer home in the Hamptons? I'm sure the pay is sufficient to keep up my RV."

"Enough shop talk. Great, he's hired. Alright, go and arrest that guy – Mercer or another – and throw the book at him." Ric glared at God like his command was about to be followed.

"Didn't I already tell you I'll handle this?" God gritted through a tightly clenched jaw. "We can't just go and arrest someone. Most of the information he got was obtained illegally. We'll need—"

"Then why bother doing it? Y'all flew this guy here just so he could show off and get a ton of inadmissible evidence!" Ric fired off, his big arms flailing with each word he yelled.

Free was next to Tech as soon as Ric started up, inching behind him and Steele.

"Hey! If you got all the answers, then you go get him!" God snapped again. "Otherwise, stop trying to tell me how to do my job. One more insult to me or my team and it's over! I don't work this way!"

"No. No, please. He's just scared." Blair stepped in between Ric and God. Pres had dropped back into his chair, looking dejected. "God, Day, we're going to do it your way. No more outbursts or demands. Right, Bear... Right?" Blair snapped at his partner, making the fury in his face melt to sorrow.

God didn't wait for an apology from Ric; instead, he turned to Syn. "How long before Ro gets here?"

Syn checked his phone. "Maybe another fifteen minutes."

"Okay. Ruxs, y'all go get this guy. We'll have about an hour to make him talk before he lawyers up and we gotta let him go. All we have legally is that he was at the café at the time the address was hacked. It's not enough. We need him to talk. Bring him in, show him who you guys really are. Maybe he'd rather take his chances in jail than ever see you three again."

"We'd love to." Ruxs clapped his hands together.

Tech watched them go. He was supposed to be shadowing, but right now, he needed to be here with Free and get him started on paperwork. Tech turned to his friend when the commotion had cooled down. His light caramel skin looked ashen and his eyes darted back and forth between God and Ric. "Are you sure about me being here, Techy?"

"I'm sure. You're safe here. I swear it." Tech smiled at his friend, excited to be with him, to have the great honor of working with one of the greatest hackers in the world. What Free had just done in a matter of minutes was nothing short of amazing.

Day walked up to Free and lightly tapped him on his shoulder and pulled out his raggedy cell phone with the cracked screen. "Hey, do you think you can fix this? And for some reason, it keeps dropping calls, too."

"Jesus, lieutenant." Tech looked at Day like he'd lost his mind. Asking Free to do that was like asking the President to get you out of a parking ticket.

Free just smiled and took the phone from Day, looking it over. "Sure. When my home arrives I'll get it straight for you."

Day pumped his fist like he'd just won the lottery.

"Really, Leo?" God stared at him.

"They wanted a one-hundred-dollar deductible to give me a new one." Day looked at everyone like it all made perfect sense.

Chapter FORTY

Day

Day and Pres were sitting outside talking privately while they waited for the Enforcers to come back. Day had reassured his best friend many times over that everything was going to work out. He could imagine how frightened he was. Day had been under the gun more times than he liked to remember, and it never got any less terrifying when you felt your life might end at any second.

"Where's Ric?" Day asked, scanning the parking lot.

"He walked up the block with Blair." Pres kicked at colorful leaves and twigs while they walked around the side of the building, dust and grime covering his expensive shoes, but he didn't look like he cared. Day guessed shoes were pretty trivial right now. "I'm really sorry about how he's been behaving and arguing with you guys."

"Pres, the guy walked into a room and found a man pointing a gun at the men he loved. If he had been five seconds later, he'd be completely alone right now... planning a funeral. I think we can cut him some slack. I personally wanna kiss him. He saved you, Pres. I don't blame him at all for wanting results."

"*You* won't blame him, but God probably won't take much more. I mean, you guys are getting married in days. I'm sure he doesn't want the added pressure."

"This doesn't stop anything. God will have this wrapped up in a day or two, tops. My gut is telling me it's your business partner, too. Tech and his friend are still digging into his financial records. I'm really sorry if it comes down to arresting him, Pres."

"He's never been a friend. When I was blind and alone, he was perfectly okay with keeping our relationship professional, no personal calls or invites to his frequent parties. I was the name behind the business that he got paid well for. We actually spoke personally maybe once or twice a year. We corresponded through our secretaries and emails. If I saw him on the street, I'd probably walk right by him, not knowing it was him. He… he was a business partner, Leo. That's it. Maybe that's why it wasn't difficult for him to get rid of me. If he goes to jail, I can't say I'd be devastated. It's depressing but more for him than me. What the hell made him think he could pull off a conspiracy to commit murder?"

"I don't know. In this line of work, I stopped asking that question long ago and trying to understand why people commit the crimes they do. Criminal psychologists are still stumped by that question," Day said sadly, wishing his friend wasn't going through this. Day's business was narcotics. The entire organization of drug lords had one root cause… money. People did horrible things to get it.

"Ya know, the more I think about our past meetings, the more it's making sense and pointing at him. He's been wanting to do way more critiques overseas and advertise in more publications. Even suggested starting our own magazine, which would, no doubt be lucrative, but I've been focused on other ventures. Damn, what a shark. I never saw this coming." Pres turned to look at him. "So, if God's plan goes right and this Mercer guy confesses or has proof it was Adam, then what happens?"

"He's arrested and the district attorney presses charges. There'll be a trial, but he'll probably have his attorneys plead it out."

"Will I have to talk to him?" Pres asked uneasily.

"Absolutely not. For one, it's prohibited… you're the victim. You won't have to face him. But when you go to court, you'll see him."

"That's it. He's arrested and that's the end of it?" Pres shook his head.

"Yeah, honey. It is. You'll need to contact your lawyers to handle his share of the critique business. Obviously, he'll lose his rights to it when he's found guilty." Day hugged his friend. "You don't deserve this."

Pres hugged him for a long time before pulling back and cupping his face. "Enough about that for now. Let's talk about your wedding. For instance… who's catering it?" Pres flashed that gorgeous smile.

God

God let Ro hug Pres and his partners. They'd all hung out in the past, and like all men, Pres loved Ro's company. God had known Ro would get in here and do everything he could to help. After they were done with pleasantries, Ro was handed the file containing all the information that Free and Tech had gathered. They were quiet again around the large conference table while Ro fingered the papers quickly.

"This looks pretty clear-cut." Ro shrugged. With his blond hair a little longer on the top and his beard grown out to more than just stubble, Ro looked good, rested and ready to work.

"You can get a confession out of him?" Ric asked, pacing back and forth.

"Oh, he'll talk." Ro nodded. "He has no record at all. Even the threat of going to jail will rattle the shit out of him."

"We don't have a damn thing useful, Ro. One image of him at a public café isn't probable cause to arrest him. Question him, yes, but that's it," God told Ro, although he was sure he already knew it. Ro was a vet at this.

Ro straightened his holster and walked with the rest of them to the interrogation rooms. He turned to Tech. "Tech, in three minutes come give me a few pieces of paper and say it's from the cyber division and leave. Day, come in two minutes after with more papers and say it's from forensics, then Syn, if he hasn't cracked, come in with a CD and say it's from the backup camera at the condominiums." Ro nodded when they all agreed and turned the knob into room four.

The rest of them hurried into the viewing room. Ro's entire face had changed from handsome and fun to uninterested. He looked at the man in front of him. Mercer had a bruise on his right cheek and a painful looking cut over his left eye and God was sure no one would know how they got there. Ro sat down, his sharp eyes locked on their suspect. He sat back and crossed one leg over the other like he was at a lounge and waiting for a waiter to bring him a cognac. Ro casually flipped through each page of the file. He took out the one legal piece of evidence they had, an image of Mercer in the café, hacking Pres's security system, and slid it in front of him. Mercer looked at it and shrugged, rambling on about how he always went there... so what. Ro had yet to speak. Right on time, Tech went in with some papers he probably got from the recycling bin, said his lines and left. Their suspect's Adam's apple bobbed while Ro nodded his head and looked across the table at him. Mercer asked questions, but Ro didn't answer.

"That's it. I want a lawyer. This is bullshit," Mercer snapped. "I want a fuckin' lawyer in here, right now!"

"Why isn't he asking him anything?" Pres whispered into the dark room. "He has to hurry up."

"It's one of his many tactics. Works every time he uses it. Ever been looked at for so long you began to squirm? The unknown making you crazy nervous?" Day asked.

"No," Pres responded.

"Then keep watching, you're about to." Day left the room to do his part.

Ro stared, his eyes blinking maybe once a minute.

Mercer shifted. "What? What was that from cyber?"

Ro kept staring.

"Say something. Whatever it is, it wasn't me."

"He's already cracking," God said. "Come on, Ro."

Day went in next but let Ruxs and Green go in with him, the Enforcers doing their usual intimidation.

Mercer jumped back in his seat, shaking his head for no apparent reason. When Day turned and left, Mercer clenched his fists repeatedly, the metal of the handcuffs clinking. "Hey, hey, I want to talk to that officer. Come back! What forensics did he give you?" Mercer snapped, looking more and more afraid.

Ro looked at the papers, still as silent as a mouse.

"I don't know what's going on here." Mercer paled, his body reacting to the situation, his chest rising and falling like he was running a race. "Say something, goddamnit. Talk!"

Syn went in and slammed a CD down in front of Ro, his dark eyes staying on Mercer's until he left the room. The man stared at what was most likely a blank disk; his face turning a sickening pale shade, thinking it was a video of him. "Oh my god."

Ro began to put everything back in the file like he didn't even need to ask any questions, he had all his answers.

"No. No. Wait, this wasn't my idea. I didn't do it. There's someone else!"

Ro began to stand, the file tucked under his arm, the exact same expression on his face that he'd entered with like Mercer wasn't saying enough to make him stay.

"Don't leave! No, I'm not the one you want. Hold on, please! The guy you want is still out there." The man was begging to be interrogated. "I have his number. He's expecting my call."

Ro silently slid a piece of paper across the table and Mercer began scribbling fast. "I'll tell you everything. I didn't do this. I swear. But I know who did."

Ro took the paper, got up, and left the room.

"No. Don't go," Mercer yelled at the closed door. "I got proof!"

Ro met them in the hallway and handed God the paper with Mr. AC – *Mr. Adam Carbone* – written on the front along with a phone number, probably a throwaway cell. But with the positive ID from a witness, they had enough to arrest him.

"Is this admissible, even though he asked for an attorney?" Ric asked.

"Yes. You have to stop interrogating immediately after they ask for counsel. Ro never asked a single question, before or after he asked for a lawyer. It's all one hundred percent admissible. He got a confession and never uttered a single word."

"Damn." Ric went over and shook Ro's hand before coming back to stand in front of God. "I... I have no words. I'm sorry. I underestimated you, doubted you... it'll... it'll never happen again."

God shook Ric's hand. "I understand. I'm glad we could help."

They headed back to the office while Ruxs and Green took Mercer to processing. They'd get him to make the call and set Pres' business partner up. They'd have Hart and his men at the man's front door to arrest him as soon as he did.

Chapter FORTY-ONE

Steele

Steele called his shot and sank the number six ball in the corner pocket. "So what does this mean for your company? It'll be a lot of negative press, won't it?"

They'd all gathered at Ruxs and Green's to wait for Hart to call and tell them the situation was contained. The set-up call by Mercer had been a success and Hart's arrest of Carbone was an easy one, apprehending him right there in his office. Hart insisted God and Day stay out of it, not wanting any force that may have to be used on Carbone to come from men so closely connected to Prescott. They needed a clean arrest. Once Pres' business partner was in custody, they'd let the DA handle it from there. Their work was done. Pres would meet with the DA to give his statement, and their office would handle acquiring Carbone's records and evidence to build their case.

"No. This probably won't be negative. I don't want people feeling sorry for me, though. It took a long time for the public to stop seeing me as blind and vulnerable. I'll see if my publicist can keep it quiet." Pres pulled one of his partners between his legs, holding him around his waist while the bigger one held him from behind.

Steele wondered, briefly, what it was like to have two men all over you, but any thoughts of that quickly vanished when he heard Tech come through the front door with Free. Steele stood up, dropped his cue, and began walking towards him.

"Hey, asshole. We're in the middle of a game. Tech's scrawny ass ain't going anywhere," Day bitched, standing there with his arms out at his sides.

"Let Blair finish the game," Steele yelled over his shoulder.

"No. I'm going back into the kitchen with Green. The food's almost ready." Blair detached from Pres' grip.

"Okay, then Ric, you play." Steele wasn't paying any further attention to Day's complaining when Tech turned in his direction and headed straight for him.

"Hey."

"Hey," Steele said, kissing Tech softly on his mouth. Those moist lips making Steele want some alone time. They'd had a very long day and even longer evening. "Did you get Free all settled in?"

Tech nodded, both arms still wrapped around Steele's waist. "I did. He's having his RV shipped here in a couple days. I told him he could stay with me but he loves his home."

"Come outside with me while I smoke."

"It's cold out there." Tech frowned, still wearing his jet-black pea coat.

"I'll keep you warm," Steele whispered in his ear.

"Okay." Tech bit his bottom lip, his eyes looking Steele up and down.

He watched Tech look to be sure his friend was okay and noted that he was already chatting it up with Furi and Ro. Steele took Tech's hand and pulled him outside, ignoring the catcalls that followed them.

When they got to the bottom floor, Steele led them to a small opening between the two buildings where he usually smoked, sheltering them from the biting wind. Steel maneuvered Tech so that his back was pressed against the wall and crowded the front of him, spreading his legs wide and tilting his hips in so that their pelvises were connected.

Tech stared up at him, watching while Steele lit his cigar with the heavy Zippo and flipped it shut, stuffing it back in his inside pocket. He took a long inhale of the cherry-infused tobacco and blew it in the opposite direction. When he turned his head back, Tech was staring at his mouth, and Steele pressed in tighter, smirking at the rigid bulge that could be felt even through the thick layers of Tech's clothing.

"Is it too cliché to say your smoking turns me on? I think it's hot." Tech's hands were inside Steele's leather jacket, his fingers digging into the muscles of his lower back.

286

Steele's voice was low and gritty when he replied, "You like that, huh?"

"Yes."

Steele kissed Tech hard and long, letting him taste the sweet smoke that lingered in his mouth. Tech sucked on his tongue while he thrust against him. Steele took his other hand and pushed open Tech's coat, brushing the back of his hand over Tech's nipple, making him arch and hiss loudly. Steele smiled against his mouth. "You still a little sore here, baby?"

"Hell yeah, I am. You practically sucked my nipple off my chest today." Tech moaned, still letting Steele rub circles over the tender point.

Steele took another pull. "Let me come over tonight and make it better."

Tech shook his head and Steele pressed in even tighter, making Tech shudder at the feeling of being trapped by him. "Why not?"

"Because it's Free's first night. I want to make sure he's comfortable. Hearing you fuck me into the mattress in the next room probably wouldn't make him feel all that welcome," Tech said, nuzzling against the warmth of Steele's body.

Steele reached down and cupped Tech's dick through his khakis and squeezed hard enough to make him grunt and close his eyes behind those sexy glasses. "You'll miss my mouth here tonight."

Tech groaned. "Unh. I already do." Tech rocked back and forth as best he could, but Steele didn't give him much moving room with the way he had him covered. "I told Vasquez that I was seeing someone. That I had a... a boyfriend."

Steele pulled back and looked at Tech's face. He looked unsure of the word he'd used. Steele didn't think anyone had ever called him their boyfriend, no scratch that, he was sure of it. He liked that Tech thought of him that way. Maybe it was too soon to be considered partners, so he'd take the boyfriend title for now. Getting to know the man in his arms made coming to Atlanta the best decision he'd ever made. And to think, when his uncle called, he almost hadn't come. Next week, while they had some time off, he'd start looking for his own place. Between work and wanting to spend as much time with

Tech as he could, they hadn't been able to do any apartment hunting. He couldn't stay with Ruxs and Green forever – besides, he liked his privacy. He wanted to walk around his place with his balls and ass out whenever he felt like it. Maybe he'd check out the condos across the street, that way he could still come over and have breakfast in the morning. He was starting to get used to that. He was getting used to his team… his friends… his new family.

Steele kissed Tech on his red cheeks. "Good. Now he can find his own and leave *my* boyfriend the fuck alone."

Tech's smile warmed his heart like it always did.

They heard a vehicle pulling into the parking lot and Steele began putting out his little cigar. "Come on. Since everyone else is already here, I think Hart just pulled up. Let's go back in." Steele took one more kiss. "You'll call me before you go to sleep tonight?"

"It'll probably be late, but yes, I'll call. I'm sure Free and I will catch up tonight."

"Late is good. That way, you can dream about me." Steele licked Tech's mouth, their noses and lips brushing together while they nestled against each other and stole a few more kisses.

Chapter FORTY-TWO

God

"Hey, Hart. Thanks, man. You always come through for us. I owe you," God told the big captain and his lieutenant when they stopped in front of him. He noticed a few other guys from Hart's team were coming through the door with coolers, their arms loaded down with brown paper bags. God looked at Day, who shrugged. "Hart, what the fuck are y'all doing?"

"You didn't think we would let you guys get married without a proper send-off, did you?" Hart's devious but charming grin had God groaning and dropping his head in his hands. Day threw his head back and laughed, just as the door buzzed again.

"That's right you slave-driving motherfuckers! Bachelor party!" Ruxs yelled from across the room. Everyone threw up their hands and yelled along with him. A couple seconds later, some of the lights went down and the music came on, blasting through Ruxs and Green's monster sound system.

No wonder Pres and Green were making so much damn food, but God hadn't thought twice about it. How'd they do all this in such a short amount of time? They couldn't've known everything would go smoothly with Pres' case, so what the hell?

"Ahh, look at you guys' faces." Ruxs slung his arms over God's broad shoulders. "As soon as Hart said everything was a go and Carbone was in custody, we started making calls. You know it doesn't take much for guys to drop whatever the hell they're doing and come have drinks and act like asses for a few hours."

Day shoved Ruxs away, looking as stunned and amused as God. "You guys are nuts."

A few more guys showed up, ready to party. One guy from vice thanked them for saving him from a boring night of Family Feud with his lazy brother. Another detective actually admitted to canceling date night with his wife, lying that there was a last minute, job-related emergency. There were a lot more rounds of what they were doing before they got the call, and next thing God knew, there were at least thirty guys hanging around, drinking and congratulating them. The later it got, the drunker everyone got and the more outrageous the stories became.

God had to admit he was having fun. Day was in his arms, warm and inebriated. His ass pressed against his cock while he sat on the stool and Day leaned against him. God couldn't resist licking on his neck while Vasquez and a few of his buddies stood in front of them complaining about the process of getting in with their team.

"We're not looking for new recruits right now, Vasquez." Day half chuckled and half moaned when God bit at the back of his neck.

"Can you guys stop that for a second?" Vasquez's buddy asked, turning his head.

"No," God growled.

"Not hiring? Come on. You just picked up two new members in the past few months," Vasquez bitched, tossing back the last of his drink and slamming the glass down a little too hard on the bar.

"You just want to get in so you can flirt with Tech, but you can let it go, man. That ship has sailed." Day nodded towards the pool table where Tech was practically wrapped around Steele's body while he waited to take his next shot.

"I see. Whatever, though, his loss. But his friend is a pretty good substitute." Vasquez's ogle was predatory and he adjusted himself in his pants.

God ignored it for now – Vasquez was drunk – still, he was getting on his nerves. The beat officer was a pig, a horny pig that used his uniform to chase ass. God and Day both despised officers like that. Now that he thought more about it, he didn't know why Vasquez was even there. He'd probably caught wind of a party and invited himself.

Free sat on the couch – all that wild hair barely contained by the headband – with Furi and Ro, playing a spirited game of Call of Duty, several of the other guys watching and shouting strategies at them. The young man was already fitting right in. His smile was huge and he finally wasn't stuck to Tech's side, looking a little more comfortable around them. God had been a little leery of his skittishness when he'd first come into the office, but thank the heavens for Ro and Furi. They could make anyone feel relaxed. The guy was going to be a huge asset, he could feel it, and with Tech in the field…, his team was growing and getting stronger with each new addition.

But these asshats in front of him didn't stand a chance. He'd talked to Syn and Day about getting a couple demolitions experts and another sniper, but that was a ways off. Regardless. When he did start to recruit again, there was no way he'd look to them. They'd be in it for the wrong reasons. The recognition and commendations weren't the reason they risked their lives every day, it was because of their love for this city and respect of the job.

"You're a vulture, dude," Day threw back at Vasquez. "You're treating our squad like it's a fuckin' orgy you want in on. Go on, we're done with this conversation, you're bringing down my buzz."

Vasquez jerked his head back, his face a contorted mask of anger. "Fuck you, Day."

God rose up from his seat and Vasquez put his hands out in front of him, sealed his ignorant mouth, and backed away, pulling his friends with him. God stared at them with a look that said, "Don't bring your asses over here again," and eased back down in his seat, pulling Day back into him. "Piece of shit. I don't want him in the department anymore. Something about him, now. He's changed."

"I agree." Day turned around and ran his hands through God's long hair. "Now forget about that and give me some more of what you started."

God leaned in and kissed his soon-to-be husband. After a couple lingering presses of their lips, he gripped the back of Day's head and pushed his tongue inside, tasting the vodka and a hint of strawberries from the fruit tray. God closed his eyes and lost himself in the headiness of his partner. And didn't break apart until the whooping and beer bottles banging on hard surfaces made him smile against Day's mouth.

"Hey, what kind of bachelor party is this? Where are the strippers?" someone yelled from the other side of the loft. God couldn't see who it was, but it made him laugh. He didn't need a stripper, the hottest man there was already in his arms.

Syn stood on top of one of the bar stools and yelled over all the raucous laughter. He wasn't drunk, but he wasn't entirely sober, either. Ruxs lowered the music and everyone turned their attention towards them. The music changed to that annoying ass song God hated, the one made notorious in the movie *Magic Mike*. Ginuwine's "Pony" started up and God had an urge to run. What had his team done now? The lights went low and someone turned on a slow-moving, white strobe light and shone it on them.

"What do we need some ratchet strippers for, when we have two of the sexiest men alive right fuckin' here!" Syn yelled.

Green and Ruxs pulled God and Day to the two huge recliners that'd been positioned in the center of the room. The guys were already forming a wide circle around them, ready to watch whatever his team had cooked up.

"You've got to be kidding me," God grumbled, slouching down in the chair. He looked over at Day and saw a look that mirrored his own. Ready to be humiliated.

"Gentlemen, brace yourselves and get ready for your dicks to harden to the point of pain!"

After they'd all finished laughing, Syn continued, pointing towards the steel steps that led upstairs. "Gentlemen, I give you Furious and Blair!"

God turned his head and saw Blair and Furious slowly walking down the stairs. He knew both of these men were once professionals in the world of sex, but he'd never thought he'd see them in action. He swallowed hard when Blair turned the corner. He had a wild look of hunger in his exotic light brown eyes, a gold barbell pierced in his brow and large diamond earrings his ears. God looked down at long legs encased in black leather pants and – oh hell – bare feet. Both of them. Blair's shirt was an ultra-thin, starched white button up, but the last two and the top two were already undone. His hair was tousled all over his head like he'd just had a good time in the bedroom, and

God had to admit, he wore the hell out of that look. Furious came around the stairs next, and as soon as he was in view, he pulled at the band that confined his hair in a bun and shook his head, letting that thick, dark gold mane fan down his back and around his face. A round of cheers exploded and the music went up louder. Furi had on tight blue jeans that had holes in so many places they left very little to the imagination. He had on a snug black tank top that God had a feeling was going to come off soon to show all those delicious tattoos inked over his chiseled abs.

The sexy rhythm and erotic words of the song put Furi and Blair in motion. They moved their bodies in sync with each other, like they'd been practicing this for a while, or maybe it was natural, God didn't know and to be completely honest, he didn't care. He watched them grind on each other, getting the crowd into it. Furi was slightly taller than Blair. He stood with his legs braced apart and clasping his hands behind his head while Blair nestled in extremely close and ran his hands up Furi's chest, pulling his tank top off in one smooth movement. Another round of yells and whistles blasted from the room when Furi's pierced nipples came into view. But if they thought Blair stripping Furi was hot, Furi leaned in, his forehead pressed against Blair's, his bottom lip clenched between his teeth, slowly popping one of the buttons on Blair's shirt, teasing the guys with more skin, and before they could all calm down from that, Furi gripped Blair's hips and yanked his body into him, dragging his hands up his chest, clamping down on his shoulders and in one skilled move, shoving Blair to his knees.

The crowd erupted and God finally had to pry his eyes away and look over at Prescott and Syn. Both of them looked proud and extremely turned on. Blair and Furious together should be fucking illegal. None of the men went too far and threw money in their direction, either. This was a show God and Day's friends were putting on for them. It was no secret that Furi had once been in the porn industry to make money to buy his garage or that Blair had worked as an escort to put himself through culinary school. They did what was needed to achieve their dreams, so no one in that room better disrespect Syn's or Pres' partners, or there'd be trouble.

God and Day looked at each other and smiled. Blair was practically tucked between Furi's spread legs, running his hands up and down his thighs, looking up at Furious like he wanted him so badly he could hardly stand it. Furi played it up beautifully. That gorgeous hair hung around his face while he smoothly cupped Blair's chin and brought his face to his pelvis. Furi looked up and grinned wickedly, popping the button on his jeans, splaying them open, revealing silky, light-colored hair covering his lower belly, leading down into the top of his low-cut briefs. Underwear that would make God chafe, but he liked them on Furi's slender frame.

The crowd egged them on, wanting more, and Furi gripped the back of Blair's head and pulled him into his open jeans and ground his pelvis into his face in the most obscene way. As if he'd just had an actual mouthful, Blair leaned back and pulled in a hard breath, panting and licking his plump lips. Furi wound his body to the music and leaned in like he was going to kiss Blair, but stopped just an inch before their mouths could connect, and both of them turned their heads to stare greedily at God and Day.

Blair smoothly got to his feet and walked over to the recliners, Furi right next to him. Staring into God's eyes, Blair popped open the last couple buttons on his shirt and let one side hang of a shoulder inked with colorful flowers. Blair opened his X-rated leather pants and spread them just enough for God to see that he wasn't wearing any underwear.

Jesus, help me.

Furi tweaked his nipples in front of Day, making them hard and red while he stood over him, still dancing slowly and sensually to the music. They both turned around at the same time when the music started in on the last hook. Furi and Blair each straddled them and dropped down on their laps, leaning all the way back against them. The guys laughed and hollered while he and Day sat there as still as statues, both of them stunned beyond knowledge. Blair smelled like the ripest Georgia peach and he felt just as good. He grabbed God's big arms and placed them on his hard thighs, then lifted his arms and clasped them behind God's neck while he wound his body like a snake on top of him. Blair's cheek was pressed against God's and

God could hear him moaning. *Holy shit.* God turned for a second and he could see that his fiancé wasn't fairing much better than he was. Furi's long frame was splayed on top of him, his back pressed firmly against Day's chest. Day had his hands in the same place on Furi but his face was buried in his hair. It was common knowledge that Day loved Furi's hair. He ran his hands through it at every opportunity. Over time, Syn finally stopped threatening Day's life for doing it. Day buried his nose even deeper while Furi held the back of his head captive.

When the song came to an end, the clapping and noise everyone made were loud enough to be heard for two city blocks. Blair and Furi got up, buttoning their pants and righting their clothes. God stood when his mind finally began to work again and hugged Blair, kissing him on his temple, then did the same with Furi, thanking them both, Day following suit. That was definitely better than any professional stripper could possibly do. A stranger coming in and grinding all over him would be extremely uncomfortable. Furi and Blair kept it sexy but clean. And because he admired Furi and Blair so much, it made it fun but, most of all, it made it special. Those guys really showed up for them and God appreciated it.

It took a long time for the men to calm down, all of them wanting to admire Furi and Blair or joke with Syn, Pres, and Ric for being the luckiest sons of bitches. There was a lot more drinking and toasts made to them as the night began to wind down. God was drunk by the end of the night and so was his partner, so he made sure he kept him tucked in close. It had been the best bachelor party he didn't know he wanted and he was touched everyone went to so much trouble. The food Pres and Green made was amazing, and all his friends pitching in with booze and beer made it not be a strain on his team's pockets. God felt truly blessed and fortunate. He'd had a hard life and a difficult journey before he got to this place in his life. He'd found his world in Day.

Chapter FORTY-THREE

Lennox Freeman – "Free"

Free kept looking through the window, wondering how much longer Tech would be here and if he was spending the night with his boyfriend. He didn't want to be a pest and make Tech feel like he had to cut his evening short. It was his bosses' – and he guessed *his* bosses', too – bachelor party so he didn't want to appear antisocial. Obviously, everyone here was very close. If he wanted to go back to Tech's, he was a big boy; he'd figure it out. Free took another sip of his grapefruit juice, having steered clear of the liquor. He wanted to keep a fully alert mind. His belly was full of great food and the entertainment had been a blast. He did like Furi, Blair, and Ro. The guys seemed cool and were all amazingly gorgeous, but not wrapped up in their appearances. He respected that. They were men he wouldn't mind hanging out with, at least until he really got to know everyone on the team.

Free watched Tech interacting with the guys, while Steele stared at him like he hung the moon. He knew his friend was in love with that big guy, and he was happy for him. Tech hadn't had the chance to develop relationships with the guys he'd dated in the past since none of them stuck around long enough. After that last prick took off, Free thought he'd have to come back and spend some time with Tech, but his friend had refused. Free was in the middle of a huge job and it would've cost him a lot of money, but he'd have done it for his Techy. The younger man meant the world to him. He was a true friend with a good heart. What he'd done for him and his mom could never be repaid, but Free was here now, hoping that showed just how thankful he was. Tech wanted him here, so he was here. But damn, getting used to all these giant men was not going to be easy. He didn't know what he'd been expecting from a room full of law enforcement, why wouldn't they be fit and muscular? And most of them weren't just officers, they were specialized officers. Free wasn't entirely relaxed with men like that. It was nerve wracking to be attracted to that type of man and to also fear them. So Free just stuck with twinks or men who were at least under five-ten, five-nine… it was usually safer.

He was standing on the fire escape getting some air. Although it was pretty cold out, it was too stuffy and overloaded with testosterone inside. Most of the men were past drunk and were getting louder while they talked about police stuff.

The door opened and a man came stumbling out with a beer bottle in his hand. Free had noticed the obnoxious guy making rounds in the room. It didn't look like he was well liked, especially by the members of God's team. He looked at Free for a couple seconds before making his way over to him, bumping his shoulder when he leaned on the space beside him. Free eased over but there wasn't much space on the small landing. The guy smelled like a brewery. He wasn't completely unattractive. He had a nice face and a thick upper body, but warning bells pinged in Free's head, and he'd learned long ago not to ignore them. "I'm gonna head back in—"

"Hey. I'm Ramon, a good friend of Tech's. Ramon Vasquez. Has he mentioned me?" he slurred.

"Um, not that I know of, but it's my first day. We haven't had the—"

"Probably too full of that hot shit Marine of his. But forget that. So, how's it been going with your new team?" Vasquez asked, cutting him off. The question didn't sound right like Vasquez didn't care either way, and the sneer he'd worn with the words was another clear sign he may not be the friend of Tech's he claimed to be. "You just popped up out of nowhere and got right in with God's team."

Free didn't answer, looking through the glass to see if anyone was paying attention to them, but it didn't look like it. He checked his watch, a universal sign that he was ready to go. Besides, it was going on two in the morning. He'd had a long flight and a long day. He hadn't expected an impromptu bachelor party. Right now, he just wanted to get some rest in a comfortable bed. "It was nice to meet you," Free said, his tone final, and went to leave, but Vasquez blocked his path, putting one hand on the brick wall and the other on the railing. Free's throat tightened at the feeling of being closed in.

"Hey, what's your rush, pretty man? I was only talking with you. You have a sexy ass accent, you know that? Did you fly here from England?"

Free didn't answer. He didn't want to talk with this guy another second. Obviously, he was drunk and didn't know what he was doing was making Free nervous. He tried to calm himself down; after all, this guy was a cop. *So was your father.* Free swallowed the nervousness and shook those thoughts from his mind. His dad was a monster. There was no way Tech would place him around men like that. Vasquez was a guest at the party; he wasn't going to hurt him. Free cleared his throat. "I think I'm gonna go. It's late."

"You're right," the man blurted loudly before toning it back down. "I think maybe we should get out of here. It's late and I'm… I'm thinking maybe I can take you back to your hotel or whatever, seeing as you're new to the area. Besides, Tech looks pretty busy."

"I'm good," Free said curtly. "I'm staying with Tech."

Vasquez's creepy eyes were looking all over his face. "You have nice skin. Are you… are you black...? Or um, what nationality are you?" Vasquez corrected himself like he was trying to make the question politically correct. "I'm a half-breed, myself."

Free frowned. "Excuse me?"

Vasquez's eyes narrowed a fraction then he waved his hand around in the air. "Never mind, forget that. Came out wrong. I meant I'm Hispanic and Irish. Weird combo, huh?"

"If you say so." Free went to move again. "Have a nice night."

"Man, I could listen to you talk all night." Vasquez reached out and tried to touch his hair, but Free batted his hand away. "Oh, easy now. You're a feisty one. What's the problem? You already got your eyes locked on one of God's guys? Well, you can forget that idea, they're all taken. I saw you all cuddled up with Ronowski, he's taken, too."

"I'm not fixated on anyone. You need to move now," Free said sternly. He didn't like feeling this way. He wasn't a weakling and he had some muscle on him, but anytime he was met with this type of threat his body shut down and his mind followed shortly after. After all the self-defense courses he'd had, he'd never been able to apply them when confronted, especially by a larger person. Confrontations didn't happen often in his life, but those that had happened when he was younger screwed him up good. Now that he had an obnoxious asshole in front of him, he had no clue how to handle it.

Vasquez inched in closer and ran his hand down the center of Free's chest, right between his thick pecs. "You don't have to be so mean, pretty. I won't hurt you... unless you're into that." Vasquez's laugh was cold and eerie.

Free tried to hurry past but Vasquez caught his arm and held him back.

"Let go," Free hissed, his forehead breaking out with a fine sheen of sweat, even though his body was freezing. He closed his eyes when Vasquez leaned in. Next thing he knew, he was jerked hard, his body was knocked back a step and a rough, angry voice laced with danger followed.

"Get your hands off him, Vasquez. Have you lost your mind?!"

Free opened his eyes but saw nothing except the broad back standing in front of him, blocking him from Vasquez.

"Chill out, Hart. I was only talking with him," Vasquez replied with more than a little irritation.

"Didn't look that way to me. Leave, now. He said he's not interested, I'm going to take that to mean permanently. You better hope I never see what I just saw, again."

"This is none of your business. I forgot. You love doing God's dirty work, don't you, Hart? Just like all the rest of them. Riding his goddamn coattail." Vasquez's tone was full of venom. Free couldn't see him – Hart's massive body standing between them – but he could hear him.

"Do you think you're insulting me?" Hart's arms were crossed over his even bigger chest. "You're drunk. You need to go sleep it off. Last warning. Stay away from him."

"Or what?" Vasquez threw his arms out.

300

"Or I'll level you, idiot." Hart took a step closer, towering over the shorter officer. "Get him outta here, Joe."

"I'm not ready to go."

"Yes you are, and there's two ways you can leave. Over that railing or out the front with Joe. I suggest you do it before I let everyone know what the fuck is going on. I'm going to chalk it up to you being drunk. But trust me, you don't wanna push me on this."

Vasquez turned and left, Hart watching him the entire time. No one had been paying attention to the minor altercation outside and Free was somewhat happy about that, he didn't want to bring down the party, but he wasn't looking forward to telling Tech tomorrow that he didn't think he'd be staying. He'd really wanted to be close to his friend again and try to return the favor he owed, but this might not be the best thing for him. He'd come a long way in healing from what had happened to him but he hadn't come far enough to deal with situations like that.

"I'm really sorry that happened."

Hart's deep voice made his head snap up from his depressing thoughts. The man stood at a polite distance, giving him some breathing room, and Free was thankful. Surprisingly, he wasn't nervous with Hart. His eyes were too kind, too clear as if Free could see his intentions and there was no malice there. Free stared up at him, neither of them saying anything, maybe Hart was trying to get a read on him, as well.

The door opened again, breaking the intense staring. "Hey, Free. You okay?" Tech asked, his eyes glassy and dancing with excitement. The music drifted out the door and Free could see the party was still in full swing, although the crowd had thinned a bit.

Free looked up at Hart, who was still watching him. "Yeah, I'm good. Go on and enjoy. I'm going to head back to your place."

"Oh. You wanna leave already?" Tech asked, looking slightly disappointed. "Why don't you come back inside, it's cold out here."

"You don't have to leave. I'll call a cab. I know my way back."

"I'll take you back if you want. I didn't drink anything, I don't mind. I was just getting ready to tell the guys bye and I was looking for you," Hart admitted to him.

Free liked him. Hart's look was everything he'd go for if he actually weren't afraid to go after what he wanted. His shiny bald head clashing with the scruffiness of his long beard. His inviting, muscular body was blocking most of the frigid wind whipping between the buildings. He looked amazing and full of power in his SWAT gear, but dressed in dark denim jeans and a short-sleeved shirt, he looked easy-going and handsome. He took his thick coat off and wrapped it around Free's shoulders, careful where he touched him. He hadn't even realized he was trembling from the temperature drop, but Hart had. Free thanked him, his body inching closer to get more of the warmth that emanated from Hart. He was a big man with a gentle touch. *Perfect*. But Free had no clue if he was gay. He could just be an exceptionally sweet and chivalrous guy like Tech had told him earlier.

"Are you okay with that, Free? Riding with Hart?" Tech asked more seriously.

Free kept his eyes trained on Hart when he answered softly, "Yeah. I think I am."

Chapter FORTY-FOUR

God

God's Special Day

"God relax. Everything is fine. Gen hit a lot of traffic driving in but he'll be here well before the ceremony." Syn tried to calm God down while he got dressed in his suit.

"He should've been here a week ago," God snapped, yanking his tie off and tying it again. He'd almost choked himself on the last try. Syn moved his hands and took over.

"Curtis' boss was being a jackass again and wouldn't give him the time he'd requested months ago, so they had to come this morning, but as long as he gets here, that's what matters. Sit still, I'm trying to tie this and I can't do it with you seething."

"I'm seething because I want to kick Curtis' boss' ass. He keeps giving him shit, and for what? It's a volunteer job, who does that?" God fumed.

"Let's not worry about that, right now. Stay calm."

"What's Day doing?" God asked for the fifth time in an hour.

Syn sighed, still working on tying the off-white tie to God's black suit. "He's getting dressed, just like you are. He's with his brother in Steele's room, Furi's in there, too."

"What are the guys doing?" God asked, his hands wringing nervously behind his back while he held his head up to give Syn better access.

"You don't have to keep track of everyone, God."

God glared at Syn.

Syn closed his eyes and blew his own calming breath. "Again. Ruxs and the guys are finished positioning the arch, now they're just standing around waiting. Green's in the kitchen with Blair and Pres—"

"Prescott should be with Day," God cut him off.

"He'll have plenty of time to get changed and ready to stand with Day. You know he's going to make sure the staff is doing what they're supposed to in the kitchen, first."

"I can't believe he's doing this," God mumbled. Pres had insisted on providing the food and catering the service with his own staff from some of his restaurants. It already smelled delicious, the scent of baking and of searing meat permeating the entire loft. God agreed to let Pres do the catering, as long as he kept it simple. Nothing fancy or over the top and Pres quickly agreed. Blair did an elegant but modest cake, as well. God was looking forward to just saying "I do" and going to the gorgeous hotel where they were staying, right next to the airport so they didn't have a long drive to catch their flight at five in the morning. He was ready for days of stretching out under the Aruba sun while Day rubbed oil on his chest, and long nights of hot sex.

"Better." Syn looked up at him, smiling slyly like he knew where God's thoughts had gone.

"I'm nervous, man," God admitted to his good friend. "I don't want anyone here that wasn't invited. Make sure Ruxs and Michaels know that. Judge knows to watch the door, right?"

"They know. Everyone knows what they're supposed to be doing, God. You need to stop. It's only us for the ceremony, and then a few others will come for the reception later this afternoon," Syn reminded him. He was glad Syn wasn't getting tired of repeating the same thing, but as usual, Syn was his voice of composure and reason.

"I'm so fuckin' nervous. Shit," God gritted out.

"I know. Hey, hey, look at me." Syn finished the tie and clamped his hands on God's shoulders, making sure he was looking at him. "Remember. This is just Day. When you meet him at the bottom of those stairs, keep your eyes on him and nothing or no one else. He's your other half; he'll take you all the way through this."

God breathed deeply, nodding his head. Syn let him go just as he heard the front door open and Curtis' voice yell out to his dads.

"Gen is here. And there're still two-and-a-half hours before it's time to start." Syn sat down on Ruxs and Green's bed and began using the lint roller on God's suit jacket. He was doing everything Vikki told him to do. When God and Day's former assistant got over the fact she was no longer planning an extravagant wedding for them, she became a pleasant help, organizing the seating and rearranging Ruxs and Green's loft to fit the guests and make the most of the minimal decorations.

Gen busted through the door with his garment bag slung over his shoulder and his luggage in the other hand. God looked at his baby brother – which was hard to say now because Genesis was almost as tall as him and still well built from his years as a college ball player. His brother collided with him, wrapping his arms around him. "I'm sorry I'm late, bro. I really am."

"You're not late," God replied, happy to see his brother again. It'd been a few months since Gen had been able to make the drive from Richmond. He worked long hours at Apple and his partner, Curtis, had a demanding school schedule. Now that he was here, God didn't care that he hadn't been here for the bachelor party or here a week ago, he was here now.

Day

Day stood at the bottom of the stairs next to his brother, Jackson. There was jazz playing quietly on Ruxs' sound system and it only took him a second to realize it was one of Day's favorites… one from his collection. God must've given it to Vikki to play today. He looked around the loft at the few people who were there to witness the ceremony, most of them already seated and waiting. Their team and their significant others were chatting quietly with each other and God's mom was sitting in the front between Curtis and the captain. Small and intimate. This is what made God comfortable, and him, as well. In Green's kitchen, the wait staff was silently filling champagne flutes, smiling professionally. He saw Vikki standing off to the side in a long, silky silver dress, talking quietly with the chaplain. Day winked at her and she gave him a sweet smile.

"He *is* still here, isn't he? You're sure he didn't sneak out the back." Day leaned over and whispered to his older brother. He smiled to show he was kidding, but his stomach was still fluttering like crazy.

"Of course, he's here. He'll be down in a second. We're a little early," Jackson whispered.

Day cleared his throat and smoothed his hands down his suit jacket. They'd opted out of tuxedos and had chosen nice suits from a shop Blair recommended. They were classy, but not too much. He was sure God would look wonderful in his. Day stared at the wedding arch his team had made for them. He shook his head and smiled at the handcuffs and badges intertwined in the green garland and white Cherokee roses. He had to admit it was eclectic and perfect for them. Day fought the urge to check his watch. He was pretty sure God would come down on time. He felt his brother tap him on his shoulder.

"Yeah?" Day turned. Jackson pointed to the top of the stairs.

Day looked up and had to clutch the banister to keep from falling over. He saw him. Saw his soon-to-be husband. Standing there, larger than life. In a suit that hung from his broad shoulders the way every suit should fit a man. God looked down at him, his hair falling to the front. Day hadn't seen it like that before. Luxurious and soft. Like he'd just come from a salon. It was tucked behind his ears, but thick, soft strands still fell forward as God smiled down at him. A smile most people didn't get to see. He looked like he was just as relieved to see Day standing there. Genesis stood behind him with his hand on his shoulder the exact same way Jackson was supporting him. Day finally breathed when God began to descend the stairs. When he reached the bottom, Day saw God's chest deflate like he'd been holding his breath. They stepped in to each other, needing the closeness, the reality of what they were about to do flooding their bodies with anticipation and nerves. God never looked into the room, didn't glance around to see who was there. His vibrant green eyes stayed on him when he lifted Day's hands and gently kissed his palm, pressing Day's hand to his face. There were a few soft sighs from the room, but Day couldn't look away. He ran his hand through God's

306

hair, feeling the silky strands ease through his fingers, not a tangle to be found. He looked amazing.

"You're beautiful," God whispered just for him.

Day's feelings rode him. He wasn't going to cry, he'd sworn it, but he felt the moisture in the corners of his eyes. He held it back by feeding off God's strength, letting his presence soothe him, knowing it would work, as it always had. God intertwined one of their hands and turned them to walk down the makeshift aisle. When they got to the archway, Vikki turned the music down low just as God looked around the arch, noticing the decorations, and turned back to look at his guys with a "really" expression and laughter burst from most of them. Just that fast, the situation lightened to a relaxed vibe, and the precinct chaplain started to speak. It was only fitting he presided over their nuptials. Neither he nor God was very religious or even had a church home. Chappy had counseled them from the very beginning when they first became partners. He watched them grow and become who they were today; he'd seen them at their best and at their worst.

After Chappy told a few stories about them, and how he hadn't seen a couple more suited for each other, he segued right into the traditional vows. They didn't want to write their own or have any long drawn out speeches, that's why they asked Chappy to say whatever he felt was right. And he covered their life and growth together even better than they could have. When it came time for the ring exchanges, God's hand shook a little when he placed Day's ring back on his finger. But when God looked him in his eyes and adoringly whispered, "I do," Day couldn't stop the single tear that ran down his cheek. God wiped it away with his thumb, keeping his large hand on his cheek while Day agreed to honor and obey, love and cherish him for all the days of their life.

The part he'd been waiting for was finally spoken and God tilted Day's head and gently kissed him, lingering with their mouths pressed together until Day felt God's arm slide around his back and the tip of his warm tongue at the crease of his lips. Day submitted and opened for him, letting his husband... *Oh, Jesus...* his husband deepen the kiss.

Their friends and family stood and clapped for them while they embraced and quietly spoke promises in each other's ears. Promises of love and fidelity. Trust and honesty. Day believed every word God said. Knew he was safe with this man, always had been, and always would be.

As soon as their family members finished hugging and congratulating them, they were quickly seated for dinner at the beautifully decorated table placed in front of the tall windows at the back of the loft. The servers brought out the meal that Prescott had carefully constructed. The roast was succulent and tender, a favorite of both of theirs. Three sides of homemade macaroni and cheese, old-style mashed potatoes, and fresh green beans that melted in your mouth. Classic and simple, like them.

The champagne toast immediately followed, both his and God's brothers saying a few words to their family. Jackson's was more humorous, telling everyone about the trouble Day's and his stunts used to get them into with their parents. Jackson told Day that if their parents were still here they would be proud of him and welcomed God to the family. Thankfully, he didn't make Day weep too badly. But Genesis' speech brought tears to everyone's eyes.

"... My brother and I were separated for a long time. He was everything to me when I was young and I lost him for a while. I'm blessed to have him back in my life, fortunate to have such a wonderful man looking out for me. No one deserves happiness more than him and I know my new brother, Leo, will continue to give him that. Cashel is an inspiration to me... to all of us. I strive every day to be half the man he is. To my big brother and his husband."

While the family clinked their glasses, God stood and hugged Genesis, Day following right behind him. No one else knew what Gen and God had been through when they were younger. No one but Day, and God's mother. Their team didn't have the details, but they knew it was something really bad.

When they were finished, the table was broken apart and the loft was set up for the guests arriving later for the reception as the wait staff piled hors d'oeuvres and finger foods onto black and chrome serving trays.

Chapter FORTY-FIVE

Steele

The reception wasn't as rowdy as the bachelor party, everyone mingling with the newlyweds while Day's jazz collection played quietly in the background. The crowd, however, looked similar, with a few women sprinkled in. Steele was full from the amazing dinner Prescott's staff had prepared but he couldn't help sampling some of the intricate foods that the reception attendees were indulging in. He was beginning to understand why Pres and his restaurants were so famous. The guy was a wizard in the kitchen. He wasn't even cooking, only tasting and giving an instruction or two here and there.

Steele looked at his watch. It was going on five. He figured if he disappeared for a little while and popped back up before the cake cutting, no one would know. He had to do something to loosen the tightening in his slacks. Tech had the audacity to show up in a dark royal blue suit with velvet lapels – which appeared black in dim lighting – and matching blue suede loafers. And he'd be damned, Tech had on a goddamn bow tie made from the same material as the lapels. The pants stopped an inch above his ankles and Steele could see he wasn't wearing socks. He took another swig of his drink and placed the glass back on the counter, one of the kitchen staff snatching it right up.

He walked over to Tech, not interrupting whatever he was talking about with Free and Furi. When they finished, Steele leaned into Tech's back. "Come with me."

Tech turned and looked behind him, giving Steele a skeptical look. Tech knew Steele's voice. Knew when it was full of want. He took Steele's hand and let him lead him up the stairs while most of the guests weren't paying attention to the front of the loft. He really didn't care if they were seen or not. Steele opened his bedroom door and hurried Tech inside. He closed and locked the door, then stepped back so he could look at his boyfriend. Steele had long ago shed his borrowed suit jacket and was rolling up his sleeves like he was about to do something serious to Tech.

Neither of them said anything while the sexual tension built around them and saturated the air. Tech leaned against the door, his hand drifting down to the front of his pants, rubbing himself there, like just looking at Steele made him hard. Steele stalked forward and brushed his hand over the bow tie, his eyes hooded, his dick rock hard. He wrapped one arm around Tech's back, still caressing the fabric of his suit. "You look breathtaking, dressed up like this. I couldn't keep my eyes off you," Steele whispered. He methodically removed Tech's suit jacket but didn't touch his black dress shirt or that tie. He walked Tech to his bed, watching his eyes behind those frames cloud with lust.

"Edwin," Tech moaned, leaning into his neck and sucking at his throat.

Steele growled, easing Tech down on the bed and covering his body, pressing firmly against him. Steele kissed Tech with all the built up passion he'd kept contained for the last eight hours. Breathing hard and grinding against each other, Steele couldn't take it another second. He sat up, pulled one of Tech's legs up on his shoulder, and slid his loafer off his foot. Tech watched him closely while he did the same with the other.

Tech took off his glasses and placed them further up the bed, moving to unbutton his pants, but Steele stopped him. He wanted to do it. He wanted to do it all, wanted Tech to fall apart under him. He finished what Tech had started, pulling his pants off, butterflying his thighs open.

"Oh god. Edwin, do something," Tech pleaded, his hips thrusting up into the air.

Steele licked his lips, staring at Tech's hairless balls and his long, leaking cock, bobbing and begging for his attention. Steele bent and swallowed Tech whole, slamming the thick head to the back of his throat. Steele was glad there was music playing downstairs because Tech's yell of shock and pleasure was loud, as Steele sucked him. He buried his nose in Tech's groin, staying there until he had to come up for air, while Tech continued to curse and call out his name.

"Fuck, fuck, fuck. Babe, damn." Tech twisted on the bed when Steele devoured his balls next. Sucking both into his mouth at the same time. Steele wished he could take his time, but they had to get back downstairs. He let his saliva drip over Tech's hole, coating it while he kept laving at his balls. It was becoming one of his favorite things to do to him. Tech went wild for it every time.

Steele moved back up and kissed Tech, licking around his mouth the same way he did his cock. Tech's taste made him crazy, made him insane, made him ache. He rubbed his finger around Tech's wet hole, eating up the moans that spilled between their joined mouths. Steele looked in Tech's eyes while he pressed a little harder at his tight bud.

"Yes. Do it," Tech begged, sucking on his bottom lip.

Steele pressed his mouth against Tech's ear. "Shawn. Tell me, baby. Tell me what you feel about this," Steele whispered and pressed two fingers deep inside him, going for his prostate. "Tell me, Shawn. How do I make you feel?"

"Oh god, Edwin. You make me feel so good." Tech's back arched, his cock turning a dark red.

Steele rubbed over the spongy gland again and had to clamp his mouth over Tech's to muffle the shouts of passion. "I make you crazy, don't I?" Steele's voice was thick and rough as he ground his own rigid dick against Tech's thigh. He pulled out his fingers to the tip and thrust them back in. "Say it."

Tech bucked against him and Steele knew he was getting ready to come, and he swore he wished he could prolong it. Make his lover suffer, make him beg. But he'd do that later tonight, this was just an appetizer.

"Yes, fuck. Ohh, I'm gonna come so hard." Tech clenched his teeth, his neck muscles straining while his orgasm roared through his body. Steele swiftly moved back down and placed his mouth over the head of Tech's dick, sucked once, twice, before his mouth was flooded with warm come, coating his tongue as he tried to swallow it all. The sounds Tech made when he came made him suck even harder, made him suck until Tech had to grab his face and pull him off his spent shaft. "Shit," Tech gasped

Steele licked his lips just in case he'd missed any. He could leave the lingering taste of Tech in his mouth the rest of the evening and be satisfied. Tech's eyes parted, his smile lazy, his body limp beneath him. Steele noticed Tech's eyes drop to the bulge in his pants, his look going from sweet and sated to ravenous and starving.

Tech sat up and pushed his hand against Steele's chest, moving him back. Steele stood up and lost all words when Tech dropped down to his knees in front of him. Steele's growl was husky as Tech made quick work of his belt and pants, pulling them down around his thighs. He cupped Tech's chin, tilting his head up to look at him. He looked so sexy down there. On his knees for him, ready to please him. Steele's heart beat at a crazy rhythm and his breath caught in his throat. He was happier than he'd ever been and it was all because of the man looking up at him with a look that said he was his. And at the moment, he realized why he felt so good all the time. Why he laughed so much and looked forward to working every day. He knew, looking into those baby browns why his life was damn near perfect now. He had the urge to confess something, something real and of the utmost importance. He'd missed his opportunity to say it before. He wasn't going to miss it again. If he'd learned anything in his lifetime, it's that tomorrow wasn't promised.

Steele lightly stroked Tech's smooth cheek with his other hand, then bent down to kiss him passionately. Pressing his forehead against his, he whispered into Tech's mouth, "I love you, Shawn."

Tech sucked in a sharp breath, clutching Steele's thighs tighter like he needed stability. Tech blinked and stared back at him. His voice hushed and throaty when he asked, "Say that again?"

"You heard me the first time, *armastaja*." Steele licked the tip of Tech's tongue and repeated, "I love you. God, I love you so much."

Tech made the most delicate, appreciative sound he'd ever heard and rubbed his face all over Steele's lower body. Tech gripped his waist and kissed over his stomach, down the trail of dark hair that led to his cock. Steele threw his head back with ecstasy when Tech breathed over his shaft, his hot breath simply letting Steele know what was coming. Tech wrapped his hands around him and cupped his ass, pulling him forward. Steele almost lost it when Tech timidly flicked his tongue out, looking up at him as if he was shy and innocent, but Steele knew the fierce man who was his lover. A man who could take on two or three thugs at a time and put them all at his feet. He was underestimated by criminals and Tech enjoyed nothing more than proving himself every time. Tech was physically well trained, masterfully taught by experts. Pair his agility with his brilliance and his Tech was a dangerous disguise on the streets. Steele loved working with him, partnering with him, watching him become a warrior right before his eyes. A beautiful fighter. Impeccable for him. Steele had the best of both worlds in Tech.

Tech took him deep in his mouth, his peach lips spreading wide to fully take him. "Fuck, I love watching you like this. So strong and sexy… on your knees for me." Steele panted while Tech moved his hot mouth over his cock at a steady pace, bringing Steele to the edge faster than he wanted. "Mmm. This is gonna be over fast, *armastaja*. You feel too good."

Tech sucked harder when Steele said that. He hissed and pumped his hips at Tech's encouragement. He felt those thin fingers caress his ass and inch inside his crease, brushing over his hole. He wasn't a bottom and Tech was happy with that, too greedy to give up Steele's dick and trade places, but he liked the way Tech touched him there. His palm still over Tech's jaw, he rubbed his thumb across Tech's bottom lip, his finger gliding over the saliva running down his chin. He was gonna blow. Steele gripped the back of Tech's head and thrust into his mouth, his control slipping as Tech tapped on his hole. "Oh fuck. It's coming, baby."

Steele's knees gave out at the first jet of come exploding from his shaft and down Tech's throat. He took his hand from Tech's cheek and bent his upper body over his head, bracing himself on the bed. With each spurt, he pushed Tech's head into his thick bush, holding him there as the last drops leaked from him. Tech leaned back, his mouth slack while he harshly breathed in and out, trying to fill his lungs back up with oxygen. Steele finally gave up and dropped to his knees in front of Tech, dropping his forehead onto his shoulder. "That was amazing. It's like I come harder each time."

"Must've been the bow tie this time." Tech turned and nuzzled Steele's jaw, his smile pressed against his cheek.

Steele turned and looked at him, his own amusement showing on his face. "I really think it was. I've been wanting to see you in a bowtie for a while."

"I will never understand why my clothes turn you on." Tech smiled warmly, letting Steele help him up so they could get their clothes back on.

"You don't have to understand it," Steele finally said when they were dressed and he was helping Tech back into his suit jacket.

Tech turned in his arms and watched him closely for a long time like he was at a loss for words. When he finally opened his mouth, he said exactly what Steele hoped he would say. "I love you too, Edwin. For a while, actually." Tech dropped his eyes but Steele tipped his chin back up.

"You have? Why didn't you tell me?" Steele rubbed down Tech's arms, his hands smoothing over the soft material of the jacket, and intertwined their fingers.

"I don't know. Nervous about saying it too soon. Didn't want to run you off, I guess." Tech laughed doubtfully.

"I'm not going anywhere, Tech… not without you."

Chapter FORTY-SIX

Tech

He and Steele snuck back downstairs just as everyone was crowding around for God and Day to cut the cake, so they simply slid into the crowd like they'd never been gone. Free sidled up next to him and bumped him with his elbow, looking over at him with a conspiratorial smile.

"And where did you disappear to for…" Free looked at his watch, which was exactly like Tech's. "… Forty-five minutes?"

"We had some things to discuss. I didn't miss anything, right?" Tech asked, unconsciously straightening his bowtie.

"No. You're just in time for that good-looking cake," Free said, craning his neck to watch God and Day cut the first piece together.

Tech looked around and caught Hart's eyes looking past the main show and staring at Free. Hart didn't notice Tech, but he could see something in the SWAT captain's eyes. Myriad reactions. Confusion, admiration, and something else. Perhaps infatuation. Tech wasn't sure what was going on with him. He was one of God's closest friends, so Tech knew he had no problem with gay men, but he was straight and had said so a few times. Tech frowned. So why was he staring at Free? Why was he sticking up for him? Offering him rides home and coming by the department more often than usual to ask if Free was settling in well? Tech chalked it up to Hart being an awesome guy. Like he'd said, there wasn't anything he wouldn't do for another, it was just his nature.

Over the past week, Free had fully learned Tech's system and had made quite a few upgrades, too. He was amazing, just like Tech knew he'd be. When they were out in the field on their first test run, Free was cool and collected. God and Day were happy with him, but most of all, the entire team was impressed with him. Tech wouldn't've entrusted his system to anyone else.

Free was still living with him and Tech loved having a roommate again. He and Free got along just like brothers. It'd been that way since they were in college. It was going to be some time before Free could get his RV here because two of the wheels needed replacing and Free hadn't had the time to get back to Miami – where his last job was – to get it taken care of. It didn't much matter because neither of them seemed in a rush to change their living situation.

Everyone clapped when Day wiped a smudge of cake on God's face, bringing Tech's attention back to the room. While more pictures were snapped of the happy couple, Tech looked over at Steele standing next to Syn and wondered if they'd get there one day. Sure, it was way too early to think about it too hard, but Steele said he loved him. Said it first. He couldn't help but hope. Next time he went, he was going to ask Steele to go home with him to meet his father. He'd told his dad about him, so much so that his father was insisting on it.

Tech looked around the room while the servers passed out the cake and more champagne. Watched his family laugh and surround each other with love. They were brothers, all of them. Now he had Free here, too. Life was good.

Chapter FORTY-SEVEN

God and Day

God put the card into the scanner and waited for the light to turn green. He opened the door to their hotel suite and stopped Day before he could walk inside. "Hey. Isn't someone supposed to be carried over the threshold to the wedding bed?"

Day leaned against the doorjamb, his laughter filtering down the empty hall. "That's quite traditional, and usually it's the bride."

God smiled down at him. "Alright, then. Get your damn arms up and carry me inside."

Day shook his head at him. "You're crazy."

God swooped down and grabbed Day around his waist, lifting him so his legs straddled his hips, and walked them into the room. He let the door close behind them and turned, pressing Day against the door.

"Mmm. I've barely had time to kiss you properly today," God said, holding Day up with his mass.

"So, rectify that now," Day retorted.

God turned them and moved Day into the large room. The bed was huge and covered with red rose petals in the shape of a heart. He looked down at it, rolling his eyes – Day still clinging to his body. "Vikki is such a sap."

"You know she had to do at least one thing she wanted." Day laughed, staring down at the bed.

God laid Day down on top of the fragrant petals and leaned over him, staring into the beautiful eyes he had the rest of his life to gaze upon. His brown and blond hair fell around their faces and Day tucked both sides behind his ears before caressing the long strands around his shoulders.

"Your hair looks so gorgeous today," Day whispered.

"Blair did it. He went on and on about it's all in the conditioner, then he used a blow dryer that looked scary as shit, but this was the end result." God ever so gently brushed their lips together. "Don't get used to it. No man should spend that kind of time on his hair."

Day's eyes glistened as he smiled up at him and God's smile fell slowly. He was so in love. *Christ.* "My husband," he whispered roughly, an edge of wonder to his tone, like life couldn't be this amazing to him. "You are my husband, Leo."

Day rubbed his calloused fingers over the course hairs of God's goatee. "Yes."

Day wasn't sure how long they laid there holding each other, the magnitude of the day sinking into their souls. They were one now, but only officially. He and God had been connected for years. From the first day at orientation when they locked eyes across the room. Day had known, even then, that God was a man he wanted around him for a long time, in whatever capacity he could have him. But only in his dreams did he see *this*.

Day reached up and pulled the already slackened knot of God's tie and removed it the rest of the way. He kept his eyes on God's while he unbuttoned his shirt.

"Aren't you supposed to go and slip into something sexy for me?" God questioned.

Day couldn't stop the burst of laughter again. "What is going on with you? When did you learn all this traditional stuff?"

God shrugged. "It's common knowledge."

Day nodded, a sneaky grin on his face. "Okay. You put on something sexy and so will I."

God rolled over and let Day get up. Their luggage had been brought to the room earlier that day by one of their guys, so Day grabbed his duffle bag and went in the bathroom, throwing a seductive look over his shoulder at God before he closed the door.

I'll show him my sexiest outfit, God thought after Day closed the door.

God took off his suit, removed every stitch of clothing and laid across the bed amidst all those fucking flowers. Naked as the day he was he born. His sexiest outfit. He heard water running and Day moving around, taking his sweet time. God wondered if his husband had packed a thong or something. His cock was thickening at the thought. He reached down and tugged on his balls, groaning at the shock that shot through his entire body. He was worked up already. The fact that he was going to make love to Day as his husband for the first time almost had him getting up and bursting through that bathroom door to toss Day over his shoulder. God spread his legs wider, his toes curling the harder he pulled on his sack.

"You starting without me?" Day's deep voice cut through his heat.

God jerked his head up to see Day dressed in the exact same outfit as him. "That's the hottest look you got, sweetheart." God crooked his finger at him. "Come're."

Day crawled up God's body, dragging his tongue over his shaft as he went.

"Fuck," God hissed.

Day laid down over him, sealing their hard bodies together from toe to mouth. "You're everything to me, Cash. You're my husband."

God held him close while he ran his hands all over Day's willing body. Manipulated every erogenous zone he had – he knew his spouse's body better than he knew his own. He stroked Day between his legs and between his ass cheeks, knew his weakness for that double assault. God teased him and licked him until Day released continuous moans into the large suite, calling out his name and his love for him. God rolled them, laid his husband down tenderly, and made love to him in what felt as powerful and real as their first time.

When they were finished, sweaty and covered in red rose petals, God reached over and grabbed a couple Kleenex from the holder on the bedside table, wiping Day's come off his stomach and chest, too exhausted to stand and get a washrag. It was extremely late or extremely early, however you wanted to look at it, and they needed to sleep. They had a plane to catch to Aruba soon. A much-needed vacation after way too long. Their task force was the most important thing to them besides each other, but they needed a break. They could trust Syn to hold it down until they returned next week. God stretched out on his back – his best friend, his partner… his husband in his arms – and pulled Day's leg up over the top of his thighs, sleeping in the same position they did every night. Fitting together effortlessly.

Chapter FORTY-EIGHT

Tech

When the bosses are away, they never hesitated to play. Syn wasn't to be screwed with, but he was also a big pushover. He loved them too much to not give them what they wanted.

"Come on, Syn. God and Day come back on Sunday, we've been sitting around here doing shit for three days. Just say yes." Green was practically whining.

Syn was at his desk flipping through a magazine, eating a bag of chips like he was barely listening. But they all knew he was.

Tech was sitting with his back to his desk, smiling longingly, his feet propped up on Steele's lap while he massaged them. They didn't hurt, but for whatever reason, Steele had started rubbing them.

"I can't sit here with these two another minute." Ruxs pointed at Steele. "It's getting on my nerves. Why don't they run off and start a 'love is grand' cult or something? It's nauseating."

"Don't be jealous, Ruxs... it's not attractive." Steele smiled, but never took his eyes off Tech.

"We haven't had a four-day weekend in a year. Come on, man. God won't care. When they get back, they're going to be so well rested and high off newlywed crack, they won't care you gave us a few days off." Ruxs kept hammering away at Syn's resolve.

Syn turned to face them. "What if a department needs back up and you guys are... who knows where, huh? Then what?"

Ruxs looked like he was contemplating that. "Call Hart. He'll cover for us."

Syn nodded like that was a reasonable solution.

Free leapt up from his chair. "I'll go ask him. Be right back."

Tech shook his head at his best friend, watching him hurry through the bullpen to the elevators to head upstairs to Hart's department.

"Shouldn't someone tell him Hart's not even bisexual?" Ro looked at Tech before he tossed the small rubber ball to Michaels. Yeah, they were really bored.

"Hell no," Green piped up. "Let's see how this plays out. Hart has been acting a little strange if you ask me. I've caught him staring at the guy more than once."

"Me too," Ruxs agreed.

"That's only because he's sexy. Doesn't mean Hart wants to do him." Ro shrugged. "I just don't want Free to get his feelings hurt."

"He *is* an adult, right?" Tech glanced at his brothers. "Let him decide."

They all looked at him with sour expressions. "Well, fuck us for caring." Ro threw the ball at Tech, but Steele reached up and intercepted it.

"My hero," Tech said softly.

"Okay. Be back on Monday," Syn blurted. "Hell, even I don't wanna watch them any longer."

"Yeah! Way to go, Tech!" Ruxs ran over, high-fiving him and Steele.

They had been playing up the lovey-dovey to annoy everyone, especially Syn. When Ruxs said Syn had mentioned their terms of endearment and overly obnoxious affection were driving him crazy; Ruxs and Green asked them to turn it up a notch more so they could start hammering at Syn to get off early Thursday for a four-day weekend. Looked like their devious plan worked.

Tech walked with Steele to the parking lot. He leaned against his driver's side door waiting for Steele to light his cigar. "So we have four whole days. What do you wanna do?"

"You."

Tech rolled his eyes. "Obviously. What else?"

Steele shrugged, taking a deep inhale. "I didn't have shit else planned. Wanna grab some grub tonight, hang out?"

"You sweet talker, you. How can I refuse, since you asked so nicely?" Tech looked indignantly at his boyfriend, his arms crossed over his chest.

Steele eyed him for a few seconds, a sexy quirk curving his mouth. He moved closer until he was pressing Tech into the door. "*Armastaja*. Will you let me take you to dinner tonight?" Steele kissed Tech's chin, leaning back for his answer.

Tech smiled. He enjoyed giving his lover crap about his roughneck ways. Steele was a wonderful man, a great boyfriend, and Tech was turned on by every aspect of him, even his rough demeanor, but he still liked ribbing him on it sometimes.

"Yes, I'd love to, thank you," Tech teased.

"Then, after dinner… will you let me fuck you until you scream my name?" Steele thrust his hips hard enough to make Tech grunt.

"You couldn't resist, could you?" Tech laughed, pushing Steele back before he caused some permanent damage to his pelvis or the door of his truck.

Steele flicked away the last half of his cigar and crowded back against him. Gentler this time, he dipped to kiss Tech just under his nose, making his way to his mouth. Steele held Tech's face in his hands, tilting his head and smoothly sliding his tongue inside. Tech closed his eyes and moaned, quickly sucking on that smoky tongue, riding high off it.

"Steele! Bring your ass. Let's go before Syn changes his mind," Ruxs yelled after bringing his truck to a jerky stop right behind Tech's truck.

"I'm going to wait on Free." Tech pecked him one more time.

"Okay. You want to take my bike out tonight?" Steele grinned. "Furious has it riding nice."

"Hell no. It's too cold. I'll pick you up."

"That's cool. Later." Steele turned and jumped into the backseat. Ruxs sped off before Steele even had the door closed all the way.

Tech was thumbing through his phone while he waited for his friend. He jumped at the sound of loud knuckles rapping on his window, his hand instinctively going for his 9mm. He turned, frowning at Vasquez. He hit the button and dropped the window down halfway.

"Don't kill me." Vasquez smiled. "That Marine of yours has you jumpy."

Tech didn't bother to respond or appear receptive to conversation. Free had ended up telling him how shitty Vasquez treated him at the bachelor party and why Hart intervened, so Vasquez was officially on Tech's shit list. "Did you want something?"

Vasquez looked taken back, his eyes squinting like he was pissed off. "Damn. I just wanted to say hi to a friend. We used to be close, now you act like you can't stand me. What's up? Since you got your little boyfriend and your new job title, you act like you're too good to speak to anyone."

Tech wanted to roll his window up in his face. Was he for real? Vasquez's posture was defensive. His thick arms crossed over his chest, the dark blue uniform stretched to the limit over his straining biceps. "First of all. There's nothing little about my boyfriend. And two, me being a field officer has no bearing on anything. I'm still me. I haven't had much to say to you Vasquez, because of how you treated my best friend."

An angry frown penetrated Vasquez's tan forehead. "Did Hart tell you a lie?"

"This has nothing to do with Hart," Tech said. He was done with this conversation because it wasn't going to go anywhere good. "I'll see you around, Vasquez."

"Here comes Free. I'll clear this up right now." Vasquez backed away from Tech's window but paused when he noticed Free wasn't alone. He was followed by Syn and Hart.

Free's steps faltered when he noticed Vasquez walking around the truck. Syn leveled a hard look at Vasquez before putting his hand on Free's shoulder, moving him forward again. When they got to Tech's truck, Vasquez tried to speak, but Syn gave him a look that implied, "You better not say a fuckin' word." Hart's posture was very similar. Tech wondered if Free told Syn what had happened. Maybe Syn just picked up on Free's unease. One way or another, it looked like Syn knew because he opened the door for Free and ushered him inside, closing the door when he was fully seated. Syn hit the hood a couple times, signaling Tech to drive off.

Looking in his rearview mirror, Tech saw that Syn didn't bother acknowledging Vasquez, who was still standing there looking disrespected. Syn shook Hart's hand and both men gave Vasquez their backs as they turned and walked off in different directions.

Chapter FORTY-NINE

Steele

Steele reclined in his chair and clenched his hands in his lap. He was full, but he was far from relaxed. His full rack of ribs was delicious, but it was the bottle of Stella that was keeping him from jumping up and shouting for the staff to turn the goddamn music down. He could barely hear his own thoughts. Tech was still working on his burger while flipping through the dessert menu. Steele watched the people come and go in the brightly lit, too loud, overly decorated Hard Rock Café in Downtown. Tech chose the place, contending he'd been wanting a good burger for days and this place had the best. Whatever Tech wanted, he'd do. But if he never came back to this restaurant, he was good with that.

Tech turned to him, wiping his mouth. He had to practically yell his question to be heard over the incessant chatter around them. "You good? You want dessert?"

"No." Steele mouthed.

Tech frowned, pushing his plate away, leaving only a couple bites of his huge burger. Steele didn't know where he put all the food he ate. "What's wrong? You look like you're about to fight someone."

"Nothing. It's just extremely loud and bright in here." Steele leaned over so Tech could hear him over the classic Aerosmith song blaring from the sound system. Multi-color, crazy strobe lights, people toe tapping, singing, and customers bumping into his chair every five minutes while he ate wasn't the way he liked to dine. It was too much going on and he felt out of control. Being disoriented wasn't good for him. He looked around again, his eyes darting to the front door every few minutes. Out of his peripheral vision, he saw Tech's hand go up, signaling the server for the check. Steele rubbed his palm on his jeans when he was jolted again, a server bumping his chair when he tried to ease through at the same time a customer did. Steele gritted his teeth, closing his eyes against the harsh light and taking a slow breath. Next thing he knew, Tech's hand was in his and he was being pulled from his seat and out the front door. Tech didn't stop until they were around the corner and away from the pedestrian traffic on the sidewalk.

Tech stopped them against the side of the restaurant and turned to look at him. "Babe, are you okay? Why didn't you tell me you were uncomfortable in there?"

Steele's jaw was locked tight while he tried to calm himself down. He didn't have full on episodes, he knew how to prevent them, but it was good he got out of there when he did; he simply wasn't at ease in environments like that. It was amazing, he could efficiently move through a chaotic war zone but he couldn't sit in a crowded restaurant full of over-stimulated patrons and servers.

"Okay. I got it," Tech whispered, wrapping his arms around Steele's neck and pulling him close.

Steele gripped Tech's waist, tucking his face into his neck, rubbing his cheek against his soft, clean-smelling skin. Steele didn't need to voice anything, admit anything. Tech already understood, and Steele loved him even more for that. He could feel his body relaxing under his lover's touch. A partner was supposed to be able to do that for you. Put his hands on you and make the discomfort disappear. Tech could already do that to him.

"I'm all right." Steele turned his mouth into Tech's throat, just barely brushing his lips across the skin so opposite from his own bristly stubble. "I hate that fuckin' wild lighting."

Tech squeezed him harder as if apologizing for taking him there. Steele rubbed Tech's back, bringing one hand up behind his head, smoothing down the already neatly arranged hair. He took Tech's chin between his thumb and forefinger, applying a bit of pressure to open his pretty mouth. He slowly placed his lips on his, closing his eyes at the first touch of those tender lips. The feeling just as incredible as the first kiss he'd stolen in the equipment room. Tech moaned lovingly, burying his fingers in Steele's hair. He kissed him until he felt Tech shiver in his arms. He couldn't resist swiping his tongue across a couple more times before pulling back. "Come on. You're cold."

"Hey." Tech leaned in, his lips curved in a sensual smile, breathing his warm breath against Steele's oversensitive ear. Tech's lips brushed his lobe when he spoke, his sexy *armastaja* knowing what it did to him. "Why don't we go someplace a little darker and quieter?"

Steele held Tech's narrow waist in a death grip, his groin pressed firmly against him so he could feel exactly what Tech's sly move was doing to him. He felt the moist tip of Tech's tongue, drag across the outer rim then gently dip inside.

"You must want me to fuck you right here in this parking lot," Steele hissed, grinding their pelvises together. It was dark outside and the parking lot was small, tucked farther between the buildings, but it wasn't that isolated. Someone would probably walk by any minute.

Tech's lips curved again, and just like that, Steele had long forgotten his anxiety.

Chapter FIFTY

Tech

"Where are we?" Tech asked Steele, looking over at him. He looked a lot more relaxed and content now. He couldn't believe he'd misread Steele's mood the entire time they'd been in the restaurant. He noticed he didn't talk much, but Tech had just chalked it up to him enjoying his food. He'd pay more attention to Steele when they were in new surroundings. But now he knew: his boyfriend didn't like those types of places.

"Didn't I ace my quiz? Why do you still ask me where we are?" Steele grinned over at him.

Tech shrugged. "Yeah, you passed it, but I only had a hundred questions on it. I didn't cover everything."

"You covered enough." Steele looked out the window. "We're on Mooreland. If you turn right up there on Fayetteville and take Constitution, the Metro detention center is on the right... no, left."

Tech nodded his head in approval. He knew his map had been a good idea, regardless of how the guys on the team had ridiculed him for it.

"But I still don't know where we're going. You said someplace dark... I thought you were talking about your bedroom."

"Free has a business call tonight with a company in San Diego, so I don't want to disturb him. He's going to be helping the tech team troubleshoot a system he set up there last year. It might be a tad unprofessional if the client heard sounds of hot sex going on in the next room."

"I told Green and Ruxs I'd be out the rest of the night. I think Green wants Ruxs to fuck him in the kitchen." Steele cringed.

"What?" Tech choked on a startled laugh. "Did he say that?"

"No. But it's probably still true. I need to give them their privacy back."

"So we're both homeless tonight." Tech shook his head. "Great."

"We'll think of something." Steele shrugged like it was no big deal.

Tech turned into the entrance of the Starlight Drive-In, shooting Steele a devious smile. He told the attendant after he paid that he'd been there before and didn't need the instructions. He pulled into the spots designated for large vehicles. He put the truck in park, turned off his lights, and killed the engine, turning it to accessory mode. He quickly tuned into the drive-in's FM station and adjusted the volume to low. He looked over at Steele. "Dark and quiet."

Tech adored the way Steele was gazing at him. There was no mistaking the love in his beautiful gray eyes. Tech reached over the console and laid his palm on Steele's cheek. "You like drive-ins?"

"I do. Haven't been to one since before I enlisted." Steele chuckled, turning to look at the screen. "Nice idea, baby."

"Come on, let's get in the back." Tech grabbed his remote and anxiously jumped out of the truck, ignoring Steele's questioning look. Tech tilted the driver's seat all the way forward, motioning for Steele to do the same. When they climbed in the back, Tech took his shoes off and reclined back, propping his feet up on the front seat. "This is better, there's no huge console between us. A lot more room."

Steele spread his legs wide and leaned back with him, opening up his arms so Tech could rest his body against him. The movie was just beginning and Tech saw a few more trucks had pulled into the back row. Didn't matter, his windows were entirely too dark to see inside. "Let me know if you get cold. The back rows have warmers, too."

Steele somehow pulled Tech even closer, nuzzling behind his ear. "I'm plenty warm enough."

With his back against Steele's chest, Tech leaned his head back, resting it on Steele's shoulder, letting him drag his nose along his neck. "We're going to at least watch the opening of the movie,

332

right?" Tech said, stretching his head higher to give Steele more room.

"Mm hmm. Maybe," Steele murmured, his teeth grazing Tech's delicate flesh.

Tech let Steele have his fun. With his head all the way back, Tech pushed a button on his remote and the cover of the moon roof slid open. Steele stopped his ministrations and looked up. The air was crisp on the beautiful fall night and the stars were bright high up in the sky.

"That's cool as hell. You have a remote control for this thing?" Steele took it out of Tech's hand, looking it over.

Tech put his hands up in a take it easy gesture. "Careful. You don't want to shoot the missile and take out the screen."

Steele jerked upright. "What?" he barked.

Tech laughed hysterically. "Kidding. I'm kidding."

Steele grabbed Tech and yanked him against him, gripping his chin and laying a brutal kiss on his mouth as punishment. "That wasn't funny."

"It sort of was. Why in the hell would you think I have a missile in here?" Tech managed to say between laughs.

"You have every-fucking-thing-else," Steele argued, finally relaxing in his seat. "You have a shitty sense of humor, you know that?"

"You love it." Tech reached up and cupped the back of Steele's neck, directing his mouth to where it was on his neck before the moon roof opened.

The movie was five minutes in and they settled down to watch. Tech had paid for whatever the next movie was that was starting, which ended up being some type of drama. Steele had clearly lost interest about midway through. Tech felt Steele's hand inching under his sweater.

"Did I tell you looked nice tonight?" Steele said close to his ear.

"Yes. But thank you again." Tech looked down at his light brown Calvin Klein sweater and black jeans. He looked plain, but for some reason, Steele repeatedly complimented his look.

"You smell good, too." Steele licked at the base of Tech's hairline.

Tech squirmed, his balls tightening. He couldn't help but reach down and adjust his cock, which was growing at an awkward angle in his pants.

"You getting hard for me, baby?" Steele asked him thickly.

"I'm always hard for you," Tech said on a stimulated breath.

"I like how that sounds." Steele's hand was under his sweater and t-shirt, his thumb brushing tenderly over his nipple. "Will you do something for me, *armastaja*?"

Tech moaned his response. "Anything."

Steele growled appreciatively, like Tech's answer was perfect. "Take your dick out. Let me see you."

"Oh fuck." Tech twisted back and forth against Steele's hard body. With shaky fingers, Tech undid the button of his pants.

"Slowly." Steele nipped Tech's ear. "I can feel how hot your body is, but I don't want you to rush."

Tech inched his zipper down and splayed his pants open. Despite the fact that it was a chilly fifty-two degrees outside, the inside of his truck was quickly heating up.

"Take it out... all of it... wanna see those smooth balls too." Steele's voice dripped like honey around him.

Tech tucked his underwear under his sack, gasping with relief at the release from restriction. Biting his bottom lip, he used both hands, one massaging his heavy balls and the other stroking himself as slowly as Steele asked. "Oh god."

"Yeah... just like that." Steele pinched Tech's nipple harder while sucking on his neck.

Tech gazed up at the stars over their heads, feeling like he was floating in outer space, the sensation of being under Steele's control feeling beyond amazing. He naturally stroked faster, his fingers taking him towards his climax. He could hear Steele's moans mixing in with his own erotic song.

"That's it. Show me how you get yourself off when I'm not with you. When I'm not in your bed. Do you think of me, *armastaja*, when you have your dick in your hand?"

334

"Edwin," Tech whimpered. He squeezed his balls and the tip of his cock, pulling a thick drop of precome from it and using it to slick his way to ecstasy. Tech couldn't hear the movie anymore, didn't know anything happening around them, it was only him, his desire, and his Marine.

"Do you cry my name like that when I'm not with you?" Steele asked with Tech's earlobe between his teeth.

His sex throbbed in his hand, his breathing labored and fogging the windows. Tech moved faster, couldn't slow down, couldn't hold back whether he was ordered to or not. Steele was whispering stern words in another language in his ear, words of his Estonian heritage. It sounded forceful and racy. Tech jerked wildly, but Steele's strong arms kept him in place as his orgasm stiffened his spine and shot through his engorged shaft. Tech had barely gotten Steele's name out of his mouth when he was pushed back against the seat and Steele swept down and captured the head of his dick in his mouth, just in time to catch the first jet of come to erupt from him. Steele sucked him hard, sucked the shouts of passion from him with each release of his seed. When he was too over-stimulated to take any more, he gripped Steele's chin, urging him to let his cock slip from his tight suction.

Steele finally sat up, wiping his mouth with the back of his hand, looking pleased and predatory, like he was about to pounce on him any second. Eyeing the thick bulge in Steele's jeans, Tech realized that an attack was highly likely. Tech was splayed against the seat, trying to catch his breath from one of the most powerful orgasms he'd ever had… but when he thought about it… didn't he think that every time Steele made him come?

"If you only knew what I want to do to you right now," Steele growled, massaging himself through his denim while Tech lay there recovering.

"Give me two minutes," Tech answered, his chest still heaving.

"Fuck that. We're leaving." Steele jumped out of the truck, leaving Tech breathless in the backseat with his cock lying lifeless on his thigh.

Steele got in the driver's seat and started it up, easing from the space. "Where… where are we going? I thought we were gonna have drive-in sex."

"You're too special for me to fuck you in the back seat of a truck surrounded by eleven other vehicles."

Tech smiled lazily, chewing on his lip while his boyfriend sped them down the highway to who knew where.

Chapter FIFTY-ONE

Steele

He had to stop looking at Tech in the rearview mirror before he veered off the road and crashed. His boyfriend was just so damn sexy, sitting back there with his dick still out, writhing back and forth on the seat. He couldn't hear what Tech was mumbling to himself, he looked lost in his own erogenous world. Coming that hard was a potent wave of euphoria taking over your entire body, but coming down from a powerful climax was an amazing sensation in itself.

Steele pushed hard on his erection, pressing the gas a little too much as he merged onto the twenty. He'd wanted so badly to flip Tech's ass over and push inside him, but he meant more to him than that. Fooling around at a drive-in, fondling, sucking, kissing, was fine – thank heaven for Tech's darkly tinted windows – but Tech's body was his to cherish. He wouldn't demean their coming together. Every time Tech gave himself to Steele, he was thankful for it, knowing now what it meant to make love. That didn't mean they could only do it in a bedroom underneath Egyptian cotton sheets, only that it was all still so emotional right now.

"Edwin. Where are we going? Hurry up," Tech moaned.

Steele quickly glanced back and saw Tech was almost fully hard again, stroking himself. "Fuuuck." Steele shook his head, gripping his dick so hard it hurt. He looked at the map on Tech's display screen and saw he was only two minutes away after he took his exit onto West Peachtree. "Almost there, baby."

Steele stopped at the light and chanced a peek in the rearview, seeing drugged brown eyes looking back at him. Tech sucked his bottom lip into his mouth and released it slowly, his teeth grazing the tender flesh. *Ungh, fuck.* Steele adjusted himself in the seat, still staring. Tech was leaking on his leather seats, his legs gaped open so wide Steele could see his hole. *Motherfucker.* Tech knew what he was doing to him because while his eyes were filled with yearning, his wet lips were curved into a smile that meant trouble. Tech pinched the head of his dick, another clear bead drizzling over and down the underside of his full shaft. Tech smeared it over his middle finger and inched closer to his hole, teasing Steele with torturously slow movements. "Yeah," Steele said gutturally. Tech pushed the tip of his—

A horn blasted behind him and Steele jerked back forward, looking up at the green light that had just turned yellow when he stomped on the gas. He hadn't realized how long he'd been sitting there engrossed by his lover's show.

Steele pulled into the Aloft Atlanta Downtown and parked in one of the back parking spaces. He turned off the truck and turned around, reaching for Tech. He gripped him behind his neck and yanked him forward, crashing their mouths together, biting him hard enough to jolt him out of his haze. Tech slid forward like he was going to climb over the center console and into Steele's lap. Damn, he was so in love with this man. An intellect paired with the insatiability of a sex addict.

"I'm going to get us a room." Steele reached for Tech's dick, firmly stroking it a couple times. "Put this away… for a few minutes."

Tech simply nodded like he was too horny to speak the words.

Steele pulled his cock upwards in his jeans and closed his leather jacket before he went into the lobby to register for a room. He asked for a king-sized suite, thinking they should stay here a couple days and enjoy some of their unexpected time off. The desk clerk smiled suggestively at him, her long red hair swept up into a large bun on her head with tendrils hanging around her delicate face. She was very attractive, but Steele hardly paid attention to her soft rambling about the heated rooftop pool, billiards room, Wi-Fi passwords, and complimentary breakfast.

"You look like you'd enjoy our exercise room." She smiled, putting his set of key cards in an envelope.

"My boyfriend probably would," Steele said casually, taking the envelope and thanking her.

Tech

"What made you pack a bag?" Steele asked, sticking the card into the door scanner.

"I thought I was staying with you. Why do you have your backpack?"

"I was staying with you." Steele chuckled.

"We need to communicate better." Tech smiled up at him, walking into the room.

Steele let the door close behind them, dropped his bag and pulled Tech into his arms. "Oh, I think we communicate just fine." Steele's touch was calmer now, unlike ten minutes ago. It was adoring and romantic as he held the back of Tech's head while lightly rubbing his back. He looked into Tech's eyes and affectionately kissed him. "I love you."

"Mmm," Tech moaned. "I love you."

They held each other for a moment, not in a rush, realizing they had the whole night; actually, they had a few days. He didn't know how much the room was, but the Aloft hotel was nice. Located in Downtown amidst a ton of restaurants, shops, clubs, there was a lot they could do. Tech let Steele go and walked farther into the room. It was beautiful. The bed was huge and draped in starched white linens, looking like it'd never been used before. There were orange and blue decorative pillows to give it a splash of color, which matched perfectly with the colorful drapes. The art was chic and modern, as were the furnishings. He wanted to stay there with Steele their entire break and made a mental note to talk with him later about splitting the costs. He wanted to be fair.

Steele gave Tech some space while he looked around. The back wall was floor to ceiling windows. Tech turned the heat on low to knock the chill off the large space. The room was on the twelfth floor and Tech couldn't resist opening the heavy curtains and staring across exquisitely lit Downtown at night.

"That's sexy, huh?" Steele came up behind him, laying a soft kiss on the back of his neck. It was another part of Tech's body he was obsessed with.

"Yeah." Tech sighed. He turned around, looking further into the room and gasped at the massive Jacuzzi tub right outside the bathroom door. "Oh, come on, let's take a bath together. That one's exactly like Day's tub."

Steele looked quizzically at him. "First of all, how do you know what Day's tub looks like and second, I don't take baths."

"Well, to answer your first question. Everyone knows what Day and God's bedroom looks like because it's where Day keeps his prize jazz collection that he can never resist showing off along with the model cars that he builds. I'm sure as soon as you go there, he'll drag you up to see it."

"Oh. Alright, then." Steele released Tech and retrieved his backpack from the floor.

Tech went to the tub and started to fill it with water. He sat on the edge looking expectantly at his boyfriend, trying to look pitiful and pleading at the same time. "You going to make me get in this huge tub all by myself? Why would you get this amenity if you didn't plan to use it? I love these; they make me feel so... good."

Steele stopped searching in his bag when he heard the suggestiveness Tech projected in his voice. "It came with the suite. Never mind how it makes you feel, grown ass men don't take baths."

"Right. Because only two-year-old toddlers should get in this thing."

"Smart mouth makes a soft ass, Shawn." Steele stared at him.

"That's the spirit." Tech winked. "Get undressed. I'm gonna use the bathroom. It'll take a while for this to fill up."

Chapter FIFTY-TWO

Steele

Steele watched Tech practically floating in the deep tub, grinning excitedly like a kid in a toy store. He'd removed his glasses, his wet hair slicked back from his face. He didn't know which one of them looked more ridiculous. Tech, playing in the chest-deep water or him, standing there butt naked with a petulant scowl and his hands on his hips.

"Come on. You know you want to get in. The water feels great," Tech purred.

"If you tell anyone, I'll deny it," Steele said, climbing in.

"Promise. I won't tell anyone you bathed this weekend." Tech slid between Steele's legs as soon as he was settled in.

Out of sheer stubbornness, Steele didn't moan when the hot water encased his body, but fuck it felt good. Lying there with Tech in his arms, he felt like he was actually on vacation. They let the water relax them while they talked about any and everything.

"What do you wanna do in the morning?" Steele asked, rubbing soapy circles over Tech's chest.

"I'm supposed to go to Chen's, but I can call and cancel. It's at noon since I don't have a personal session."

"No. Don't do that. If you want to go, I can go with you. I'd love to see it."

"Really? You want to go with me?" Tech asked eagerly.

"It's important to you. It's where you honed your skills to become the badass you are today. I'd be honored for you to show me where you've worked so hard the past couple years. Show me the designs your brilliant mind came up with for the program." Steele ran his hands through Tech's hair. "Then I think you should take me to those neighborhoods you marked last week. Since we have a few days, I want to take a look at some of them. I need my own place, baby. Need a lot more uninterrupted time with you."

Tech craned his head to the side, looking up at Steele like he was the luckiest man in the world, but Steele felt like it was the other way around. Tech cupped his cheek, leaning in for a kiss. Steele held Tech's palm, kissing his wrinkled fingers. "Let's get out of this tub. We're turning into raisins."

Tech stood up and held his hand out to him. They dried off and pulled back the soft cotton sheets on the bed, climbing in right behind each other. Tech reached up and turned off the light on his side of the bed. Steele left the dim light of his bedside lamp on, wanting to see Tech's face until he closed his eyes. He yawned at the thought of sleep. He'd gotten up early; it'd been a long day.

"You not going to sleep yet, are you?" Tech asked around a yawn.

"I think it was the bath. I'm feeling real relaxed right now." Steele pulled Tech into his body, enclosing him in his warmth.

"Don't you want me to—?"

"Shh. Sleep, *armastaja*." Steele was already dozing.

"I want you to be satisfied," Tech whispered, grinding his naked lower body on his thigh.

Steele popped him on the ass. "Be still. I'm satisfied just like this."

Steele felt Tech smile against his chest. He waited until he heard Tech's deep breathing before he succumbed to his own peace.

Steele was getting some of the best rest he'd ever had. In his subconscious, he knew he didn't have to be anywhere early and he could feel his sweetheart in his arms. He teetered between half-asleep and half-awake for most of the night. He thought he was having a wet dream and might've even moaned a few times, he wasn't sure and he didn't care. Steele was warm and comfortable, the feeling of hands on him kept him on the edge of being fully awake, but would soothe him right back into slumber. He was floating in that lustful state where he thought he heard sounds of pleasure but wasn't sure if it was him making them since he felt so good. His body was gently rocked back and forth like he was being lulled back to sleep every time he came to. He knew his dick was hard, he could feel the stimulation, the tingling in his balls, but his languid mood kept him from reaching for it, he was comfortable where his hands were. On supple, soft skin. His head rested on a fluffy pillow, his face nestled in silky hair. Steele wanted to stay like this for as long as he could.

Another moan, louder this time, pierced through his fog, causing his eyes to flutter. It was still pitch dark outside, not even a sliver of daylight breaking. It must be two or three in the morning. Lying on his side with Tech's back against him, movement drew his attention lower. In and out motion – the reason for his body rocking back and forth – a slicking sound... a lewd moan. Steele looked down his body, past his chest, to his hard cock that was pointed at Tech's hole. A hole that Tech was pushing two fingers deep inside of.

Oh, he was awake now. Steele slowly ran his hand up Tech's chest. "You bad boy." Steele's voice was as rough as sandpaper from sleep, but Tech's response to him was obscene.

Tech reached for Steele's dick and nudged back until its head was right there at his slippery entrance. Steele had his arm under Tech's head, he brought it up and held a handful of his sleep-tousled hair in his hand while he squeezed Tech's hip with the other. Tech pushed back onto him, controlling the entry, easing Steele inside him... with no condom.

As if they both realized it at the same time, Tech paused midway, his breath hitching from either the realization or the penetration, Steele didn't know. But he did know that he trusted Tech. He loved him and he knew they were both good. This was right. "Keep going," he ordered hoarsely.

Tech moaned loudly, and in one move, pushed back and sheathed Steele's dick in an amazing, hot restriction that made him grunt and fold in over Tech's back. "Fuck," Steele cursed, squeezing his eyes shut, trying to get a handle on the feeling that had just taken hold of him.

Steele was so wrapped around Tech's body he didn't know where he began and where Tech's frame ended. Tech lay there, motionless, breathing through the feeling and Steele didn't dare disrupt him. This was all about Tech, he'd let him direct this show.

After a few more tense seconds, Tech began a lazy sway of his hips, moving back and forth in shallow pumps, pushing his ass back into Steele's pelvis. It was glorious. Steele kept a hold of Tech's hair but he moved his other arm up Tech's chest and held him there so their upper halves never parted. He kissed Tech's shoulder, licked across the back of his neck, and sucked on his collarbone while he made slow love to him. Moving his pale hips in unhurried motions, taking his sweet time.

"Edwin. I love you so much," Tech whispered into the darkness.

Steele squeezed him tighter, Tech taking his hand from over his chest and kissing Steele's palm before settling back over his heart. An overwhelming sense of déjà vu hit Steele. He remembered this scene, walking past a parted door. An insanely in love couple, lying in a gorgeous bed, wrapped in the same exact embrace, savoring a bond that most men only dreamed about having with another. Whispering words of heated passion and love. Steele had seen this before and he remembered closing himself in the bathroom down the hall, wishing he could have it, too. Hoping that a man with impeccable style, an incomparable mind, and the fierceness of a lion would love him and fight by his side. After losing Ack he never thought he'd have that chance. But he did have it and it was right there in his arms. For the first time since that tragic day, his soul didn't cry when he thought of Ackerman. Reflexively, he squeezed Tech tighter to him, knowing he was the reason why.

"I love you too, baby," Steele confessed, giving Tech his heart and soul. He reached down and pulled on Tech's hardness, feeling it expand even more. "Come with me."

Tech pushed back and ground his ass against him, moaning deeply into the pillows, spilling his hot release onto the cool linen. Steele turned Tech's head so he could taste him, so he could see the rapture on his face when he came inside him for the first time. Holding his hip firmly to his, Steele's mouth dropped open, the sensitivity, the emotion devastating him. His entire body clenched tight and he could hear his lover, encouraging him to let it go.

"Edwin," Tech cried when the warmth flooded his channel.

"My *armastaja*. Shawn." Steele held on, emptying more than just his seed deep inside Tech. He was his forever. There was nothing he wouldn't do for him. He'd love Tech until his last breath, he'd protect him… they'd protect each other. The man in his arms held his heart, and he knew it was safe there.

The End… for now.
Coming Next: Nothing Special VI ~ Free's story.

Continue for the Bonus Read

BONUS
Chapter
ONE

A Genesis and Curtis Short Story

Genesis Godfrey

Genesis dropped the luggage in their spacious Washington DC apartment and kicked off his Jordan slides, pissed that he was back home already when he'd only left two days ago. Traffic had been hell leaving the city, but it was a bitch coming back in. He wasn't supposed to have needed to worry about that so soon, but his partner mucked that up. They'd had two weeks of vacation planned. Planned it three months ago, and still, Curtis had managed to let his boss tank their happiness. It was becoming quite regular now. Anything they tried to do, that jerk would pop up like a big zit and ruin everything.

Genesis hardly had any time with his brother and new brother-n-law. They'd missed the bachelor party, missed Prescott again. *I MISSED FURI AND BLAIR DANCING!* The video that Green took of it – he refused to show him because he was so pissed with him – probably wouldn't have done the actual visual justice, anyway. Genesis grabbed the luggage back up, stormed past his boyfriend, and tossed it into the bedroom. He plopped down on the recliner and tried to get his anger under control. The way Curtis' dads looked at him before they left was getting under Genesis' skin. It wasn't his fault that Curtis was letting his boss make their lives a living hell. He was just as much a victim. They hardly went out, hardly had any time together in the evenings, the asshole keeping Curtis there way beyond the time he was supposed to leave, they hardly even made love because Curtis was beat every night.

Genesis understood the community center Curtis volunteered at was in desperate need of caring people like him, people willing to sacrifice their time because those kids deserved it. His lover was compassionate like that. The center was one of the biggest in the city, but also one of the most understaffed and underfunded. Curtis had made so many suggestions on how to better the center only to have them shot down by the director each time. Programs that made perfect sense to Genesis, programs that benefited not only the kids but the community as a whole, were repeatedly rebuffed. Even the proposed night GED prep course for adults had been called silly and unnecessary, right to Curtis' face.

"You still mad at me?" Curtis asked from the door, looking just as exhausted as Genesis.

"Yeah, Curtis. I am mad. This was my brother's wedding. You know how important it was for me to be there." Genesis sighed.

"You were there."

"You know what I mean!" Genesis yelled. He closed his eyes, immediately regretting raising his voice. "I was supposed to be there longer than forty-eight hours. Now I have over two-and-a-half weeks of vacation time and nothing to do. I'll be here alone all day, sitting on my thumbs because that dick really enjoys monopolizing your time when you have a break from school."

"I can't keep having this conversation with you, Genny." Curtis went to their walk-in closet and began shedding his clothes. "I need the volunteer hours for my degree, too."

"There are a lot of other community centers," Genesis combatted uselessly. He'd said this a million times before. "I did my fair share of volunteering too when I was in college, but I never had to deal with bullshit like this. The center I participated in, the volunteers were appreciated, not tortured."

"I'm not letting him beat me. Those kids need me. I'm not walking away." Curtis squared his shoulders, looking back at him with determination in those usually dreamy blue eyes.

His partner may be a petite, beautiful man, but he was strong and brave. It's what attracted Genesis to him in the first place. Curtis hadn't grown up like most kids. He'd been a child, a teenager who'd had too much responsibility put on him when his biological father walked out on him and his mother. He was at his lowest and most desperate when God and Day found him trying to rob a mom-and-pop convenience store – with an IOU note in his back pocket – to pay the electric bill for his mother. He'd worked and gone to school from the time he was fourteen, but his meager wages weren't enough to support them all the time. Curtis still said God and Day saved his life. They took him under their wing, and that's where he met his dads, Ruxs and Green. They were there for him while his mom fought her kidney disease, adopted him when she died from it. The entire team made sure he had everything he needed, including a job that allowed him to still focus on school. Genesis knew Curtis was missing his fathers as well, but he wasn't going to disappoint those kids that relied on him every day. Genesis understood, he really did, but he at least wanted Curtis to stand up to the guy. Everyone had superiors. He needed to file a complaint or something, but he refused.

"I'm sorry, Genny. I said it earlier, I'm saying it for the fourth time. I'm sorry." Curtis closed himself in the bathroom, a few minutes later Genesis heard the shower turn on.

He wanted to go after him, hated to see him look like that, but he was still upset. He changed clothes and put on his favorite pair of lounging pants and left the room. He walked down the long hallway, through the open space that was their living room and dining room, and through the double doors to his den. It was his sanctuary. Almost a shrine to his days as the G-Man. All his awards, trophies, and plaques from high school through his four years as a Georgia Bulldog. The furniture was all browns and dark reds throughout the nice space. His mid-size, brown leather sectional had four recliners and a chaise lounge on the end, was positioned in front of his seventy-inch curved television. A housewarming gift from his brother's team when they helped move them in. He had framed pictures on the wall of his mom and brother, of his teammates and his spreads in everything from *Sports Illustrated* to *OUT* magazine. There was hardly space left anywhere. Especially after his latest addition, an old-school popcorn stand. He loved it in here. He turned on his television, typically tuned to ESPN, picked up his ratty nerf ball he'd had since peewee, and began tossing it in the air while he decompressed.

Next thing Genesis knew, he was opening his eyes to slivers of daylight breaking through his blinds. Shit, he'd fallen asleep in there. He hadn't meant to. His first thought was Curtis. He was probably heartbroken, thinking he was so mad he didn't even want to sleep beside him. Genesis wiped the sleep from his eyes and picked up his cell phone. It was a quarter to six. *I must've been beat.* It had to be the drive, especially after staying up until almost three with the guys after his brother and his new husband left to the hotel. He saw he had a missed text message from Curtis around one in the morning.

You coming to bed, Genny? I said I was sorry.

Genesis got up and left his room. *Oh, baby. I didn't mean to stay in there all night.* He was going to make Curtis the best breakfast he could. He wasn't as good as Green, but he could make a helluva short stack and some bacon. Curtis didn't have to be to the center until two, maybe they could see an early movie. Genesis walked through their bedroom door to a freshly made bed. *What the hell?* There was a note on his pillow in Curtis' neat handwriting, waiting for him.

Charles asked me to be in at six this morning. I'll try to call you at lunch time. I missed you last night. Love you, Genny.

Genesis crumpled the paper up in hand and threw it across the room. "Jerk!" he yelled. There was definitely something up with Curtis' boss. Genesis wanted to call him every curse word he knew. The kids didn't even get there until school let out at two, what did he want Curtis to do? Sweep all the rooms again? Restock the supply closets? There were at least fifteen other volunteers there and from what Curtis said, the director was disrespectful to all of them, but he didn't treat any of them near as badly as he treated him. Genesis paced back and forth, his mind racing. Was the guy a bigot? Was he a racist? Did he just loathe his job so much that he had to make everyone else miserable? Genesis wasn't a violent person but he wanted to go down there and bust that guy's head in. But if he did anything to get Curtis fired, he'd be sleeping in his den for a lot longer than one night.

BONUS *Chapter* TWO

Curtis Jackson

Curtis drank his triple shot latte, trying to give his body a little extra boost to stay awake. He hadn't gotten much sleep last night when Genesis didn't come to bed. They always slept together. It wasn't often they fought and when they did, it was cleared up pretty quickly. He knew his partner was getting fed up with his boss, Charles, but what could Curtis do? He pulled on the door to the center, but it was locked. He cupped his hand on the tinted glass, trying to see inside. Charles' office was the first door on the right, so he knocked a couple times and waited. It was freezing out and his body was already trembling. He went around the corner and noticed that Charles' Mustang wasn't in his spot. *He's not even here!* Curtis got back in his car and called Charles' number. After four rings he answered with a curt, "Yeah."

"Good morning, Charles. I'm here, but the door is locked. Is any—?"

"Tony will be there in an hour. You need to help him get the chairs set up in the rec room for movie day. Shawn's wife had her baby last night so he won't be in to do his job."

"So you called me?" Curtis was so stunned he didn't care how that sounded. He wasn't the custodian. He was an educational volunteer. "What do you mean in an hour? You asked me to be here at six."

"I called a few people but they weren't available. Is this a problem, Curtis? Tony is coming in, too. He'll help you get it set up. I'm late for a meeting. Goodbye."

Curtis stared at the home screen on his phone. He held it so tight in his hands he had to put it back in his book bag for fear he'd crush it. He wanted to call Genesis, but he was probably still asleep. Instead

351

of sitting there stewing, he pulled out his laptop and went back to working on his next proposal for the center. He wanted to start a computer education program. Learning computers and software was instrumental to this generation's success in the future. Most of the schools in this neighborhood couldn't afford computers or the newest technology. Curtis knew this center had money, he just had to figure out how and where Charles wanted it to be used… so far he hadn't.

"Curtis, Curtis, look. I passed, dude. I passed my geometry test. Coach said I can play in this week's game!" Jamal yelled at him when he burst into the rec room. The kids were shushing and throwing popcorn at him while he made his way back to the table where Curtis was sitting with his laptop open.

Curtis quieted down the kids and pulled Jamal into the hallway, smiling broadly. He took the paper he'd been waving and clamped his hand over his mouth, stunned speechless at the bright B+ in bold red ink at the top of his test paper. "Oh my god, Jamal. You did it. I knew you could."

Next thing he knew, Jamal threw his arms around Curtis' waist and grabbed him in a bear hug, the huge six foot one linebacker lifting him off his feet. Curtis yelped, slapping Jamal on his broad shoulders to put him down. Susan, who volunteered in the library, walked by, laughing at their theatrics, stopping beside them.

"What in the world is so exciting? I wanna know." She smiled, looking back and forth between them. She was in her usual knee-length skirt and long-sleeved turtleneck, her long black hair up in a messy ponytail sitting high on top of her head.

"Only my first good grade in geometry all year, that's what." The big eleventh grader thrust the paper in Susan's face. "I thought I was gonna be put on the bench the rest of the season. Mr. Graham said if I pass the next test it'll bring my grade to a C."

"Way to go, Jamal! I knew you'd get that grade up," she congratulated him.

"All because of this smart dude, right here." Jamal threw his heavy arm around Curtis' neck, yanking him in and running his knuckles over his hair like he was his little brother. "He even used football plays to help me understand angles."

"Jesus. Get off me." Curtis pushed at him, Jamal's huge body not budging.

"Yes, he has a way with you kids, that's for sure," Susan agreed.

"He did it." Curtis pointed at Jamal. He was so proud of him. "He buckled down, stayed focused. You did it, Jamal. First, your world history class, and now, geometry. You're on your way to honor roll, man."

"Curtis, my mom is going to be so happy, you just don't know." Jamal playfully shoved him and Curtis could see the sentiment on his face. Jamal was proud of himself and most importantly, he was proud to take some good marks home. Curtis pulled Jamal into another hug, patting him encouragingly on his back. "I'm so proud of you. I really am."

"Curtis. I'd like to see you in my office."

Curtis stepped back at the sound of his boss' tight voice, looking around Jamal's big frame to see him standing there with a pinched look on his face.

"What this sucka want now?" Jamal grumbled.

"Be quiet, Jamal, before he suspends you again," Curtis shushed him, turning back to Charles, he pointed at the open door. "I'm monitoring the rec room right now."

"Doesn't look that way to me," Charles snapped back.

"I'll watch the kids for you until you get back, Curtis," Susan offered nicely, pulling Jamal in the room in front of her, but Curtis didn't miss the daggers Jamal was shooting at the center director.

Curtis walked down the long hall, making the unwanted trek back to the front of the building. When he stepped inside Charles' office, he moved a few papers out of one of the chairs in front of the cluttered desk and sat down. He thought it might be about this morning, but Curtis was sadly mistaken when Charles finally sat down, clasping his hands in front of him.

"Curtis. I can't have you behaving inappropriately with the students. Because of your sexual orientation, one so-called innocent gesture could be perceived in the wrong way." Charles' thin lips barely moved when he spoke, his voice laced with loathing.

Curtis blinked stupidly, wondering for a moment if he'd actually heard right. "I'm sorry. Excuse me?"

"I saw you embrace Jamal several times." Charles leaned in; one eyebrow going up into his nonexistent hairline like what he was saying was spot-on.

"I didn't *embrace* him. I was congratulating him on his test grade." Curtis slid to the edge of his seat, shaking his head in disbelief. "This is insane. I didn't embrace him in that way, and if you were watching, I'm sure you could see that."

"Oh, I was watching. He spun you around like you were lovers."

Curtis coughed, almost gagging at the thought. "That is a kid." Curtis clenched his teeth, fighting not to yell or flat out curse his boss out. But the look Charles gave him said, "That's my point." Curtis stood up. "What the hell is this? Because I'm gay you think I'd... have you lost your mind, Charles?!"

"This is only a warning, but I will still have to note it in your file. I think you should go home for the rest of the day, I can see you're upset." Charles opened up a thin manila file folder and clicked the end of his pen and began jotting down something in chicken scratch.

"In my file! Put what in my file? You can't do that." Curtis ran his hand through his hair, completely baffled by everything. Charles couldn't outright ban him for nothing, so he was completely fabricating something. Something extremely serious. Something that could get back to his school and possibly hinder him getting his social work degree. "Wait a minute. Susan was right there. She'll tell you."

"I don't have to speak with anyone else, Curtis. I witnessed it," Charles said in a monotone, still writing.

Curtis wanted to rip that pen away and stab him through his hand. "You know this isn't right. I was not doing anything like you're insinuating. I would never," Curtis hissed the last word. "Even think along those lines. That is sick. It's sick for *you* to think it. To make up a story like this."

354

"Careful." Charles' head snapped up, his eyes locking in on Curtis. "I can make this an official write-up of inappropriate conduct."

"What is it you want from me, damnit? I'm here every day, weekends too. Putting in the work and time with these kids. Why are you here? I'm here because I care. Why? Why are you even here, Charles?!" Curtis fumed.

Charles shot up and pointed to the door. "I suggest you close your mouth and take the rest of the day off. Before I decide to not allow you back."

Curtis wanted to dump that desk on Charles' head, but if there's one thing he'd learned over the years, it was to not let anyone control your life. That's what his boss was trying to do. Curtis couldn't walk away. Couldn't tell his boss to shove it, even though that's what he wanted Curtis to do. He couldn't let this bully chase him away. Those kids needed Curtis here. Jamal needed him here. He had another test to pass to get that C and Curtis was going to make sure he was here to help him. Jamal had a real shot at getting into college by way of football and passing grades, a chance to get an education and a way to help his single mother, who worked two jobs to support them. They'd earned this, they'd put in their dues. Curtis thought about the B+ in Jamal's hand and clamped his mouth closed on the tirade of slurs and curses on the tip of his tongue, turning around and storming out the door. He went back to the rec room and quickly gathered his belongings. Susan looked at him with confusion, standing to walk him to the door.

"What happened? Curtis, are you okay?"

"Curtis, what's up, man. You leaving?" Jamal asked. "Did you get fired?"

Curtis couldn't talk because of the massive boulder in his throat but he could hear the worry in Jamal's voice. He reached his hand out to pat Jamal on his shoulder to let him know he was alright but yanked it back quickly. Having to do that shot a world of hurt through Curtis' chest strong enough to make him double over, but he held his spine rigid and barely whispered that he'd see them tomorrow and turned to hurry back down the hall.

When he was in his car, he dropped his forehead on the steering wheel and beat his hand on the dashboard, releasing all the anger and frustration he'd wanted to unload on his boss. He cried angry tears into his shaking hands. He'd never been accused of anything so vile and degrading. The thought of anyone getting wind of the accusation his boss had made was making his stomach cramp up.

He put the key in the ignition, but his hands were trembling so badly he knew it was dangerous to try to drive, so he sat back and rested his head against the headrest and tried to calm himself down. After a couple minutes, his phone rang in his backpack. Tears still streaming down his face, he tapped the speaker button and tried to put a little cheer in his voice when he answered his dad's call. "Hey, Dad. How's it going?"

"What's the matter, Curtis?" Green asked.

His father knew him too well. Green was the one that always could pick up on even his slightest discomfort. "I'm fine, Dad."

"No, you're not. You're crying. What's wrong, Curtis?" Green's voice was getting louder, his anxiety coming through the line and making Curtis wish he was there so his dad could wrap him in his arms. But he was grown. He didn't need his dads coming to his rescue. He'd be a man like they'd taught him to be.

"Crying. Curtis is crying? For what?"

Curtis sighed at the sound of Ruxs' deep voice in the background. He heard shuffling then Ruxs' angry voice blasted through the speaker. "Curtis?! Buddy, what's going on? Where are you?"

"I'm alright, Dad, calm down. It was just a really shitty day at work. One of the... the kids, he... the director...."

"Curtis calm down, just tell us slowly."

He could hear Green's compassionate voice mixing with Ruxs' pissed one.

"What did that motherfucker do? Tell me!"

"Mark, chill out, let him talk. Go on, Curtis, nice and slow," Green said softly.

"He said I was inappropriate with some kid. All the kid did was hug me because he was happy about me helping him pass his test. It's disgusting, Dad. That asshole knows it wasn't like that. He wants me to quit, but I'm not quitting. I'm not gonna quit!" Curtis yelled, trying to hold in more frustrated tears that only welled up in his eyes and spilled over anyway.

"Oh, he's dead. He's fuckin' dead!"

Curtis squeezed his temples. He knew Ruxs would go there. "Dad. I can handle it. Will you just let me handle it, please?"

"Okay, okay. We know you can handle it, son. I just hate this guy is doing this to you and getting away with it. He has a boss too ya know," Green said.

"It's alright to fight fire with fire, Curtis," Ruxs added.

"He sent me home for the day, okay. I just want to go home and forget this happened and come back tomorrow to help Jamal with his next test. I promised Shelia I'd help her with her food chain project on Wednesday. I told the kids last week if all of them brought in items to donate to the Goodwill, that I'd bring Krispy Kreme on Friday and I'm not going back on any of that. Most of them have brought bags full of stuff already. I am a man of my word and that's why those kids trust me. I know the director's just pissed because they like me and hate him."

"I'm so proud of you, Curtis. I know you'll figure this out," Green said, but Curtis could still hear the pain in his voice. His dad wanted to intervene, to come in and crack some skulls, but he didn't need them to do that for him anymore.

"I'm proud of you, too. But say the word, buddy, and we'll be there first thing in the morning."

"I know. Trust me, though. I'll handle it." Curtis said goodbye, sagging down in the seat of his Malibu.

He hoped Genesis wasn't still mad about him ruining their vacation and was willing to have a quiet night with him. He needed him desperately.

BONUS
Chapter
THREE

Genesis

It was a little after three and he was just about finished making his wonder burger surprise. It was one of Curtis' favorites. He always went on and on about how juicy it was with all the rich, infused flavors. His favorite part was how Curtis begged for the recipe anytime he made it, offering up all kinds of sexual favors for it. Little did his partner know, all Genesis added to the fresh ground beef was A1 Steakhouse and a little Heinz 57. Nothing more, nothing less. He'd done it by mistake one day when Genesis couldn't remember which steak sauce he'd used the first time and ended up adding them both, only for it to come out tasting delicious. He smiled at the memory and formed the last patty, tucking it into the refrigerator to marinate. He'd throw them on the grill a few minutes before Curtis was supposed to be home.

Genesis took off his Falcons apron and hung it on the hook next to the pantry door, just as his cell phone rang. *Please don't be calling to say you're working late.* Genesis hurried to the living room and yanked his phone off the table. He slumped when he saw it was Ruxs. Swiping the screen, he answered cautiously, never knowing what his partner's intimidating fathers were going to say.

"What the fuck, Gen? Why's my boy still getting the business at that goddamn center?"

"Hi Ruxs, it's nice to hear from you, too." Genesis sighed. Terrifying was a gross understatement to describe Ruxs' voice at that moment.

"Cut the crap. I asked you to handle that prick months ago," Ruxs growled.

"Curtis is a grown man, Ruxs. You know he doesn't like anyone stepping in to fight his battles. He may be smaller than us, but he can solve his own problems."

"I know he can! You think I don't know that? He's the strong man we helped him become, but Curtis will keep taking the abuse from that dick because he'll do anything for those kids. He'll never risk losing that job. Did you know he's sitting in his car right now, angry and upset because that motherfucker had the audacity to say Curtis touched one of the kids inappropriately?"

"What?" Genesis jerked back like Ruxs had virtually sucker punched him.

"Yes. You fuckin' heard me right. So now, I want you to go and put the fear of God in that piece of shit. He's probably treating him like this because he's gay or who the hell knows, I don't give a damn. Just handle it, Gen… without Curtis knowing."

"Alright," Genesis growled back, his own anger bubbling to the surface so fast his body heated and sweat started to trickle down his temples.

"I mean it. I don't want to hear him so upset again. Either you do it… or we're coming to do it," Ruxs snarled.

"No! No, no, no. I like this city. I can handle it," Genesis said quickly. He didn't need the Enforcers coming to DC. No damn way.

"Good," Ruxs conceded. "Hold on, someone wants to talk to you."

Genesis walked back and forth across the soft beige area rug in their living room while he thought about how he was going to manage this. He could only imagine how his baby was feeling. That crooked boss had gone too far now.

"Hello. Good afternoon to you."

Genesis frowned at the slight British accent. "Hello. Um, who's this?"

"It's Lennox. Lennox Freeman. You can call me Free. I work with Ruxs and Green. I met you at the wedding this weekend, albeit briefly. Sorry to barge in on the conversation like this."

The guy's accent wasn't as thick as some he'd heard, just enough for it to be smooth and fun to listen too if Genesis weren't in such a foul mood. "I remember, yes."

"Well, Green was telling me about this director at that community center and what he's been doing to your boyfriend. Being rude and rejecting his proposals. So I took a couple minutes and did a little digging. There is plenty of money available for that center that's just sitting there not being used. Federal and state, I'm afraid. Three point two million dollars to be exact, available to those young lads to better their center. I don't see where this director – Charles McMillian – approved any funds for upgrades or programs in the last eighteen months, but I did find some other interesting things. Like, he has a daughter that goes to a pretty impressive private school in Massachusetts and a wife that took him to the cleaners in a divorce two years ago. I'm sure if I keep going I'll find something he doesn't want anyone to ever know, especially the police."

Genesis' eyes got wider the more the hot Brit spoke.

"And, since Mr. McMillian is so good with tossing around accusations, Genesis, I thought I'd give you one to toss back at him. How can a pay band 3 *State* employee afford his daughter's nineteen thousand dollars a year tuition and also pay out two thousand dollars a month in alimony to his ex-wife, while still being able to afford a 2016 Mustang GT? He probably couldn't, unless he was embezzling money from his place of employment."

Genesis was stunned. Shocked that one, this guy could get this kind of information in only a couple minutes, and two, Curtis' boss was a damn thief. Now it was all making sense. "Holy shit."

"Holy shit, indeed," Free said smoothly.

"You know what. Next time I'm in Atlanta, Free, I'm taking you out for drinks. Thank you so much. I gotta go. Tell Ruxs and Green I'm on it."

"Will do."

Genesis hung up and went back to preparing their dinner. Tomorrow, he'd surprise his heart at work with a nice lunch to eat in the park, but before they did that, he'd make sure to introduce himself to Curtis' boss and maybe have a little discussion with him.

All during dinner, Genesis was extra sensitive to Curtis' mood. He'd only told Genesis he'd had a bad day and wasn't feeling well. Genesis didn't like that Curtis wasn't being completely honest with him, but he'd let him have his time. He couldn't imagine how it felt to be accused of such a thing. It was deplorable for his boss to do that.

Curtis barely ate his burger, never commenting on the flavors or teasingly offering up his body in exchange for the recipe. After they finished cleaning the kitchen, Genesis offered to run him a bath and rub him down good before bed. Curtis turned and hugged him tight, tucking his smaller body into his, and Genesis could feel him shaking, could sense the overwhelming heartache and disappointment pouring off him.

"Whatever it is, you can tell me, Curtis. What happened today?" Genesis tried to pull back to look in Curtis' eyes but his lover wouldn't let him, holding him in a death grip.

"Not right now, okay. But I swear I'll tell you. I just need a couple Motrin and some rest, my head feels like it's about to explode."

Genesis rubbed Curtis' back and turned to guide him to their bedroom. "Sure. I'll get the bath started and bring you the pain reliever."

"I love you, Genny."

"I love you too. I'm sorry I fell asleep in the den last night, I didn't mean to," Genesis confessed.

"You're not mad anymore?" Curtis looked up at him, his pretty eyes red and swollen from the challenging day.

"I just want you to be alright. I'm not mad at *you*, I'm mad at the situation. We'll discuss it tomorrow after you've rested. I hate seeing you like this. Come on."

While Curtis laid there in his arms, his body soft and warm from his long bath, Genesis wished he could make him feel good. They lay on their sides facing each other. Genesis had one arm around Curtis' back while he soothingly caressed his head and shoulder with the other until Curtis was almost asleep.

"I know you want to make love," Curtis said softly. "I'm sorry, I'm not—"

"Shh." Genesis kissed Curtis' forehead, tucking his head back into his chest. "It's not about that. We have a lifetime to do that. Try to relax, okay."

"Okay."

BONUS *Chapter* FOUR

Curtis

"You didn't have to take me to work today; I could've driven and met you at the shop during my lunch." Curtis smiled over at Genesis. He'd been adamant about taking Curtis to work today, something about wanting to get his car tuned up and detailed. Curtis kept his car clean enough, he didn't need it detailed, but it *was* overdue for a little maintenance.

"I don't have anything else to do, so why not. That way, you don't have to lose your break. How about I come back in your nice clean car and take you to that Mediterranean place on 9th that you liked." Genesis held his hand while he easily steered the car with the other.

"Oh, I loved that place." Curtis sighed. "Might not be a good idea, though, I don't want to get back from lunch late."

"I'll make us a reservation."

Curtis didn't want to keep refusing all of Genesis' nice gestures so he'd agreed. Genesis pulled up to the door of the center and pulled him to him before he could reach for the handle.

"I hope your day is better." Genesis kissed him on his lips, pulling back a fraction to stare at him before he leaned back in again and licked his tongue out to swipe it across Curtis' bottom lip. His neglected cock jerked in his jeans at the feel of Genesis' firm lips on his. He couldn't help leaning in a little further, wanting more, wanting to start his day off on a better note than yesterday in hopes he didn't constantly think about his boss' nasty comments. Genesis slanted his mouth, giving Curtis a deeper taste before pulling back and whispering against his parted lips, "I'll see you at lunch. I love you."

"Love you too," Curtis answered and took his backpack from between his legs. When he got out of the car, he took his hoodie and pulled it down as far as he could to cover his half-hard erection. Genesis leaned over the passenger seat, smiling devilishly before he pulled off.

Curtis was feeling lighter when he walked inside the center. He didn't know how he landed a man as great as Genesis Godfrey, but he was thankful every day. He hurried past Charles' office and straight to the recreation room to get ready for the first of the high school students to arrive. He was working on his sociology law and conflicts research paper when Jamal and a couple of his buddies came barreling through the door.

"Hey, where's the fire?" Curtis asked, grinning up at them.

"We didn't think you'd be here," one of the other seniors said, taking off his letterman jacket and hanging it on the back of one of the chairs.

"What happened yesterday, man?" Jamal asked, looking serious.

"Nothing you need to concern yourself with. Doesn't your mom always tell you to stay outta grown folks' business?" Curtis laughed, remembering Jamal's mom's favorite quote from the one dinner he'd had at their house with his family.

"Shut up." Jamal shoved and horsed around with his teammates.

"Hey, calm down in here," Charles said from the door, his hands on his hips. "Don't you all have homework to do? You should."

None of the guys budged. Curtis couldn't even bear to look at his boss, but the guys scowled back, none of them moving from standing around Curtis like bodyguards.

"Alright, guys. Let's get those books out and get started on securing your futures. Markus, you have a Biology test on Friday, hop to it," Curtis said, closing his laptop. The boys immediately moved over to the long table and began opening up their backpacks.

The afternoon went smoothly, the other volunteers showing up and helping Curtis with study period before the kids were allowed to have some fun. He didn't see Charles again and he was glad about that because he didn't want anyone picking up on his discomfort and change of demeanor when he was around.

"It's the G-Man!" He heard one of the guys yell.

Curtis looked up to see Genesis standing in the door of the game room, wearing light blue jeans and a green collared shirt that molded wonderfully to his thick chest and made his already stimulating green eyes appear even brighter. He looked like a ray of sunshine, his smile full and cheerful. Curtis let several of the high school football players crowd around Genesis while he stood back and watched. His partner was always a huge hit wherever they went. It was rare that there wasn't at least one guy that recognized him.

"Do you think you can toss the ball with us soon?" Jamal asked, giving Genesis an enthusiastic handshake and shoulder bump.

"I'm sure I can do that a few days this week," Genesis agreed.

There was a loud round of cheering from all the students, even the young girls grinning and making sweet eyes at the guys. No doubt, they'd be out there watching and cheering on the fellas while they played with a professional.

"Hey, what's all the noise? Settle down!" Charles bellowed, coming through the doors with an angry expression... that is until the crowd parted and Charles noticed Genesis standing there.

"You're Genesis Godfrey," Charles said stupidly. "What are you doing here?"

"He's obviously here to see his boyfriend, duh," one of the girls said.

"What?" Charles frowned. "Who?"

"Curtis, dummy. G-Man is *his* boyfriend."

"Sharice, be respectful," Curtis said with little heat. He didn't want his boss to discipline her for name-calling.

Curtis was surprised when Genesis' smile widened and he went and introduced himself to his boss like he was his favorite person in the world.

Genesis

"How you doing? I don't think we've had the opportunity to officially meet. I'm Genesis, Curtis' partner, but you can call me Gen." Genesis put on his best camera-ready smile, not wanting anyone to see his disgust for this man. And it wasn't just his shifty eyes that Genesis didn't like, either. Nothing about the man screamed good. When he thought about Curtis' solemn mood last night, this wasn't a man Genesis wanted to ever see again, nor did he want his boyfriend to.

"I know who you are. I was a huge fan when you played for Georgia," Charles said, shaking Genesis' hand enthusiastically. "I thought for sure you were going to the NFL, but boy did you really shock the sports world when you turned it all down."

"Curtis is more important to me than anything. Certainly more than a multimillion-dollar contract." Genesis' smile was fading as he spoke; he wanted this man to know the depth of his love and feelings for the man he'd been mistreating for months.

A few of the guys behind Genesis teased Curtis with mocking, cooing noises, and the girls were swooning at his admission. Charles however, looked confused, but nodded anyway, his laugh taking on a trace of nervousness. He cleared his throat before he spoke again. "I can't believe I didn't know you were his... his...."

"Partner," Genesis filled in again.

"Yes. Right. Ya know, if you're not too busy, I'd love to get an autograph. It's been a year since you left Georgia, but they still mention your stats and compare the current players to you."

Genesis barely refrained from glowering, needing to keep up appearances around the young people. "Oh, absolutely." Genesis turned to look at Curtis, who was watching with a slightly disappointed expression. "Baby, would you mind going out to the car and getting one of the footballs from the trunk? I think I got a couple back there, so I can sign it for your boss."

"I only have a little time for lunch," Curtis said, his eyes trying to convey a message to Genesis. A message that said, "Don't give that piece of shit anything."

"Oh, take an extra hour." Charles waved at Curtis like he was always so generous.

Genesis clamped Charles on his shoulder, turning him back towards the door. "Awesome! Thanks, man. Come on, Curtis. We got plenty of time." Genesis began walking towards the front with

Charles, Curtis brushing past them. Genesis could read that body language and knew his boyfriend was annoyed with him.

"How about we talk a little football while Curtis fetches that ball for us," Charles suggested with a laugh.

Genesis' steps faltered right along with Curtis', but he recovered quickly. Curtis looked hurt and taken aback but oh, Genesis couldn't wait to get that asshole alone. Curtis barreled through the double doors and out into the parking lot. Genesis had parked in the last space, all the way to the back, so he'd have enough time.

"My office is right here, G-Man," Charles said, turning into the last door on the right.

As soon as Genesis was inside, he slammed the door shut and grabbed Charles by his collar, throwing him back against it and shoving his forearm over his throat to keep him from yelling. Genesis hated violence, loathed it, but his brother had taught him how to use his bulk to his advantage if he had to, and right now, he wasn't afraid to use it for Curtis.

Charles' eyes were wide with fear, his laugh cut off instantly. "Hey what the fu—"

"Shut. Up," Genesis snarled, his face just inches from Charles'. So close he could smell the old coffee on the man's breath. "You have no idea what I want to do to you right now." Genesis' voice was surprisingly calm. He thought he'd have to struggle not to yell, not to let anyone hear him, but he was impressed with the tone his voice had taken on. A composed but terrifying tenor. Like the one Green often used. It certainly had more of an affect, because Charles looked like he was waiting for Genesis to go insane and snap any second.

Charles' feet were almost off the ground, forcing him to balance on his toes as Genesis held him in the air with his huge arms. Staring down at the pitiful man, he scowled, his lips curling up into a snarl. "I hate violence, Charles. I really do. So you making me resort to this is only making me angrier. You've been torturing and harassing the love of my life for months and I've sat idly by waiting for Curtis to handle it on his own. But yesterday, you crossed the fuckin' line." Genesis yanked Charles away from the door only to throw him against a tall bookshelf and crowd him, putting him back in the same

369

position, corded forearm over his throat, his other hand with a fistful of his blue dress shirt. Charles grabbed onto Genesis' biceps, holding on to him.

"Get your grimy fucking hands of me. GET 'EM OFF!" Genesis yelled. Charles raised his hands as if he were in a stick-up. Genesis lowered his voice back to hissing. "You had the audacity to accuse Curtis of touching one of these kids. You motherfucker. All he's done, all the time he's put in here. What's your beef with him, huh?"

Charles was barely able to breathe, much less speak. Genesis wasn't really interested in an answer, so he didn't let up. "I know some very scary people, Charles. Smart, but scary. And you know what they told me? That your slimy ass is embezzling money from this center to pay for your daughter's fancy education and your wife's alimony."

Charles turned an interesting shade of green like bile was rising up in his throat and Genesis knew without a doubt – without a verbal confession from Charles – that Free was right in his assumption. Curtis' boss shook his head frantically like he was denying it. Genesis took the hand gripping Charles' shirt and popped him on the side of the head a few times, the way his coach used to do to his helmet when he messed up.

"Stop lying. You'd rather ruin a good man like Curtis' reputation and education by spreading despicable rumors. Rumors *you* made up." Genesis pushed harder, Charles's feet struggling to gain purchase. "You'd rather steal from underprivileged children just so you can drive a new car. Over three million dollars available for these kids to have a nice, safe place to go after school, to stay off the streets, and you won't even approve a request for them to get balls for the basketball court. What kind of man does that? I should do more than choke you. You deserve to be beat to shit, but I'm not going to do that." Genesis turned to look out the window and saw Curtis was just making it to the car. "I'm not going to fuck you up, although you sure as hell deserve it, but beating you to a pulp wouldn't do a damn thing and that's not my purpose for coming here today."

Charles was gasping for air and Genesis eased up on the pressure just a fraction. He didn't want the weasel to have a heart attack. "You are officially done here, Charles. Do you hear me? My connection was able to get that information in five minutes. Imagine what he could find on your dirty ass in an hour. And I'd take great pleasure in turning it all over to the police. You ever been probed up the ass with a goddamn microscope, Charles?" Genesis bared his teeth. "Do you want to be?"

Charles looked like he was about to cry as he shook his head no. "Then quit. Effective immediately. You call whoever you need to call, the city supervisor, a deputy, the director of parks and rec, you can call the fuckin' modern major general for all I care, just be gone before four o'clock today. That's one hour. And you better not even think about applying for another state or federal job again. Believe me; I'll make sure my contact is watching. Work at a dollar store, you goddamn crook."

Genesis glanced out again and saw Curtis was halfway back. "I'm going to take my baby to a nice lunch. I don't care why you hate him so much, it's irrelevant to me because the reasoning is coming from a man with no morals. So you aren't worthy to ever speak to him again. You can curse me for the rest of your miserable days, but you be sure to keep his name out of your mouth, or you'll definitely see me again." Genesis' voice dropped lower, scarier. "And if I have to come for you, Charles, I won't be coming alone. Believe it or not, there are a few men who are even madder than me over how you've treated Curtis, and they're just waiting on the word."

Genesis stepped back and Charles dropped to his knees, clutching his throat and gasping for air. "Now, get up, thief. You don't have long to get the hell outta here. Do we have an understanding?"

Charles struggled to his feet and scurried behind his desk like the measly object would protect him if Genesis attacked again. He was still coughing and straightening his clothes, probably trying to understand how Genesis' visit went from pleasant to threatening in two point five seconds. "You're not going to the police if I leave?" Charles asked pitifully.

"Fuck you! Say the words. 'Yes, I understand. I'm getting the fuck out of town'," Genesis bit out. This guy was the lowest of the low and he couldn't stand to be around him anymore.

"Yes, I understand," Charles said in a hushed, sad tone, but Genesis didn't care how the man felt; Curtis felt worse all last night.

"When Curtis comes in, you better play it off like we were simply talking about football. Go ahead, put a smile on, and hurry up," Genesis snapped.

Charles wiped the sweat from his forehead with a Kleenex and plastered on a pained, phony smile that looked like Heath Ledger's when he played the Joker. Curtis didn't even look at his boss when he cracked the office door, which was a good thing because Charles wasn't fooling anyone with that terrified look.

"There were no footballs in the trunk, Genny." Curtis stared at him and backed out the door.

Genesis rubbed his temple. "Oh, I must've run out and didn't realize." He turned Curtis to leave and looked back at Charles. His voice said, "Maybe next time." But his eyes said, "You never wanna see me again."

BONUS
Chapter
FIVE

Curtis

Lunch at one of his favorite restaurants was tainted. The food had no taste and he had very little to say to Genesis. He didn't know how he could be so chummy with his boss after everything he'd told him. Disregarding that he hadn't told him about yesterday, he'd told him plenty over the last few months. Genesis got more upset than *he* did most nights, yet somehow he wanted to chat up Charles and sign autographs. He was still bristling when Genesis pulled back up to the center. He was glad he only an hour left at work because once again, he was in a shitty mood.

"Hey, baby. I can see you're not speaking to me. I'm sorry, okay." Genesis gripped Curtis' hand before he could get out of the car. "Before you go back inside. Will you please just understand that anything I do, I do it because you mean everything to me?"

Curtis turned and looked at his partner with a perplexed expression. He'd been with Genesis long enough to know he wouldn't betray him. There had to be a reason for this insanity, but he had no clue what. "I know."

"Have a good day. I'll be back to get you at six," Genesis told him.

Curtis shook his head. "Charles will probably make me work late to make up the extra time he said I could have for lunch."

Genesis held his chin and kissed him gently. "I'll see you at six."

Curtis nodded and climbed out of the car, walking back inside the building. The halls were buzzing with activity. There was a cluster of volunteers standing at the entrance to the lunchroom, talking animatedly with each other. Curtis looked in a few of the rooms, noticing quite a few of the younger students had already been picked up for the day, or left for home, but a lot of the high school kids were still there.

Jamal was the first to hurry up to him. "What did you do?" Jamal's dark brown eyes were shining with humor, his voice hushed like he had the best secret ever bubbling inside of him, anxious to burst out. "What happened to Mr. Charles? Did you get him canned?"

"What?" Curtis yelled before he realized it.

"Hey, I don't know. About an hour after you left, a guy comes in here in a suit with about five other official-looking adults and says that he's going to be our new director and that Mr. Charles had to leave unexpectedly… for good."

Curtis frowned, looking around. This couldn't be real.

"It was Genesis, Curtis. I know it. He don't take no mess. The G-Man pops up for five minutes, next thing we know Mr. Douchebag is packing up a box and high tailing it out of here like his ass was set on fire. That's wild, Curtis. Your boyfriend is the man!" Jamal yelled.

Curtis shushed him loudly, ordering him to stop cursing. He shoved Jamal back in the rec room. "Be quiet. Let me go see what's going on. Just stop saying that, Jamal. Genny didn't tell me anything of the sort."

Jamal jogged back over to his buddies, all of them huddling around him to see if he'd gotten any answers. Curtis walked back towards the library. Susan would know. She always had the right information. Curtis pushed through the doors and saw Susan talking to a man in a navy blue suit. She pointed at him and the man turned around, plastering a welcoming smile on his face.

"Ah. So, you're Curtis," he said, extending his hand and grasping his in a firm grip. "I'm Michael Woodard, your interim center director. Call me Mike."

"I-I'm—"

"Susan here says that you're the man I need to speak with," Mike cut in. "That you practically run this place and know every student."

Curtis was still at a loss for words. He could see Susan beaming and giving him an enthusiastic thumbs up behind Mike's back. "I'm

not sure what's going on. Charles was here when I left and now…
he's what?"

"He quit. They didn't tell me the details. The deputy director
sent me over. I'm more than happy to discuss my credentials with
you, Curtis. If you have the time. I had no clue I'd get a center so
quickly. Let me tell you, I'm really excited to work with you. Susan
was telling me about your great ideas. I don't know what happened
with the last director and why these programs aren't already up and
running, but I'm going to see that they are, real soon. I've already
spoken with maintenance as I walked through the building, noting
their concerns." Mike looked at his legal pad, where he'd scribbled a
lot of notes. "But I've been wanting to speak with you. If you can
round up some of the employees and whatever volunteers haven't left
yet, and see if they have time for a quick power meeting. I know it's
late…. unless you think we should just wait for tomorrow. I'm just so
excited to get started. What do you think, Curtis? I'll defer to your
judgment."

Curtis could probably catch flies with his mouth since it'd been
hanging open the entire time the man spoke.

"Or, I'll just meet with you in your office," Mike threw out,
instead.

"I, um… I don't have an office," Curtis admitted.

"Oh. Okay. We'll rectify that later. Let's see who's available to
meet, shall we." Mike extended his hand, gesturing for Curtis to lead
the way.

He felt like he was dreaming. He knew Genesis had something
to do with this, it just didn't make sense that he didn't. He texted his
boyfriend and told him he'd get a ride home from Susan after the
meeting and went about making plans to upgrade the center with a
new director who was genuinely interested in making it better.

Genesis

When he saw headlights illuminate the wall, he set his magazine
in his lap and checked his watch. It was after nine. Genesis hoped he
didn't take one mess and create an even bigger one. What if the state

replaced Charles with an even bigger prick? *Holy shit.* That thought hadn't even crossed his mind until just now.

Curtis came through the door and set his laptop bag on the floor, peeling out of his jacket and tossing it on top of the bag. Curtis stood there at the door, looking at him long enough to make Genesis tense. He wasn't sure what had happened when Curtis went back to work, but he was starting to feel like he may have acted too quickly before weighing every consequence.

Genesis swallowed a wave of nerves. "Hey, baby."

"Don't hey baby me." Curtis' eyes looked him over and Genesis wasn't one hundred percent sure he was reading Curtis' expression correctly. "What did you do?"

"Huh?" Genesis said, ridiculously. If all else fails, play dumb.

"Gen." Curtis walked across the room, not stopping until he was practically standing on top of him. He lovingly ran his hand through Genesis' hair, looking deep into his eyes.

Genesis wasn't misreading that look at all. Curtis was turned on.

"What did you do? Tell me." Curtis' voice was thick with lust as he straddled Genesis' big lap and sat his pert ass directly over top of his cock. "What did you say to him? Tell me, right now."

"Oh, shit." Genesis clutched Curtis' waist when he began to grind down on top of him. How was he supposed to formulate a complete thought? It'd been a few weeks since they'd made love and the way his sexy partner was writhing on him, Genesis was liable to come in his lounging pants from the contact. "Damn, baby."

"Yes. I know it was you. It couldn't've been anyone else. I told you to let me handle it," Curtis whispered, arching his neck when Genesis sucked at his throat, biting over his Adam's apple. "I'll have no choice but to punish you for this," Curtis moaned.

"Jesus Christ." Genesis was so hard his eyes were crossing.

Curtis gripped Genesis' chin and closed his mouth over his, taking a long, passionate kiss before pulling away and gasping for air. "I'm going to go take a quick shower. Be in the bed, naked and aching for me by the time I get out."

Genesis was left there hard and panting when Curtis got off him and strolled down the hall, his bubble ass making him lick his lips in anticipation of burying his tongue and his dick inside it. After a few moments, Genesis was finally able to stand. He locked up their home, turned off all the lights and got in the bed just like he'd been ordered to do.

Usually, he was the aggressor when it came to sex, so it was a rare and fun treat when Curtis took the lead. Genesis dimmed the lights and stripped out of his pants and tank top, yanking back the covers and spreading across their queen-sized bed. The shower was still running and his anticipation skyrocketed at finally being able to connect with his lover in that special way again. His baby had been so overworked and hassled that Genesis hadn't been an ass and hounded him for sex. He just hoped he lasted longer than two minutes.

Curtis came out of the bathroom, his hair wet and slicked back. He had on the long blue silk robe Genesis got him for Valentine's Day. It was more of a present to himself because he loved the way Curtis looked in it. The light from the bathroom filtered into the dark room, just enough for Genesis to see the yearning blazing in his partner's eyes. Genesis' cock was hard and standing proudly, jerking every time Curtis licked his lips while he stalked over to the foot of the bed.

He watched him climb on top of the bed and up his long body, like a cheetah sneaking up on his prey. Curtis' body was just as sleek and sensual. The way he moved made Genesis want to cut out all the angst and grab him. Flip him over and ravish him. But he'd take the punishment Curtis was dishing out, every tormenting, seductive bit of it.

Curtis stopped his ascent, his beautiful face directly over his pelvis. He bent and rubbed his smooth cheek against his shaft, making his cock bob and dip all over Curtis' face. His eyes were closed like he was lost in the sensation of having his lover's cock violate his face, Genesis' precome leaving trails over his lips and chin. Curtis breathed a deep sigh. "You are so amazing, Gen. Everything about you."

Gen arched but didn't thrust. He wanted his dick inside Curtis' pretty mouth. So much so that a fine sheen of sweat broke out across his forehead. He kept his hands clenched in the sheets. Curtis kept talking, praising him, his warm breath gusting over Genesis' extremely sensitive head. "Thank you, baby, for whatever you did. Thank you for taking that risk… for me."

Genesis reached up and caressed the side of Curtis' face. Guiding him down, he hissed as Curtis swallowed his head into his mouth. There was hardly any suction, just moist softness. "Please."

"I'm not gonna make you beg, Genny… yet." Curtis smiled around the cock head resting on his lips.

Genesis' body shook at what was to come and what was being done right now. Curtis took him down as far as he could, slurping and sucking like he'd missed this part of their lovemaking. Did it with enthusiasm, like he was getting an award for it. Genesis twisted and thrashed under the carnal physicality. His climax was taking hold already; he clenched his teeth together, fighting the devastating urge. He wanted to pull Curtis off and he wanted to keep him there forever.

Curtis popped off his dick. "Come in my mouth, Genny. Don't worry, I'll be far from done with you."

"Oh shit," Genesis whispered, watching his shameless lover like he'd never seen him before. They'd had some amazing lovemaking fests, but this was definitely going to be in his top five and they hadn't even gotten halfway in yet. "Curtis, I'm gonna—"

Curtis hummed around his mouthful. Working Genesis' base with one hand and rolling his balls with the other. Genesis' toes curled painfully as he shot with the force of a cannon. Curtis took it all like a professional, swallowing and sucking, then swallowing even more. Genesis moaned loudly, crying out with each breathtaking jolt of his orgasm. This was so worth the wait.

Curtis licked at him until Genesis couldn't take anymore, covering his flaccid dick. "Okay, okay," he breathed rapidly.

Curtis' soft chuckle blew more air over his damp skin, giving him chills all over. With a couple kisses as he went, Curtis climbed up Genesis' body, nuzzling into his neck, just beneath his ear. "Tell me," Curtis panted.

Genesis' heart was still beating wildly. His lover wanted an answer, wanted to know how he'd done it. He knew Curtis wasn't thinking he'd beat him up because that wasn't in Genesis' nature. Even the little he'd done in grabbing the guy had felt horrible. He'd done it for emphasis.

Curtis allowed him to catch his breath, resting there quietly on top of him.

"He was stealing, baby," Genesis finally said, absently rubbing his hand up and down Curtis' spine. "That new computer wizard in my brother's department told me about it. All I did was tell Charles to leave and never come back, or else I was coming back with the police."

Curtis sat up, looking at Genesis' face. "He was stealing... you mean the center's money?"

"There's still plenty left, but he was definitely dipping into it," Genesis said sadly. Though that bastard was gone, it was hardly a victory. It was sad. "What happened when you got back?"

Curtis smiled. "We have an interim director, who's really great. I think he's going to do really well for us."

Genesis took a sigh of relief. "Oh, good. Thank the lord. I thought for a minute my plan may have backfired."

Curtis' smile fell slowly. "You can't always intervene in everything. Are you going to threaten everyone that gives me a hard time?"

"Yes," Genesis said seriously.

Curtis shook his head, a slight smile creeping back on his face. Genesis softly placed his hand over Curtis' heart. "This is mine to protect, and I always will. No matter the consequence. He was hurting you too much. I couldn't take it. Your dad told me what he wrongly accused you of doing to one of the students. What kind of partner would I be to let you go through that alone? The word partner means something to me, baby. It means everything *you* go through... *I* go through. And him disrespecting you was disrespectful to me... so I yoked his ass up until he was blue in the face."

Curtis' smile got huge, excitement gleaming in his bright blue eyes. "Did you really? Was he scared? Tell me."

"Curtis," Genesis admonished, rolling so he was on top. He sealed his mouth over his, the mood quickly turning back to where it was supposed to be. Curtis wrapped his legs around his back, moaning into their kiss. He was enjoying the taste of his lover, but he needed a deeper taste. Genesis slithered down Curtis' tight body, stopping over his chest to bite at his dark pink nipples.

Curtis sounds were making his dick twitch back to life already. He sucked harder on the left, pinching the right one between his fingers. "Yesss," Curtis whined, clutching the back of Genesis' head, keeping him there until he absolutely couldn't take it anymore.

Genesis didn't swallow Curtis' flushed cock too long. He wanted to see him spray his come when he was inside him. Genesis flipped Curtis over so he was on his stomach. He rubbed those supple mounds, dragging his lips over the lightly furred cheeks, loving the feel of it on his tongue. "Jesus," Genesis murmured. He pulled Curtis' straining cock between his legs and pushed him down flat against the mattress.

Curtis' cheek was against the pillow, his hands tucked underneath it. Genesis ran his hands up and down Curtis' slender body before stopping again at his cheeks, spreading him wide open. Curtis moaned 'yes' repeatedly as Genesis ate him like he hadn't had a meal all day. He ran his tongue over the quivering hole, loosening him up real good. Curtis loved this part and so did he. "You taste so sweet," Genesis whispered, then blew a little air over the wet trail he'd left from Curtis' hole to his balls. He ran his tongue along the shaft of Curtis' erection, nestled between his thighs, giving his tight balls the same treatment. He wasn't sure how much time he spent thrusting his tongue in and out of Curtis' tight bud, but the way he was forcibly pushed off told him when his lover had enough.

Curtis maneuvered Genesis so he was on his back and grabbed the lube from their bedside table. He groaned when he saw Curtis straddle him backward. He had the perfect view. Curtis positioned his hardness at his hole and slid down on top of him, hissing and moaning at the same time. "You're so big, Genny."

Genesis massaged Curtis' cheeks while he took him inside his body. When he was fully seated, Curtis positioned himself comfortably, moving up and down with shallow pumps. "Yeah, baby. Damn, you're so tight."

A.E. VIA

Curtis leaned back, showing off his flexibility, turning his head, seeking out a kiss. Genesis wrapped his arms around Curtis' chest, holding him close to him. Enjoying their connection. He sat buried inside Curtis, his lover not moving until he wanted to. After a few more strained seconds, Curtis brought his knees up and placed his feet flat on the bed so he could raise his hips up. Genesis hooked his arms under Curtis' armpits, his face nestled in his wet hair.

"You like it when I ride you like this," Curtis said huskily. Raising his hips up slowly and sliding down the same way. Genesis' chest tightened at the sensation, his legs quivering with restraint. He wouldn't buck… he liked Curtis this way… in control. He wasn't looking for Genesis to answer – it wasn't a question. He'd told Genesis exactly what he wanted and how he wanted it and Curtis was exactly right. "You want me to make you crazy."

Genesis nodded, barely remembering how to speak. "Mmm." Curtis kept the pace slow and romantic, made the pleasure build between them. Genesis clamped onto Curtis' waist, feeling his muscles contract. "Yessss. More."

"You're begging already. I haven't even gotten started," Curtis said seductively, his ass grinding down on him. As soon as he confessed that, Curtis picked up the speed, not enough to make Genesis blow again, but enough to make him curse.

"Damnit. Just like that," Genesis encouraged. He buried his nose in Curtis' neck, smelling the clean scent of his soap. He sucked on the satiny skin, his balls tightening the louder his lover's moans got.

"Oh, Genny. I'm so close," Curtis warned, pressing the back of his head into his shoulder. His body shook and his legs jerked and he tried to keep up the frantic pace while his orgasm hurtled through him.

Genesis added his hips to the motion, knowing it wouldn't be long now. He met Curtis' downward thrust with his own, pounding into his tight heat. Curtis cried out to take him harder, faster, wanted the roles reversed, begged Genesis to take back control. It was too much for him to hang on any longer.

Genesis stilled Curtis' wild movements and eased him off his cock, then quickly and effortlessly lifted him and changed their

381

positions. He did love Curtis riding him but this was by far his favorite – call him old-fashioned. He reached down and pulled the covers up over half their bodies and settled between Curtis' legs, watching him closely while he slid back inside him. He'd never tire of the look his lover made when he entered him. Curtis bowed and whimpered, his cock an angry red, nestled between their stomachs. "Oh my god, it's so good. It's been too long, Genny."

Three-and-a-half weeks was too long. Especially for them. "I wanna watch you. Watch you come so hard for me." Genesis kissed Curtis' slack mouth.

"Now, please." Curtis gazed longingly at him.

Genesis knew what he was feeling. Curtis slid his hand between their stomachs, his fist moving rapidly to Genesis' deep strokes. He cradled Curtis' head in his arms, kissing his cries of pleasure, living in his shouts of ecstasy.

"Oh god." Curtis squeezed his eyes shut, his hole tightening around Genesis' girth. His body tensed and stilled until the first burst of release erupted between them. Genesis kept pumping while he brought them both to the height of euphoria, the warmth from Curtis' seed slickening their jerky movements. Their foreheads pressed together, Genesis yelled Curtis' name, his dick shooting again, this time even more powerfully than the first. His pumps were light, shallow, making sure he'd emptied himself completely inside his sweetheart's hot body. When he was well drained and fatigued, he slid out and rolled to the side, pulling Curtis with him. Oh, yes. This was absolutely going in the top five.

"How do you expect me to walk tomorrow?" Curtis huffed, sounding content.

"Carefully," Genesis teased in response.

Curtis laughed against his chest. "God, I needed that so much. You have no idea."

"Yes, I do." Genesis stroked Curtis' hair, kissing the top of his head then pulling him in for a warm hug, ignoring their messy bodies.

"It has been a while."

"Meh. Twenty-four days. But who's counting?" Genesis smiled, nuzzling Curtis' temple.

"Wow." Curtis went to move out of Genesis' grasp but he tightened his grip.

"Mmm. Where you think you're going?"

"Shower. Come on. Let's clean up, so we're not stuck together like this in the morning."

Genesis tucked his hands behind his head and watched Curtis climb from the bed on shaky legs, ambling to the bathroom. He was looking forward to a peaceful sleep and waking with Curtis in his arms. Maybe even a little morning love before breakfast. Then he'd go to the center with him on the pretense of tossing the ball around with the kids, but he was really going to check out this new director. Curtis said he was cool but Genesis was going to see for himself. Possibly have Free do a background check. Genesis wasn't taking any more chances. Curtis was his heart, his world. He'd protect him, no matter what he said. He was Curtis' partner; he was only doing his job.

The End

Blue Moon I: Too Good to be True

Blue Moon II: This is Reality

Blue Moon III: Call of the Alpha

You Can See Me

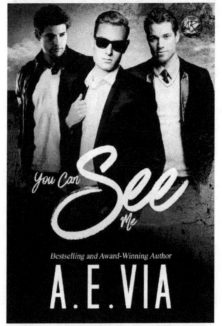

Nothing Special (Nothing Special Book 1)

Embracing His Syn (Nothing Special Book 2)

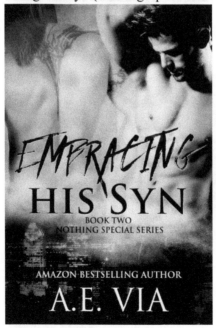

Here Comes Trouble (Nothing Special Book 3)

Don't Judge (Nothing Special Book 4)

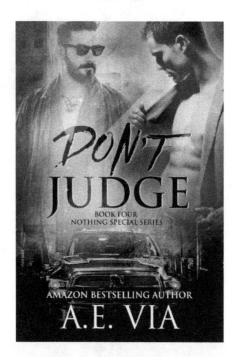

Promises

Promises 2

Defined By Deceit

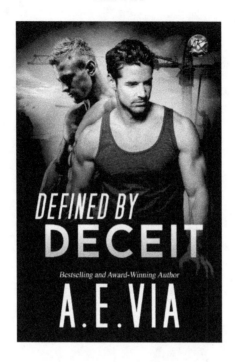

The Secrets in My Scowl

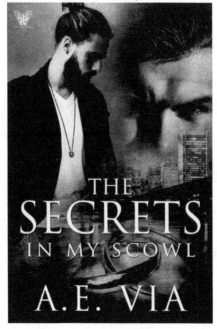

CPSIA information can be obtained
at www.ICGtesting.com
Printed in the USA
BVHW041448190520
R10816800001B/R108168PG579811BVX1B/1

9 781540 416261